Somebody to Love

Sheryl Browne

Safkhet Publishing

First published in 2012 by Safkhet Soul, London, United Kingdom
Safkhet Soul is an imprint of Safkhet Publishing
www.safkhetpublishing.com

1 3 5 7 9 10 8 6 4 2

ISBN 978-1-908208-11-8

A CIP catalogue record for this book is available from
the British Library.

Printed and bound by Lightning Source International

Typeset in 11 pt Crimson and Worstveld Sling Extra with Adobe InDesign

Find out more about Sheryl on www.sherylbrowne.com
and meet her on Facebook at
https://www.facebook.com/pages/Sheryl-Browne-Author-Page/245372252189480

Production Crew:

Sheryl Browne	*author*
Nora Neurohr	*cover model*
Kim Maya Sutton	*managing editor*
William Banks Sutton	*copy editor*

 The colophon of Safkhet is a representation of the ancient Egyptian goddess of
wisdom and knowledge, who is credited with inventing writing.
Safkhet Publishing is named after her because the founders met in Egypt.

A Note from Sheryl

As a writer, I admit there are days when I so wished I had a bijou little studio-flat (room only for me) overlooking the sea. But would I want to be on my own, really? Minus dogs, rabbits, fish, son, partner, window cleaner (no, he's not part of the family, but a real nuisance, appearing at the window when I'm having an intimate moment with my hero). Would I want a magic wand to make them all disappear? Well, the window cleaner possibly, but my family? As tempting blissful solitude might seem, I think not. If I didn't have my family around me, I don't think I could write. For me, writing is about more than creativity and research, it's about life; experiencing life and its sometimes tumultuous events, and bringing that into play in my storytelling.

At least until the housework is beyond ignoring, then, and the human contingent has mysteriously disappeared, I'd like to thank my family for giving me a wide berth when I do need a little 'me' time. I would like also to thank the person who was the inspiration behind Somebody to Love: A lost little boy, who threw his shoes over my fence in order to make the acquaintance of a three-legged dog called Sadie. Thank you, Kyle.

I would also like to thank the gorgeous cover model, Nora Neurohr, and her equally gorgeous rabbit, Findus, who gamely agreed to pose, and remained professional despite the many retakes and kisses.

Lastly, thank you Kim and Will Sutton of Safkhet Publishing for loving this book as much as I loved writing it ~ and for believing in me.

A dog for an autistic child and somebody to love for the father; that's heartwarming romcom at its best
Sue Quinlan

Danemere Animal Rescue

Registered Charity
No: 1065072

For Sadie, Max and Buffy

A Lost Little Boy...

The bell tinkled overhead. The soft murmur of voices slowed and, somehow, Mark could sense his son's nearness. He glanced at the shopkeeper. 'There wouldn't be a young boy?'

'We wondered whose he was.' She nodded, indicating a room beyond the shop-fronting area they were in. An Aladdin's cave, stuffed full of toys and magical to a child's eyes. 'We were just about to call the police.'

'Mine. My son,' said Mark, his throat tight as he watched Karl wander through from the back room, his clear blue eyes wide with wonder, before they alighted on Mark. Then, they grew disconcerted, as if Karl knew he was in trouble, and Mark couldn't bear that. He knew he should talk to him. Try to instil in him through firm repetition, that he should not do this sort of stuff. Instead, he walked over to Karl and bent down to hug him so tight, he could feel his son's heartbeat next to his own.

'Hiya, mate. Did you get your model car?' he asked throatily, knowing Karl wouldn't, couldn't hug him back. Trying hard not to mind, Mark stood to ruffle Karl's hair. His fringe was tickling his eyelashes again, he noticed.

Time for a trim, he guessed, recalling how, with his long dark eyelashes, Karl had often been mistaken for a girl as a baby. How his wife had joked he'd grow up to be a heartbreaker. Mark's heart seemed to have broken, that was for sure.

Karl shook his head. 'No,' he said, in that gruff, grainy voice that drew people's stares. Mark didn't care. At least Karl was speaking. He was two when he'd stopped, and Mark's life changed forever.

Chapter One

'She's fine now. Good as new.' Trying not to mind the icy plop of rain trickling down the back of her parka, Donna O'Connor reassured a concerned pensioner that her wobbly, three-legged dog wasn't about to keel over.

'She's a miracle.' The little old lady blinked watery eyes, opaque with old age. 'And so pleased with herself. Her little tail's wagging, see?'

'Yes, she is.' Donna beamed, quite proud of her courageous dog, too, who'd adapted amazingly well after major surgery.

'Here,' the old lady said, ferreting in her Tesco bag, from which she produced a sock, from which she produced a pound coin. 'I normally have lots of balls,' she went on, confusingly, since she didn't seem to have a dog, 'but take this, instead. Buy her a new one.'

'No, I couldn't possibly.' Touched, Donna declined the old lady's generosity, whilst quietly hoping she didn't look like a charity case in her moth-eaten dog-walking gear.

'I insist.' Resolute, the old lady reached for Donna's hand. 'You're a good girl,' she said, pressing the pound coin into it. 'The world would be a better place for more people like you.' So saying, she turned to totter off.

In slippers in the rain, Donna noted, her hitherto flat mood buoyed up a bit. 'Come on, hon. Let's go and buy you a new ball.' She gestured Sadie on. It was the little things, she decided, glad her special dog brought some joy to the old lady's probably otherwise lonely existence. Smiling, she turned towards the car park, and her buoyancy deflated like a pricked balloon.

Oh, wonderful. Donna groaned inwardly and debated whether to dive behind the nearest bush or about-face pronto. With her actual face devoid of make-up and wearing her bang-on-trend — not — unflattering leggings, *he* was absolutely the last person in the world she wanted to bump into.

Still, at least her face had features to enhance, Donna supposed, steeling herself as her ex-husband strolled towards her, arm-in-arm with his latest featureless girlfriend, aka the Twiglet, who was leading an equally anorexic Pekinese by the lead.

Deep breath in, Donna told herself, counting slowly to seven. *And out.* Exhaling to a count of nine, she tried to ward off a threatening panic attack. The sight of Jeremy wasn't enough to induce one, normally. It was his glib attitude on the phone this morning, glossing over her concerns for their son as her 'usual neurosis,' again that had her almost hyperventilating on site of him.

'Well, well, Donna. Fancy meeting you here,' Jeremy exclaimed, looking surprised.

The surprise was all Donna's, Jeremy having phoned barely an hour since, citing some emergency or another as reason for letting their son down again. Matthew was used to his father's excuses, of course. He didn't bat an eyelid anymore. He had better things to do with his time, chatting with his current cyber-crush or lusting after Buffy the

Vampire with pet-friend and best-friend, Findus the rabbit perched on his chest, being infinitely more interesting than discourse with Jeremy, who seemed only to work at breaking the father–son bond. Donna, though, was fuming — and feeling inclined to verbalise her feelings. But knowing Matthew might be caught up in the middle of more animosity, she gritted her teeth and bit hard on her tongue.

And the emergency that had taken priority over taking his son shopping for the new ice-cool trainers he'd promised him for his birthday? The Pekinese wasn't well and needed to go the vet, Jeremy had said, leaving Donna thinking the poor dog must be close to death. Yet, here they were, the happy trio. Jeremy smiling away — apparently not a care in the world, the Peke looking not at all peaky, and the Twiglet looking... well, blank, her botoxed face having all the expression of a boiled egg... and wearing hair. Lots of hair. Glossy, truffle coloured, extremely long hair. Hmm? New extensions, Donna wondered. She squinted a bit. Yes, definitely extensions arranged artistically around breasts that would still be up and out there when the rest of her had given in to gravity.

Implants. Donna would bet her life on it. At least Donna's were all her own. She promptly breathed in, trying to look thin, whilst thrusting her own less abundant frontage up and out there.

The Twiglet was dressed in designer, presumably. Not that Donna had a clue about labels, beyond which High Street stores labelled generously. She looked the woman's attire surreptitiously over: a horse print tee — Stella MC possibly, black tailored jacket over, and figure-enhancing jeans under, she looked every inch what she claimed to be: An ex-model, with her own stables and rich daddy, who would make sure she and her horses were well-shod for life.

Realising she was on a mission impossible, Donna breathed out, before she expired. She couldn't hope to measure up. Nor would she aspire to, had Jeremy not constantly measured her up, even to past women in his life, all of whom seemed to have been younger, thinner, bubblier and cleverer than she.

That wasn't the Twiglet's fault though. Reluctantly, Donna retracted her claws. The woman couldn't help it if, like the others before her, she'd been taken in by Jeremy's broody good looks and smooth repartee. She'd learn in time that the 'broody' was more moody and the repartee was designed to impress.

So, what was he doing here? Jeremy didn't do dog-walking, any more than he did monogamy.

'Just back from the vet's,' Jeremy enlightened her. 'Thought we'd give the poor little chap a quick walk before taking him home, didn't we, Leticia?'

Leticia batted tarantula lashes and manoeuvred her mouth into a smile.

'I see.' Donna waited for Jeremy to mention the other not-so-little chap in his life, his son. Jeremy didn't.

Fine. Donna wasn't about to remind him he'd got one. 'He doesn't look too poorly, though, does he?' She glanced down at the Pekinese, who looked perfectly bright-eyed and bushy-tailed.

'Gippy tummy.' Jeremy patted his own, and petted the Peke, which was up on its little hind legs begging attention. He didn't pet Sadie, even though she was wagging her tail, having known him all her life.

'Right. Well...' Donna swallowed a little lump in her throat. 'I'd better get off,' she said breezily, clapping her gloved hands in front of her. 'Things to do, errands to run.'

'Boyfriend not in tow, then?' Jeremy enquired interestedly, glancing past Donna, who braced herself for one of his unfunny little witticisms.

He knew very well she hadn't got an actual boyfriend. He was referring to her work colleague, Simon, presumably, whom Jeremy had spotted her out walking with in Worcester last Saturday. 'No.' She smiled tightly. 'Simon's not with me today. It's a work day, Jeremy. I'm on a day off.' Of which Donna had few, and Jeremy, who ran his own accountancy business, seemed to have many.

'I meant heterosexual men, Donna.' He dripped sarcasm, smiling that smarmy smile Donna had actually once thought attractive.

Damn. She should have known better than to rise to the bait. She'd been trying to deflect the open insinuation that no man would be in tow, because no man could possibly be interested. Simon, a dear friend as well as a work colleague, didn't qualify as a man in Jeremy's xenophobic opinion, though Simon was twice the man Jeremy could ever be.

'If you're asking whether I'm dating, Jeremy, then the answer is yes.' Tired of his condescension, Donna lied through her teeth. 'For your information, since you're obviously so interested in my personal life, he's good looking, tends not to like being towed or pushed around — anymore than he would dream of towing or pushing women around.'

She paused in hopes of making the point. 'He's definitely a sex-addict like you, Jeremy, but *unlike* you he's well-endowed and rather good at it. He's also a gentleman.'

Noting the flash of humiliation in Jeremy's eyes, Donna turned with satisfaction to the Twiglet. 'Attentive in bed,' she explained, with a smug little smile.

'Yes, well, let's hope his *attentiveness* reaps some reward, hey?' Jeremy remarked, with soul-crushing sarcasm. 'Nice to see you, Donna,' he went on, before Donna could retaliate. 'Better get off though. Clients to see and whatnot, you know? Do give my best to your mother.'

Oh, dear. He'd got a plum stuck in his mouth. Upset though she was, Donna almost laughed at Jeremy's regal tones, quite obviously adopted to impress the Twiglet.

Donna oozed plumminess back. 'Oh, I *do* know, Jeremy. I'm doing overtime now, as well as fulltime. But then, one does love one's little luxuries, *you know?* Like food. How about you? Do you work, um?' Donna turned to the Twiglet, deliberately forgetting her name.

'Leticia.' The Twiglet supplied. 'I'm in equitation, actually.'

Donna blinked. 'Pardon?'

'I ride.'

'Ah.' Donna nodded, enlightened. 'I do, too, *actually*,' she said chummily. 'I have a little fold up I carry in the car. It has a puncture at the moment, but I'm a dab-hand with a bicycle pump.' Honestly, did the woman have to have an exotic job to match her eyebrows? Couldn't she have worked in an estate agent's?

'Horses, Donna. She rides horses,' Jeremy informed her, with an elongated sigh.

'Really? How very brave of you. 'Aren't you afraid you might fall off and burst something?' Donna studied Leticia curiously.

Jeremy rolled his eyes, apparently not impressed. 'Come on, darling.' He sighed and took hold of one of the Twiglet's offshoots. 'Don't you have a horse to put through its paces for the British Open? I'm sure Donna's far too busy to stand here chatting.'

The darling had come out dah-ling. God, he really did think he was Prince Charming.

'Yes I do, as it happens,' Donna informed him flatly. 'I have to pop to the garage to oil a mechanic by way of payment for my clapped-out car. Lovely to meet you, Patricia. By the way, do be careful if you're joining her in the riding lark, dah-ling.' She turned back to Jeremy, her brow knitted in concern. 'I've heard it can do terrible things to a man's virility.'

'Very witty.' Jeremy shot her a derisory glance.

Donna thought so, for her anyway. But then, she had learned from the best. 'Would you like a wet wipe?' she asked him.

'What?' Jeremy looked at her now as if she were mentally challenged.

'A wet wipe,' Donna repeated, nodding down at his shoes as she ferreted through doggy supplies in her pockets.

She handed Jeremy a good handful of wipes, which he'd certainly need. 'Well, bye, bye. Must trot off. Do have a nice day.'

With which Donna turned away, leaving Jeremy gingerly lifting one tarnished patent leather loafer.

'God, Leticia?! Can't you put a nappy on it or something?' Jeremy's miffed, and rather less regal, tones drifted after her.

'Titan is a *he,* not an *it,*' Leticia informed him shortly.

Titan? Donna's mouth curved into a delighted smile. Well, well. The woman obviously had a sense of humour. If it wasn't for Jeremy, Donna had a feeling she could even like her.

'What on earth do you expect anyway, wearing your business shoes to walk through the park,' Leticia went on, obviously peeved. 'I didn't ask you to come to the vet's, Jeremy.'

Donna snuck a peek over her shoulder, at Leticia plucking up her midget-sized Titan and strutting off, which wasn't terribly helpful to Jeremy, who'd been holding her shoulder for support while he cleaned off his shoe. Yes, under different circumstances, Donna and Leticia might definitely have bonded.

As for Jeremy, served him right. Hoity-toitying it all over the place. If there were any justice in the world, Leticia's horse would dump on Jeremy's other shoe.

'Come on, Sade.' Donna walked on, glad that Jeremy at least didn't get to saunter off with the upper hand, as he usually did. 'Let's go and fantasise about our attentive, well-endowed lover on the way to the boring old library. Not that Donna was sure she'd know what to do with an attentive, well-endowed lover if she fell on one.

****

'Sh... *ugar!*' Donna balked at the patrol car parked behind her suspect PT Cruiser, as she came out of the library an hour later. Oh, no, not again. She noted the police officer emerging from the post-office her car was smack-bang in front of, and her heart sank. She couldn't afford any more points on her driving licence. She'd already achieved the impossible, notching up six points in two weeks. Panicky, she broke into a run, cleared the six or so yards between them in five seconds flat, and skidded to a halt just short of bowling him over.

'*He-llooo!*' she sing-songed cheerily, hoping to distract him from the double yellow lines someone had thoughtlessly parked under her car.

The officer looked at her bemused, as if no one in the world ever said hello to a policeman. Well, they probably didn't quite so effusively. Nice eyes. China blue and sort of... twinkly. Donna tried to dismiss a disconcerting little flip in the base of her tummy and come up with a halfway intelligent statement that might keep him distracted.

'Have you got the time?' she asked, earth-shatteringly.

'If you've got the place,' he answered as quick as a flash, which left Donna distracted, not least because the smile that accompanied his quip was so sexually charged he could have any flesh-and-blood female panting without even removing his cap. He could certainly have her. Donna was tempted to tell the alluring officer she *had* got the place — a spacious double bed that hadn't seen much action, apart from snoring with her dog, and drag him off by his tie.

Mathew though, who, at the grand old age of just seventeen, fancied himself as man of the house, might not be impressed if he emerged from his bedroom to find a semi-naked policeman on the landing.

As if. She'd need implants first, boobs plus self-esteem, which her tumultuous marriage had left sloshing about in her shoes. Donna knew the hurtful comments Jeremy had made re her performance in bed — or lack of — were manufactured to excuse his own adulterous behaviour, but from seeds of doubt...

Thus her visit to the library for an instruction manual.

Her shoulders slumped as the police officer squinted interestedly past her to her illegally parked car. That was it. The game was up. Short of draping herself over the bonnet or fainting, there was nothing else she could do to distract him. She might as well go quietly.

'I, um...' She searched for a lie that wouldn't sound contrived, and came up with nothing.

The officer squinted some more, then cocked his head to one side.

'Unbelievable,' he said, pushing his cap back. 'Your dog only has three legs.'

'What?' Donna blinked, surprised, then quickly rearranged her face lest he think she hadn't noticed her dog's leg-less predicament. 'I know.' She smiled fondly as Sadie hopped from one seat to another, her tail swishing manically. 'Gorgeous, isn't she?'

'Amazing,' he said, walking around to the driver's side to get a better look. 'She was sitting up so straight, I didn't notice at first.'

'She's very proud.' Donna joined him, peering through the window next to him. Head level with him. Very close to him. Mmm. What was that aftershave? Scrummy. Donna's nose twitched. Oops, she was in terrible peril of having a closer sniff of him.

'Labrador, isn't she?'

'Labrador/Old English Mastiff cross,' Donna confirmed, preferring her tri-legged non-pedigree to the Twiglet's Pekinese any day. 'That's why she looks so proud. She has a big, um, chest, you know.' Actually, that wasn't the whole reason why. Sadie had a strong disposition and a huge personality, which was why she'd been sitting so tall. Despite her missing front leg, Sadie didn't give in easily, which was why Donna loved her, unequivocally.

'Road accident?' he asked, his brow furrowed in concern as he continued to look Sadie over.

'Cancer. She's fine now. Loving life. But they had to remove the leg to save her. I wasn't sure I'd done the right thing at first. You know, I got her home from the op and I thought Oh, my God, what have I done? She looked so frail. But the next day, she was up and hopping, and she's never looked back.'

He gave a low whistle. 'Lucky dog,' he said, 'to have an owner with such a big heart.'

'Yes,' Donna agreed, a bit giddily as he turned his face towards her, a warm smile now dancing in his pretty blue eyes. Good Lord, he was growing tastier by the minute. If he came any closer, she'd be tempted to have a little bite of him. Donna's heart expanded to fit his description of it, pitter-pattering against her ribcage.

'I'd better get off.' She dragged in a breath and straightened up before she drooled on his shoes. 'I'm just on my way back from the vet's and I don't want to leave her in the car too long. I just had to run into the library and renew my book.' She waved her free hand at the car door.

'Oh, sorry,' he said, stepping back.

She made a grab for the handle, hoping to make a quick getaway, and that's when it happened. At the exact same time, he reached for the handle, too, and sparks literally flew.

He snatched his hand back. Donna almost jumped out of her skin. The book slipped from under her arm. He bent to retrieve it and — poof went any hopes of Donna doing demure.

Horrified, Donna clamped her hand over her mouth as he glanced curiously at the book, then back to her. *Sex and the Single Girl* stared up at them from the pavement.

'PC Mark Evans,' he said, standing up.

Donna froze. Oh, God, he was going to charge her, here in the street. Totally humiliate her, in front of everyone.

He offered her the book — back cover discreetly upward, his smile now rather elusive. 'I'm just going off duty. Don't suppose you fancy a quick coffee, do you?'

Chapter Two

In deference to Sadie, they plumped for a table outside the *Café Vienna*, where Donna assured him she would never, ever park illegally again.

'Good,' Mark said. 'I'd hate to have to drag you off in handcuffs.'

'Me too,' Donna said airily, then choked inelegantly on her mocha.

Her coughing fit over, assisted by an able policeman patting her on the back, they continued to chat, swapping small-talk and smiles. Finally, they swapped coffees. And a man that would part with the flake on top of his vanilla Frappuccino and give his biscuit to her dog scored high, as far as Donna was concerned.

The cream-coated flake tantalised every taste bud. Mark's thumb trailing over her lips tantalised more. 'You missed some,' he said. Such a cliché, but with his twinkly eyes fixed firmly on hers — not tired. Not tired at all.

Smiling again, uncertainly this time, he glanced down and then back up. 'I, er, don't suppose you'd like to go out properly sometime, would you?' he asked, now looking very uncertain, making Donna's heart pitter-patter all over again. 'Dinner, maybe?'

Donna blinked, astonished. By God, he was a fast mover. He was asking her *out* out? To dinner, when she looked like the dog's dinner? Dressed in her moth-eaten leggings, now sporting more hair than her dog, and a top under her parka that was mislabelled size fourteen instead of age fourteen, she doubted she'd be anyone's fantasy come true. Less so, if she took her unflattering ensemble off, but *oh, my God* — he was. And he was looking so delectably self-conscious, she might just be forced to eat him wholesale and done with.

Loosening his collar, and looking as though he'd quite like something to swallow him up, Mark glanced away again. 'Sorry. I, er... Bit presumptuous.' He reached for his coffee cup and swirled the contents around. 'You're probably with someone. I just thought I'd...'

'Actually,' Donna cut him short, her confidence suddenly bolstered so high, it had grown wings, 'I quite like you,' she said quickly, feeling her own face flush right down to her freckly décolleté.

'Oh.' Mark stared at her, his coffee cup halfway to his mouth.

Great! Now he'd probably got her down as a desperate tart who didn't do sex very well. Donna dropped her gaze, wondering how she could make a discreet exit with her three-legged dog, now she'd made a complete idiot of herself.

'Right,' Mark said, lowering his mug and planting it on the table. 'Likewise.'

Donna's head snapped back up. 'Sorry?'

'I'm not. I'm flattered.' Mark's mouth curved into its bone-melting smile. 'The feeling's mutual, but then, you probably gathered that.'

Was he having a laugh? Donna scanned his face, looking for a hint of mockery in his pretty blue eyes. 'No. No, I didn't,' she said, noting nothing but sincerity there. 'I mean, I do now that you've, um, you know, but I... Ahem.' She stopped, before she started babbling and beamed a smile at him, then tried to tone it down, lest he think her a complete imbecile.

He laughed not unkindly, reached for his mug again, and did his swirly contemplative thing with the contents. 'So,' he asked, locking eyes with hers, 'are you married?'

'No.' Donna squinted at him, wondering at the question. Was he in the habit of asking women out before he'd checked out their availability? She hastily dropped her gaze to his ring finger, squinting harder as she searched for the tell-tale white band. Upon which, he reached quickly into his inside breast pocket, fumbling ever-so-conveniently for something therein. 'Sorry, mobile,' he offered by way of explanation.

Oh, hell. Donna closed her eyes. *He was.* She sighed heavily inside. Unhappily married, no doubt. Wife's a horrible cow who doesn't understand him and who he's never had sex with, ever — except to produce two-point-four children, who are doing their exams right now as he sits here and lies, and so he can't possibly leave her, not now. Not ever.

Whatever. Donna tugged in a breath and steeled herself. She wasn't going there, not now. Not ever. 'I was married,' she said quickly, averting her gaze, because she really was beginning to feel naïve now and extremely idiotic. 'I have a son,' she went on, opening the door quite wide enough for him to introduce any wives or children of his own he might be neglecting to mention.

'I know.' He gave her another one of his elusive smiles. 'I've seen you around.'

Neat move, thought Donna. 'You have?' Where? She didn't get around that much, apart from the supermarket. Was he a supermarket cruiser?

'Once or twice,' he expounded, looking serious. 'The last time driving the wrong way down a one-way street.'

'Ahh…' Donna nodded, and swallowed.

Mark smiled. 'I've never seen a sixteen point turn before, I have to admit. It was different.'

'Sat nav,' Donna offered by way of weak explanation.

'Of course. I have the same trouble all the time,' Mark assured her — the soul of understanding.

Donna smiled back, despite herself. She liked him, she really did, and she couldn't help it. So what on earth did she do now? *Ask* him. Suspicion gave her a quick shove in the right direction. There was nothing else *to* do. 'What about you?' She braced herself and took the bull by the horns. 'Is there a Mrs PC Mark Evans?'

Mark hesitated, dropping his gaze to his coffee cup — and Donna's heart plummeted.

She waited.

Studying him hard.

Mark shifted uncomfortably, tugged in a breath, and debated. He should tell her now, up front. He knew he should. He ran his thumb pensively over the rim of his mug and debated some more. And then what? And then, he'd see her eyes cloud over with uncertainty, as he'd seen happen so many times before. She might go out with him. Chances were, though, she'd consider the wisdom of getting involved with a man there could be no future with and say, thanks, but no thanks.

'No,' he said, finally. Over dinner, he decided, that's when he'd tell her, if she would go out with him. Maybe then, if she knew him a little better, liked him enough, she'd want to take things further. Yes, right. He sighed inwardly. Not likely though, was it? 'I, er...' he started again, knowing there really was no way forward if he wasn't honest at outset, then paused.

'What?' Donna's urgent tone snatched his attention back to her face.

'Nothing,' he said quickly, bottling out — and feeling like a complete coward, but was it really that wrong to want to delay the inevitable? To want to spend some time in a woman's company where his complications weren't the topic of conversation? There was Michelle, of course, who didn't mind spending time in his company — when her schedule at the hospital allowed it — but they rarely had much time for verbal intercourse, both always on the clock, snatching time to meet up when they could. The sex was... well, good... but Michelle had made it clear that, as a young junior doctor chasing promotion to clinical lead, she had no time or inclination for anything more, i.e. his life and all the baggage that went with it. Mark couldn't blame her. He'd been almost relieved when she'd come right out and said so. The thing was that he *did* want more. He'd even considered taking up smoking on the basis that the odd post-coital conversation might be nice.

'I was married once,' he continued, choosing his words carefully and hoping that this time things might be different. That Donna might possibly be interested in a relationship that was more a relationship. 'But it didn't work out.'

'Oh?' Donna nodded. 'Do you want to talk about it?'

'Not much to tell, really.' Mark ran a hand over his neck. 'We, er, grew apart, you know? I'll bore you with the details some other time.'

She stared at him, a puzzled look on her face. A very cute face. Mark smiled quietly, noting the smattering of freckles over her nose, her pretty green eyes. Her lips, which curved easily into a smile. He liked her. He really did want to see her again, and he would tell her. He promised himself that. Next time.

'So what do you do?' he asked, changing the subject, not too obviously, he hoped. 'For a living, I mean?'

'Single parent and office worker at a care centre at the moment,' she smiled apologetically. 'Nothing special, but I'm looking at training.'

'Don't underrate yourself,' Mark replied, curiously searching her eyes. She didn't exactly exude confidence. No surprise there. Mark knew a little of her history. Should he tell her he did? No. He supposed it was fair to assume that if he didn't care to share his private life in public outside a coffee shop, she wouldn't thank him for sharing hers. 'What kind of training?'

'Childcare,' she said, with a self-effacing shrug. 'Not rocket science, I know, but the centre caters to children with learning difficulties and I think it's something I could be good at, you know? Assuming I can get my bitchy manageress to OK my application, that is.' She rolled her eyes despairingly.

Mark smiled. Knowing the special qualities needed for that particular line of work, he didn't doubt it might be something she would be good at. 'Would you like me to drop by and harass her?' he asked, with a mock scowl.

Donna laughed. 'I can fight my own battles thank you, but I'll call if I need you.'

'I'll make sure to give you my number,' Mark said, serious now. He scanned her eyes — kind eyes, vulnerable, yet determined — and found himself not wanting to look away.

She held his gaze for a second, and then glanced down.

Damn. Too pushy. 'So, do you have any interests?' he asked, steering the subject back to safer ground.

'Apart from picking up policemen, you mean?' Donna's eyes flickered bashfully back to his. 'No, except...' she hesitated '... self-interest, maybe.'

Mark finished his coffee, and wondered whether he should offer to get another. 'How so?'

Donna took a breath. 'I, um, don't want to rush into anything.' She glanced uncertainly at him. 'I mean, I'd quite like to go out with someone. With you, if you'd like, assuming you are, um, currently unencumbered,' she hurried on, 'but I don't want... complications, I suppose.'

Mark nodded, careful to keep his expression neutral. 'So, you'd like to take things slowly, then?'

'Yes.' Donna furrowed her brow. 'I think so.'

Mark nodded again, thoughtfully. 'No problem. I understand,' he said, wondering whether he should do the cutting and running, now, before he made her life as complicated as hell.

He checked his watch. Force of habit, juggling home and work as he always seemed to be. Karl was due at the respite centre. He could get back comfortably enough to relieve the child-minder. But Jody would only wonder why, he supposed. And Karl really wouldn't notice one way or the other.

Dammit, he owed himself a little off-duty time, didn't he? And if he was reading the signs right, Donna was hinting she wanted more than dinner. 'I'd better make a move,' he said, trying to work out — assuming she did — how to pin her down to a time and a place.

'Oh.' Donna's eyes shot wide... with alarm? Mark smiled and took that as a positive sign. 'Right. Yes, me too,' she said, glancing away. 'Things to do, dog's to, um, hop. Come on, Sade.' She visibly hoisted her shoulders up and attempted to scrape her chair back, the leg of which, unfortunately, seemed to be wedged between paving stones.

Mark's smile widened. 'Doesn't do for policemen to be seen hanging around coffee bars in uniform for too long,' he said, standing to walk around the table to assist her. 'Would you allow me the honour of escorting you to your car? And the further honour...' he said, his mouth close to her ear '... of seeing you again, after whatever amount of time you deem appropriate, of course?'

'Pardon?' She blinked up at him.

'As long as it's not too long.' He offered a hand and helped her to her feet. 'Don't want you picking up any more policemen in my absence, do we?'

'No,' Donna said, her eyes on his, her lips slightly parted, far too close to his. 'I've got the place,' she blurted, just as Mark was wondering what she might taste like.

Mark twanged his attention away from her mouth. She'd got the... 'What?' He shook his head, confused.

'The place,' Donna repeated, with a determined nod, 'if you've got the time.'

'Right,' Mark nodded, now feeling totally confused. 'Donna, I'm not sure I'm getting the drift.'

'Coffee,' she said, two little bright spots appearing on her cheeks. 'Would you like one? Another one, I mean. Or tea? I might have some juice. Or wine, if you'd like. Only white, though, I'm afraid. And it's only the boxed stuff but...' Donna stopped as Mark continued to study her, confounded. Was she inviting him back to...? *Christ,* so what did he do now?

Donna dropped her gaze. 'I was just wondering if... but, if you're busy...' She stopped, chewing worriedly on her bottom lip, whilst distractedly stroking her beloved dog's head. The dog panted, glared at Mark — he would swear — then gazed lovingly up at Donna

Mark could see why. 'I adore coffee,' he said softly. 'Can't get enough of the stuff.'

****

'I haven't read it,' Donna announced, coming back into the kitchen after checking her son wasn't home.

Trying hard to look cool, as if a rabbit appearing from nowhere to park itself at his feet and make meal of his bootlace was nothing out of the ordinary, Mark glanced at her curiously.

'The book,' Donna clarified, plucking the rabbit up and peering worriedly through its ears.

Mark's mouth twitched into a smile. 'What, the one you renewed today? What was it?' He decided on diplomacy, rather than embarrass her further. What was he doing here? Apart from Michelle, his sexual encounters with women amounted to not many lately, but he wasn't convinced Donna was into casual sex.

Was it some kind of ego-boosting exercise on her part maybe? In which case he'd be happy to oblige, but couldn't help thinking it might not boost her ego very much. He'd thought his being here in situ might jog her memory, but she obviously didn't remember him from the call out they'd had a while back, a domestic reported by the neighbours. He definitely remembered her though. Remembered very well the guy she'd been married to: a posh twat with a temper. A nasty bastard if ever Mark saw one. Nothing but cocky contempt in his eyes, for Donna or the law. For obvious reasons, Mark had taken an instant dislike to him, keeping the pompous prick in the dining room while a WPC waited in the kitchen with Donna for her sister to arrive. She hadn't sustained physical injury. But she was shaken. And from what Mark had seen of her, her self-esteem had been badly bruised. Still was, obviously. So what *was* he doing here?

He glanced at his watch. He probably shouldn't be. Donna was clearly nervous and, though Karl was being safely looked after, he really ought to get back.

Mark felt a fresh pang of guilt at the thought of his son. He should have mentioned Karl. But then, whenever he had in the past... Announcing he had a child with autism spectrum disorder tended to ensure there was never a second date. And God knew, Mark really would like a relationship that didn't end before it started.

He certainly liked Donna, liked her a lot. He'd been so tempted to kiss her when she'd stood up to face him outside that café. He'd certainly like to try his luck here and now, if only she'd stop kissing the rabbit. She hadn't just brought him back for that though, surely? She was as shy as a mouse for a start. That was obvious a mile off. And, as well as being obviously fond of her buck-toothed little friend, she had a kid of her own and three-legged dog she would probably die for, which didn't make her sexual predator material. *Did* she mean she wanted more when she'd said she didn't want to rush into anything? Mark was less sure now. Maybe this was what she wanted. A no strings kind of thing. He really couldn't tell if he was reading the signs right at all.

'So?' he ventured, as Donna gave her furry puffball another smooch before lowering it gently to the floor.

'So, um...' Donna straightened up, shrugged and smiled; and looked as if she was about to bolt for the nearest door.

'Coffee,' Mark reminded her gently, as the rabbit hopped under the table to chew on a carrot, clearly contented. Mark could see why.

'Oh, yes. Sorry. Brain's not working very well.' Donna skidded over to the working surface. 'Not working at all, actually,' she said, peering into the coffee tin. 'I'm out, sorry.'

'No problem,' Mark assured her. 'Tea's fine.'

'Right. Good.' Donna nodded, reaching for the tea caddy.

'Is that where he lives?' Mark asked in awkward silence that followed, bar the crunching of carrots.

'Who?' Donna glanced over her shoulder. 'Oh, Findus. No, he lives in the utility, but his second name is Houdini.'

'He doesn't like solitary confinement,' she clarified, in answer to Mark's puzzled frown. 'Escapes his cage whenever he can and hops upstairs. I found him in my bed yesterday. Didn't I, naughty little Findus, hmm?'

Clever little Findus, thought Mark, wondering whether he should work on the doe-eyes and maybe grow some fur.

'Oh,' said, Donna a second later. 'I only have Earl Grey though. Will that do?'

'That will do nicely.'

'Good. Sorry.'

'But what would be nicer is if you'd stop saying sorry.'

'Right.' Donna turned back to the kettle. 'Sorry.'

Mark smiled. 'Donna,' he walked up behind her, placing a hand gently around her shoulder, 'you have nothing to apologise —'

'Crap!' Mark stepped back again, fast, as Donna whirled around.

But not fast enough.

'*Jesus*... Ouch!' He clutched his drenched jacket away from his midriff. '*Christ, that is* hot.'

'Ohmy*God*! I am *so* sorry! You took me by surprise. I... *Hell*!' Donna flew at him, dragged his jacket open, grappled with his shirt.

'Ahem.' Mark glanced down, as she fumbled with his buttons. Well, if she was a sexual predator, she wasn't very good at it. 'Donna?' Despite his best attempts at hiding his amusement, Mark's mouth twitched up at the corners.

'Ooh, *bloody* things.' Donna cursed, frustrated.

Mark laughed then, out loud. He couldn't help himself.

Donna gawped at him. 'You're burned,' she said, aghast. 'Why are you laughing?'

'Because you look as if you're about to saw my buttons off with your teeth.'

'I can't get them undone,' Donna said, obviously mortified as she fumbled some more.

He caught her hands. 'Donna, it was just a drop of tea. I'm not burned.'

She glanced down. 'Sorr...'

'Shush,' Mark said, easing her chin up. 'Never apologise, Donna. You have absolutely nothing to apologise for. Be confident. Believe in yourself. You're a beautiful woman.'

She blinked. Then blinked again. Then stood up on tiptoe and kissed his lips, a soft sweet kiss, which salved the scald under his shirt in an instant.

Jesus, now that was an invitation he was definitely hard-pushed to refuse. He searched her eyes as she looked expectantly into his, then, hesitantly, he pulled her into his arms and pressed his mouth against hers, his tongue gently probing, exploring.

Sweet Jesus, she tasted fantastic. Donna's tongue darted into his mouth. Boldly she thrust her tongue deeper and Mark suspected if she stopped now he might well die on the spot.

Tentatively, he trailed one hand the length of her spine, then stopped, his heart pounding, his thoughts colliding. She'd pulled away, dropped her gaze. He sucked in a breath.

'Donna, what is it?' he asked, his throat tight. 'What's wrong?' He lifted her chin to look into her eyes, and the ground beneath him shifted slightly off kilter. Jesus Christ, she had tears in her eyes.

'Hey, hey, gorgeous, what is it?' He wiped a tear from her cheek with his thumb and pulled her hard to him, holding her, hoping to comfort her. What the hell had he done? He wrapped his arms tight around her.

'I'm not gorgeous,' Donna mumbled into his epaulette.

'Excuse me?' Mark spoke gently, breathing deep the sweet scent of her.

She pressed her face closer. 'I'm sorry,' she said, grazing her thumb idly across his chest, which did nothing to dampen his arousal. 'I mean... I'm just not sure...'

'Not sure what?' Mark eased back. Panic setting in, he tried to ease her chin back up.

She wouldn't look at him.

'Donna? Do you want me to go?'

'No!' She snapped her head up, looking as bewildered as he felt. 'I don't want you to go. It's just... I'm not sure I'm doing this right.'

'What?' Mark laughed. Her gaze hit the floor again. Wrong reaction, Mark. 'Donna, you're crackers. Crackers and utterly gorgeous.' He cocked his head to one side to try and catch her eyes. 'You don't need to read your *how-to* guide. Whatever you're doing, you are *most* definitely doing it right for me. And if you don't believe me, I can give you hard evidence, trust me.'

'It's not a *how-to* guide. It's a... sort of hint.' She laughed. Thank God.

'That's better. Now, shall we take a step back, do you think?'

Donna blinked at him — and stepped back.

Mark scrunched his eyes closed, then peered at her through one eye. 'No, Donna. I didn't mean...' He trailed off. If he wasn't careful he was going leave her with less confidence than she'd had when he'd arrived.

Sexual predator? She was about as capable of molesting him as her three-legged dog was.

He took her hand, glanced down at it, trailed a thumb over it. 'Donna, don't get me wrong here, but are you sure you didn't mean *this* isn't right?

Donna chewed on her lip. 'Sorry,' she mumbled apologetically, again.

'No apologies required,' he reminded her. 'Come on,' he folded her into his arms. 'You know that saying *worth waiting for?*'

'Uh, huh.'

'Well, I am.'

She looked up at him, a smile on her face and the light back in her eyes. 'You're lovely,' she said.

'I know. And modest.' Mark laughed, then, ignoring his phone beeping in his pocket, he brushed her beautiful lips with his — and couldn't help feeling he might have found a little bit of heaven.

Chapter Three

Dammit, he should have known it was going to be one of those days with Karl when he'd practically had to wrestle him away from the cooker this morning, Karl's latest obsession being fire, which meant he was going through a pyromania phase when most kids would be getting into football.

Agitated, Mark flicked his siren again, frightening shoppers out of harm's way, and then humped the patrol car up on the kerb. 'Sorry about this, Phil.' He raked his hand through his hair and turned to his partner, who had offered to help Mark search the area for his now missing son. 'I had no idea Jody would...'

'Stop apologising and get going.' Phil shoved the passenger door wide, ready to climb out. 'He can't be far away. We'll find him.'

'Thanks, Phil. I owe you.' Mark nodded his appreciation and climbed out of the driver's side, panic knotting his stomach.

'You do the top end. I'll take the bottom. We'll cross over and come back down the opposite side.' Phil gestured Mark on, then headed for the lower end of the High Street.

Mark didn't need telling. He ran, fast, his heartbeat escalating to a steady thud as he went from shop to shop.

'We're looking for a small boy,' he shouted across to the owner of one of several gift-shops, all with the same glitter of memorabilia that would attract Karl like a moth. 'Aged six. About so high.' Mark indicated with his hand. 'Dark-haired. Wearing jeans, red tee-shirt, and a white hoodie.'

Also recognisable by the hand-flapping and spinning he'll be doing if he's stressed, Mark didn't get the chance to add before the owner shook his head.

This was hopeless. Mark pushed his cap back, frustrated, as he came out empty-handed. With the annual jazz festival on, Upton was chock-a-block with sightseers. What if Karl had headed for the river? Dread sliced through Mark's chest. Water might not be Karl's current fascination, but it had been a while back, running taps and flushing loos wherever he went. Might he have been attracted by the spectacle of boats bobbing at the water's edge? Crammed in at the water's edge, more like, at this time of year. Mark tried to quell a sudden queasiness. Narrow-boats mostly, shoulder-to-shoulder. Tons of heavy, bone-crushing metal.

Christ, he needed to call it in, radio for help. Mark swallowed hard, total panic gripping him now, as he turned in the direction of the river, then fleeting relief as he caught sight of Karl's carer.

'Mark!' Jody waved frantically, pushing towards him through a throng of onlookers.

Mark caught her by the shoulders as she reached him. 'Anything?' he asked, scanning her face, hoping against hope that Karl might be with her, behind her. Anywhere, for pity's sake.

She shook her head. 'No. I... I'm sorry, Mark. I didn't...'

'For Christ's sake, what were you thinking!?' Mark struggled to hold on to his temper. 'He can't stand crowds, Jody. You know that! The slightest thing sets him off.'

'I know. I do know.' Jody pressed a hand to her mouth. 'I'm so sorry,' she said, her hand trembling as she pulled it away. 'I needed to pick up a prescription for my mum on the way to the respite centre, and Karl seemed okay. I'd promised him a new toy, and we have brought him here before, so I...'

'Out of season, Jody, when the shops are empty and the crowds are gone.' And that was bad enough. Mark recalled with crystal-clear clarity how Karl had bolted as they'd tried to cross the road, narrowly missing an oncoming car.

Mark dragged a hand over his neck. He was tense, every muscle in his body taut with frustration and anger, but this wasn't Jody's fault. Karl was as unpredictable as he was predictable. If it was anyone's fault, it was his. Christ, even the boy's mother hadn't been able to cope with the day-to-day stress of caring for Karl. How was Jody supposed to cope day-in-day-out if Emma had finally admitted she couldn't be what Karl needed and quietly disappeared from his life?

She wouldn't be back either. She wrote occasionally. Called... less occasionally, now she'd met someone else. No, Emma wouldn't be back in Karl's life. Mark had faced that fact head on. He needed to face a more fundamental fact now. As much as he wanted to, and even with a sergeant understanding enough to cut him some slack, *he* couldn't cope.

Karl was growing up, getting bigger, stronger, becoming more demanding. Mark needed to get more help, rather than insist on keeping Karl home and entrusting his day-care to Jody.

'We'll find him.' Mark sucked in a breath, gave Jody what he hoped was a reassuring smile, then scanned the street behind her.

Jody nodded and wiped at a tear on her cheek.

'This toy,' Mark tempered his tone, knowing he was the cause of her tears and not liking himself for it, 'what was it going to be?'

'Just another model car to add to his collection.'

Figures, thought Mark, squinting as he noticed a rocking horse outside a second-hand shop, which would definitely indicate toyshop. An old-fashioned, glorious grey speckled affair on rockers. Similar to the horse depicted in Karl's *Sugar Takes Flight* bedtime story, which he insisted on hearing over and over each night.

'Was he using his own money?'

'Yes, his piggy bank...'

'In which case, I have an idea where he might be.' Mark scrambled around Jody so fast he almost fell over her. Please, God, let him be there.

Trying to slow his rapid breathing, Mark opened the shop door calmly. He didn't want to scare Karl. Karl couldn't relate to emotion on any level, but Mark knew that his son could see anger in his eyes. And he was bloody angry.

The bell tinkled overhead. The soft murmur of voices slowed and, somehow, Mark could sense his son's nearness. He glanced at the shopkeeper. 'There wouldn't be a young boy?'

'We wondered whose he was.' She nodded, indicating a room beyond the shop-fronting area they were in. An Aladdin's cave, stuffed full of toys and magical to a child's eyes. 'We were just about to call the police.'

'Mine. My son,' said Mark, his throat tight as he watched Karl wander through from the back room, his clear blue eyes wide with wonder, before they alighted on Mark. Then, they grew disconcerted, as if Karl knew he was in trouble, and Mark couldn't bear that. He knew he should talk to him. Try to instil in him through firm repetition, that he should not do this sort of stuff. Instead, he walked over to Karl and bent down to hug him so tight, he could feel his son's heartbeat next to his own.

'Hiya, mate. Did you get your model car?' he asked throatily, knowing Karl wouldn't, couldn't hug him back. Trying hard not to mind, Mark stood to ruffle Karl's hair. His fringe was tickling his eyelashes again, he noticed.

Time for a trim, he guessed, recalling how, with his long dark eyelashes, Karl had often been mistaken for a girl as a baby. How his wife had joked he'd grow up to be a heartbreaker. Mark's heart seemed to have broken, that was for sure.

Karl shook his head. 'No,' he said, in that gruff, grainy voice that drew people's stares. Mark didn't care. At least Karl was speaking. He was two when he'd stopped, and Mark's life changed forever

But now, with speech therapy and hard work, Karl at least had some vocabulary.

'Dog,' Karl went on bluntly, his brow furrowed in concentration as he took hold of Mark's hand.

'Dog?' Mark furrowed his brow in turn. 'Okay, so show me,' he said, knowing Karl would drag him there anyway to show him what he wanted.

Karl paused outside a glass display case. 'Dog,' he repeated, pointing a finger at a ceramic creature with huge, beguiling eyes.

Mark crouched down to Karl's level. He placed an arm around his son, his own eyes full of wonder now. 'That's right, Karl. Dog,' he said, looking from the dog to his son's face, carefully gauging his reactions. 'And this one...' he pointed to another dog, similarly hand-crafted, but a different breed, '... what's that Karl?'

Karl pointed at the original. 'Dog,' he repeated, resolute.

'Right.' Mark smiled. It was too much to hope that Karl might be able to hang something that was a different shape and colour on the same family tree, but one miracle was enough. Karl was here, in one piece, in a shop, with people. No sign of claustrophobia. No rocking, hand-flapping or temper tantrum in sight. And he was communicating. Rudimentary it might be, but he was exchanging dialogue. As miracles went, this one was more than enough.

'So, shall we buy the dog, Karl? Forget about the car for today, maybe?'

Mark held his breath and waited. Karl needed routine. Knowing what was going to happen next kept him on track. Buying a model car while out shopping was the 'right' way to do it in Karl's mind.

Karl nodded, at length. 'Yes,' he finally said.

And Mark breathed out.

The day, he decided as they left, Karl clutching the dog that had cost and arm and a leg, might not have turned out so badly, after all.

Draping an arm over Karl's shoulders, Mark nodded his reassurances to Phil and Jody as he approached the car where they waited.

Should he ring Donna, he wondered. Check she was okay after he'd checked his text and made what must have seemed like a sharp exit?

He could still taste her; smell her, an intoxicating mix of perfume and pure feminine essence. He reached for his mobile, which seemed to be burning a hole in his pocket. Wouldn't it seem a bit too keen though, ringing her barely an hour after leaving her? He hadn't had that much practice at the dating game. Had no idea what the protocol was. He must already have seemed pushy. Way too pushy. He didn't want her thinking he was desperate, some kind of obsessive who was going to plague her with calls. Didn't want to have to explain right then either why he had had to leave in such a hurry. Because he'd have to gloss it over, or out-and-out lie, and he definitely didn't want to do that.

Tomorrow, he decided. That wouldn't seem too soon. He'd ask her what food she liked, book the restaurant, and come clean over dinner. And then…

What would be would be.

****

Up bright and early the next morning, Donna popped Sadie on her favourite chair — opposite the patio windows where she could see out, popped a generous helping of cabbage and cucumber under the kitchen table for Findus, then dashed for the stairs to get ready for work, glancing casually at her mobile parked on the hall cupboard as she went.

She had given him the right number, hadn't she? She knitted her brow. He had put it into his mobile correctly, hadn't he? It was possible he might have... No, Donna, it is *not*. You gave him your home phone as well. The man said he'd ring and he will. Of course he would. She trudged on up. Wouldn't he?

Yesss! Donna whooped as, magically, the telephone rang behind her. She back-stepped, ecstatic, then deflated as she noted the number on her caller display.

'Hi, Mum,' she said brightly, not wanting to sound disappointed as she picked up.

'Oh, dear, still in the doldrums, then?' said her all-seeing, all-knowing mum.

'No, Mum.' Donna said sharply, wishing her mum wouldn't assume she spent her life lamenting the lack of a man. Mark had piqued her interest... a bit... but she could manage without one. She'd much rather manage without one than leap gaily out of the frying pan into the fire. Slowly was how she'd wanted things to progress with Mark. Assuming he wanted to take things further, that was. Did he? Her heart skipped a beat.

'I'm fine, Mum, honestly,' she said, feeling guilty. Her mum was concerned for her; that was all. It came with the territory, Donna knew it did. 'It's just that I'm a bit...'

... *late for work*, she didn't get the chance to add, before her mother said, 'down, I know, darling, but that's why I've rung.'

Oh, no. Donna groaned quietly. Not another suggestion to get herself out and about and join a pottery class or something. *Why?* Donna wanted to know. Demi Moore might have pulled it off on Sky Movies the other night, but Donna hadn't got a snowball in hell's chance of looking sexy with clay oozing through her fingers and caked on her face. She didn't want to join anything, for goodness sake. She didn't need to now, in any case. Did she?

Donna was halfway into a profound worry, when her mum announced, 'I've put your profile up on *Datamate*.'

What!? Had she gone completely mad?

'Now, before you think I've gone completely mad, you can take it down at any time, and you don't —'

'Mum!'

'… have to respond to any of the winks, or even —'

'Winks!?'

'… reply to emails, if you don't want to, but we are living in a technically-savvy age, darling. It was Dot's idea, and I do have to say I think it's a splendid one. We thought it might give you a chance to chat, you know, without putting yourself out and about.'

Dot. She might have known. Donna studied the cracks on her badly-in-need-of-decorating ceiling. Her friend Dot and her mum together were like the blooming dynamic duo, unstoppable. Advocates for charity courses, fund-raising efforts — the riskier the better, as in risqué-r — they were a force to be reckoned with. Possibly the only sensible activity they undertook since they'd met whilst out walking their own respective dogs, was the dog crèche they now ran together at Dot's house. It suited her mum, being retired from teaching, and it actually bought in a decent income as word spread and business picked up. And, the best spin off of all was, it kept her mum too busy to meddle in Donna's luckless love life. Or it had.

'Take it down, please, Mum,' she said remarkably calmly.

'But, Donna…' Her mum faltered for a nanosecond. '… it's perfectly safe. An excellent way to see what's out there without actually *going* out there. I know you're terribly shy, sweetie, and I thought —'

'Out where?' Donna scowled, noticed her reflection in the hall mirror and straightened her face. 'Cyberspace is the whole world, Mum!'

'Well, obviously you'd narrow your choices down by location.'

'Mum, I don't want to…' Donna stopped and breathed in… and out, in… and out. 'I don't want to get winked at. I don't care whether it's safe. It's sad! And I'm not.' Donna wasn't sure whether online dating was actually sad, each to their own, but what was definitely sad, was that everyone must think *she* was.

'I'm not in the doldrums, Mum.' She softened her tone, trying to sound less ungrateful. 'I just…' Should she mention Mark? Donna chewed on her lip. Yes, but mention what, exactly? That they'd had a sort of date and then watch while her mother put Mark through the third degree before they'd had another? If they had another. If he rang. 'I'm late for work, that's all. Please take it down, Mum.'

Her mum sighed resignedly. 'All right, Donna. Of course I will, if you really don't like the idea. But don't blame me if Matt Demon is out there, winking away as we speak.'

'Damon. It's Matt Damon, Mum, and he's married.'

'Is he? Oh, well, never mind, there are bound to be plenty of other winkers,' her mum quipped jocularly.

Donna shook her head, despairing. 'Yes, mum, but I don't want one. Look, I've got to go. Talk later. Bye.'

'Bye, darling,' her mother said, through another audible sigh. 'And try not to get too down, hmm? Having a man in your life is not the be all and end all, after all, is it? Oh, that'll be Dot at the door. See you later.'

Donna went cross-eyed as she put the phone down. Honestly, did she look desperate enough to be 'chatting' to a flipping computer?

'Ring, will you?' she growled at her mobile, then headed huffily back upstairs.

Truthfully, Donna half-expected Mark not to. No, she fully expected him not to. That was okay. She swallowed hard. She'd mentally prepared herself anyway.

She must have totally confused him, inviting him back for coffee followed by not-so-hot sex and then actually offering him nothing. No wonder he'd done a runner.

She hoped he hadn't.

He'd seemed so nice. Straightforward, uncomplicated, courteous and... Donna sighed longingly... utterly scrummy. Profiteroles drenched in fresh cream and hers for the eating — if only her mum knew. Pity Donna hadn't had a clue what to do.

Glancing wistfully back at the bed she fantasised Mark in all night, her attention snagged on the clock, sending Donna into a flap. Damn, where did the time go? Work aside, she'd her doctor's appointment to go to. She'd already put it off twice, her bitchy manageress always seeming to be watching her timekeeping. Well, she couldn't put it off any longer. Suspicious little lumps shouldn't be ignored. Donna's poor hoppity dog was testament to that.

Heading swiftly for the bathroom, she stripped off her dog walking clothes, tossed them out onto the landing ready to take down to the wash, then threw herself under the shower. She was just stepping out when the doorbell rang. Perfect. Donna was stark naked on the inside of the bathroom, and her clothes were on the outside.

Dabbing at her hair, she squeaked the open bathroom door. 'Matt, could you get the door please?' No response. 'Matt?!'

Still nothing. Donna assumed her son either had his iPod stuffed in his ears, or he'd already left for college. Sighing, she wrapped a towel around herself and headed for the stairs, to find Matt, who obviously hadn't yet left, scrambling up them, Findus in arms. *Hell.* Being highly superstitious, Donna's heart sank. She didn't want to tempt fate when she'd just met the nicest man she was ever likely to meet. The hall mirror crashing to the floor the morning she'd discovered Jeremy was bonking the Twiglet was evidence of the terrible luck that befell people who did. But then, the mirror had broken *after* she'd found out. And they had been in the middle of that dreadful door-slamming, fist-banging last row, Donna remembered with a shudder.

No, she assured herself, this wasn't a sign. She was just being neurotic. Mark would ring. He'd said he would. Everything was absolutely fine.

'Don't cross on the stairs. It's bad luck,' she hissed at her son, sandwiching herself against the wall to try to negate said bad luck as Matt squeezed past.

'Sorry,' he mumbled, glancing over his shoulder as he hastened his way upward.

Rather too urgently, Donna noted. Matt didn't move with any sense of urgency. He sloped. During an earthquake he might notch it up to a brisk walk. But bounding, whether joyfully or otherwise, was just not in his adolescent nature.

Donna narrowed her eyes. He was cuddling Findus very close to his chest, she noticed, which, from experience, read: *you wouldn't hit a man who loves fluffy animals, would you?* 'Matt, what have you been up to?'

He turned on the landing, hoisted Findus higher and peeked over his ears, the epitome of virtue. 'Moi?'

'Yes, you. You look far too innocent not to be guilty. What have you done?'

'Nothing,' he assured her, blinking beguilingly, then bolting for his bedroom. 'Much,' he added, kicking the door closed behind him.

Oh, no… Donna's shoulders slumped. She tightened her towel, and trudged on down to see which neighbour he'd annoyed now with his clunking, exhaust-blowing VW, which he insisted on starting at least ten times a day, even though he was barely past lesson two. Please don't let him have reversed it down the drive and over next-door's prized plant pot again. Or worse, their cat.

Donna swung the door open, hiding her trepidation with a cheery smile. It was just the postman. She smiled proper. And Matt obviously hadn't reversed over him.

The postman smiled back, rather flatly, and handed Donna the buckled wheel of his bike.

Oh, not so fine then.

****

He *had* rung. Donna couldn't quite believe it. She shut down her computer, ready to go home, outwardly calm, but inside her emotions in turmoil. She'd been perfectly relaxed all morning, nervous, yes, but desperate for him to ring. Convincing herself she could do relationships should — by some miracle — Mark want to take things further. On the basis that neither party could be entirely blameless, Donna conceded that she might have been responsible in some part for the breakdown of her marriage, but she had to believe she wasn't mostly to blame. That Jeremy's insinuation she was unresponsive, ergo a total turnoff in bed was dire tripe, concocted to get himself off the hook.

The thing was, though, even acknowledging it was hard to respond sexually to a bully, she didn't believe she wasn't deep down. Insidious little things that they were, those seeds of doubt had taken root, and as hard as her mum and her sister had tried to convince Donna the problems in her marriage had been Jeremy's, not hers, Donna couldn't help thinking they might be.

By lunchtime, she'd felt so nauseous, she'd gone off her tuna and cucumber on white. She didn't even feel the inclination for a cheese and onion crisp, which she generally devoured by the big-bagful. Mark wasn't going to ring. She'd managed to convince herself that much.

By mid-afternoon, she'd convinced herself she couldn't do it anyway, even if he did ring, which he wouldn't. She really had no clue how to... just be, naturally. Inarticulate is how she felt. Unworldly — and scared.

'I thought Italian, maybe,' Mark said into her mobile, as she tried to formulate a sensible sentence. '*Benedicto's* in Worcester. What do you think?'

Ultra posh nosh, Donna thought, followed by coffee... Oh, God! 'I can't, Mark,' she blurted. 'It's a nice idea, but...' Donna trailed off, glancing at Jean, her work-shy manageress, who glanced from Donna to the clock, pointedly, her unspoken message being, *it's five minutes to five. You're still on work time.*

'Oh,' Mark said, followed by a loaded pause. 'Did I do something wrong?'

'No! I —'

'But you're not interested?'

Donna closed her eyes, her heart beating a steady drumbeat in her chest. What did she say? He'd actually rung. She'd thought it about as likely as winning the lottery. But he had. She'd so wanted him to.

'Donna? Talk to me.'

Donna swallowed. 'I have to go, Mark,' she said quickly, as Jean harrumphed and demonstratively shuffled papers. 'I can't talk right now. Can I call you back in about ten minutes?'

'Okay. No problem,' Mark said, a curious edge to his voice.

Donna signed off, and tried hard to convince herself she was being pathetic as she filled the last five minutes of her workday filing. She'd found one: a perfectly lovely specimen of the rare breed of late-thirtyish men, whose intentions seemed honourable, and she was about to turn down an invitation to go out with him?!

Was *she* mad?

No... She filed an 'E' document under 'H', extracted it, and tried again... she was truly scared. Terrified he'd see her as her husband obviously had, i.e. a not-so-perfect specimen of a not-so-rare breed of mid-thirtyish women, who wasn't quite so honed as he. In fact, totally unhoned and with stretch marks she couldn't hope to hide unless she made love with him in the dark wrapped in a duvet.

Oh, God, what on earth did she do? He'd be bound to want to get naked; sooner rather than later, since she'd so brazenly thrown herself at him. And if it wasn't sooner, it would be later, and then he would move on... sooner or later.

And she'd be lonely and upset all over again.

Because she'd let him in - and this man wouldn't leave with a little bit of heart. He'd take all of it. Break it.

Because, she suspected, PC Mark Evans quite easily could.

Donna trailed to the loo to ring him back, knowing it was hopeless. Even with spray tans and Posh Spice's bone structure, she couldn't hope to pass herself off as fresh fruit. And, even if he didn't mind what he saw, the reality was he'd like it much more if what he saw was ten or fifteen years younger.

No, she simply couldn't go that route. Whatever dignity she did have, she needed to hold onto it.

'Mark, I like you,' she said immediately when he answered. 'I like you a lot, but...' she hesitated, no clue how tell him but the way it was. 'I'm not ready for a full-on relationship, Mark. I thought you understood.'

'Oh, right. I, er...' Mark paused, for what seemed like an eternity. 'Maybe we could... go for a drink then, sometime?'

'Yes, that might be nice.' Donna chewed hard on her lip.

'Good.' Mark paused again, and Donna so wanted to fill the gap, to tell him how she really felt. *So tell him!* An inner voice screamed.

Cursing her ineptitude, Donna opened her mouth and, 'Okay,' he said, drawing in a terse breath. 'I'll catch up with you, then. Bye.'

And then he rang off.

Donna blinked at her mobile forlornly. She'd hurt him. She could hear it in his voice. She hadn't meant to. He'd been considerate and caring, more caring than any man she'd ever known, but... He would change, she told herself resolutely. Hadn't he already, going swiftly from dinner tonight to a drink 'sometime'? He wouldn't 'catch up with her', not now that he realised he hadn't got access to the full menu. And what about Matt? Mark might not have responsibilities, but Donna certainly did. Was a man like Mark, good-looking, apparently childless, ergo footloose and fancy-free, really going to be interested in anything beyond a sexual relationship? Would he really want to be embroiled in the life of a single-mum and all the problems that went with it?

Not a chance. Of that much Donna was totally convinced.

Chapter Four

'Great!' She'd given him the brush off. Why? Surely she must realise he liked her? Could care about her — a lot. Dammit, he'd really thought Donna might... Obviously not. Dejected, Mark ran a hand over his neck, pocketed his mobile, and headed back towards the lawned area outside the Blossom Tree Respite Home. They'd agreed to keep Karl for a few days, which would give Jody a break while her mum was ill. It would give Mark a break, too, which he badly needed.

He glanced up from his contemplation as he approached a group of five children, Dr. Lewis overseeing them and... what was that in the middle of the group? Blimey, a real live dog? Mark smiled, surprised, as he got closer. A Labrador, from the look of it, sitting slap bang in the middle of them, wagging its tail, quite content being petted... by Karl?

Surprise gave way to out-and-out shock. Mark hardly dared to breathe as he locked eyes with Dr. Lewis. Karl was actually stroking the dog. Touching it. Feeling? How? Mark swallowed back a lump in his throat.

'It's a PAT dog.' Dr. Lewis answered his unasked question, walking across to place a reassuring hand on Mark's arm.

'A PAT?' Mark's voice was slightly strangulated. He coughed and tried again. 'A what?'

'Pets As Therapy. They're volunteer dogs. Well, that is, the owners volunteer their dogs for service. Karl coming in clutching his new doggy friend prompted me to contact one of our volunteers. What do you think?'

'I think I may be hallucinating.' Mark laughed, disbelieving. 'The most I've seen Karl do lately is line up his cars, turn endlessly around in circles, try to set fire to the place or throw himself on the floor.'

Dr. Lewis nodded. 'That's where I'm hoping Ben might come in and help Karl stop being a hostage to his rituals. Dogs like Ben are used all over, to bring comfort to people: in hospitals, hospices, residential homes and special-needs schools. They allow kids to express themselves in ways they otherwise couldn't.'

'Right,' Mark looked doubtful. 'And if the kids get a little over-expressive and try to part the dog with its tail?'

'Oh, I'm sure one or two of them will, but we don't worry if the dog doesn't. They all have to pass an assessment test, undertaken by an accredited assessor. Karl won't come to any harm. In fact, I'd say it's doing him some good, wouldn't you?'

Mark nodded, the ability to speak seemed to have temporarily deserted him. He pressed a thumb and forefinger against his eyes.

'We've been assessing Karl over the last few months...' Dr. Lewis wrapped an arm around Mark's shoulders and walked him away from the group, nodding at a volunteer to step in as he did so '... and we think he might benefit from an Autism Assistance dog.'

'An assistance dog?' Marked looked at Dr. Lewis dubiously.

'Autism Assistance Dog or AAD, as we call them. They're trained to assist people with autism. Much like service dogs are trained to perform tasks for people with other sensory-processing disabilities, to help them gain independence and confidence, ultimately the ability to perform day-to-day activities, much like everyone else.'

Mark drew in a deep breath. 'Karl isn't like everyone else, though, is he?' He stopped, looked Dr. Lewis straight in the eye, then looked back to Karl, who'd now wrapped his arms around the dog's neck. Jesus. Now, that was a miracle. Mark glanced at the sky. One he'd never allowed himself to hope for. 'Do you think it can help him?' he asked, daring — after so many despairing, draining years of trying to keep Karl safe — to hope for more.

'Well, it can't cure him, but...'

'I know that,' Mark snapped, and immediately regretted it. The guy was just covering himself, but the fact was, Mark did know. Caring for Karl was for life, an almost indescribable task to anyone but Dr. Lewis: The uphill struggle to get the diagnosis, the constant assessments, the roller-coaster ride of not knowing where and what might bring on a tantrum.

The constant ritual they lived their lives by, making sure Karl's daily routine wasn't detracted from before he was ready. He was scared of traffic, of crowds, of shops, the noise seeming to close in on him and cause a total meltdown sometimes. Even background noises — noises most people couldn't even hear, could drive Karl to distraction.

Mark wasn't ashamed of Karl. He could never be that. Karl was the same child he'd loved before he heard the word autism, after all. But Mark wanted more for his son. He wanted Karl to be the best that he could. He didn't believe Karl was happy cocooned in his own little world, when the outside world was such a mass of people and places he couldn't make sense of. Mark wanted Karl to learn, at least learn new ways of coping with daily activity. Because, at the end of the day, Mark knew he wouldn't always be around — to hold Karl when he was scared, to stop him from bolting in front of that car, to find him when he'd wandered too far.

Mark massaged his temples. 'Dr. Lewis, I apologise. It's been a long day and... I'm struggling, to be honest. It's hard to allow myself to hope, you know?'

Dr. Lewis nodded. 'Autism is hard on the children, but it's sometimes harder on the parents. We don't know whether it can help Karl until we try, though. And whilst Karl might tire of Ben, he certainly doesn't seem to be in danger of doing so imminently.'

Mark glanced back to the group. 'No,' he conceded, watching Karl stroke the dog with repeated consistent, soft strokes, from his head to his tail. 'Okay, tell me more.'

'Good.' Dr. Lewis smiled. 'Well, it is a relatively new thing, but it does seem to be getting results. Obviously, the dog provided is fully-trained, assuming there's a dog available.'

Mark nodded, trying not to feel disappointed before they'd even got started.

'The parents or carers have to have the correct training and support, along with the child, of course,' Dr. Lewis continued, 'but basically, whilst being aware that every autistic child is unique, we're looking to help with behaviours in common that lead to social isolation, both within the family and with other people. Mobility issues, lack of awareness of danger in everyday situations.'

Mark nodded again, understanding, but not quite getting how. 'Can it stop him from wandering, or bolting, when he's out in the open?' he asked, that being one of his major fears.

'That's the idea. The child and the dog share a harness and, initially, you control the child by commanding the dog.'

Mark looked at Dr. Lewis, not sure he wanted Karl to be tethered to a dog.

'It might seem a bit extreme at first,' Dr. Lewis said, 'but remember these dogs are highly trained. And the benefits are enormous. Increased safety for the child, increased independence. The amazing thing is, from case studies, it does appear to teach the child responsibility. We've seen positive changes in behaviour, lower aggression levels, and of huge benefit is that the dog seems to offer comfort to the child when he gets upset. They're allowed full access to public places, as are other sensory assistance dogs.'

'So he'd be with him wherever he goes?' Mark stopped to look back at Karl.

'Yes, by and large. The ultimate aim is to reduce the stress associated with interacting with people. An autism dog, given it works out, can allow a child to participate in education, social, and leisure activities.'

'... to lead a more fulfilling life.' Mark finished, his gaze on Karl, who'd curled up on the lawn with Ben now, and seemed to be sleeping.

'So, how do we apply?' he asked, choked, because if ever he'd been looking for evidence there was a God, this had to be it.

****

Donna pulled up on her drive feeling miserable. Then, marginally better as she imagined Jean getting her artistically-knotted scarf caught in the shredder. The Chief Executive was so besotted with her, he'd probably think it was some kinky sex game and try to bonk her. Donna sighed. She didn't care if they were having an affair as long as Jean didn't keep offloading her work onto her. She had no hope of her application for childcare training succeeding if she couldn't keep on top of her workload, thus ensuring a decent reference.

Ah, well, she was home now. She'd try a little one-on-one assertiveness with Jean tomorrow — or email her — possibly.

Coward. Donna despaired of ever getting ahead as she trudged through the front door. She just didn't do confrontation well.

'Sweetie!' she cried, spotting Sadie hopping precariously up the hall. 'You came to greet me. Aw, hon...' Donna bent down to stroke her faithful friend and felt a lot better, until she remembered tonight was Pilates night.

Oh, she really did not want to go. She'd much rather stay at home and examine her heart about her feelings for Mark; and her conscience about her treatment of him.

Why had she turned him down? She was a grown woman. She didn't have to give all of herself, heart, body, and soul, until she knew him, knew whether he was interested in anything long term. And surely she could have handled it if he didn't turn out to be as perfect as she needed him to be. Perhaps she could have, in time. She wouldn't have time though, not now she'd pushed him away.

She sighed, a shuddery sigh. She'd have to go to Pilates. Her sister would be insistent, being the *healthy body equals healthy mind* sort and determined to keep in shape. Not that Alicia ever looked out of shape, as Jeremy hadn't been slow to point out. Unlike Donna, Alicia was tall, beautiful and slender, even after having a baby.

Donna sighed again and tried not to mind. Alicia was as mad as a hatter, as eccentric as their mother, always there for her — and Donna loved her to bits. No, she couldn't let her sister down.

Like she had Mark.

Awash with guilt, Donna headed for the kitchen to check whether Findus was home or under the table. The table invariably, dining out on a carrot.

'Hey, little one, how are you doing, hmm?' Donna crouched down to trail the pad of her finger the length of his velvet-soft nose.

'All right, hon?' She blinked lovingly at him. Findus stopped gnawing his carrot to fix her with one sideways bright eye.

'You're all fur, aren't you, sweetie, hey?' Donna continued to stroke him, gentle strokes over his head — careful to avoid his sensitive ears — and down his back, feeling the fragility of his little bones beneath her fingers. 'A big furry fluff-ball, aren't you?'

She reached to gather him up, as Findus warmed to her touch, always a bit wary, being a one guy kind of rabbit. 'A gorgeous, big, furry fluff-ball,' she cooed.

Findus observed her, unmoved, bar a twitch or two of his nose.

Donna smiled and twitched, and then kissed him; she couldn't resist. 'Smitten, aren't I, sweetie, hey?' She laughed as Findus offered her another startled twitch back, then held him close to pop him back safe in his cage.

'Between you and me, I think I might be smitten with another gorgeous guy, Findus,' she confided, nuzzling his cheek as she carried him there. 'And I'm not sure I want to be,' she fluffed up his hay and encouraged Findus to find his way home, 'because I'm not sure I can give all of me.

'So what should I do?' she asked herself more than Findus, as she closed the cage door. Not that there was anything much *to* do, now she'd more or less told Mark where to go. She sighed again, then smiled, as Findus demonstrated his thoughts on the subject and hopped merrily into bed.

'Hmm? I suspect this is more the male point of view, Findus,' she told him, making sure the door was closed tight, then checking Sadie was safe on her chair, before trailing upstairs in search of sports gear that wouldn't make her look like the back end of a bus. Should she ring Mark back, she debated. She could always say she was calling about the damp jacket he'd left behind when he'd read his urgent text. He couldn't be very authoritative in only half a police uniform, after all. She walked over to where she'd hung it on the wardrobe door to dry. Brushed a bit of fluff from it. Trailed her hand over it. Sniffed it.

It smelled of him. She breathed deep the citrussy scent of his aftershave. *Joop Homme.* Yes, definitely, *Joop.* She'd identified it in her lunch hour at Boots. Orange blossom, cinnamon, jasmine accented with amber, cedar, vanilla — and pure essence of man.

It suited him.

No, she couldn't ring him. Even if he wanted to speak to her, she'd be doing it for all the wrong reasons. She had another quick sniff, then wandered across the room to peer into drawers, hoping for inspiration. She'd be ringing him out of guilt and guilt was a problem she'd struggled with throughout her marriage. Jeremy always seemed to make her feel as if everything was her fault if they argued, jumping on her every mood, asking casually if it was 'that time of the month' whenever she'd been upset over things he'd said, and done, and had been doing for a very long time behind her back. She'd been such a fool to let him treat her so badly.

But Mark wasn't Jeremy.

Mark was nice. She was beginning to think that that's what she would have found at the core of him, if only she'd given him a chance. No hidden depths or dark secrets, just niceness.

Jeremy was most definitely not nice.

His overt condescension hadn't taught her that. It was a combination of things. The way he'd laugh at her, belittling her in front of friends. Drawling, 'Donna's domestic Goddess gene doesn't work very well, does it, darling?' when she'd spent hours in the kitchen and things had gone a bit awry. He'd create situations where he *could* laugh at her. He knew she was terrified of spiders. He'd pretended to throw one at her once. It was just a crinkled-up leaf from a plant, but Donna hadn't known that when it landed in her hair. They'd had company around that time, too. She'd been hysterical and the man she'd once thought herself safe with had laughed at her.

And then, when the guests had gone, they would argue and Jeremy would stomp about and bang things and shout.

He'd scared her. Donna shuddered involuntarily and reminded herself never, ever, would she go there again.

Mark scared her too, she supposed, though in a completely different way than Jeremy. No one could be as perfect as he seemed. Donna didn't want be there when the gloss wore off. When Mark got bored and stopped trying. The opposite of love, it seemed to Donna, wasn't hate. It was indifference: Treating a person as if they were nothing more than a mild irritation, or didn't exist at all.

No, she wouldn't ring him, she decided, pouring herself into her too-tight sweatpants and vowing to diet immediately after she'd finished her bar of Cadbury's Whole Nut.

What happened with Jeremy wasn't Mark's fault, but she couldn't go through that again. Donna honestly didn't know whether she was damaged goods now, or whether she'd never functioned properly in the first place, inviting a man into her life who didn't truly care for her. Whatever, she didn't feel able to cope with the aftermath if she made the same mistake all over again with Mark.

And she could, quite easily.

Except... it was all history now, wasn't it? And if it wasn't, it soon would be if he caught a glimpse of her in this little lot. Donna appraised herself in the mirror, rolled her eyes and hastily tugged off a breast-flattening vest in favour of baggy. Finally, as ready as she could be in mismatching sports gear, she wrestled her hair into a band and dashed downstairs.

'Bye, baby.' She kissed Sadie, left Matt pizza money — he being out, having progressed from Facebook to face-to-face with a girl, and plucked up her car keys.

Just as she reached the front door, the phone rang. Donna's mouth went dry. She glanced at the caller display. It was Mark. Her heart boomed against her chest as she plucked up the receiver.

'Hi,' he said. 'It's me. How are you?'

Donna took a breath. 'The same as I was earlier. Okay, you know.'

'Any chance you've changed your mind? About dinner?'

Donna chewed on her lip. *Say yes. Say yes,* a little voice said in her head. *Go back upstairs, put on some make-up, pick out your best dress and say yes.* 'I can't, Mark, not tonight. I...'

'Look, Donna, don't blow me off again,' he said quickly. 'I understand. You don't want to get too involved. Can't we just talk though, over coffee maybe?'

Donna agonised. 'Mark, I can't tonight, really. I have to meet my sister.'

'Tomorrow?'

Donna closed her eyes. 'I... I'm not sure. I have something on,' she said, part of her backsliding already. 'Can I call you?'

'Okay,' Mark said, with an audible sigh. 'I'll wait to hear from you, then. Bye, Donna.'

****

Would she call? Mark didn't think so. Well, he'd tried. There was nothing else he could do, short of driving past her house with blue lights flashing and a banner flying behind saying, "Donna O'Connor will you please give me a bloody chance?'

Not much point if she really wasn't interested. He supposed he should just forget about her and move on. He'd got too much on his plate already anyway. Pulling in a breath, he started the engine, then switched off again as his mobile rang. Noting the number he didn't hesitate to answer, though he was disappointed it wasn't Donna.

'Hi, Dad. What's happening?'

'Power's gone off.' His dad sighed. 'Lights, TV, cooker, the lot. Just wondered if you knew of a decent electrician, rather than me sticking a needle in the old Yellow Pages?'

'Not one who's likely to come at short notice, no. You're sure it's not just a bulb blown, or something?'

'Oh, that would do it, would it?' his dad asked, sounding slightly embarrassed.

Mark guessed why. Working away from home most his married life meant his dad didn't have a clue about maintaining a house. It had been hard on his mum sometimes, harder when she'd realised it wasn't all work that kept him away. It was hard on the old man now though. His guilt weighed heavy, Mark knew.

'That, or a short in the supply somewhere,' he suggested. 'You'll need to flip the switch on the fuse... No. No, leave it.'

Mark pictured his dad struggling to climb the ladder to reach the fuse box. Uh-uh, not with his dodgy hip. 'Stay where you are, Dad. I'm on my way.'

****

Twenty minutes later, Mark headed through his father's kitchen with the stepladder. 'All done,' he said to his dad, who was standing at the table, looking awkward and out of place in a room that was once solely his wife's domain.

'There's a torch in the utility,' Mark offered, noting his dad was scraping spilled candle-wax from the table. 'Mum kept one in the cupboard for emergencies.'

'Ah.' His dad smiled. Stiffly, Mark noticed. His dad hadn't smiled much since his mum died. That was the trouble with regrets, Mark supposed. Life had a habit of moving on before you could do anything about them.

No point in his dad beating himself up about it now though, or for Mark to be laying blame. His dad was getting older, confused sometimes, and, God knew, Mark had a few regrets of his own. The past was the past, best left where it was, he reckoned. Life was just too short to be agonising over stuff you couldn't change.

'Do you fancy some tea?' he asked, trying to ease the awkwardness between them.

'I'll get it.' His father insisted, turning to stride to the cooker, still the proud man with a razor sharp memory Mark had always known his father to be, so long as he wasn't trying to recall what happened yesterday.

Years ago, no problem. That was his dad's yesterday nowadays. 'Brought Emma with you, have you?' His father asked as he filled kettle, confirming Mark's fear that he was getting more confused.

'No, Dad.' Mark dragged a hand through his hair. 'We, er… We split, Dad, remember?'

His dad furrowed his brow. 'Oh. Yes. Sorry, lad. I get a bit forgetful sometimes.'

'Don't we all?' Mark made light of it, because he knew his dad hated being reminded about his incompetent memory. He'd have to organise some home help for him at some point. 'I'll just go and…' He nodded towards the stairs, then went off to scout about for other candles that might inadvertently be left burning.

'I've got some of that walnut coffee cake in, if you fancy some,' his dad called after him. 'Your mother's cake was always better, of course.'

Mark paused on the stairs.

His dad didn't often talk about his mum, but when he did his tone was always tinged with remorse. Mark had been furious with him, initially, but now… Whatever he'd done, it was enough for Mark that he knew how much hurt he caused.

'Man after my own heart, Dad,' he called back, then swallowed quietly as he peered into his parents' bedroom; at the bed where his mum had sat once, quietly crying. That was the only time Mark had seen her cry. He'd known she was, though she wouldn't admit it, dabbing quickly at her eyes when he came into the room.

She was fine, she'd assured him, telling him to get off and see to his own problems, of which she knew Mark and Emma had plenty,

Karl being at the stage where he seemed to be unlearning all that he'd learned. She hadn't been fine though. Mark had heard the arguments and the loaded silences when he'd visited thereafter. He'd gleaned his dad had had 'a fling' while working away.

It was later though, while his dad kept up a vigil at his mum's side at the hospital, that Mark had learned how much of a fling.

His mum had been taken ill so suddenly, it shocked both of them. Mark recalled with familiar sadness how she'd seemed to lose weight overnight. She wasn't going to make it, they'd realised that as they'd watched her slip silently into unconsciousness. Needing to confess, Mark supposed, his dad had started talking to him, telling him how, as the sales director for Mercedes Benz in Japan — where there was cachet in owning a European car, he'd been kept busy; too busy to come home sometimes. There were times, though, he'd admitted, not meeting Mark's eyes, when he could have come home, and he hadn't... because he'd had a longstanding relationship with another woman.

That's what had made his mother cry openly that day, Mark realised then. She'd obviously found out. And his father had examined his conscience every day since, living a frugal existence, donating all of his mother's insurance payout — other than that which he'd put in trust for Karl — to the hospice. Cutting himself off from the company.

Mark knew it was his father's way of trying to make amends. He wished he wouldn't; isolation seeming only to exacerbate his confusion. Knew also that he had to let any resentment he might have go. At the end of the day, hadn't he walked away from his responsibilities, too? He didn't blame Emma for leaving, not really. He should have been listening, not getting to work as fast as he could, leaving Emma to cope on her own with Karl, to feel utterly alone. Mark knew how that felt now.

He closed the bedroom door and went back down to the kitchen, where his father was slicing up the coffee cake. He definitely looked older. The perpetual swarthy tan had gone and there was a slight stoop to his shoulder. No, there was no point raking over old coals.

'Your mum was a good cook, you know?' his dad said, glancing at Mark, nostalgia shot through with sadness in his eyes.

'I know, Dad.' Mark nodded and went to pour the tea.

'Upstairs, is she?' his dad asked.

Mark tensed. This was not good. 'No, Dad. You know she's not,' Mark reminded him gently. He looked back at his dad now seated back at the farmhouse table. The same table his mum had stripped of 'atrocious' gloss paint and lovingly restored. That was the abiding smell of home Mark always remembered, wax polish, and home-baked cake.

'There's plenty,' his dad said, eyeing the cake, then Mark hopefully. 'I like to keep some in for...'

... when Mark ever bought Karl round, Mark knew his dad wanted to add. He would bring him, he decided, at the weekend, though the chances of Karl eating anything unfamiliar were nil. His last tantrum in mind, when his food wasn't arranged on his plate as he needed it to be, coffee cake would be more than Mark dared to put in front of him. He'd need to visit before then though, he suspected, his father forgetting — or more likely not bothering — to keep much else food-wise in.

'Cheers. Looks good,' he said, plucking up the cake to take a bite, and remembering that he hadn't thought much about food himself that day. 'Tastes pretty good, too.' Mark checked his watch as he downed the last mouthful. 'I've got to go, Dad,' he said apologetically. 'Will you be okay?'

'Yes, of course. Go on.' His dad waved a hand. 'You get off. Karl will be waiting. All right, is he, young Karl?'

'Yes,' Mark assured him, dusting crumbs from his lapel and feeling much better for having broken bread of sorts with his father. 'A handful, you know, but nothing I can't cope with.'

'Good. Good. And how's that woman who looks after him, Gemma?'

It was Jody now, but Mark despaired of his father ever remembering that. Gemma had retired to become a full time mum six months ago. And what an adjustment that had been for him and Karl. But it was over now, and Jody and Karl were getting on famously.

'She's fine, Dad. Got her hands full with Karl, too, as always, but doing okay. I'll see if Mrs Bruce can pop round, shall I?'

His father gagged on his tea. 'Bruce the Brute!' he spluttered. 'Your mother would turn in her grave. And I'll probably jump in mine if that woman comes around fussing and flicking her duster. Go on. You go. I'm not incapable yet. I can get myself fed and watered and off to bed.'

'Okay, I'm gone.' Mark held up his hands in surrender, as his dad clattered his cup up and marched to the sink. 'Make sure you lock up though.'

'Oh, I will.' His dad assured him as Mark headed for the door. 'Don't want The Mighty Bruce sneaking in.'

'To have her wicked way with you.'

His dad shuddered. 'God forbid.'

Mark laughed as he left. He'd drop by tomorrow, but... He tapped on the next-door neighbour's door, nevertheless. Better to be safe.

Mrs Bruce squeaked her door open an inch. 'Oh, it's you, Mark.' Her expression went from wary to warm when she recognised him. She flung the door wide and had him pressed to her ample bosom in two seconds flat.

'How are you?' she asked, finally releasing him before his ribs cracked.

'Fine, thanks, Mrs B,' Mark assured her, glancing past her to where her friend, business partner, and fearless leader of every local campaign, was shooing three barking dogs back into the kitchen. 'Hi, Evelyn,' he called. 'How's things in the dog walking business?'

'Dog sitting,' Evelyn corrected him, turning from the kitchen door and dusting herself free of dog hairs. 'And business is slow with *madam* here...' Evelyn rolled her eyes towards Mrs Bruce '... stopping to pee every time we pass the loo in the park.'

'I do not!' Mrs Bruce blustered.

'Dot, you do.' Evelyn collected a wine bottle and corkscrew from the coffee table and strolled towards the door, looking trendy and elegant, in a belted thigh-length jumper and leggings. 'No point being embarrassed about it. No shame in old age, is there, Mark?'

'Er, no.' Mark glanced at his shoes.

'So have you come to show an old girl a good time?' Evelyn made suggestive eyes at him.

'I'd love to. Unfortunately, my heart belongs to another, doesn't it Mrs B?' Mark gave Mrs Bruce a wide smile and a wink.

'Oh, get on with you.' Mrs Bruce blushed. 'I'm old enough to be your grandmother. Mind you,' she mused, 'I could do with getting myself a boy-toy.'

Evelyn sighed. 'Toy-boy, Dot. Toy-boy. Honestly, how on earth is a girl supposed to pull any kind of man with her tagging along?' She handed Mark the bottle with an amused smile, indicating he should pull the cork, presumably.

Mark laughed. She was a strange woman. If he had to describe her, he'd call her a glamorous battle-axe, one he couldn't help but admire. Last time he'd seen her, she was stopping traffic trying to get a new school crossing in place. Evelyn Thompson took on local causes as if they were her own. He doubted she'd allow herself to be put out to grass any time soon.

'You're on, Mrs B,' he said, handing the open bottle back to Evelyn. 'I'm yours, so long as you do me a favour in return.'

'Oh, dear, been playing up again, has he, our Mr Independent?' Mrs Bruce nodded towards his dad's house.

'No, he's doing all right,' Mark assured her. 'Just a bit forgetful.'

'And cantankerous.' Evelyn added.

'And that,' Mark acknowledged with a smile. 'I just wondered if you could keep an eye out for him?'

'I always do.' Mrs Bruce assured him. 'Even though he obviously thinks I'm after his body and shuts himself in his loo.'

'Ah.' Mark said, a tad uncomfortable.

Mrs Bruce gave him an affectionate pat on the cheek. 'Stop worrying,' she scolded. 'I'll check on him. Your mum would never forgive me if I didn't. Though I'm not sure it will be a pleasure.'

'Thanks, Mrs B. But don't bother yourself tonight. He's just going to…'

'Batten the hatches?' Mrs Bruce rolled her eyes. 'I'll pop around in the morning.'

'Cheers Mrs B. You're an angel.'

'Yes,' said Mrs Bruce, as Mark planted a kiss on her cheek. 'And I'm sure I'll get my reward in heaven.'

'How's Karl?' she called after him as Mark headed for his car.

Mark turned. 'Good,' he said, his stock answer, anything more being too complicated sometimes.

'Bring him for tea one Sunday.' Mrs Bruce waved him off. 'And if you've got a young lady, bring her along, too.'

She was fishing, Mark knew. Said the same thing every time she saw him. 'Still looking.' He smiled half-heartedly as he turned back to his car, wondering how it was he thought he'd finally found someone, and then lost her in such a short space of time.

Chapter Five

Donna sighed, highly fulfilled by her scintillating night out — not. Couldn't get much more enjoyable really, could it, she thought obliquely, as she puffed her way along the hard shoulder in her "not desirable footwear for Pilates" according to the instructor.

Donna glanced down at her cheap feet. Cheek. She didn't have the financial resources for prominent logos. And nor would the snooty instructor if she had a son who thought child abuse was not having a PS3.

Oh, gosh, more joy. She glanced up. It was raining, again, a fat splat, followed by a deluge, landing on Donna's head as testament to which. Perfect.

Abandoning her car had been a no-brainer. Against the law to leave vehicles unattended or not, Donna had been out of there in a flash, minus all worldly goods, including her mobile. Breathing hard, she peered over her shoulder, just in time to see her car puke out an acrid cloud of black smoke. Oh, God, it was well and truly — terrifyingly — on fire! Carless of her juggling bum-cheeks on display to passing traffic, Donna cranked her sprint up a gear.

Please, Lord, she prayed, as her feet pounded on the tarmac, *don't let anyone open the door and be burnt to a crisp, and please, please, let me reach the emergency phone soon.*

At last, there it was. Donna strode the last few yards like a gazelle — a heavily pregnant one, clutched at the receiver, and then paused to wheeze and pant.

And then almost wet her sweatpants as a voice in her ear said, 'Keep calm,' before she'd even dialled. 'The burning vehicle at your location has been reported,' the voice went spookily on. 'The emergency services are at the scene.'

'They are?' Donna glanced behind her, and there indeed were flashing blue lights. Two fire engines worth of flashing blue lights.

'Are you all right?' asked he who was obviously trained to soothe in such situations.

'Yes, fine,' Donna assured him, breathlessly.

'Good. Now, can you tell me whether there is anyone else in the vehicle?'

Donna knitted her brow. 'Sorry?'

'The emergency services need to know whether there's anyone in the car.'

What?! Did the man think she'd actually leave someone in a burning car whilst she wandered along the hard shoulder in search of extinct emergency phones?

'No,' she said flatly.

'So, there's no one travelling with you, then?'

'No, no one,' Donna confirmed, peering worriedly into the dense wooded area on the opposite side to the traffic. Oh, God! There might be a made axe-murderer sharpening his axe, right now, even as she spoke! She took a step sideways, then another back sharpish, as a car shaved past.

'Right, well, keep calm,' the voice said, as Donna's stomach tied itself in a knot. 'I'll make contact with the emergency services and inform them you're a lone female.'

'Thank you,' Donna said, suddenly all too aware of the loneliness of being alone.

'Meanwhile,' the disembodied voice continued, 'could you make your way back to the vehicle and let them know you're safe?'

'Yes, no problem,' Donna croaked, reluctant to let go of the phone as the call ended. She was sure she could feel evil eyes watching her.

An icy chill prickling the back of her neck, she turned ready to flee, and then froze. There, before her eyes, a miracle occurred. Trundling towards her, blue lights rotating, was a police patrol car. *Thank you, Lord.* Donna prayed earnestly, utterly relieved and tremendously...

Gobsmacked.

Mark was out of the vehicle, racing towards her, almost before she'd closed her mouth. 'What happened?' he asked, catching hold of her shoulders. 'Are you all right?' He searched her eyes, so much concern in his, Donna was shocked.

'Yes. I think so,' she mumbled, her teeth suddenly chattering down to her toes.

'Good.' He nodded. 'Good,' he repeated throatily, then, right there on the hard shoulder, spotlighted by the beams from his headlights, he wrapped his arms around her and pulled her tight.

Donna swallowed back a lump in her throat, which was stuffed full of remorse. He cared. He really did care. And she'd refused to even go out with him.

'Come on, you're freezing.' Mark eased away from her to tug off his jacket. 'Come and sit in the car,' he said, wrapping the jacket around her and leading her there.

Donna didn't resist. She didn't want to. She felt snug tucked under his arm. Safe by his side. She studied him as he helped her into the passenger side. He smiled. Donna watched him walk around to the driver's side, climb in, check the heater. Quietly authoritative. Quietly caring.

'Okay?' He smiled again, his face turned towards her, one hand draped over her seat as he readied himself to reverse.

Donna nodded, still watching him, unable to take her eyes off him. Was it possible that Mark Evans *was* all that he seemed?

'I'll take you back to your car,' he said. 'You'll need to give a few details to my colleagues. Nothing to worry about. You just need to tell them what happened.

'Are you okay with that?' he asked, concern flooding his eyes again as he obviously noticed the confusion in hers.

'Yes, but... Why can't I just tell you?' Donna didn't fancy speaking to anyone who was going to be all detached and official when she actually felt quite vulnerable.

'Not my patch.' Mark turned his attention to reversing back along the hard shoulder. 'I caught the call. When I heard it was a red PT, I, er...' He glanced at her, embarrassment flitting across his lovely concerned features. 'Well, I thought I'd just check it out, you know?'

Donna did know. Just because she'd had the misfortune to pick a rotten apple didn't mean they all were. Mark had ridden to her rescue. He *was* nice at the core and she'd tossed him away.

'Mark, I...'

'Jesus *Christ!*' Mark slammed on the brakes, then pulled her bodily towards him as something whooshed, then exploded behind them with such ferocity it popped Donna's ears.

'Your windscreen just blew out,' he said tersely, his heart beating so loud Donna could feel it. 'You all right?'

'Yes,' Donna mumbled to his chest, her eyes scrunched shut and her own heart pounding.

'Sure?' he asked, stroking her hair, lifting her chin.

She opened her eyes. Donna had the feeling she'd never be sure of anything again. Had her car just *exploded*?

46

'You were bloody lucky, you know?' Mark's China blue eyes darkened almost to cobalt. 'If it had been a petrol engine, it would have gone sky high ages ago.'

****

It was whilst trying to extract Matt from her toasted car the next morning — Matt having insisted on checking out whether her CD player was salvageable, that Donna noticed a sparkling new Jaguar cruising towards the house.

She squinted at it, then almost dropped to the floor as she realised that Jeremy was at the wheel, the Twiglet adorning the passenger seat at his side. Just what Donna needed with her wearing soot-covered scruffs and her own car a scrapheap on the drive. *Damn.*

'Jeremy.' She dredged up a smile as the car pulled up — for Matt's sake, who was loitering behind her, Findus in arms and an incredulous look on his face. No doubt he was wondering to what he owed the pleasure. She nodded at Leticia, rather than call her by name. The only name springing to mind being lettuce, draped in a green fitted slip dress as she was.

Jeremy nodded through the open driver's side window. 'Donna,' he said, looking her up and down as if he'd encountered a bad smell. 'Had a bit of an accident, haven't we?' He looked past her to her cremated car.

Yes, I married you, Donna resisted saying for the sake of their son. 'Did you want something?' she asked, as civilly as she could.

'Yes, I did, as it happens. I came to drop off some cash for Matt.'

Donna glanced over her shoulder at Matt, who duly raised one pierced eyebrow, bemused.

'Can't stop, unfortunately,' Jeremy came out with his stock phrase. Sticking around long enough to exchange two words with his son was too much to hope for, Donna supposed.

She looked over her shoulder again. Matt's expression as he turned to slope back indoors told her he hadn't hoped for much more either.

'We have to shift one of Leticia's horses up to the stud at Feckenham,' Jeremy went on snootily. 'Hunter. Good breeding stock, you know? Then I have to get back to the office. Make some money to pay the bills and whatnot. A man's work is never done.' He smiled stoically.

Donna fumed quietly. He wouldn't have to work very hard to pay his child support payments, which fluctuated between meagre and non-existent. 'The whatnot being your new car?' She speculated.

Jeremy sighed wearily. 'It's Leticia's, Donna. Mine's in for a service.'

Yes, and Donna would bet he could afford to pay for his service, too.

'I did stop by last night, but I saw you had company,' Jeremy informed her, with a pointed glance.

Damn. He must have seen Mark dropping her off. The last thing Donna wanted was Jeremy privy to her private affairs. He'd use that as ammunition for facetious remarks for sure.

'Bit desperate, wasn't it, setting fire to your car to attract the attention of a man?' he dripped on cue.

'One would have to wonder *why* I'd be that desperate though, Jeremy, wouldn't one?' Donna countered calmly.

Jeremy smirked. 'I hope you gave him his jacket back. Not quite proper attire, is it, for an officer of the law, shirtsleeves?'

Donna folded her arms. So he'd hung around long enough to get a good look, then? At Mark gathering up Findus as he hopped through the open front door in his bid for the great escape. Handing him gently over to Donna and then kissing her tenderly, reassuringly on the forehead, before dashing off to go back on duty? 'I thought you had to go,' she said, her gaze fixed stonily on his.

'I do,' Jeremy said, chuckling away, apparently still amused by his wit. 'Here you go.' He reached for his wallet and extracted his conscience money. 'I'm sure Matt would prefer not to have his dad tagging along while he shops for his *cool* trainers in reality, don't you?'

'I don't know. Why don't you try asking him?'

Jeremy's brow creased. The Twiglet's face remained bland, but she did at least try. 'Do you want to pop in and have a word, darling?' she suggested. 'I mean you are here, after all. I'm sure my groom will be able to get Black Rum boxed and ready for the orf.'

'Don't bother yourself. Matt's about to leave anyway.' Donna offered him a get-out, knowing Jeremy looking for reasons to leave as soon as he'd walked in would only make matters worse. 'I'll pass him your regards along with the money though.'

She held out her hand.

'Yes, do that.' Jeremy passed over the cash with that awkward little smile of his that said he knew damn well what he was doing.

'Thank you,' Donna said icily, making sure to stand tall. 'Goodbye, Jeremy. Leticia.' She nodded at Leticia, glad the woman had at least acknowledged that Jeremy had a son.

****

Donna had always thought living in a cul-de-sac was akin to living in a goldfish bowl. Her life was a soap opera on free-view to the world. She'd noticed a distinct twitching of curtains opposite as Jeremy drove off. She couldn't fail to notice the knowing looks and gossip on doorsteps, which stopped abruptly whenever single parent Donna walked by.

It was as if they were waiting for her to trip up, which inevitably she did, spectacularly rolling from disaster to disaster. Or, in this case, one disastrous relationship to another, which it was bound to be if she fell into one with Mark.

Was she really proposing to go down that road again? Get intimate enough with a man for him to turn around and say, I know you, Donna?

She would see Mark tonight, she decided, sifting through her melted CDs for something to do until she could get her emotions back under control. She wanted to, and not out of any sense of obligation because he'd been so caring. But she would have to spell out to him that no complications meant just that, for now.

Donna sniffled, set the CDs aside, and then got busy sweeping at shards of glass and globules of blackened gunk that had landed on the drive along with the car deposited there by the breakdown man.

'Mum!' Matt poked his head back around the front door. 'There's some bloke on the phone.'

'Oh, right,' Donna said casually, dusting herself off, despite the fact that Mark couldn't actually see her.

'I've washed my combats,' Matt announced proudly, as Donna walked back to the house.

'My God, you don't mean you've discovered the kitchen?' She blinked, astonished, sure her son must be gripped by some strange malady. 'What did you do? Use satnav?'

'Nah. Just shouted *choccy drops* and followed Sadie,' Matt quipped. 'So, how do I get them dry?'

'You put them in the oven, Matt, obviously.' Donna rolled her eyes, but smiled nevertheless. She was glad he seemed to be bouncing back, though she couldn't help thinking it was a bit of a front.

'Good idea.' Matt headed back inside.

'Switch it to high heat, for forty minutes,' Donna called after him, aware that these were his *cool* trousers, in which he hoped to impress his "crush" tonight. Matt was making an effort to help out, bless his socks, but the tumble dryer, she suspected, might be a kitchen implement too complicated. 'Oh, and Matt...'

'Huh?' Matt turned back.

'I'm sorry about your dad.'

He smiled wanly. 'Not half as sorry as I am.'

****

Mark selected Donna's number and switched to hands-free. 'Hi, it's me,' he said, when she picked up. 'Have you got a sec?'

'Yes, as long as it's a quickie,' Donna quipped, sounding quite cheerful, despite the previous night's events, which made Mark feel bad. He wasn't sure how she felt about him, but she'd seemed keen to see him when he'd finally plucked up the courage to ask her out again last night. The last thing he wanted to do, if she was warming to him, was to put her off. But then, he had no choice. On this occasion, Karl's needs had to come first.

'Love to oblige,' Mark joked, taking a left off the main road towards the city hospital. 'It's just that I don't think I'm going to be able to make it tonight. Can we postpone until tomorrow, possibly?'

'Oh,' Donna said, now sounding distinctly flat. 'I'm not sure. I'll have to find out whether Matt will be home. It's a bit soon for introductions, you know?'

'Of course. No problem. I'll call you back later. I'd better go. I'm on dut...'

'Unless I come to your place, of course.'

Shit. Mark ran his hand over his neck. 'No, no good,' he said quickly, wracking his brain to think of an excuse. 'I have a lodger, a work colleague. He works the late shift. Needs his beauty sleep, you know?'

'Oh,' she said again.

'So, can I call you?'

'All right,' Donna said, at length. 'Later though. I'm at work.'

Mark breathed out. 'Great. Gotta go. Catch you later.'

He signed off, relieved and full of trepidation at the same time. A small cut but quite deep, the respite home had said. Mark wasn't surprised. Getting Karl to keep his shoes on was a struggle, indoors or out, especially if they were new. No matter how much Mark scuffed them before putting them on him, they still looked unfamiliar, so off they came again.

He parked outside the main doors, killed the engine and headed quickly into Casualty. With luck, Michelle would be on duty and help him short-circuit the system. It was handy having a girl-*friend* who was a doctor and understood the problems of having an autistic son, even if she didn't want to deal with those problems on a personal basis.

He couldn't blame her. Would any woman?

Would Donna? Or would she walk away when he told her, which he was going to have to do when he saw her, whatever the outcome?

****

'Donna, you're being paranoid,' Simon assured her, popping a mug of tea on Donna's desk. 'The man's a policeman. Something obviously came up.'

'Do you really think so?' Donna asked, typing at warp speed as she worried. Jean was otherwise engaged with the chief executive, going through the staff rota, which they'd been going through for rather a long time, meaning Jean's workload had landed on Donna's desk.

'Donna,' Simon sighed, with a theatrical roll of his eyes, '*you* made the rules,' he reminded her of what she'd told him vis-à-vis her *no complications* stipulation, then dunked a chocolate biscuit. 'From where I'm sitting, it looks as if your Adonis is just following them.'

Donna knitted her brow. 'How do you mean?'

'Well, I assume if you cancelled, you'd expect him to ask no questions but be ready and primed when you did meet, yes?'

Donna flushed and typed faster.

'So give him the benefit of the doubt. If he doesn't call back, you can assume he's lost interest and you won't have lost anything, will you?'

Donna stopped typing and swallowed hard.

'If he does, you'll have your answer. So smile when you see him, wear nothing but the merest wisp of lace,' Simon paused to indulge a lick of melted chocolate, 'take him to bed and enjoy, sweetie. It will do wonders for your complexion.'

Donna's complexion was feeling distinctly heated, actually. 'Um, we haven't actually got that far...'

'Then get on with it,' Jean interrupted her, appearing behind Simon, who promptly stuffed his biscuit wholesale into his mouth. 'But it's probably best done *and* discussed in your own time, Donna, don't you think?' She shot Donna a meaningful glance, which translated read: You're on thin ice. Watch your step.

'Bitch,' Simon mouthed to Donna, followed by, 'Sorry, Dons.'

Donna smiled wanly. Oh, dear, looked as if her card was well and truly marked. She could type until she'd worn her fingernails up to her elbows, but Jean, she suspected, wasn't about to write her a glowing reference to back up her application for training.

****

Donna was walking back from the train station with Alicia when she saw him. Alicia had decided retail therapy was called for after Donna's traumatic events with her car. So they'd met up along with Matt in Worcester and shopped until they were ready to drop. Matt had got his new ice-cool trainers, and then headed back home to bathe in aftershave and make himself into a babe magnet for the nightclub.

Alicia had purchased the entire *Next* new season collection, and Donna had splurged the birthday money their mum had given her on a new, slightly risqué bra and panty set, and was now blanching at the thought of Mark possibly seeing her in it.

What *had* she been thinking, allowing Alicia to talk her into showing off her assets? She hadn't got any assets. Alicia had been first in that filial queue. And whilst the lacy lingerie might adequately cover her 'bits', they wouldn't be covering her more embarrassing bits. The only hope she had of that would be to wear pyjamas buttoned up to her skull.

'Donna, did you know there's a policeman outside your house?' Alicia interrupted her ponderings, nodding over her two-year-old son Jack's pushchair as she clacked alongside Donna in peep-toe ankle boots.

'Um, yes, actually,' Donna said casually, though her heart did a little Highland fling in her chest. He'd come, after all. She was so pleased, she forgot to be peeved that Matt might still have been in and seen him.

'Well, sort of,' she added with a nonchalant shrug, as if good-looking coppers beating a path to her door was an everyday occurrence.

Alicia stopped in her tracks, one eyebrow arched curiously. 'Donna O'Connor, you dark horse, you. That's him, isn't it, your sex-toy-in-blue?'

'Alicia! Shush!'

'Oh, he can't hear me from here. So, tell me,' Alicia went on, pushing her chocolate-coated toddler purposefully onwards. 'How many marks out of ten?'

'Alicia!'

'Nine and a half, I bet. Oh, honey, I can see what the attraction is, apart from the uniform, of course.' She waggled her eyebrows and clacked on. '*He is hot.*'

So was Donna. Her cheeks must look like a set of blooming brake lights. 'Alicia, shut up,' she hissed, glancing down at her passé trainers. 'He will hear in a minute, and then he'll know we've been talking about him.'

'What's not to talk about?' Alicia looked Mark appreciatively over. 'If I were you, I couldn't *not* talk about him. I certainly wouldn't be keeping him under wraps.'

Alicia stopped again, flicking back her naturally sun-flecked golden tresses as Mark stepped back from Donna's front door to glance in their direction.

'Definitely hot,' Alicia said out of the side of her mouth, then flashed him an ultra-white smile.

'Yes,' Donna said, trying to fix her own smile in place, but feeling like an ugly duckling next to a swan in Alicia's presence. Pluck and preen as much as she might, Donna could never hope to compete for a man's attention side-by-side with her sister. She sighed and tried not to mind that Mark would be bound to look at Alicia and like what he saw.

'Hi,' Donna greeted him as he walked towards them. He *was* quite hot, now she came to think about it. Not that she had, more than once… or thrice.

'Hi,' he said, stopping a step away, his mouth curving into his lovely smile and a breath-taking twinkle in his eyes… which were fixed firmly on Donna.

She waited for them to stray to Alicia, who'd turn heads dressed in a sack. They didn't. He kept looking at Donna.

'Well, this is nice,' Alicia said brightly, several silent seconds later. Donna could almost feel her curious gaze flicking back and forth between them. 'I'm Alicia, Donna's sister. And you must be?'

Donna's gaze was locked firmly on Mark's, which was locked on hers, mischief tempered with something pulse-racingly deeper therein.

'Right,' Alicia said, shifting from one peep-toe to the other. 'I'll get off then. Nice to meet you, um...'

'Oh, hell. Sorry.' Mark snapped his gaze away from Donna's. 'Mark,' he said, turning to Alicia and extending his hand over Jack's pushchair. 'Donna's, er...' He trailed off, obviously not sure who he was in relation to Donna.

'... dream come true, I imagine,' Alicia finished, with a knowing smirk. She nodded a greeting in the absence of usable hands. 'Lovely to meet you, Mark.'

'Likewise. And this is?' Mark looked down at the pushchair.

'Jack,' Alicia introduced her son. 'But whatever you do, don't disturb him. He never normally sleeps unless he's in the car. If you come across a demented mother on the motorway at midnight, that'll be me.'

'I'll give you an escort.' Mark smiled at Alicia, then his gaze... complete with China blue eyes so twinkly Donna felt sparks fly all over again... slid right back to hers.

'You'd better take him in, before you both get arrested for indecent glances.' Alicia smiled indulgently. 'See you soon, honey.' She presented her cheek to Donna's. 'I like him,' she whispered.

'I'll ring you later,' Donna promised.

'You'd better,' Alicia assured her. 'Now, take him in and do unspeakable things to him, before he implodes. And, trust me, I want details.' She turned back to Mark. 'Bye, Mark. Be gentle with her.'

Mark glanced at her, then down, embarrassed. 'I will,' he said, glancing back to Donna. 'I'd never be anything but.'

'Besotted.' Alicia sighed audibly as she clacked off. 'Utterly besotted.'

Chapter Six

'Made for sharing,' Mark mumbled, his indecent blue eyes lasering into hers, his lips — most definitely made for kissing — sucking sexily on the other end of her noodle.

Donna smiled, tempted to reel him in and slurp him, which might not go down terribly well with their neighbours, at *Wagamamas* noodle bar.

'Sorry about *Benedicto's* being fully booked,' he said, fishing around in their shared bowl for a prawn. 'Maybe next time?'

Donna smiled. 'Maybe,' she said, doing likewise.

'Is that maybe *Benedicto's*, or maybe a next time?' Mark asked, his gaze now fixed on his chopsticks.

'Maybe *Benedicto's*,' Donna confirmed, her smile widening as she watched him. He was nervous. She couldn't quite believe it. Nervous that she, plain, ordinary Donna O'Connor might say no? Did he not realise how delicious he was, even when not dressed in his bite-the-buttons-off uniform, which he'd changed at her house and left hanging in her bedroom — where Donna fancied it looked quite at home.

'Thank God.' He glanced up, mischief now dancing in his eyes. 'My chopsticks would be devastated if this turned out to be a one-night stand.'

Donna followed his gaze back down, to where her chopsticks had been getting seriously entangled with his. 'Oh.' She laughed, looking back at him, amazed at how easy it was to be with him.

Mark smiled a warm, sunny smile, which Donna would be quite happy to bask in the glow of forever. 'And *I'd* be devastated, if I ever did anything that made you not want to do that,' he said, reaching across the table to take her hand.

'Do what?' Donna asked, her scalp prickling pleasantly as his fingers made contact with hers.

'Laugh,' he said, caressing the back of her hand softly with his thumb. 'You do it beautifully.'

Oh, Lord. Donna gulped, in danger of bursting into tears, right there in front of the little Japanese waiter. It was such a small thing he'd said, but so poetic in its simplicity, her disorientated heart felt full to overflowing. He hadn't been gushing, full of false compliment designed to impress. He'd picked on the one thing she quite liked about herself: her smile, which she hadn't had a reason to use much lately.

'So tell me more about yourself,' she asked, aware that she hadn't told him much about *herself*. She liked him. More than liked him. He was kind, and obviously caring, but was he true? Or too good to be? It was too early to tell. She didn't know him that well. She wasn't ready yet to share her past with him, or for him to start defining her based on her history.

Mark nodded slowly. 'Okay, I'll tell you all my deep, dark secrets, but you first.'

'Oh.' Donna knitted her brow. 'There's not that much to tell really.' She shrugged evasively. 'Marriage, divorce, you know? Usual story.'

'Ditto. Not easy to know where to start, is it, telling your life story?' Mark suggested astutely.

'No.' Donna shook her head and glanced down.

'Tell you what,' he squeezed her hand, 'why don't we get to know each other slowly? Make a promise to reveal one secret every time we see each other? Sound good?'

'Sounds good.' Donna nodded, relieved, and added perceptive to his list of qualities.

Mark nodded in turn. 'Right, me first,' he said, 'but, I have to warn you, it might be a bit... off-putting.'

'How off-putting?' Donna asked warily.

Mark scanned her face, his expression serious.

Oh, no. Donna's shoulders drooped. He was still married. Addicted to lap-dancing clubs. Escaped from an asylum.

'I, er...' Mark started, then stopped. 'There's something I need to tell you, Donna, and it's... well, like I say, off-putting... possibly. Something that some people... women wouldn't be able to, er...' He trailed off awkwardly.

Donna glanced down, then back at him.

Mark raked a hand through his hair, clearly uncomfortable now.

Don't stare at him, idiot. Donna shifted her gaze to her plate and idly plucked up a prawn. 'I'm sure it can't be more shocking than anything I've done,' she said, attempting to put him at his ease. 'I have been around the block a few times, you know.' She waved her prawn airily. Then took her foot out of her mouth and popped the prawn in.

Mark cocked his head to one side. 'Just a few times?'

'Oh, you know, one or two,' Donna trilled nonchalantly.

'Right.' He nodded. 'So is that one of your secrets? Or is it general knowledge?'

What? Donna blinked at him, panicked, not least because of the marine crustacean wedged in her windpipe. 'No,' she spluttered. 'I didn't mean around, around. I meant around, um...'

'A bit?' Mark suggested helpfully.

56

'Yes.'

'Ah.'

'No! I mean...' Donna trailed helplessly off.

'You're a woman of considerable experience?' Mark offered, his mouth curving into a slow smile.

'Oh, ho, ho, ho.' Donna couldn't help but smile back. 'I thought we were supposed to be serious.'

'We are. I am.' Mark laughed, an easy comfortable laugh.

'Right, go on then.' She nodded him on, trying to look more worldly-wise woman of substance than woman of considerable experience.

'Right.' Mark straightened his face. 'It's, er, personal,' he said, his voice low against the hum of conversation in the restaurant. 'And not something most people would be comfortable with, to be honest.'

Donna stared at him, wondering whether now might be a good time to leave.

He beckoned her closer. Donna obliged, realising the only way not to, without making it obvious, would be to fall backward in a dead faint off the bench chair — which really wouldn't translate *worldly woman of substance*.

'What?' she whispered, so close to him now, she could smell his intoxicating aftershave, which would haunt her senses for the rest of her life if he told her anything terrible.

Mark moved closer. 'I, er.' He stopped, his breath so warm on her cheek, Donna felt goose bumps the length of her spine.

'I have a... My s...' He drew in a breath, then, 'I... like rom-coms,' he finally said. 'Sorry, I can't help it. It's a compulsion. It's pathetic, I know. I'm thinking of getting professional...'

'Rom-coms!?' Donna pulled back. 'You like rom-coms? That's your deep dark secret?'

'Shush,' Mark said, glancing hurriedly around, closely followed by 'Ouch!' as Donna prodded him with the blunt end of her chopstick.

'Ooh, *you*...' She narrowed her eyes, about to give him another prod, when the girly table next door broke out into rapturous applause.

'He could watch rom-coms with me anytime,' one of the girls shouted as the other girls whooped.

Donna folded her arms. 'You're over-egging it,' she suggested as Mark feigned dying of embarrassment, face down on the table.

'I think we'd better leave, before you have to fight them off,' he mumbled, glancing up with a smirk.

****

'Stick with me, kid, and we'll get through this,' Mark drawled in a terrible American accent as they surveyed the rain pebble-dashing the pavement around them 'Ready?' He glanced from where they stood outside his car to Donna's front door.

'Uh, huh.' Donna nodded bravely from under the jacket he was holding cape-like over them.

'Good man.' Mark switched to military British. 'Okay, on my count we make a run for it. Agreed?'

Donna saluted. 'Wilco.'

'Good chap.' Mark nodded. 'One, two,' he counted — then ran. Then, obviously noticing a certain good chap was missing, skidded to a halt halfway to the front door. '*Shoot!* Donna? What're you doing?'

'Getting wet.' Donna informed him — wetly, then shrieked as an icy drip snaked its way down her spine.

'You said on your count. Ooch! Ouch!' She scrunched her head into her neck and caught up, ducking too late under his cape to be anything other than seriously flat-haired.

'I counted,' Mark insisted, tugging her close and holding the coat over them as they made a final bolt for the house.

'To two, Mark,' Donna pointed out this all-important detail. 'I thought you meant three.'

'Whoops, sorry,' he said, as she pushed the key into the lock.

'Three,' he said hopefully, as they scrambled in from the rain. 'Er, you're wet...' he pointed out unnecessarily, as she turned to face him '... a bit.'

Donna went cross-eyed as another icy trickle dripped off the end of her nose. 'Gosh, I never would have noticed.'

'Sorry,' Mark said seriously, then promptly opened the door and stepped back out. 'Does that help?'

'Mark!' Donna laughed, and tried to drag him back in. 'You'll get pneumonia.'

'Bound to,' sighed Mark, back-stepping in as she tugged at his shirt. 'You're a hard woman, Donna O'Connor.'

****

'Here you go.' Donna offered Mark a towel, as she came downstairs dabbing at her wet tendrils with a towel of her own. 'And consider yourself lucky. Messing with a girl's hair is practically a hanging offence. A lesser woman would have left you shivering on the doorstep.'

'So you're saying forget the flowers and chocolates, just make sure to bring the sun next time. Tall order.' Mark said, towelling his own hair as he followed her up the hall.

'Well, any man worth his salt would bring the sunshine and make sure the chocolates were in a cool bag.' Donna laughed, though the words *next time* gave her a jolt, next time being nearer the time when she might have to reveal more of herself. 'I thought you were going to call anyway. Not just turn up here.' Not that Donna minded now. She'd had a wonderful evening.

'I did call. Your mobile was off.' Mark paused behind her to give Sadie a fuss. 'Hey, girl, how you doing? Clever girl, aren't you, hmm?'

'Oh.' Donna turned around, her heart melting at the sight of this most masculine man fawning over her three-legged dog. And he was still smiling, despite that he'd got wetter than she had. It was nice to have a man smiling around her.

'Oh,' Mark repeated, his smile broadening as he straightened up.

Donna cocked her head, perplexed. 'What's funny?'

'You,' Mark said, hanging his towel on the stair-rail and taking a step towards her. 'And that *oh* of yours. Kind of like a full stop, isn't it?'

Donna was none the wiser.

'Everywhere there should be a question or a statement, you insert, *oh*. Complication avoidance technique?' Mark asked, moving closer.

'No,' Donna said, her gaze drawn irresistibly to his.

'Sure?'

Donna nodded, the very closeness of him causing her heart to flip in her chest.

'So your mobile wasn't switched off on purpose, then?'

'No.' Donna gulped as he reached out to cup her face with his hand, grazing a thumb skin-tinglingly across her cheek.

'Good,' he said, weaving his hand through her damp hair, trailing the other down her back and pulling her towards him. 'Because I've been thinking,' he said, his voice deep and smoky, 'if it is just a casual acquaintance you want, with no complications, I'll do it. And I'll keep on doing it until you trust me.'

Donna's heart was racing so fast it was in danger of leaping right out of her mouth as he searched her eyes, the look in his igniting every nerve in her body.

'I like being with you,' he murmured, grazing her cheek with his, pressing his lips to her temple so softly it caused a low moan to escape her. Sweetly agonising, Mark took his time, trailing his lips slowly the length of her neck, then back again to find her mouth. Then pausing.

'Are you okay with this?' he asked, cautiously.

'Yes,' she said, her voice barely a whisper.

Mark nodded, rested his forehead briefly against hers, then kissed her, hard, hot and hungry.

'OhmiGod! Stop!' she cried, as one hand found its way tentatively under her top.

Alarmed, Mark snatched his hand back. 'What?' He quickly scanned the hall, searching for lace-eating rabbits, whose great-escape plans he could possibly curtail with a sidestep.

'Matt,' Donna gasped, cocking an ear as someone walked up the drive. 'He's back early.'

'*Hell.*' Mark looked this way and that, looking totally panic-struck. 'Do you want me to slip out the back?'

'What, and give my son the impression I have a secret lover?'

Mark scratched his head. 'You don't, do you?'

Donna gave him a look. 'I don't want Matt to *think* that I do, Mark. Sends out all the wrong signals. He'll be thinking I have a string of lovers coming and going while he's out, and a turnstile in the hall.'

'Ah.' Mark nodded, as if enlightened. 'I thought it was some kind of safety gate to keep Sadie downstairs,' he quipped, then held up his hands in defence as Donna shot him her best withering glance.

'You'll just have to meet him,' she said. 'But please promise not to do or say anything controversial. Okay?'

'I'll do my best not to embarrass you.' Mark sounded a touch hurt.

Oh, dear, that didn't come out quite right. Donna felt bad for him. 'I meant anything that might upset Matt, Mark, not me. He's very vulnerable right now, though he'd rather die than admit it.'

'As teenagers do.' Mark nodded understandingly. 'I'll do my best, promise.' He gave her a reassuring smile.

'Do you mind waiting in the kitchen?' Donna handed him her towel and quickly straightened her top. 'Give me a chance to set the scene?'

'Right,' Mark said, disappearing swiftly through a door, then reappearing. 'Toilet,' he said, smiling wanly and heading for the kitchen.

Two minutes later, Mark hovered at the lounge door, loosening his collar and looking more nervous than Donna felt.

'Matt, I'd like you to meet Mark,' she said, stepping in.

Casting Mark a cursory glance, Matt continued to stroke Findus, who was nestled in the crook of his arm, nibbling at his tee shirt.

So far, so good, Donna thought. 'Mark's a policeman.'

'You don't say,' Matt replied, disinterested eyes fixed back on the TV.

Mark ran his hand over his neck and glanced at Donna in a what-do-I-say-now sort of way. 'Findus looks comfortable,' he tried.

Matt remained mute.

'Looks like whatsitsname?' Mark pondered. 'Mr something. You know, in the James Bond film?'

'Bigglesworth,' Matt supplied, with a roll of his eyes. 'And it's not.'

'Right,' Mark nodded, and looked puzzled. So did Donna. 'Er, not what?'

'Not the James Bond film,' Matt informed him dryly. 'Mr Bigglesworth was Dr Evil's cat, not Blofeld's. He was also bald.'

Matt continued to run his fingers through his rabbit's abundance of fur, now definitely looking like Mark's archrival.

'Ahh? Er, right.' Marked nodded, and looked completely lost for words.

'Austin Powers,' Donna chipped in, by way of explanation. 'You know, the, um... films? Ahem.' She clapped her hands jollily in front of her as silence ensued, smiled apologetically at Mark, then bemusedly as Mark glanced at the TV, said, 'Wow! Cool. *The Wrath of Khan*,' and bounced on in.

'Have you seen *Search For Spock*?' he asked, plonking himself next to Matt on the sofa.

Matt's gaze slid suspiciously sideways. 'Downloaded it,' he said guardedly.

'Yeah? Blimey, wish I'd thought of that.' Mark turned towards him, impressed. 'What about *The Voyage Home*?'

'Yep,' Matt confirmed, now looking rather smug.

'Cool.' Mark went all sixties hippie again. 'Did you see the bit where Scotty thought the computer mouse was a communicator?'

'Yeah. Brilliant, wasn't it?' Matt nodded enthusiastically, warming to his subject, and towards Mark, if the volume dropping to enable hearing level was anything to judge by. 'Have you seen the latest?'

'No, not yet.' Mark looked heartily disappointed. 'You?'

'Yep. S'good. Leonard Nimoy's in it.'

'So I heard. And the guy who plays Captain Kirk... Whatsisname?'

'Chris Pine,' Matt supplied.

'Yeah, him. He's supposed to be quite funny, isn't he? So, have you seen all of the others?'

'Yep.' Matt looked suitably proud. '*Nemesis, Insurrection...*'

'*The Final Frontier*,' Mark picked up.

Generations, Donna thought, next and current, sitting side-by-side with gleaming eyes glued to the telly. Well, they were obviously bonding. She decided to leave them trekking happily together while she made herself presentable in the bathroom.

Which was not going to be easy. Her hair was as flat as a pancake and with half her make-up washed off she was as pale as a ghost. Donna sighed and decided on *au natural...* ish. Just a teeny dab of bronzer and her hair tied up in a top knot.

Five minutes later, she walked back into the lounge, trying hard not to look like a sun-kissed pineapple, only to be greeted by Matt's, 'Oh my God, it's hair Jim...'

'... but not as we know it,' Mark finished, hilariously.

Obviously a girl's hair being a sensitive subject, Donna made a big show of not speaking to Mark.

Not that he would have noticed, she thought, sitting side-by-side with Sadie and Findus in arms, watching Mark stroll past, giving her a distracted smile and still talking animatedly with Matt as they headed to the hall. Having apparently decided Mark was all right, Matt was now keen to show him the other passion in his life — his clunking VW.

'I could have pranced around in front of the TV stark naked with tassels on, couldn't I, hon, and still he would have strained his eyes around me in search for Spock.' Not that Donna would have pranced, unless they were extremely large tassels.

'I wouldn't,' Mark said, coming back into the lounge ten minutes later to beam his best twinkly smile at her.

Donna, trying to work out who Khan was and how Spock was going to feature in the next film when he was dead, had lost the plot. 'Wouldn't what?'

'Search for Spock in favour of you stark naked.' Mark walked towards her, his eyes wickedly sexy as he bent to tease her lips with his. 'Though you might have to lose the rabb… Ahem.'

Mark straightened up smartly as Matt waltzed into the lounge, his eyes sliding from Mark to his mother, then suspiciously back.

Mark coughed awkwardly. 'I'd, er, better get off. Early start tomorrow, you know.'

'Right.' Donna scrambled to her feet and deposited Findus on the armchair, to Sadie's befuddlement.

'Right.' Mark ran his hand through his hair, hesitated, then shook Donna's hand. 'Bye,' he said, turning to shake Matt's hand manfully, before heading to the hall.

Donna glanced at Matt, who rolled his eyes so high they were in danger of disappearing under his Bench cap. 'You'd better go after him,' he said, his mouth twitching into a smirk, as he retrieved his beloved rabbit in case Sadie sat on it, 'before he finds a hole in the hall floor to disappear into.'

Donna laughed. Matt obviously approved. He must do if he considered Mark worthy of a whole energy-sapping sentence. 'I'll see you out,' she called, scooting quickly after him.

****

Mark had started his engine when his mobile beeped from the hall floor. Uh, oh. It had obviously slipped out of his jacket pocket as they'd scrambled in from the rain. Donna turned to scoop it up, then waving it, dashed out of the front door. 'Mark?!'

Damn. Too late. She ground to a halt as his tail-lights disappeared around the corner. Ah, well, never mind. She'd just ring him and… *Yes, excellent idea.* Not really likely to answer though was he, given she was clutching his mobile. So how was she going to get in touch with him? She hadn't got his home number. Donna felt suddenly a teensy bit adrift.

Well, that was just silly. His number would be in his phone, somewhere. And if she couldn't find it, she'd just reply to the last text sent, tell whoever it was he'd lost his mobile and ask them to contact him if they had another number. Simple.

She headed for the fridge for a snack — the events of the evening leaving her rather peckish, whilst trying to do the decent thing and not read the incoming text in too much depth. Perhaps she should send a message to all his contacts, she thought distractedly, reading it anyway, then almost choking on her Cadbury's Whole Nut. *What time do U want me 2 come over tomorrow?* She read it again. *Will I need my toothbrush? Jody xx*

Excuse me?! Who the bloody hell was Jody-kiss-kiss!?

Donna almost regurgitated a nut. And what the bloody hell was she doing *coming over* to his house? With a toothbrush?

Cleaning her teeth, obviously. Donna stuffed the last of the whole nut in her mouth and closed the fridge door. Then opened it again, extracted the leftover Easter egg she absolutely wasn't going to eat and trailed into the lounge.

Checking to make sure there were no Findus-shaped cushions, she sank dejectedly onto the sofa. So what did she do now? Devouring half the egg in three seconds flat, Donna guiltily rewrapped the foil. She could hardly ring the woman and make slitty-eyed accusations, and she couldn't ask Mark, because, apart from the fact that she shouldn't be reading his texts, she hadn't really tried that hard to find out anything about him. She had no rights, whatsoever. If he had a harem queuing outside his bathroom brandishing toothbrushes, she had no right to question or judge him.

Miserably, Donna picked at the foil and slowly peeled it back. She should have known. Did know, deep down. That he... That any man, especially a good-looking man, would cheat on her sooner or later and she'd be hurt all over again.

Thank God she'd protected herself, stipulated no complications from outset and not allowed herself to get too emotionally involved. She'd just cut her losses and, um... Ahem.

Donna dragged a hand under her nose, tugged in a deep breath... but a great, fat tear plopped into her eggshell anyway.

****

Detached. Donna reminded herself what she should be when doorbell rang half an hour later. Emotionally unfettered.

He'd come back for his mobile, presumably. Well, she heaved herself off the sofa, stuffed all evidence of chocolate over-indulgence under a cushion, braced herself and headed for the door.

She wouldn't demean herself anymore. Uh,uh. Absolutely not. No way was she about to turn into a snarling green-eyed monster; demanding to know why he had a woman staying over with no luggage bar a toothbrush and a fictitious lodger to back up his lies. She didn't care.

At all. '*Sniffle*'.

Hoisting up her shoulders, Donna quickly checked her face in the hall mirror, then swung the front door wide — to find Alicia and Evelyn standing side-by-side, Alicia with her tongue hanging out, in anticipation of juicy details, no doubt, and her mum wearing half Alicia's new Next collection and *what-have-you-been-up-to* expression on her face.

Chapter Seven

'Has he gone?' Alicia peered interestedly past Donna up the hall.

'Definitely,' Donna reported gloomily, not sure she was ready for a *post mortem*.

'Good. The doorstep's a bit drafty, Donna. Do try and answer a bit more quickly next time.' Evelyn stepped in, painted toes protruding from peep-toes — Alicia's — and a bottle of *Sauvignon Blanc* in hand.

'Give us the goss, then.' Alicia followed, wheeling a pyjama-clad Jack before her.

'And a corkscrew, darling.' Evelyn handed Donna the wine and headed for the lounge.

'Oh, and some cheese and biscuits would be nice,' she called. 'I'm starving. Dot's trying to diet, so we're both on a diet. I left her watching Kelly and Flavia's Strictly Dancing DVD, trying to jive her way to a honed backside. I think she quite fancies getting down and dirty with that little Italian one. Personally, I'd prefer a few hot moves with that moody Brendan Cole myself.'

'In your dreams.' Alicia laughed, handing Donna her Yummy Mummy baby bag, then heading after Evelyn. 'I think he prefers tall women to mature ones, Mum.'

'I know.' Evelyn's voice drifted from the lounge. 'Never mind though, I can live with substituting food for sex, especially if Donna can find me a bit of chocolate for afters. Oh, not to worry, I've found some.'

Donna sighed and heaved her baggage to the kitchen. Cheese and crackers, she suspected, even with chocolate for afters would be no substitute for Mark.

****

'Come on then, spill the beans.' Alicia helped herself to wine and patted the seat beside her. 'What's he like?'

Donna checked on Jack, who, with his thumb in his mouth, was contentedly watching his *CBeebies* DVD form his pushchair. Sighing again, heavily, she plucked up a cheese cracker, and plonked herself down. 'Quite nice,' she said, guessing she was going to be grilled about Mark whether she liked it or not.

'Riveting, I'm sure, but I meant in the bedroom department.'

'Alicia!' Donna spat cracker. 'I haven't... We haven't...' She trailed off, flushing furiously.

'Done it?' Alicia gawped, her wine glass halfway to her mouth. 'Why ever not? The electricity between you two could light up the streetlights.'

Donna's shoulders slumped. She so didn't want to be reminded of Mark's twinkly-eyed smile, which had lit up her world, for a little while.

'Donna, I know you're not the sort to leap into bed willy-nilly,' Alicia said, gently, 'but a second date's not too soon, you know, honey. Unless he's married, of...'

'He's not,' Donna cut in. But then, he might as well be. There she'd been agonising about how she was going to bare all, emotionally as well as physically, and he'd probably wanted no complications more than she did. She might as well have had a blooming one-night-stand. At least then she might have laid a few ghosts in the process.

'Hmm, well, I wouldn't leave it too long, if I were you,' Alicia suggested. 'He is rather attractive, isn't he? Most single women of a certain age would kill for him. A few married women I know would kill their husbands for him. If you don't bag him, he might just be tempted to go off with...'

'In which case, he'd be a very shallow man, wouldn't he? And I won't have lost out on much other than a quick bonk.'

Donna humphed, took a huge slurp of wine, and choked on it.

'Leave it, Alicia,' Evelyn said, scrambling out of her recliner to give Donna a hearty slap on the back. 'Donna doesn't have to compromise her principles just because men are bound to go off with slimmer, dimmer young things, do you darling?'

Donna choked harder.

Evelyn nudged Alicia over, who shrugged and went to check on Jack.

'So what's he really like, this new man, hmm?' Evelyn cajoled, wrapping an arm around Donna. 'Trustworthy, I hope.'

'Tall, dark and handsome,' Alicia supplied as she rolled Sadie's ball for her, which Sadie duly hopped after, which delighted little Jack, who clapped his podgy hands excitedly.

'I gathered he might be. And?' Evelyn looked expectantly at Donna.

'Blue eyes,' Donna imparted, after a more discreet sip of wine. 'Really blue, you know, and kind of... twinkly,' she said, hoping to distract Evelyn from a character assassination of Mark.

She knew her mother was only trying to be protective, her own marriage being one she'd suffered for the sake of her daughters. Their father had never been very supportive of Evelyn, complaining about the 'state of the house' when she'd gone back to teaching, necessarily. He drank and moaned, and — the girls suspected — womanised, and had finally given Evelyn an ultimatum. *Me or the teaching.* Evelyn, though, would rather have cut off her arm than her means of earning an income. Of a generation of women who'd learned to be economically independent, she'd never compromised her principles since, nor would she.

Donna admired her, yet felt sad for her sometimes, that Evelyn seemed not to know how to let down her defences.

'Just eyes?' Evelyn asked, with an amused glance. 'One would hope he has a bit more about him, Donna.'

Donna blushed as Mark's touch, smell and feel flashed through her senses. 'He's got a lovely smile.' She sighed wistfully.

'And he wears a police uniform. What more could a girl want?' Alicia sighed in turn, and batted her eyes.

Evelyn, though, didn't look quite so ecstatic. 'Does he, indeed? Hmm, almost sounds too good to be true, doesn't he? So, does he have a name, this twinkly hunk in a uniform?'

'Mark. Mark Evans,' Donna supplied, droopy-shouldered.

'Good Lord!' Evelyn eyes shot wide. She shook her head bemusedly. 'Well, there can't be two of them.'

'Two of what?' Alicia asked, crawling after Jack, who — set loose on the world — was crawling across the floor after Sadie.

Donna eyed her mum quizzically, who seemed to have drifted off somewhere. 'Mum?'

Evelyn snapped back to attention. 'I know him,' she said, a smile on her face, but her eyes troubled, which sent a tingle of trepidation down Donna's spine.

'You do?' Alicia sat back on her haunches.

'How?' Donna asked cautiously, wondering whether Evelyn had perhaps had a run in with him, defending one of her many causes. Crikey, she hadn't been arrested by him, had she?

'He's Robert Evans' son,' Evelyn enlightened her. 'Dot's next door neighbour. Small world.'

'He lives there? With his father?' Donna blinked, puzzled. So where did his lodger and Jody-kiss-kiss fit in?

'No. He looks in on him. Brings his son sometimes, too.' Evelyn glanced worriedly at Donna. 'In fact, Dot invited them both to...'

'His son? He has children?!' Donna's heart plummeted to the depths of her soul. She knew this would happen. Knew it!

Hardly able to breathe, she steeled herself to ask. As excruciatingly painful as it was, she had to know... just how many lies he had told her. 'Is he?' *Oh, God.* 'Is he married, Mum?'

'Good Lord, Donna?' Evelyn stared at her, disbelieving, 'You mean you don't?' She stopped, obviously noticing her daughter's slightly demented look. 'No. Divorced, I gather.'

Donna reached for the bottle and poured a wine. A large one. 'No fiancés knocking about the place, then? Girlfriends waiting in the wings?' She took a huge swig, wiped her arm across her mouth and snarled, 'Harems queuing on the landing?'

Evelyn eyed her curiously, then tried to coax Donna to let go of her glass.

But Donna wasn't parting with it or the bottle.

'Donna, as far as I know, no, there are no girlfriends lurking anywhere,' Evelyn said gently. 'No women in his life, apart from his child-minder — Gemma, I think her name is. So, come on, darling, there's no need for all of this over-indulgence in alcohol, is there?'

Donna sniffed, then head high and bottle hugged tight to her chest, she stood up to walk to the coffee table. Wherefrom, she picked up Mark's mobile, selected his *inbox*, walked back with a slight weave, handed Evelyn the mobile — and waited.

'Oh, I see,' Evelyn said, reading the text with an unimpressed look on her face. 'Thank you.' She took a large slug from the glass Donna handed her without further ado.

****

Evelyn walked straight past Robert Evans when he opened his front door the next morning.

Mark turned from his endeavours restocking the fridge to eye her curiously as she came into the kitchen, looking purposeful. 'Everything okay, Evelyn?' he asked, concerned that Mrs Bruce might have had a fall or something. It was a bit early for a social call.

'Mark.' Evelyn nodded, marched across the kitchen, eyed him quizzically, then slapped him, hard.

'*Christ*!' Mark dropped the carton of milk he was holding. 'What the *bloody hell* was that for?!' He ran a hand across his abused cheek, and stared at her, shocked.

'Whoa, steady on.' His father came into the kitchen behind Evelyn. 'You can't just barge in here, throwing punches. What in God's name's got into you, woman?'

'Don't you *woman* me,' Evelyn said, eyeballing Mark furiously. 'For *your* information, that was most definitely *not* a punch. If it had been, he'd be flat on his back, which is where he was trying to get my daughter, I've no doubt.'

'Oh, don't be ridiculous.' Robert scoffed. 'Mark's a good lad. He would never do anything to disrespect a woman.'

'Like father, like son, you mean?' Evelyn gave his father a good eyeballing, too, then turned back to Mark to drag a disdainful glance the length and breadth of him. 'Running around like he hasn't a responsibility in the world. In my day, a father worth his salt would have taken his *good lad* outside and given him a good thrashing.'

'Bit old for that, don't you think?' Robert suggested dryly, obviously quite lucid right then. 'Now, would you like to sit down and discuss this civilly over a cup of tea, or are you going to stand there ranting like an old witch?'

'I don't want tea!' Evelyn growled. 'I want *him* to move on.'

'I'll round up the posse. Meanwhile, I'll put kettle on, shall I?' Robert made *gone loco* eyes at his son.

Mark shook his head, glad his dad seemed not to be taking this too seriously, though the fact that he'd just been assaulted was serious in Mark's book. If the shoe had been on the other foot, though. 'Would that be before dawn, Evelyn?' he asked. 'And shall I take my *responsibilities* with me when I move on? It's just that Karl's pretty settled in this neck of the woods, you know?'

Evelyn looked contrite, albeit for one second.

'Would you like to tell me what this is all about,' Mark asked, much more calmly than he felt, 'because either I'm going nuts or you are.'

'Oh, I'm *far* from gaga, PC twinkly-eyed Evans, though I concede my daughter must be to have seen anything in you!'

'Daughter?' Mark shook his head. 'What daughter?'

'Do you know how I left her last night? With her confidence in tatters. You did that, Mark Evans. And after all she's been through with that horrible little toad Jeremy. You should be ashamed of yourself.'

'What on God's green earth are you talking about?' Mark asked, utterly exasperated.

'I'd say fifteen calls to Jody-kiss-kiss and as many or more text messages in return in one week tells the tale, wouldn't you?' With that, Evelyn planted Mark's missing mobile pointedly on the kitchen table, glared at him, and turned to the door.

Jesus. Mark ran his hand through his hair, realisation dawning as he stared at the phone. 'Donna?' he asked, disbelieving. '*You're* Donna's...'

'Mother, yes.' Evelyn turned back. 'You've abused her trust, PC Evans. Lied to her. Mislead her. Broken her heart, I suspect. If you have any respect for her at all, please don't see her again.'

****

Donna drooped downstairs a full day later, Sadie plopping tri-leggedly down after her. 'I'll take you out, baby,' she promised, knowing that a leg missing here or there wasn't about to stop Sadie wanting her walkies. She'd gotten away with taking a sick day from work, but she doubted it would wash with Sadie.

Turning to make sure the dog was safe on all threes in the hall, Donna's puffed up eyes fell on the flashing answering machine. She chewed on her lip, hesitated, then pressed play.

'Donna, please call me back, will you? I have to talk to you.' Mark's voice wrenched at her heart all over again.

That was the fourth message he'd left.

Should she ring him back? Tell him she'd read all his texts and guilt be damned, several being from Jody-kiss-kiss, whom he obviously had a close and longstanding relationship with, given the content. *What time did he want her?* Some of them read. Others saying, she'd see him at this time or that time, could he pick her up, drop them off. She was taking 'K' here or bringing him there, K being Mark's son, presumably.

No, she wouldn't ring him.

No matter what he said, however many times he apologised, at the end of the day, he hadn't even mentioned his son, let alone Jody, whoever she was. Which obviously meant he didn't think Donna would be a part of his life long enough to warrant him mentioning him. She was just a passing fancy he'd hoped to have sex with and *no complications.*

Be careful what you wish for had never been more apt than it was now.

Still, she really did have no right to judge him. Hadn't she been ready to do just that to him? With him? Hadn't she bought racy lacy underwear with that exact purpose in mind?

Donna's fingers strayed to her lips. She could still taste him. How would it have been with him? She'd never know now, yet she did. He would have been gentle, and caring, and loving, she was sure, if only for a short time.

Was it possible, she wondered, to grieve the loss of a lover who never was? A man who wasn't worth shedding a single tear over, according to her mother. Donna so hoped Evelyn didn't 'give him a piece of her mind' as she'd threatened to. She'd made her promise not to. But then, the trouble with mothers is that they never stopped being mothers. Donna certainly felt like giving Jeremy a piece of her mind about his treatment of Matt.

'Come on, Sade, let's get some din-dins.' Sighing, Donna padded up the hall, then almost shot through the ceiling as the phone rang again.

She walked back and squinted at the caller display. It was him. She nibbled at a thumbnail. *Should* she talk to him?

No. Her heart might be broken, but her spirit wasn't. She didn't need Mark to fix her problems. She had a life to live. A future to secure. She was going to ring the care home — one of the charitable trust's own projects — direct, she'd decided. It couldn't hurt. It might help to get some voluntary work under her belt. Might even be a way into a permanent position alongside her training.

There. All sorted. No point wallowing in self-pity. She was going to pull herself up by her bootstraps and show mean Jean, as well as PC Mark Evans, that she damn well could fight her own battles. Donna swiped a tear from her cheek and headed determinedly to the kitchen with a plan.

She'd feed Findus and walk Sadie. Then ring the insurance company about her car, which would be another job done. Make her doctor's appointment. And then, on a better-late-than-never basis, take her-wretched-self off to work.

****

Mark debated whether to try Donna again. No, no point. She wasn't going to call back. He had lied to her. There was no way around it. Yes, he might have lost her if he had told her. Now, through his own stupidity, he'd lost her anyway. *Broken her heart,* according to Evelyn. Dammit! When, precisely, *had* he been planning to tell her about Karl, if he hadn't had the bottle to tell her when he'd had the perfect opportunity? Instead, he'd confessed to liking rom-coms.

Rom-coms!

Christ, what had he been thinking? Karl should never have been an embarrassing secret he couldn't admit to. If a woman was going to be put off at the mention of him, then she wasn't the right woman. But his instincts told him Donna wouldn't have been. Still he hadn't said anything. Mark cursed and climbed out of his car, his own heart pretty damn near breaking.

'Mr Evans, hi,' a female instructor waved, coming towards him with the Autism Assistance Dog earmarked for Karl. 'Sally.' She smiled, extending her hand. 'And this is Starbuck. He's a caffeine junkie, so whatever you do, don't leave yours lying around if you want to drink it.'

Mark smiled. 'I won't. I need all the caffeine I can get. Hey, Starbuck.' He bent to give the animal a fuss. Getting attached to the dog would be no trouble at all. He just prayed that Karl would take to him, too.

Chapter Eight

'Book Price,' the person on the insurance helpline informed Donna the amount they'd pay for her car, which meant she'd get half the amount she'd hoped for. And she'd have to send them photographs of the deceased vehicle along with the accident report before they'd process her claim.

'How ridiculous,' she told Sadie, plopping the phone down and heading back to the kitchen. 'I mean, honestly, what am I supposed to put in the report? I ran into a *fire* coming in the other direction?'

And what was she supposed to do meanwhile? Use public transport, she supposed, seated next to the local loony, no doubt. On the bright side, she couldn't fail to lose a few pounds walking to the bus stop. Not that she had reason to lose weight now that her new lacy bra and panty set would never see the light of day.

She sighed, relieved Findus of a stray trainer he was chomping and exchanged it for cucumber, then fetched a dish and Sadie's dog food from the cupboard. Still sighing, she spooned the food into the dish, then offered Matt a weak smile as he bopped into the kitchen in time to *Smile Like You Mean It* playing appropriately on the radio.

'Oh.' Matt stopped mid-bop and arched a pierced eyebrow. 'I take it you and your policeman friend had a lover's disagreement?'

'No.' Donna didn't quite lie. 'Why?'

'You're sighing a lot as star-crossed lovers do.' Matt sloped over to the working surface to eye the breakfast offerings dubiously. 'And you're about to eat dog food.'

'Ho, ho. Guess who's reading Shakespeare at college.' Donna removed the offending bowl from under his clever-clogs nose and offered it to Sadie.

Matt rolled his eyes and headed for the fridge. 'So you going to kiss and make up, or what?'

'What.' Donna opted for the latter.

'Shame. He was kind of cool,' Matt commented, emerging from the fridge with the entire meagre contents therein: one floppy sausage.

'Yes, well, you kiss him, if you like, but I'm not.' Donna relieved him of the sad sausage in order to cook it, before he went begging the neighbours for food. 'He's been... Let's just say he's been less than truthful.' She shoved the sausage under the grill pan.

'Uh-uh.' Matt shook his head, fetched two slices of bread, and placed them reverently on a plate, awaiting his sausage. 'Your gay friend, Simon, might go for a snog with your boyfriend, but dis bruvver...'

Oh, no. Donna cringed as Matt stood on one leg, a finger pointed and poised on rap moment.

'... he da woman luvver. Ain't into no uvver.' Matt twirled — and pointed. 'Check it.'

Donna looked at him, bemused. '*Ye-es*, and which woman would this be pray?'

'I'm working on it.' Matt adopted his more usual droop as he came across to where Donna stood by the cooker. 'Um, Mother,' he said after a moment standing side-by-side with her staring at the grill, 'I don't want to diss your parenting skills, but it works better when you switch it on, yes?'

He twiddled the knob.

Donna clipped his ear.

****

'By Jove, I think I'm getting it.' Mark tickled Starbuck's ear, then straightened up to smile at Sally, who seemed to be turning him into a reasonably competent dog handler.

God willing, she'd do an equally competent job during phase two of the assistance dog course, where Karl and he would take the dog out in public. Once Karl had been acquainted with him, that was, and assuming Karl took to him.

'So now I've mastered the basics and found out which way the dog's facing, what's next?'

'Well, you've done really well so far, hasn't he, Starbuck?' Sally gave the obliging Labrador a pat. 'I thought I'd try you out with the longer lead next. We shouldn't need to do too much more after that, before bringing Karl in on things. You've made a great impression on Starbuck, and that's half the battle.'

Sally glanced down to where the dog sat at Mark's feet, tongue lolling. 'Looks like he's yours for life.'

'Let's hope he feels the same about Karl,' Mark said hopefully. 'So the *sit and stay* command, I thought we did that earlier.'

'That was *stop and sit*,' Sally corrected him, positioning Starbuck in front of him and handing Mark the lead. 'The idea being that when the dog stops, the child does, too, thereby giving the parent time to assess a situation, perhaps people might be coming towards you, or Karl might be getting too far ahead.'

'Got it.' Mark nodded, stepping back away from Starbuck as Sally motioned him.

'The *sit and stay* command will give you more time. Starbuck will stay until you instruct him to walk on. If you need to cross a road, for instance, or pay at the supermarket checkout, that sort of thing. Could you step back a little further please, Mr Evans?'

'Mark,' Mark offered. 'If you're going to be almost part of the family for a while, we might as well be less formal, yes?'

'Mark,' Sally repeated, with a smile, 'could you allow Starbuck the full length of his lead, please?'

Mark did as instructed.

'Great. That way you'll be able to see clearly how things are whilst giving your son a degree of independence. He'll be to the dog's side.' Sally positioned herself thus. 'He'll have the shorter lead attached to the dog's harness. And the tether,' she clipped a small strap from a loop on her belt, also to the dog's harness, 'will be attached from Karl to Starbuck, like so.'

She turned, apparently to gauge his reaction. 'You look relieved.' She gauged correctly.

'I am,' Mark assured her. 'It looks a lot less scary than I thought it would be.'

'Nothing to be scared about. Assistance dogs can vastly improve the quality of an autistic child's life, and thereby that of the parents or carers. As well as allowing them some independence, they provide companionship, unconditional love, a source of comfort and consistency when environments change and anxiety might be high. We've had reports of children's social awareness improving, of tantrums becoming less frequent. The benefits are huge. You're here because you care enough to want to improve your son's quality of life, Mark. And you're doing a fantastic job, really.'

'Thanks.' Mark smiled, wishing he could do half as decent a job on the relationship front.

****

'Donna!' Simon dashed towards her, as she finally dragged herself into the office. 'Where on earth have you been? My God, you look absolutely exhausted. What's wrong?' he asked, wrapping an arm around her.

'Thank you, Simon.' Donna smiled wanly, immediately feeling baggy-eyed and haggard. 'Nothing's wrong, not really. I'm just feeling a bit... you know, down.'

Simon bent his head to scan her eyes at close quarters. 'Oh, dear, come on...' He propelled her towards her desk, somewhere behind the mountain of post, which it was her duty to sort and distribute. '... sit down, while I make us a nice cuppa and then you can tell me all about it.'

'*Afternoon*, Donna.' Jean paused in planning her frenetic social life on the phone to greet her pointedly. 'Crisis on the home front?' she enquired, arching an eyebrow.

'Just a minor one,' Donna lied, disinclined to discuss her majorly disastrous life with someone who didn't give a damn. 'I would have been in sooner, but I still wasn't feeling too well. I did leave a message on reception.'

'Here we go. Get this down you,' Simon said, coming back with a tray laden with biscuits and a cure-all cup of tea. 'And take no notice of her.' He nodded at Jean, who was deep into conversation on the phone re the merits of M&S lingerie. 'She's just trying to keep you in your place, because she's scared witless the CE might find her services dispensable, once he realises she doesn't actually do anything.'

'Depends which services you're talking about.' Donna took a vicious bite of her chocolate digestive, then got to grips with the million-page report Jean had thoughtfully left on her desk. And there was still the post to sort. It would be tomorrow's post at this rate.

Donna waited for Jean to disappear to the loo, make-up bag in hand, then seized the opportunity to ring the care home, and ended up talking to the doctor in charge, no less, who seemed really nice.

'Donna O'Connor, yes of course. You're at head office, aren't you? You typed up my *Practical Guide for Parents*,' he said, apparently remembering who she was. Not for the typos, Donna hoped.

'Permanently,' she answered his question vis-à-vis her location, not very enthusiastically.

He chuckled. 'I take it you're not a desk-job sort of person, then?'

'No.' Donna smiled at his perceptiveness and went on to explain that what she'd always wanted to do was work with children, ideally in art therapy. That she'd managed the art degree, but never quite got around to the post-grad and childcare courses, having had a child of her own.'

'Splendid,' he said, confusing Donna a bit, she had to admit. 'We'd love to have you volunteer, lunch times, weekends, any time you can manage. And with regard to your future employment plans, we could possibly carve out a niche for you if you don't mind being daubed in paint and following up those childcare qualifications. Pop over this afternoon. We'll discuss it.'

'Righteo,' Donna said efficiently, and then almost popped with excitement. '*Yesss!*' She whooped, just as Jean re-appeared from the loo.

'Must dash, Simon. Dental appointment,' Jean said, giving him a toothy *Clarins*-caked smile, then disappearing in a cloud of perfume and pashmina silk scarf. She didn't say any fond goodbyes to her, Donna noticed.

'Dental appointment, my eye.' Simon went across to the window to peer out. 'And the CE's going along to hold her hand, I suppose.'

Donna stopped typing and dashed over — to see Jean easing a silken stockinged leg into the passenger seat of the Chief Executive's BMW. 'She'll be doing the holding,' she muttered. 'And you can bet your bottom dollar it won't be his hand.'

'Oooh, Donna O'Connor… *Miaow.*' Simon cat-scratched the air. 'I am *sooo* shocked. I didn't think you had an ounce of bitchiness in you.'

'*You*, Simon, are unshockable. And I do, if the occasion demands.' Donna's mouth curved into a sweet and ever-so-slightly satisfied smile.

'Why don't you ring Matt? Tell him you're going to be late,' Simon suggested. 'We could pop to the wine bar and have a good old natter. What do you say?'

'Thanks, but not tonight, Simon. I've a feeling I might be doing a little online research.'

'Hmm, researching what one wonders?' Simon pondered, forefinger to chin.

'Childcare courses,' Donna informed him, before his mind ran riot. 'Um, actually, do you mind if I…' Donna nodded towards the door, desperate to *pop over* to the care home just as soon as she could.

Simon held up a silencing hand. 'Say no more. I'll square it. I suspect Scarlett and Rhett may be some time, anyhow.'

'What about that lot?' Donna nodded towards the leaning tower of post.

'Leave it to me,' Simon said, steering her towards the door. 'I'll have it sorted in no time. Five minutes and your desk will be cleared, as if by magic.'

Donna glanced at him, unconvinced. 'Five hours more like.'

Simon waggled his eyebrows. 'Not to shred it, sweetie.'

Donna blinked at him, aghast. 'Simon, you can't! You'll get sacked.'

'Do you think?' Simon looked hopeful. 'Go on, go. Oh, and if I don't get a chance to tell you later, my birthday party is a week next Saturday. Fancy dress compulsory and don't forget to tell your sister. It's going to be a night to remember.'

'As if I would forget your birthday.' Donna looked offended, though she actually had forgotten.

'Must dash,' Simon said with exaggerated campiness, tossing an imaginary pashmina over his shoulder as he headed back into the fray. 'Busy. Busy. Lots of lovely shredding to do. Talk to you later.'

****

'Hi, Donna. Glad you could make it. The dragon gave you permission to take leave, then?' the doctor-in-charge asked, with a shrewd smile.

Donna smiled back. She liked him already. 'Well, not permission, exactly. Jean's, um, otherwise engaged, so I grabbed the moment. Thanks for seeing me at such short notice.'

'Ah, so you're playing truant? Better not let on, then, hey? Peter,' he introduced himself with a chuckle, then led her through the play-room where children were being coated up to go out to the play area, bar one who was sitting cross-legged on the floor, building up alphabet blocks in columns according to colour, and clearly not as adept at social play as some of the others.

****

Pulling onto her drive later, Donna felt a huge sense of achievement, despite having her eyes opened to the reality of caring for the children. Basically, you did have to care. Really care. It would be exhausting, frustrating; but rewarding, she felt, in helping those children accomplish the little things most people took for granted.

She'd be helping a key worker out next week, painting flash cards. What a brilliant idea, using flash cards to use as visual prompts on trips so the children knew what was going to happen next. Donna had a feeling she was definitely going to enjoy learning alongside them.

She smiled, even though her feet were sore from running around all afternoon, and headed through her front door to give Sadie an extra big hug.

'Hi, my little doe-eyed beauty.' She laughed as Sadie hopped up the hall to greet her, her gait that of a horse: front leg, two back legs together, front leg, back... then an enthusiastic boinkity bounce as she jumped up.

'Aw, Sade, you're such a good girl.' Donna held onto her one front paw and had a little bounce with her, then stopped.

'Uh-oh, telephone, hon.' She lowered Sadie carefully to floor, knowing it was Mark ringing somehow, without even looking.

'Donna, hi, it's me, Mark,' he said into the answerphone. 'I assume you're not back from work yet. I, er... Actually, I'm assuming you don't want to speak to me.'

'Okay,' he went on, after a moment, 'I understand, Donna. I don't blame you. I'll try to call back some — '

Blame *her*? 'I should jolly well think not.' Oh, this was just silly.

She plucked up the phone. 'Yes?' she said shortly.

'Oh, you are there.' Mark sounded surprised.

'I seem to be, yes.' *Apart from the heart you stole and then tossed away.*

'Are you all right? I mean... I've been a bit concerned, you know?'

'Yes, I'm fine,' she assured him. 'Extremely well, actually, thank you.'

'Good. That's good,' he said. 'I, er, wondered whether we could meet up, possibly?'

Donna didn't answer. For what, she wondered. An argument? No, thank you.

'To talk,' Mark went on. 'That is, if you'd like to?'

Donna chewed on her lip, prevaricating.

'I haven't been quite straight with you, have I?' Mark filled the silence. 'I'm sorry, Donna. I...'

'I gathered, Mark,' Donna cut in, 'from you texts.'

He sucked in sharp breath. 'Sorry,' he said again. 'I didn't mean for you to find out like... Look, Donna, it's complicated. I swear I didn't mean to deceive you. Can we meet? Please? I'd like to explain. Try to, anyway.'

Explain? That he had a child he forgot to mention? That he might have been seeing someone? Might be?

'No, Mark,' Donna said firmly, though her heart seemed to be folding up inside her. 'Not being *quite straight* is lying; and lies hurt. I've been there, Mark. I can't see you again. And forgive me, but I won't say I'm sorry.'

'I am, Donna, more than you'll ever know,' Mark said quietly. 'I, er... I'd better go.'

Then there was the dialling tone. And Mark was gone.

****

'Trust, that's the problem, Sade,' Donna chatted on the next morning as she got ready for her doctor's appointment, Sadie close on her heels. 'Once it's broken, it's broken. You can't unbreak it any more than you can untell lies, can you, hon?'

'Da trouble wiv muvver, is she got da bad luvver,' Matt rapped — badly, as he passed the kitchen from the lounge. 'He's causin' bovver. And she don't want none of it. Check it.'

'*Ye-es.*' Donna rolled her eyes, then attempted to relieve Findus of her other trainer. '*Any*, Matt. She doesn't want *any* of it.'

'Yo, right on, sista.' Matt did the pointy-thing with his finger and headed for the stairs. 'Catchya lata. I'm off.'

'Off where?'

'Meeting Dad.'

Donna gawked. Good God, had neglect of his son finally tugged on Jeremy's guilt gene? 'When?' she asked, plucking up Findus plus trainer and dashing after him, incredulous.

'About an hour. Up at Hanbury Pool Farm. He doesn't have any business appointments until later, he said, so he's helping...' Matt trailed off, apparently lost for her name.

'Leticia,' Donna supplied in preference to Twiglet.

'Yeah, Leticia, that's it.' Matt nodded and headed on up the stairs. 'He's helping her put her horse through its paces.'

'How awfully spiffing of him,' Donna muttered. 'I do hope she doesn't fall off and flatten her facelift.'

'Claws, Mother,' Matt called. 'We're going to PC World after.'

'PC World? For what?' Now Donna was really incredulous. The only time Jeremy had ever ventured into PC World was to buy a new business PC.

'PlayStation 3.' Matt tripped back down, wearing his all-important outdoor accessory — his iPod. 'Belated birthday present he said. So...'

'Cool. Go for it.' Donna smiled encouragingly, but she couldn't help wondering. She nuzzled Findus around the lace hanging spaghetti-like from his mouth... would Jeremy actually live up to his word and go shopping with his son? Spend money on his son?

****

Donna got off the bus in the town centre an hour later and turned towards the doctor's surgery. She hadn't been seated next to the local loony after all. Her luck must be changing, she thought optimistically. Or not.

She froze in her tracks. There, coming towards her, if her astonished eyes weren't mistaken, was Mark. And he was with someone else. Donna gulped back her tonsils. A female someone else.

Sh... ugar! Donna immediately tried to blend with a handily placed post box, peering over it, sidestepping around it, as Mark continued towards her... walking a dog? Wonderful. The family-flipping-pet he forgot to mention, presumably.

She snuck another peek as he passed. It was a Labrador, with a harness on, which might possibly mean it was a guide dog.

Oh? Donna felt a bit guilty, then pulled herself up. No, she did *not* feel guilty. The girl Mark was with, a slim, sunny sort, with silken blonde hair — Donna suddenly felt extremely blonde-ist — was smiling away, throwing him coquettish little glances. And *he* didn't look too miserable either. This was obviously her, then, Jody-flipping-kiss-kiss.

The absolute... pig! How *dare* he be strolling about with her in broad daylight, having just broken *her* heart! Donna peered around the box again, practically elasticated herself around it, and then... *Twang...* snatched her head back as someone coughed behind her.

Hell! Donna arranged her face, rather surprised, as she turned around. 'Good God, Mark! Well, well, fancy seeing you here.'

'Donna, how are you?' Mark glanced awkwardly between her and the *Sunsilk* advert at his side.

'Oh, you know, not too, bad, considering.' Donna smiled, like an imbecile. 'I was just posting a letter.' She waved a hand at the post box she'd almost morphed with and wished she were slimmer, first-class letter weight preferably.

'Oh, right,' Mark said, looking hugely embarrassed. 'Donna, do you think we could — '

'I'll take your jacket to the station,' Donna blurted.

'Sorry?' Mark looked confused.

'Your jacket. You left it in my *bed*room,' Donna reminded him, emphasis on the bedroom, which might give his girlfriend pause for thought.

Trying though she was not to metamorphose into a green-eyed monster, this really was too much. Did he have to look so heart-stoppingly handsome, even with guilt written all over his face?

And did Jody whoever-she-was have to be so cat-walkishly stunning, she thought miserably, as the girl glanced confusedly from her to Mark.

And did they both *have* to be holding onto the dog's reins as if it were their blooming baby? She glanced down at it, noted the *Assistance Dog in Training* logo on its harness and realised it was a guide dog.

So what was Mark doing with it? Was it something to do with his work? A sniffer dog in disguise, possibly? It was quite clear the girl by Mark's side didn't need any assistance, in any department.

Forcing her mouth into a smile, Donna looked interestedly at her. 'So, you must be?'

'Oh, sorry, this is Sally,' Mark finally introduced her, raking his free hand over his neck and looking as if he'd quite like to stuff himself in the post box. 'She's an Assistance Dog Trainer. Sally, this is Donna, my, er, friend.'

One who wasn't feeling too friendly, Donna would like to have added. So this was Sally, then. Not Jody. Jolly good. He *had* got a harem.

'Nice to meet you, Sally.' Donna forced another smile. 'Right, well, I'd better get off. I have an appointment.' She turned quickly away, before her treacherous eyes gave the game away.

'Donna,' Mark called behind her. 'Donna, please wait. I...'

'Can't, sorry. Late,' Donna called back over her shoulder. 'Bye, Mark. Nice seeing you.'

But not very nice. Donna watched from the foyer of the surgery, Mark offering some explanation to Sally, raking his hand through his hair as he did, which might indicate he was flustered.

Not half as flustered as she was. Donna watched on. Mark and Sally walk towards Mr Chang's Chinese Restaurant. Go into Mr Chang's Chinese Restaurant, Mark holding the door for her. Such a gentleman.

Donna waited a minute more before going on into the surgery. Pinching the bridge of her nose, she found, forced back the tears quite well.

****

Donna felt the walls closing in as she waited for the bus to take her to work. Metaphorical walls, but they were there just the same, pressing in on her, causing that same panicky, suffocating feeling she'd experienced after losing her second child.

That hadn't happened in a long time.

Why does assertiveness desert you when you're sitting in front of a doctor, she wondered, climbing distractedly onto the bus, sitting down, then trudging back to pay the driver. She had a brain, so why hadn't she asked him for more information on whatever it was he didn't think she had anything to worry about, but wanted to get her along to the hospital for nevertheless, so they could *have a good look* at her *just in case*.

Because she didn't really want to know, Donna suspected. What she wanted to do was to pop her head in the sand and drag her body in after it. She wasn't even sure she wanted anyone else to have a *good look* at her. She was beginning to wish she hadn't gone at all, walking in with a heavy heart after seeing Mark, then walking out with an even heavier one.

Chapter Nine

Mark came downstairs wishing to hell he didn't have to back go on duty. Taking a sick day wasn't on though, not when he'd already had so much time off for emergencies.

He went into the kitchen to find Jody loading the washing machine. 'No need to do that, Jody,' he said, grateful nevertheless. 'I know I'm a single dad, but I have just about got the hang of the electrical appliances.'

Jody laughed. 'The trouble with single dads is they think they've got something to prove.'

'Oh, yes, and how many single dads do you know?' Mark grabbed the half sandwich Karl had left before Jody binned it. With no time for lunch, his stomach was beginning to think his throat had been cut.

'One's enough,' Jody assured him. She was smiling, but Mark did wonder how she did it sometimes, made some order of the chaos their lives were. Yes, she was trained. But it took a pretty special person to take on Karl with his inevitable tantrums on a day-to-day basis. He was damn lucky to have found her.

'Thanks, Jody,' he said, in between mouthfuls. 'Don't know what I'd do without you.'

'No trouble.' Jody assured him, then scowled. 'You'll have indigestion. You should sit down and eat.'

'Yes, Mother.' Mark saluted. 'I'll bear it in mind next time.'

'Go on.' Jody waved him off, as if she were his mum. 'You'll be late.'

'Tell me about it.' Mark sighed. 'I'll just check on Karl. Run through things with him again.'

'Again?' Jody eyed him curiously.

'Yes, well, you know.' Mark shrugged. 'Hope something sticks.'

He headed for the door, then hesitated. 'You will ring me, won't you? If there's a problem, I mean.'

'There won't be.' Jody set about clearing up the kitchen. 'And you know I'd ring you if there was.'

Mark raked his hand through his hair. 'Right. Good.' He started again for the door. 'You know I'm...'

'On cell-watch duty.' Jody finished. 'Yes, Mark, I know. If I can't get you on your mobile, I'll ring the station *if* there's a problem. Now go, or there won't be any point in going.'

'I'm gone.' Mark laughed and headed for the lounge.

Karl was kneeling on the floor, lining up his cars in order of colour and size as usual, never the random disorder of child's play.

'Hey, Karl, how's it going?'

Karl said nothing, his gaze intent on his endeavours.

Mark collected the sheaths of paper and photographs he'd left on the coffee table, along with the ceramic dog, which Karl seemed to have become attached to. 'Karl, do you remember we talked about Starbuck coming?' he asked, crouching down by his son's side.

'Jupiter,' Karl said, driving his Jupiter Fireman Sam engine up against an identical one.

'That's right.' Mark reached for another fire engine to park alongside it. 'Three Jupiters.'

Karl studied them, his expression unflinching.

Mark parked the ceramic dog to the side of the trio of engines. 'And what's this, Karl?'

'Dog,' Karl said, after a second, and moved the dog to a space of its own.

'That's right.' Mark nodded. 'And this?' He showed Karl some of the drawings they'd worked on together, depicting a dog, which actually looked more like a cat, but crucially it was black in colour, like Starbuck.

Karl studied the drawing, unblinking. 'Dog,' he decided, placing the drawing in the new 'dog' area.

'Good boy.' Mark hesitated, then ruffled his hair, though he knew Karl couldn't relate to affection. 'And this, Karl.' he held up a photo of Starbuck and held his breath. 'What's this?'

'Dog.' Karl said immediately, took the photo and plonked it alongside the other two items.

Mark breathed out. 'Well done, Karl. That's right. Starbuck. He's going to be your new friend.'

Karl didn't answer. He couldn't comprehend, Mark knew. He had no idea what friendship was, but the ice was broken, that was the main thing. Karl seemed to accept the idea of a dog. Mark just prayed he accepted him in the actual fur, and that maybe Starbuck would become a friend of sorts, provide at least companionship for his son. Mark couldn't help feeling that Karl must be lonely in his isolation.

****

Donna came through the door, reference books and her all-important application form under her arm. 'Babe! How are you my gorgeous beauty, hmm?' She plonked her books on the hall cupboard, bent to give Sadie a hug, glanced at the phone, then carried on up the hall.

No more messages, then? No surprise. Mark had obviously moved on. Well, she'd just move on, too, despite her heart being almost too heavy to drag around.

She should make some calls, she supposed. Let her mum and Alicia know how her doctor's appointment had gone. She didn't want her mum fussing and worrying though, which she was bound to do. And as much as she loved them, she certainly didn't want them turning up on her doorstep tonight. She wanted to chill, fill in her form, take a long bath, and she wouldn't do any of that if they did.

'Evening, Mother, beautiful, dearest. I'm wonderful, thank you. But then, you already know that,' Matt said, plodding down the stairs.

Donna waited before proceeding upwards, ever mindful of tempting fate. 'Bit early for you to emerge, isn't it?' she asked him. 'Has the Internet gone down?'

'Sarcasm, Mother, is the lowest form of wit,' Matt informed her piously. 'For your information, I've finished my English assignment, put the washing on *and* tidied my room.' He shot her his best "offended" look as he headed for the front door.

'Good Lord, you're definitely ill.' Donna dashed after him to feel his forehead. 'And if you're not, you will be now you've tackled the black-hole without the aid of an oxygen mask.'

'Very droll, Mother. Remind me not to be helpful again sometime.'

'Sorry, Matt.' Donna looked suitably apologetic. 'Just ignore me. I'm having one of those... lives.'

'Tell me about it.' Matt sighed, looking rather dejected, actually, Donna noticed as he reached for his Bench cap and jacket.

'Oh, dear, problem?' she enquired casually.

'Nah.' Matt shrugged and glanced at his feet.

'Your dad wasn't late, was he, by any chance?' Donna asked, directly.

'Nah,' Matt said, with another shrug. 'Didn't show.'

Didn't show?! The abso*lute*... 'Well, ahem,' Donna cleared her throat of a certain word beginning B, 'I'm sure there was a good explanation.' She tried to salvage her son's pride, hoping to God that Jeremy had even bothered to offer one.

Apparently not. Matt's wounded expression said it all.

'We'll get you the PlayStation,' Donna said, resolute.

'No, we won't,' Matt said, equally resolute. 'We can't afford it.'

'Where there's a will, there's a way, Matt. We'll hold a car boot sale, or sell something on eBay.'

'Like what? Matt enquired, looking none too convinced. 'Your body, again?'

'Well, that should buy us a fuse for the plug.' Donna smiled, hoping to cajole Matt into doing the same.

Matt's mouth twitched up at the corners. 'The whole plug, I reckon.' He glanced down, again. 'It's not about the PS3, Mum, you know?'

'I know.' Donna tugged his cap up, sure he had a face under there somewhere. 'It's not that he doesn't care, Matt. It's just that...'

'He's a prat,' Matt finished. 'Must be to have messed with you. I'm off,' he said, while Donna debated whether to defend Jeremy or leave Matt to his opinion based on the evidence.

'Where?' she asked, deciding on the latter — based on leopards and spots and the fact that Jeremy would never change.

'Just to Ed's to download some stuff. See you later.'

'See you later. And thanks for all your hard work, Matt. It's nice to have a son who rates me enough to care.' Donna gave him a hug, a quick one lest he die of embarrassment.

Then almost fainted when Matt gave her a hard hug back. 'You all right, Mum?' he asked, having squished her to within an inch of her life.

'Yes,' Donna assured him. 'Apart from the dead car, of course, and the decision what to wear when I advertise my body on e — '

'Mum, I'm not daft. I'm talking about Mark and you.'

'Ah, um, yes, well...' Donna glanced away now.

'So, have you definitely split?'

Donna sighed. Matt did have a right to know, she supposed. 'I think so, yes.'

'You should think again,' Matt advised her manfully. 'He was kind of all right, you know.'

'Yes. And he's into Star Trek and The Simpsons,' Donna replied flippantly, because she didn't know how else to. 'In fact, I'd say you two were an ideal couple.'

'Mum, be serious.' Matt looked as serious as he could for a teenager in a *Homer Simpson Rub-My-Tummy* tee shirt.

Oh, dear. He obviously had bonded with Mark — in the absence of any other male role model, Donna supposed.

'You should get out more. Give him a run for his money,' Matt went on, apparently clued up on the subtleties of the dating game. 'Come out with me and my mates to *Images* and have a good bop.'

Ye-es. She had had Matt quite young, but Donna wasn't sure she'd pass for his older sister nowadays. 'Don't be daft,' she replied, flattered, nevertheless, that her son wouldn't be ashamed to be seen out in public with his mad mother.

'You'd have a great time,' Matt assured her. 'And the disc jockey's a granddad, so it's not like you'd have no one to talk to.'

'Thank you, Matt. I feel so much better now.' Donna's temporarily bolstered self-esteem clanged to the floor.

'Catchya lata.' He laughed.

'Not if I catch you first.' Donna warned him as he nipped out of the door.

Right. She waited until he was out of sight, then dialled Jeremy's number. He was bound to have some feeble excuse for letting Matt down, yet again, which by the very feebleness of it, she couldn't impart to Matt, but Donna would feel a hell of lot better for imparting to Jeremy how she felt.

'Hello, Natasha,' she said, when the Twiglet picked up. 'Oh, sorry. I'm going senile, I swear. She was the one *before* you, wasn't she?' Donna paused, effectively. 'Can I speak to Jeremy, please?'

'I'll see if I can find him,' Leticia informed her coolly. 'He's in the cellar checking his barrels.'

He'll be checking his balls when I get hold of him, Donna thought furiously. 'Thank you,' she said sweetly, preferring Leticia to think her unperturbed by the obvious flaunting of her old-monied wealth.

The absolute nerve. It was pathetic. It really was. Donna drummed her fingers on the hall cupboard whilst she waited. And waited.

Totally pathetic. Oh, how well she knew the man. Even now he was playing power games. Well, Donna was *not* going to play.

'Jeremy,' she said, when he finally picked up, her anger carefully in check.

'Donna,' he said. 'How are you?'

Chafing at the bit, you self-important twit. 'Fine,' Donna informed him shortly, then waited again, in the vague hope he might realise why she'd phoned.

'Donna, did you want something?' Jeremy finally asked impatiently.

'Nothing you've got to offer, Jeremy, no,' Donna assured him, 'but I think Matt might quite like something.'

'Oh? Such as?' Jeremy asked, as if he hadn't a clue.

Ooh, now then, let me see. A father who gives a damn perhaps. 'An explanation, Jeremy,' Donna said flatly.

'A... What? Look, hang on a tic, will you?'

Donna waited, again, while Jeremy cooed to Leticia, 'Yes, thank you, darling. I'll have a red. I've opened a Merlot. It's breathing in the dining room.'

Which is more than you will be if I get hold of you. Donna fumed steadily.

'Right, now then,' Jeremy deigned to address her again, 'would you like to explain what you're talking about, Donna? Your timing's a bit off, you see. Leticia's about to serve dinner.'

'*Me* explain?' Donna spluttered. 'It's *you* who should be explaining, Jeremy! About why your timing's so off you missed meeting up with your son. Again!'

'Missed? What? Oh, good God, Donna,' Jeremy paused for an elongated and elaborate sigh, 'why on earth didn't you remind me?'

'*Me* remind!? Why, in God's name, should *I* remind *you* about a meeting with your own son?'

'Because I have an accounting office to run, Donna; which means I'm extremely busy and can't be expected to remember everything.'

'Yes, of course.' Donna tightened her white-knuckled grip on the phone. 'And a Pekinese to take to the vet's and a horse to put through its paces and a Twiglet to bed on a regular basis. You absolute bastard!'

Jeremy sighed. 'Oh, dear, here we go, histrionics and tantrums.'

'Histrionics!?' Donna almost choked.

'I'm going, Donna,' Jeremy went on before she could catch her breath. 'You're obviously hormonal or something and my dinner's getting cold. I can see I've messed up where Matt is concerned. I forgot. I'll apologise to him when I see him. I'm sure *he's* mature enough to understand I don't have time to spend my day clock-watch...'

Donna banged the phone down, then stared at it dumbfounded. She'd fallen right into it. The blame game. And he'd played her for a fool.

Damn him! She paced up the hall, Sadie hopping worriedly behind her.

She would *never* ring him again, she decided, not unless major crisis demanded it. And she would get Matt the PS3, because, it occurred to her while Jeremy was wittering on about time and clocks and busily trying to blame everyone else for his shortcomings, she did have something worth selling on eBay. Two things, actually, stuffed up in her loft. Jeremy's sixties Beatles collection picked up from a car boot sale, which he'd had valued and which was worth a bob or two, and the gold pocket watch he'd picked up at an auction.

Twice she'd told him he'd forgotten them, and he hadn't bothered to collect them — probably because he was petrified he might have to collect something else when he did, like his son — so tough! In any case, he'd got more than his fair share of equity from the house when Evelyn had helped her buy him out, the pathetic little worm.

Angrier than she'd realised she could be, Donna headed determinedly upstairs to tug down the loft ladder.

Treasure located five minutes later, she tucked the pocket watch — a Robert Pybus of London from 1790 — in her own pocket and heaved up the box of LPs, which might go some way to buying the PS3. And she *wouldn't* debate the ethics of it, because she didn't care. Jeremy obviously didn't have any ethics. Never had.

Standing tiptoe on the bed, she wedged the box into an overhead cupboard, dislodging stuff and paperwork of aeons ago as she did so. Damn. She bounced barefoot around the bed, retrieving leaflets from block-paving specialists and handymen, who might only ever be handy if she won the lottery, medical cards, birth certificates. Hers, Matt's and… Donna stopped bouncing and plopped heavily down… little Callum's. She smoothed the certificate out and re-read it, as if every detail of the two days he'd lived wasn't already ingrained indelibly on her mind.

'It's okay, Sade,' she said, squishing her close as Sadie sought to console her. 'Mummy's fine, hon,' she assured her, planting a kiss on her head and sliding off the bed.

That shouldn't have been up there getting crinkled and gathering dust. Donna padded over to her dressing table and pulled open her lingerie drawer. That's where the certificate should be, together with the photographs, two not very well-focussed photographs in Perspex frames… She fingered them, allowing herself a second's contemplation, then closed the drawer. She carried her baby's image around in her heart anyway.

Donna pulled in a catchy breath and tugged up her shoulders. Kitchen, she instructed herself.

She needed to eat. She needed to study. She needed to dismiss from her mind anything to do with the idiot men in her life. And, more importantly, she needed to work out how one did actually sell things on eBay.

****

Mark had felt like driving home blue lights flashing. All afternoon, he'd sat in a holding cell, where he should have been with Karl, listening to some pissed-up idiot, insisting he'd "hardly touched the lying cow", the "lying cow" being his girlfriend. Yeah, right. How *hardly touched* does her face look compared to your fist, you bastard, Mark had just refrained from commenting. Then, when the guy finally shuts up and slips into unconsciousness, he goes to check up on him, and the idiot rolls over and promptly pukes on his shoes.

Christ, he could still smell it.

Disgusted, Mark pushed his key into his front door, slipped inside and prised off his offending footwear.

Hang on. He cocked an ear at the unusual, all-pervading silence. His stomach knotting inside him, he walked to the lounge door and pushed it open, his apprehension growing as he noted the TV was muted. Something was wrong. Very wrong. Karl wouldn't be in bed. He was never in bed. His rituals barely allowed him two bloody hours in bed. And if he didn't have *Fireman Sam* DVDs on there was more likely to be a riot than quiet. 'Jody!?'

'Shhhush,' said a voice behind him from the stairs.

'*Shit!*' Mark gulped back his racing heart as he turned around. 'Where's...' He stopped as Jody pressed a finger to her lips and beckoned him upwards, urging him on past Karl's room as he reached the landing.

Mark did as bid, confused.

Jody stepped aside as he reached his own room, a smile playing about her mouth.

Mark eyed her quizzically, then peered inside. Bloody *Hell!!* His heart almost stopped. Shaking his head, he stared in absolute awe — at Karl lying on his double bed, one arm and one leg draped over Starbuck.

Jody squeezed Mark's arm as he glanced back to her, quite unable to believe what he was seeing. 'Go on,' she mouthed, motioning him on in and turning to slip back downstairs.

Raking his hand through his hair, Mark crept in, hardly daring to breathe, lest he should startle him. Not that he was likely to, if the steady rhythm of Karl's breathing was anything to go by. The kid was asleep, his hair plastered to his forehead, his pyjamas on back-to-front, but fast asleep.

'Stay, Starbuck,' Mark whispered, as the dog lifted its head. 'Clever boy.' He patted the dog, brushed Karl's forehead with the softest of kisses, eased the quilt over him, then headed quietly back down.

He hadn't cleaned his teeth he'd be willing to bet. Mark tried to stay grounded as he went back to the kitchen.

'Did he, er?' Shakily, he started to ask Jody, then stopped, swallowed hard, pressed a thumb and forefinger to his eyes and turned away.

'Yes, he's brushed his teeth,' Jody answered his unasked question, placing a comforting hand briefly on his shoulder.

'And no, in case you were wondering, he didn't insist on running up and down the stairs six times before he got into bed. Or touching his Fireman Sam Neeh-Nah curtains three times, turning the lights on and off, flushing the loo...'

She paused, to give him some space. Mark was grateful.

'I'll put the kettle on, shall I?' she chatted on, clinking the kettle and cups and saucers while Mark composed himself. 'Sally was fantastic. She'd got the dog eating out of Karl's hand... Or was that Karl eating out of the dog's paw? Whatever, I think Karl might just be a little bit in love. He took the dog up himself, you know? The amazing thing was, they looked at Karl's little bed... I swear they both did, then turned around and climbed right into your bed.'

Jesus. Karl had worked out that his bed was too small? *Un-bloody-believable.* Mark laughed, his heart swelling with pride of his son, yet breaking, all at once.

Chapter Ten

Fireman Sam and Starbuck to the rescue. A smile tugged at Mark's mouth as he watched Karl from the lounge door, who was watching his favourite DVD, unblinking and still in his pyjamas. Nothing new there. The amazing thing was that Starbuck was lying right next to him, practically on top of him, his head resting in Karl's lap. And Karl... Mark ran his hand over his neck. Karl wasn't just stroking him, he was talking to him, communicating with him.

'Good dog.' Mark heard Karl say. 'Dog good,' he said, as the dog nuzzled closer. Utterly incredible. Karl wouldn't know good from bad any more than he'd know love from hate. Mark felt like whooping.

'Dusty-buck,' Karl went on, his attention still on the TV.

'What?' Mark said, coming into the lounge proper.

'Dusty-buck,' Karl repeated. And now Mark was truly incredulous. He looked from his son, whose expression was much as it always was, devoid of any particular emotion, to the TV.

Mark shook his head, wondering if he was hearing quite right. 'Karl, what did you say?'

'Dusty-buck.' Karl obliged.

Mark crouched down by him, careful not to obscure his vision. 'Karl,' he glanced at the TV, where Fireman Sam's mascot dog, Dusty, was trying to avoid bath time, 'this is Dusty,' he pointed at the screen, 'yes?'

Karl nodded. 'Yes.'

Mark reached out to stroke the real dog in the lounge. 'And this is Starbuck.'

Karl nodded.

'And what are they, Karl, Starbuck and Dusty?'

'They're dogs.' Karl said, with another resolute nod.

Mark dragged his hands over his face. 'That's right, Karl,' he said throatily. 'Good boy.'

'Bone,' said Karl.

Mark furrowed his brow. 'Sorry?

'Bone,' Karl repeated. 'Karl's been a good boy, so Karl has a bone.'

He looked at Mark. And Mark smiled, then laughed out loud. He wanted a dog treat, a reward for good behaviour. How amazing was that? 'I think you've been very good, Karl,' he eventually managed. 'Starbuck, too. How about we have some of your favourite jam soldiers for breakfast?'

Mark didn't whoop, once he got to the hall, but he did punch the air. It might be not be much in some people's book, but to Mark it was monumental. Not only had Karl acknowledged another living thing, he seemed to be becoming aware of the sensitivities of the dog, of the dog's moods — a wagging tail meant Starbuck was happy, tail down or a yelp meant he wasn't, particularly when sat on. He seemed to realise that good meant reward, that dogs didn't all come in the same packaging, which must mean that the world would be a less bewildering place. Karl actually seemed to be learning *from a dog*. Was that possible?

Possible or not, it was a bloody miracle. That dog definitely deserved a treat.

Mark couldn't help wishing he had someone to share his feelings with as he headed for the kitchen. Someone close, who might confirm what his heart hoped, that his son's personality might be emerging. That Karl might have a better quality of life. That eventually he'd be able to cope with day-to-day activities without his father constantly beside him.

Mark's mind strayed to Donna as he headed back to the lounge with jam soldiers — light on the jam to avoid a sugar high — and dog treats for Starbuck. How she'd looked at him that first time in her kitchen when he'd joked he was worth waiting for. The way she'd looked at him in the restaurant, laughter dancing in her pretty green eyes. She'd made his heart feel as if it had wings that day.

What might she be doing today, with her Saturday, he wondered. Shopping on the High Street? He smiled. Then fervently hoped she wasn't. Maybe he'd try calling again, one last time; tonight when he got off work, which he was going to be late for again, if he didn't get a move on.

****

'All done. Easy peasy, Sade. Bidding to start...' Donna hesitated. Three-thousand and three-hundred pounds for the pocket watch sounded an awful lot of money, but it was valued at three-five. And also not hers, strictly speaking.

Her fingers hovered over the keyboard. So much for not debating the ethics. She was obviously rubbish at this subterfuge and underhand stuff.

Yes, and Jeremy was rubbish at providing for his own son, emotionally or otherwise. This was for Matt. If Jeremy wanted to argue about it, so be it. Donna was *not* going to be intimidated by him ever again. Shoulders set determinedly, she completed the transaction. Leticia probably paid more than that for her face anyway

Now then, the Beatles collection. Donna had another browse on the Internet. Thirty pounds? She blinked surprised at the screen. For one little vinyl record? Lord, *Sergeant Pepper's Lonely Heart Club Band* was worth forty on its own, and Jeremy had loads of records and albums stuffed in that box.

Maybe she'd just put two or three on? Or four, possibly? Oh, blow it, she'd round it up to five, why not, and save the rest for another rainy day.

There. All done, Donna logged off and dashed for the ringing phone — noted Simon's number, and swallowed back her disappointment before picking up.

****

Mark wasn't so sure Karl's efforts to relate to the dog by peeing on the lawn was such a good idea, but he'd work on that later, he decided, still not quite able to get his head around seeing Karl tucking the quilt around Starbuck when he'd woken in the night.

His son was obviously benefiting from the tactile stimulation offered by the dog, but that he seemed to respond to Starbuck, show him affection — that was almost incomprehensible.

'Whoa, slow down!' Mark span around, dropping dog-food onto his shoes as Karl came shaving past in pursuit of Starbuck, and judging by the dog's galloping gait and swishing tail he was thoroughly enjoying himself.

'*My* Sam, Starbuck. *My* Sam,' Karl said, trying to retrieve his favourite Fireman Sam soft-toy from the dog's mouth.

'Karl, slow down,' Mark repeated, as dog and boy went round in circles playing tug-of-war. On the other hand, don't. Mark's breath caught in his chest as he watched Karl chuckling softly to himself, which was an everyday occurrence for most parents, but music to Mark's ears.

Shaking his head in amazement, he continued to spoon dog-food into the bowl. He'd have to start Karl on the feeding and brushing Starbuck regime soon, hopefully teaching him that with dog ownership came responsibility. Introducing him to the idea of walking Starbuck was the first step though. He'd start him on that tomorrow when he wasn't on duty. Take a trip to the park, maybe, which would give them some space.

'Come on, guys, food,' he called over dog and boy still at noisy play. 'You know the routine, Karl. We have to clear our own breakfast things away, not leave them for Jody.'

Mark clanged the dog's bowl down on the floor, then winced as Karl bellowed behind him, '*Doooon't*! Don't *do* that!'

Karl's voice was hoarse and agitated and Mark realised his mistake straightaway. The noise; a loud, different noise, could destabilise Karl in an instant. 'Karl, it's okay.' He went over to him, to try to reassure him, but Karl squirmed out of his grasp.

'Don't do that!' he grated, backing off with his hands clamped to his ears.

'Karl, stop. It's all right. It was just Starbuck's...' *Hell*, here we go. Mark's heart sank in anticipation of the inevitable tantrum.

'No!' Karl screamed, heading straight for the wall, to bang his head against it — repeatedly against the bloody wall.

'Karl, stop it!' Mark chased him, made a grab for him, wrapped his arms around him.

Fell to his knees, and then to the floor with him.

Tried to soothe him.

To hold him.

'It's all right, Karl. It's okay.' He locked his arms around his son, rocked with him, but still Karl writhed and kicked. 'Starbuck says it's all right, Karl,' Mark tried in desperation, glancing at the dog, and then again in disbelief as the dog came closer — and placed a paw on Karl's leg.

Mark simply could not believe what his eyes were telling him.

The tantrum stopped dead.

He sucked in a breath, waited a beat, then tentatively relaxed his grip.

Karl stood up. Mark gasped, truly incredulous now. He just stood up as in nothing was happening and walked calmly over to the dog.

'It's all right,' Karl said, patting Starbuck. 'It's just Starbuck's...' He repeated what Mark had said, including the trail off, then walked casually through to the lounge, Starbuck in tow.

Mark stayed where he was on the floor, blinking stupefied for a second, then looking up as Jody came down the hall, closely followed by Sally, who must have arrived with her. Had *they* seen?

'Did you?' He shook his head and stared at them, still in a state of utter amazement. Nothing, but nothing, had ever been able to dissuade Karl from a tantrum before.

Sally smiled. 'I did mention he was trained to respond to a child's repetitive behaviour.'

Mark raked his hand through his hair. 'Yes, but I thought that would be the rocking to and fro and hand-flapping stuff, not...'

'Banging his head? Stamping his feet?' Sally gave Mark a knowing look.

Mark nodded. Of course. 'Christ, that dog is working magic nothing short of miraculous.'

'He aims to please,' Sally assured him. 'And the spin-off is, in ceasing the repetitive behaviours, Karl might interact with Starbuck more, thus becoming more perceptive of the dog's needs and hopefully transferring those accomplishments to humans. There are no guarantees, of course,' she stressed, walking across to assist him from the floor, 'but...'

'... he's making progress.' Mark grabbed hold of her hand, and thanked God he hadn't been too proud to reach out.

'You've made an awful mess of your uniform.' Jody nodded at his dog-food-spattered trousers.

Glancing down, Mark laughed. 'You know, in the great scheme of things, I don't think I give a damn.'

****

Mark's good mood evaporated as he spotted Evelyn outside his Dad's front door.

'Great,' he muttered, climbing out of his car. He needed this like a hole in the head. So, did he talk to her or ignore her? Whatever, he was obliged to walk past her. At least she wasn't here to clobber him again, he supposed, not with her daughter's child in her arms.

'Oh, it's you.' Evelyn looked him derisively up and down, as he approached the door.

Mark bent to look himself up and down. 'Yep, definitely.' He smiled, looking back at her. 'Sorry to disappoint you.'

Evelyn raised her eyebrows, clearly not amused. 'I see you're in uniform. Out to impress the girls, are we?'

Mark decided to ignore that barbed comment. 'On duty,' he said. 'If I'd known I was coming into a hazardous situation, I'd have worn full body armour.'

'Very droll, Mr Evans. For you information, I'm not in a habit of hitting people.'

'Glad to hear it. Have you knocked?' Mark nodded at the door.

'Yes.' Evelyn hoisted Jack higher in her arms, who was becoming a bit fractious. 'He hasn't answered.'

'Can't say I blame him.'

'Such wit,' Evelyn said dourly. 'He didn't answer when Dot knocked last night, either. You might want to...'

'*Christ.*' Mark fished his key out of his pocket and was through the door in five seconds flat. 'Dad?' he called, once inside the hall.

'Dad, you here?' He pushed open the lounge door, checked out the kitchen and was halfway up the stairs, when the under-stairs cupboard door creaked open.

'Unfortunately, yes.' His father emerged, with a world-weary sigh.

Mark exhaled, relieved, and trooped back down.

'Close the front door, would you?' Robert addressed Evelyn, with a tight smile. 'Preferably on your way out.' He turned to stride to the kitchen, newspaper under arm, torch in hand, and still in his pyjamas.

Stupefied, Evelyn blinked over Jack — who'd also been stunned into silence by the pyjama-clad apparition, and then turned wordlessly to close the door.

'Ahem.' Composure obviously collected, Evelyn turned back and proceeded down the hall. 'My opinion of *you* hasn't changed, incidentally,' she told Mark as she marched past him.

'Right.' Mark shook his head and wondered whether to stay or make a run for it.

Jack's wailing before Evelyn got as far as the kitchen made up Mark's mind. Clearly determined to go nowhere near the monster from the under-stairs cupboard, Jack wriggled, then went rigid and refused to bend in the middle.

'Here, let me take him,' Mark offered, sensing a toddler-tantrum coming on.

'Evelyn,' he sighed, as Evelyn struggled to hold on to him, 'I know you don't rate me, but I do have a child, you know. Do you want to hand him over before he hits floor?'

'This I'm aware of. As is Donna... *now*.' Evelyn gave him a look that could curdle milk. 'We don't see much of your child when he's here though, do we?'

'Which means?' Mark tried to quash his growing irritation.

'Nothing, I'm sure. Except, given your father has the luxury of a garden, maybe you should allow the child to act more like a child?'

What the *hell* was the woman on about now? Mark glanced angrily at the ceiling. 'Thank you,' he said, looking back at her, his temper in check. 'I'll bear your invaluable parenting advice in mind.'

He wasn't getting into this. If the woman ever wanted a civil conversation, maybe. But, right now, he needed to go to work. And, given Evelyn's last *unsocial* call, he wanted her gone before he did.

'Meanwhile, maybe we should consider Jack's welfare.' Mark nodded at Jack, who was now dangling precariously from her grasp. 'I'll take him, okay?'

'Thank you,' Evelyn managed, though Mark was reaching to take him anyway.

'Come on, mate.' He swung Jack up in his arms. 'Let's go and see if we can find you some sweets, hey? All right with you?' He eyed Evelyn questioningly.

'Fine,' Evelyn said, marching on into the kitchen. 'As long as they're not boiled sweets.'

Mark followed her, Jack still tearful, but somewhat appeased by the 'sweet' word. 'Chocolate,' he assured her. 'White. Dad's personal supply. Don't worry, I won't offer him a beer to wash it down with.'

Evelyn gave him a semi-amused glance over her shoulder, then headed over to where Robert was seated at the table, his eyes fixed on his newspaper. 'I came to apologise for my abysmal behaviour,' she said, without further ado. 'I bought you...' she paused to ferret in her shoulder bag '... these.'

Robert glanced over his paper at the box she'd planted on the table, then at Evelyn, bemused.

'Tea bags?' Mark looked at her askew.

'Williamson Duchess Grey, home-delivered by John Lewis,' Evelyn informed him. 'Nothing but the best, for someone who's obviously too high-brow to mix with us prols.'

'Harrumph.' Robert rattled his newspaper, now looking unimpressed.

'It's a joke, Mr Evans.' Evelyn rolled her eyes. 'Clearly you've forgotten your sense of humour, as well as where your wardrobe is.'

Robert licked his thumb and turned a page.

'Good God, have you no manners?' Evelyn snapped. 'Can't you at least accept them with the good grace they were intended as?'

Robert arched an eyebrow at Mark, who was in serious danger of inviting Evelyn's wrath again and laughing aloud.

'It's an olive branch,' Evelyn elaborated, with a smidgeon of contrition. 'I think I might have possibly been a touch rude when I last saw you,'

'You were.' Robert perused another page. 'You are.'

'Well no one can say I didn't try.' Evelyn shrugged and turned to Mark to retrieve her grandchild.

'Sit down.' Robert downed his paper, obviously somewhat appeased. 'I'll put the kettle on.'

Evelyn turned back, surprised. 'No. Thank you, but I can't stop. I'm helping out at St Peter's Jumble sale in aid of the church roof. Dot's watching Jack for me, isn't she, sweetheart?'

'Choclat.' Jack beamed, and offered her a sticky palm to lick.

'Ooh, lovely.' Evelyn obliged. 'Come on then, young man, let's go and play with Dot, shall we?'

She headed for the door, then stopped. 'You should come round to Dot's one evening,' she addressed Robert. 'She is a bit over-motherly sometimes, but she makes the best apple pie. We could wash it down with a G&T.'

Robert stroked his stubbly chin. 'I might just take you up on that,' he mused, 'as long as you don't leave me alone with her,' he added worriedly.

Evelyn laughed. 'I'll play chaperone,' she promised, 'as long as you behave yourself.'

'Wouldn't dream of doing anything but.' Robert got to his feet. 'Yorkshire man born and bred, and a gentleman born and bred,' he assured her, puffing up his chest.

'Like your son?' Evelyn asked archly.

'He's a good man, you know,' Robert said, walking her to the hall. 'Give him a chance to explain about... whatever happened with your daughter.'

'It's not me he has to explain to.' Evelyn glanced meaningfully back at Mark.

Mark tried a smile. 'I thought you wanted me to run out of town?'

'I'm reserving judgement.' Evelyn graced him with a small smile back. 'You shouldn't have lied to her, Mark. Chances are, you've done irreparable damage even if you do have a reasonable explanation, which, personally, I doubt.'

'I know.' Mark nodded despondently.

'Were they honourable, Mr Evans,' Evelyn eyed him levelly, 'your intentions towards my daughter?'

'Very,' Mark said, holding her gaze.

'Hmm.' Evelyn searched his eyes, a little less hostility in her own.

****

'Alicia, if we don't leave now, we'll never get there before last food orders,' Donna said, as her sister preened in front of the hall mirror.

Donna didn't even want to go. She certainly didn't want to go looking like something the cat had dragged in. Simon had sounded so excited though, that his boyfriend Nathan and he had finally set a date, she hadn't the heart to tell him the last thing she wanted to do was celebrate two people sealing their relationship.

'Two minutes,' Alicia mumbled, making a neat little "o" with her mouth and applying her lip-gloss. 'It'll only take us twenty minutes to get there, don't panic,' she went on, pressing her lips together and admiring the effect as Donna peered around her, trying to get a glimpse of even a nostril.

'And how *are* we getting there, exactly? Donna gave up and glanced at her sister askew. 'As the crow flies? Because unless we sprout wings, I'm calculating more than an hour, actually.'

'To The Swan?' Alicia glanced at Donna doubtfully.

'We're on Shanks's Pony, Alicia. My car doesn't go very well at the moment, and Mum dropped you off, remember? So unless you fancy thumbing a lift now you've made yourself irresistible, we're definitely going to be late.'

'Well, we'll call a taxi then.' Alicia turned from the mirror, apparently satisfied.

'I already did. They said half-an-hour to an hour's wait.'

'Silly question, probably, Donna, but why aren't you using Matt's car?' Alicia asked, giving her hair a final flick, then heading to the kitchen for her boots and handbag.

Donna glanced in the mirror and gave her own hair a quick flick. *Ye-es. Traffic-stopping.* All she needed now was a head transplant and she'd pass for Cameron Diaz in a flash. 'Because it *is* Matt's car, Alicia.' Donna trailed after her. 'It's also not currently road taxed.'

'So tax it,' Alicia suggested, giving Sadie a pet before plonking herself on a kitchen chair to tug on her boots.

Donna sat on the opposite chair and kicked off her passé trainers. With her heart swishing about in her tummy, she honestly didn't feel like glamming up, but she should make a bit of an effort, she supposed. At least wear some heels in the hopes that longer legs might detract from her face.

'It's Saturday afternoon, Alicia. The post office is shut,' Donna pointed out, reaching for her sister's blusher and lippy.

'Yes, but we can tax it online, can't we? It'll only take five minutes. And before you say you can't afford to —'

'I can't afford to.'

'But I can.' Alicia stood up, booted, beautifully made-up and determined.

'Uh-uh.' Donna stood up, barefoot — to the disappointment of Findus, who was in search of a late lace-luncheon, blobbed and equally determined. 'I can't let you do that, Alicia. I'm not a …'

'Yes, you can. Jack's father provides more than adequately for his son, unlike some people we know.' Alicia cut her short. 'And I know you're not a charity case. You're a stubborn Miss Independent who doesn't realise that that's what sisters are for: To support each other.'

Alicia scooped Findus up and set him down in front of a more digestible cabbage leaf, then caught hold of Donna's shoulders, twirled her around and propelled her to the lounge and the PC. 'You'd do the same for me,' she said, following after her. 'And you can pay me back when you can. Meanwhile, you need to get yourself back out there.'

What, again? Donna wasn't sure she wouldn't rather just stay in with copious amounts of pleasure-inducing chocolate endorphins. 'All right,' she reluctantly agreed, silly not to when she needed alternative transport, but, 'I will pay you back, I promise.' She nodded, resolute, as she led the way up the hall.

She would too. Just as soon as the bidding was over.

****

Mark looked the guy who was propped against the wall of the betting shop over, disgusted. It wasn't that he was so inebriated Mark's partner could barely hold him up that was getting to Mark. What had him hard-pushed not give the little runt a taste of his own, was the state of the cashier he'd assaulted.

'She wouldn't pay me me winnings,' the guy slurred, 'fuckin' bitch.'

Mark tensed, while Phil, equally disgusted, propped the guy harder against the wall. 'So you thought you'd show her what a big man you are, hey?' Phil twisted the guy's collar just a little bit tighter.

'I know what I'll show 'er next time, all right.' The guy smirked, which did nothing to enamour him to Mark.

'You won't be showing anybody anything, mate, trust me,' he grated angrily. Scum, he thought, his stomach turning over as the paramedics wheeled the cashier past them. 'Come on, Phil,' he nodded towards the patrol car, 'let's show this *gentleman* the cosy interior of a police cell. See if that doesn't cool his bravado.'

'You wanna watch it, you do,' the guy warned, as Mark reached for his handcuffs. 'Do Aikido, I do.'

'Yeah?' Mark laughed disdainfully. 'And I do Origami. Come on, you're nicked.'

'Wanker.' The guy's face twisted into a snarl. Mark saw it coming, but back-stepped too late.

'Bloody hell! *Mark…*!' Phil shouted, as the vicious head-butt sent his partner reeling. 'Are you okay?!'

'*Jesus.*' Mark shook his head, saw stars, literally, and then he saw red. 'Unfortunately, for that *bastard*, yes.' He righted himself and stepped towards the guy, no inclination this time to keep his temper in check.

'Leave it, Mark,' Phil warned him.

Mark raked a hand shakily through his hair, his cap being someway off on the pavement. '*He* is history!' he said, breathing hard.

'Yes, and so will you be, if you don't back off!' Phil positioned himself bodily between them.

Mark wasn't listening. He'd had enough. Seen enough broken bones, broken homes, and smashed lives. It never got any better. But the kind of pond-scum that bragged about talking with their fists afterwards…

'Mark! Think about Karl. He needs you! Now, for Christ's sake, get your bloody act together!'

Mark studied the guy, his chest heaving. Counting down silently, he cautioned himself… not to reach out and break the little shit's neck. 'I'm obliged to inform you I'm arresting you on suspicion of assault with intent to cause grievous bodily harm,' he instead cautioned the guy dispassionately. 'You do not have to say anything, but it may harm your defence…'

****

'Matt won't mind, will he?' Alicia asked, as Donna and she headed for the front door, having taxed the car.

'It's not that he'll mind, Alicia. It's just that Matt and I have an unspoken rule, one of mutual respect — of each other's possessions as well as opinions.' After Jeremy showing them precious little respect,

Donna felt she didn't need to add. 'And as Matt's most precious possession after his iPod is his VW...'

She dialled Matt's number as they opened the front door, to be greeted by his Indie music ring-tone approaching it.

'Uh, oh, looks like the sisters are out on the town.' Matt took in Alicia's attire and his mum's extra height. 'Lock up da menfolk.' He made imploring eyes at the skies.

'Matt, darling nephew!' Alicia exclaimed joyously, squashing his perplexed face between her hands as he walked in. 'How are you? How's college? How are the driving lessons going? How's the car?'

'All right, all right, all right. And no you can't,' Matt managed, through pursed lips.

'Oh, go on, pretty please?' Alicia batted her eyelashes. 'For your favourite aunty-wanty?'

'Uh-uh.'

'Oh, well, it was worth a try.' She shrugged and dropped his puckered face.

'Thank you,' Matt said, nipping past his mad aunty-wanty into the hall.

'I'll tax it,' Alicia offered, omitting to say she already had in favour of dangling the carrot. 'And we'll put some petrol in.'

'Umm...' Matt considered. 'Make it a full tank and you're on.'

'Done.' Alicia gave him a wink. 'He'll go far, that one.'

Chapter Eleven

'Responding,' Phil answered another callout unenthusiastically.

Mark sighed, stuffed his caffeine-kick-drink-can in the well of the door and started the engine. 'No prizes for guessing who our young shoplifter might be.'

'Well, on the plus side, we get to go back to the station and coffee,' Phil offered, cheerfully. 'That should keep you awake.'

'It'll need to.' Mark stifled a yawn as he negotiated his way through the pedestrian area of the High Street.

At this rate, he'd be unconscious before quitting time. The first shout had wiped him out, and that was without the great thumping headache.

He ran his hand over his neck. Christ, he was tired. It was a long haul most mornings, getting Karl up and dressed and into the dreaded shoes — going through the rituals. Making sure things were done in order, because for them not to be, meant Karl had to do them all over again.

Even his food had to be arranged specifically on his plate, no item to touch another and everything to be eaten with a knife and fork, which meant cereals were out. Still, it was a far cry from the day Mark realised Karl had forgotten what to do with his knife and fork. And even if Mark had cracked his shin on the chair as he went down this morning, the tantrum hadn't been a full-on one, thanks to their new four-legged friend.

He tugged in a breath as he pulled up in front of the druggist, an image of Donna and her three-legged friend reminding him painfully of what he'd taken a gamble on and lost.

Dammit, Evelyn was right. There were no excuses for lying. He should have told Donna, allowed her to make her own decisions. It wasn't likely that she'd have just said, hey, no problem, I'd love to sacrifice my life to the joint care of your son, but seeing her on a casual basis, any basis, would have been better than none. At least then he'd have been able to talk about Karl openly.

'Once more into the fray.' He sighed as he reached for his cap. Things could be worse. Karl having a better quality of life thanks to Starbuck was a cause for celebration, not maudlin. Time to stop feeling sorry for himself, Mark supposed.

'Wonder what story she'll have this time,' Phil speculated as he pushed open his door. 'Cat needs an operation? Boyfriend's car needs work, so he can turn over a new leaf and become a taxi driver?'

Mark laughed cynically. 'More like boyfriend needs a fix so he can get out of bed and she fancies some new shoes.'

****

'Stephanie.' Mark nodded at the girl sitting slouched in a chair as he came into the manager's office at the back of the shop. 'How're you doing?'

'Mmm, better for seeing you, sweetheart.' Stephanie sat to attention, adjusting her skimpy top to show a lot more cleavage as she did. Mark noted the addition of another tattoo, before averting his gaze.

'Put it away, Steph.' Phil sighed. 'He's had lunch.'

'Humph.' Stephanie slumped back in her chair and folded her arms moodily over her breasts.

'So, what is it this time, Stephanie?' Mark asked resignedly as he walked over to her pram. 'Perfume? Make-up? Electrical goods? Girl or boy?'

Stephanie shrugged. 'Dunno what you're on about. Ain't done nothing. Just shopping, wasn't I?'

'That right, is it?' Decent pram, Mark noticed. Probably nicked from Mothercare. He inched the shawl carefully away from a well tucked-up baby.

'Cute,' he said. 'What's its name, then?

'Lady Gaga.' Stephanie shot him a contemptuous glance, chewed noisily on her gum and blew out a bubble.

'Nice.' Mark pulled the shawl back, shook his head, then plucked her pop-icon from its pram. 'This nicked, too, Stephanie?' He turned back, dangling her brand new *Baby Born* doll by its leg.

'No, it's *not* nicked.' Stephanie blew out another insolent bubble and popped it. 'S'me sister's, innit.'

'That would be the long-lost sister you've just had a tearful reunion with, would it?' Mark suggested, knowing Stephanie had no sister. She was special, no doubt about it. This was good though, he had to concede. Better than the baby-sling scam, which turned out to be a *Scooby Doo* soft toy nicked from *Woolworths* tucked snugly up with a selection of DVDs. Small wonder they'd gone bust with Stephanie 'shopping' there.

'Where, is it, Steph?' Phil stepped in. 'The bloke's shaver you half-inched?'

'Don't know nothing about no shaver.' Stephanie rolled bored eyes under inch-thick mascara. 'Ain't nothing in there, either,' she said as Mark searched the pram.

'So where then, Steph?' Phil asked. 'Fell in your pocket, by any chance?'

'Might be. So what y'gonna do now? Search me?' Stephanie looked Mark languidly over.

Mark and Phil exchanged knowing glances. 'No, Stephanie,' Mark said with a tolerant smile. 'We thought we'd treat you to an all-expenses paid lunch down at the station.'

****

Donna sighed as Alicia checked her mascara through rear view mirror, again, which really wasn't terribly conducive to the careful driving of their newly acquired rust bucket.

'Alicia, do you mind?' Donna tugged the mirror back. 'One needs one's mirror in order to see what's behind —'

'Donna, watch out in front!' Alicia slapped her hands over her eyes.

'Oh, my *God!*' Donna slammed on the brakes as a feral streak flashed past. She gripped the wheel hard, then scrunched her eyes closed as the car skidded into a ninety- degree turn, before screeching to a clunking halt.

'I don't believe it.' Alicia peered through her fingers. 'Matt's car has a homing device.'

'*I* don't believe it.' Sure she must be jinxed for life, Donna uttered a silent prayer and took several deep breaths.

'Sorry, hon,' Alicia said in a little voice.

'It's all right. My fault, I should have been looking.' Donna tried to pull herself together, before an articulated lorry came along — or a freight train. Shakily, she reached for the ignition, turned the engine over, and... nothing.

'You mean the cat should have been looking.' Alicia heaved herself out of the passenger side. 'I thought black cats were supposed to be lucky anyway,' she said, walking around front, as Donna climbed out of the driver's side.

'Not if you run over them, Alicia,' Donna pointed out.

'Something's probably jarred loose. A wire or a plug or...' Alicia heaved up the bonnet. 'OhmiGod! The engine's dropped out!'

Donna laughed and headed for the tail-end of the VW. 'It's in the back, Alicia.'

'Well, how on earth did it get there?' Alicia furrowed her brow, dropped the bonnet and walked around to join her.

'I think we might need a man that can,' Donna observed after two minutes staring clueless at the engine.

****

'It could have been worse,' Donna suggested optimistically as they waited for the AA, bottoms perched on the bonnet and Alicia smiling at passing traffic. Donna would have been mortified if they'd actually hit the poor cat.

'A lot worse,' Alicia observed, sliding neatly off the bonnet. 'The man that can.' She nodded towards the AA van as it pulled up behind the VW, from which climbed a reasonably presentable dish. 'And I tell you what, *he* could, anytime.'

'Alicia!' Donna stared after her, shocked, as Alicia did her Cameron hair-flick to perfection and sashayed towards him.

'Oh, am I glad to see *you.*' Alicia smiled seductively and batted her lashes. 'I'm Alicia,' she said, offering her hand.

And I've obviously ceased to exist. Donna tried not to be too miffed as Alicia continued to bat, while he beamed.

'We're having a spot of trouble.' Alicia slid her hand from his, eventually, and turned back towards the VW, an eye-twanging wiggle to her walk. 'Our engine seems to be in the wrong place.'

'Er...' The guy dragged his eyes away from her bottom, to glance bemusedly at Donna.

Ten minutes later, Donna bobbed invisibly behind them as Michael — apparently — and Alicia peered into the engine compartment practically cheek-to-cheek.

Don't mind me, she thought. I'll just take a walk around the block while you two get better acquainted. 'I didn't realise you were so interested in engines, Alicia,' she eventually said pointedly, behind her.

'I had no idea they could be so fascinating,' Alicia replied, apparently riveted by his explanation of which thingummy connected to what whatsit and where the dipstick was.

'Me either.' Donna curled a lip. Honestly, she'd be holding his spanner for him in a minute. 'Alicia's boyfriend's quite good with engines,' she said, even more pointedly. 'He's away at the moment though, taking his black belt in karate.'

That got smiley Michael's attention. 'Shame really,' Donna went on, gleefully embellishing the facts. Alicia's current boyfriend was lovely, but actually more Hugh Grant than Jackie Chan. 'He's got such big pecs, he could have lifted the engine out and popped it in the right end in a flash, couldn't he, Alicia?'

Alicia shot her a loaded look as Michael stepped back.

Donna shot her a look back. 'You're going out with someone,' she mouthed, as Michael turned to collect up his tools.

'I know. I'm just flattering him,' Alicia whispered back. 'What?' She looked at Donna despairingly as he went to try the ignition. 'It got the car fixed, didn't it?'

'He's an AA man, Alicia. It's his job to fix the car.'

'Yes, but because it's his job doesn't mean he has to go the extra mile, does it? Did you want to be towed back home on a tow-truck?'

No, Donna conceded, certain Matt wouldn't be overly impressed if she was. *Yesss!* She whooped quietly as the engine sparked into life.

'All done,' said Michael, emerging from the car with a smile.

'Thank you. I really appreciate your efforts.' Donna offered him a grateful smile back. Perhaps a little flattery didn't hurt, after all. He had been extremely conscientious.

'No problem. We're here to serve.' He winked.

Donna glanced behind her, sure he'd be winking at Alicia. Oh? Well, perhaps he'd got a nervous twitch, then?

'You'd better get that seen to,' he said, nodding towards Donna's hand, the back of which, she was surprised to see, was scratched and trickling blood.

'Oh, it's nothing.' She smiled bravely, though it did actually look quite nasty. She must have done it pushing the car to the kerb.

'Well, you never know, you might have some dirt in it or something,' he said, plucking her hand up to examine it at close quarters. 'Hold on, I've got a first-aid kit in the van. Can't leave a damsel in distress, can I?'

Donna laughed. 'I'm not a damsel.'

'But she is in distress,' Alicia called as he headed back to his van.

'Oh, how's that, then?' Michael asked, returning with a plaster and antiseptic cream.

'She split up with her boyfriend,' Alicia informed him with a dramatic sigh. 'Heartbroken, poor girl,' she went on as Donna stared at her, slack-jawed.

'That's a shame.' Michael looked Donna over interestedly, whilst making a meal of smoothing the plaster over her hand. 'Tell you what, if you're at a loose end, why don't you come out with me?'

'What?' Donna blinked at him, amazed at his gall. Only two minutes ago, he'd been getting up close and personal with Alicia under *her* bonnet. Blooming cheek.

'You're at a loose end. I'm at a loose end. Why don't we get our ends together sometime?' he went on, winking saucily now, and still holding onto Donna's hand.

'Pardon?' Donna stared, flabbergasted.

'Go on. Go out with him,' Alicia suggested, so preposterously Donna almost laughed. 'It can't hurt. He's asking ever so nicely, and it might be just the tonic you need.'

Nicely? Donna looked disbelieving from Alicia to her expectant admirer, who was probably wondering why she hadn't swooned at his soft line of seduction. *Get our ends together?* Honestly.

'I can't. I'm, um...' Donna struggled for something to say now Alicia had announced she was single, ergo obviously up for grabs '... on the rebound.'

'You could rebound off me anytime.' Michael waggled his eyebrows.

Donna arched hers, bemused. 'Serious rebound,' she said meaningfully.

'Pity,' he said, raising her injured — and finally plastered — hand to his lips.

Good Lord. Donna gawked at him. What did she do now? Curtsey? She smiled at him wanly instead.

He smiled back and trailed a thumb over her cheek. 'Bit of oil,' he said. 'Don't want it going in your pretty green eyes, do we?'

'No. Thank you,' Donna mumbled.

'The pleasure was all mine,' he assured her. 'Look, call me if you do fancy going out sometime.' He ferreted in his breast pocket for pen and pad and scrawled his number.

Donna took the note he offered, smiled courteously as he turned back to his van, then froze.

'Uh, oh,' Alicia said. 'Don't look now Donna, but...'

But Donna was looking totally aghast — at the patrol car idling on the opposite side of the road. A very familiar driver at the wheel, looking extremely pissed off.

****

Mark tried to ignore Stephanie, smirking and slapping her mouth on her chewing gum as they waited to go through the back office.

'Wouldn't let my girlfriend get away with that.' Stephanie eyed him sideways, obviously intent on getting full mileage out of his embarrassment. 'Give 'er a good hiding, I would.'

Mark's cheek twitched. How much bloody longer did he have to listen to this? He cursed his stupid over-reaction with an audience in the back, who would remind him every second she was here that he'd just witnessed his 'girlfriend' getting up close and personal with another bloke.

Telling Stephanie, who delighted in pushing copper's buttons, that Donna wasn't his girlfriend, was pointless, particularly as he'd been close to climbing out of the patrol car and pulling the guy in on any conceivable charge he could find.

Finally, they gained access to the back room, where WPC Slater waited, as per protocol for female suspects.

'Well, well, Stephanie. Can't keep away can you?' WPC Slater gave her a knowing look. 'You into the fresh percolated coffee and haute cuisine, then?'

'Nah.' Stephanie smirked. 'It's 'im I'm into, innit? The moody, broody one. I wouldn't mind 'im strip-searching me.'

'You'd be more than he could handle, Steph.' The WPC gave Mark a sympathetic glance, as he ran a hand wearily over his neck.

'Go on, go get yourself a coffee,' she said, obviously aware he was in need of a get out. 'I'll sort the paperwork and make sure Steph here gets suitable accommodation.'

Mark smiled, relieved. 'Cheers, Rachel. I owe you one.'

'No problem,' Rachel assured him as he turned away, only to hear Stephanie taunting behind him, 'Aw, looks like someone's pee'd on his firework, doesn't he, poor sod. Never mind, luv,' her voice trailed after him, as Mark headed back through the security door. 'She wasn't all that anyway, if you ask me. You come and see me, if you're lonely, sweetheart. I'll kiss it all…'

Mark raked his hand through his hair as the back room door banged mercifully shut.

****

Alicia was driving as they entered the pub car park, Donna's faculties seeming not to be functioning.

'What was he doing there?' she said, again, her shoulders so droopy she wouldn't be surprised if her knuckles scraped the ground when she walked.

'Donna, you've asked that a thousand times and I still don't know. It was just bad timing.'

Bad timing? Donna stared forlornly through the windscreen. Some man doing... intimate things to her, and Mark drives by. That wasn't bad timing. It was horrendous. Misfortune gone mad.

He'd looked so shocked.

Okay, she wasn't actually *with* Mark, but that didn't make her feel any better. She didn't want to hurt him because he'd hurt her. To play the pathetic games Jeremy played. Most of all, she didn't want Mark thinking she was what he might have thought she was on their first meeting. A sad old slapper.

'Come on, honey. No point sitting about out here with a face like a wet weekend.' Alicia gave her shoulders a squeeze. 'Let's go on in. They might have stopped serving food now, but they won't have stopped serving wine.'

She reached for her bag and hopped out of the car. Then peered back in. 'Come on, chop chop,' she said, as Donna heaved in shuddery breath. 'Let's go and knock 'em dead.'

Alicia closed the door and clacked towards the pub, as Donna reached for her door. Then clacked back, opened her door and climbed back in. 'Or not,' she said, starting the engine.

'Alicia?' Donna pulled her door back and looked at her sister askew.

'Mark was bad timing. That,' Alicia nodded towards a sparkling new Jaguar cruising across the car park, 'is a joke.'

'Drive,' Donna said, concluding she must have been a terrible person in another life.

'Trust me, I'm driving.' Alicia reversed swiftly. 'Unless...' She stepped on the brake. 'Donna, we'll go if you want to. I'm quite happy to, but...'

'I do.'

'... .you are sure you want to do this, aren't you, hon? Run away, I mean?'

Donna stared at her sister, astounded. 'What do you mean, run away?'

'Well, I presume you're not going to spend the rest of your life avoiding public places because Jeremy might happen to be there? He'd just love that, wouldn't he?'

Donna furrowed her brow. *Good God*, Alicia was right. What on earth was she doing?! Was she going to avoid the park, too, in case she bumped into him? The supermarket?

Donna watched Jeremy climb out of their/his/her Jag, walk around and open the passenger door for Leticia. Well, wasn't he keen to please?

The only time Donna remembered him opening a door around her was when he was on his way out.

Humph. Up went the shoulders.

'Do you know, that's a very good point. Why am *I*...' Donna poked herself in the chest '... running away? I've done nothing wrong. God's gift might think he dictates the rules, but he doesn't, not anymore. Alicia, mirror.'

'That's my girl.' Alicia grinned, and hoisted the rear-view mirror passenger direction.

One nifty application of mascara later, Donna turned for appraisal. 'Better?'

Alicia scrutinised her. Fished for a tissue to wipe off a splodge, fluffed up Donna's fringe, then, 'Much,' she said, satisfied.

'Come on.' Alicia climbed out.

Donna did likewise.

They swapped supportive smiles over the roof, closed doors together, joined forces at the front of the VW, then marched, arm in arm, into the pub.

'Remember, play it cool.' Alicia paused outside the lounge door to give Donna a last tweak. 'Whatever he does, whatever he says...' She made *let it go over your head* signs, then gave Donna a nod. 'Ready?'

'Ready.' Donna nodded determinedly back.

'Right.' They reached for the double doors together, Alicia sashayed in, while Donna — coolly — peeled herself away from her locked door, stepped around it, then sashayed for all she was worth.

So where was he? She stopped mid-lounge, glancing surreptitiously around. The room was pretty packed. The last thing she wanted to do was end up sitting by him.

Ah, there. How sweet. Her eyes alighted on Jeremy in cosy conversation at a corner table. Well, Leticia was conversing. Jeremy was hanging rapt on her every word. Definitely an eager little beaver, wasn't he? Not like Jeremy, at all. Perhaps he really was smitten. Donna curled a lip and wondered whether another room might be more comfortable — in another pub.

'Right, best foot forward.' Alicia caught hold of her elbow. 'Drinks, I think are called for. If we have to spend time in Jeremy's nauseating company, we might as well try to enjoy it. And remember, if he comes out with his usual dire tripe, just play it low key...'

'Cooee! Donna!' came a familiar voice. 'Woo-hoo, Dons, over here!' Simon gesticulated wildly from across the lounge.

Well, that was really low-key. Donna rolled her eyes, then rolled them some more as Alicia waved manically back, then dashed over to him as he was halfway towards them.

'Simon, you *did* it,' she screeched, clutching his hands and jiggling up and down like a *Take That* fan in the front row of a concert. 'You did it! You did it!'

'Yes. Yes.' Simon beamed and jiggled up and down with her, then stopped. 'Um, I'm only tying the knot, Alicia,' he said, glancing at her worriedly, 'not getting a Knighthood or anything.'

'Well, I think it's sweet,' Alicia said, glancing at Donna, then nodding at Jeremy. *Ah.* Donna got the drift. Jeremy didn't hold with things not normal, they being gays, lesbians, three-legged dogs, people with disabilities, disadvantaged people, women, and was looking highly uncomfortable. Well done, Alicia.

It did beg the question, however, why was he here? Accepted, it might just be a coincidence, but why was he *still* here was what Donna was wondering. Jeremy wouldn't be likely to tolerate Simon's company for one second, without good reason.

Oh, no. Now, they were coming over, which meant she'd have to speak to him.

'Jeremy, long time no see,' Alicia gushed, as he approached. 'Not long enough, unfortunately. And... Oh?' She frowned, looking Leticia up and down. 'Well, you're not the one he was with in town. Is she, Jeremy?'

Alicia looked at Jeremy questioningly.

Jeremy looked at Alicia murderously, his chestnut brown eyes hardening to little black coals. Donna had seen that look before.

Leticia was looking quite upset, she noticed and couldn't help feeling a teensy bit sorry for her.

Alicia, oblivious to Jeremy's warning signals, trundled on. 'So how long have you two been together, um?' She turned to Leticia expectantly.

'Leticia.' Leticia smiled stoically. 'Quite a while,' she answered Alicia's question vaguely.

'Over a year,' Donna supplied, her sympathy evaporating.

'Really?' Alicia exclaimed, pseudo-surprised. 'So you met *before* Donna and Jeremy split up, then? Well, kudos to you, old girl, for 'sticking with him,' she hurried on, before anyone could comment. 'Despite his, um, little problem, I mean. Not that I'm knocking Donna. God knows, she tried, but, she's not very worldly, our Donna, when it comes to men's, shall I say, predilection to wander. Are you, Donna?'

Donna closed her eyes and prayed for someone to beam her up, then peeled one slowly open. No, no good. Jeremy's eyes were still boring nastily into hers. 'Alicia,' Donna pointed to the table, 'shall we go and, um —'

'Still persists in thinking that fairy tales exist, poor girl,' Alicia went on. 'You know, one woman – one man, kiss the frog and he turns into Prince Charming. Didn't work with Jeremy, unfortunately. Each to their own, though, hey, Leticia?'

Jeremy slammed his pint glass down on the nearest table. 'Very good, Alicia,' he seethed. 'Move over Jo Brand. Mind you, she'd have to move over, wouldn't she, you being so...' Jeremy dragged derisory eyes slowly over Alicia's breasts 'formidable.'

'Oh, ha-de-ha, ha. Is that really the best you can do?' Alicia returned the look. 'Come on, Donna, the air's a little acrid around here.'

Alicia hooked an arm back through Donna's. 'Let's go and find more salubrious company and leave Lettuce to her slug.'

'In which case, you might want to leave Donna behind. I'm not even sure she knows how to spell salubrious,' Jeremy drawled. 'Must admit I'm impressed you've managed to work out how to switch on the *home* computer, though, Donna.'

Jeremy let it hang, looking at Donna pointedly.

Donna paled.

'We dropped in on Matt,' Jeremy said, matter-of-factly, 'didn't we, Leticia?'

Leticia offered Donna a small smile. 'I thought... *We* thought it was about time he did,' she said, looking almost human.

'He told me we'd find you here when I said I needed a little word,' Jeremy went on, smiling his executioner smile.

'Another drink, darling?' he asked Leticia, pausing as he stepped past Donna, his breath suddenly so hot on her cheek it sent a chill down her spine. 'You've put my stuff on eBay,' he whispered menacingly. 'Take it off, or you're dead.'

Swallowing hard, Donna turned to glance after Jeremy as he headed for the bar, and locked eyes with Simon.

'Did he just say what I think he did?' Simon asked, his eyes narrowed.

Donna didn't answer, but her expression must have said it all.

'*Bastard.*' Simon growled. 'Right.'

Fuming, Simon turned as Jeremy came back. 'Jeremy, how *could* you?' he wailed, so overtly and over-the-top gay he could out-camp Graham Norton. 'You're supposed to be Nathan's accountant, not his *bitch* on the side.'

Jeremy balked. 'What?'

'You're sleeping with him, aren't you? Oh, God, how *could* you, after all the things you said. The things we've done?' Simon threw his arm theatrically across his brow.

Jeremy laughed disbelieving, then looked around, almost squirming with embarrassment, as the conversation in the lounge quieted to a hush. 'He's nuts,' he muttered, making to walk past him. 'On cocaine or something.'

'You said *I* was the only one.' Simon thumped himself dramatically in the chest. 'You said you loved *me*, you absolute...'

'Piss off, faggot,' Jeremy snarled.

Simon leaned in as Jeremy shoved past him. 'You know what they say about bullies and queer-bashers?' he stage-whispered, his tone now quite serious. 'In denial, sweetie — which probably explains your problems in bed.'

Oh, no. Donna froze.

Jeremy didn't say a word. Nothing at all. Just punched poor Simon square in the jaw.

Chapter Twelve

Mark hated pub brawls, especially on Saturdays. The worst element of the football crowds, more often than not, out of their heads, hurling glasses along with obscenities. He had a feeling he was going to hate this one a hell of a lot more. *Chrrrist*! He spotted the VW as he pulled up in the car park, left his door wide and ran through the foyer.

Scanning the lounge, he immediately registered that Donna wasn't in the vicinity and that one extremely agitated 'male Caucasian' was being restrained by bar staff, while another guy was being hauled away from him by onlookers.

'Right, back off.' Mark planted himself squarely between the two. 'You, sit down,' he instructed the less animated of the two.

'Come on, Nathan. Sit down, like the officer says, hey?' One of the crowd attempted to steer the man to a seat.

'I have to go to Simon.' The man pulled away.

'Sit,' Mark repeated. 'And you,' he addressed the other 'gentleman' who was spitting fury, along with liberal profanity. Mark had seen his sort before. In fact, he was pretty sure he'd had a run in with this one before, 'calm down, unless you want to get nicked.'

'Me?' The guy looked incredulous. 'It's that fucking effeminate little queer, you ought to be *nicking*,' he spluttered, nodding towards the other guy, who'd finally allowed himself to be seated.

'Sit down, please, sir,' Mark suggested politely, pointing the guy towards another chair. 'And watch the language, or you'll be up on a charge of public affray before you can blink.'

'Typical,' the guy snarled, but complied, at least, and headed for the seat. 'The snivelling little coward who starts it scuttles off to the toilets with the girlies, while decent people...'

Mark stopped listening. That's where Donna was. He glanced urgently at Phil, who got the gist and took over.

Five seconds later, Mark banged open the door to the Gents, that being closest, then seeing it was empty, he headed straight into the Ladies. Then stopped.

'Donna? *Jesus*, what the? What happened, Donna?' Mark caught her by the forearms and turned her away from the sink, where she was rinsing what looked to be a gallon of blood from a tea-towel.' His gut churning, he scanned her face, her shoulders, her arms; turned her hands over.

She was covered in the stuff. But where the *hell* was it coming from?

'For Christ's sake, Donna... Are you hurt?'

She didn't answer. She just blinked, bewildered. In shock, Mark guessed, but dammit was she *hurt* was what he needed to know? And where was the frigging ambulance?!

'Donna, talk to me.' He guided her away from the sink, the sopping wet towel dripping watery blood down her white top and jeans as she went. Mark swallowed back his panic. 'Look at me, Donna. Tell me where you're hurt,' he asked gently. 'Can you do that?'

Donna met his gaze at last, her eyes seeming to finally focus. 'I'm not,' she said shakily. 'It's not me.'

Thank *Christ*.

'Simon...' She pulled away from him, turning to a cubicle. 'Alicia...'

Alicia? Mark followed her, relief flooding through him when Alicia looked up from where she sat on the cubicle floor. Concern fast on its heels when he saw the state of the guy she had her arm wrapped around.

Jesus, that was going to need stitches. He crouched down to survey the large gash to the side of the guy's head. Yep, and some.

Mark reached for his radio. 'What happened?' he addressed Alicia, the guy obviously being well out of it.

'Jeremy happened.' Alicia shot angrily. 'He was threatening Donna.'

Jeremy? The husband? Mark shook his head and got to his feet. The idiot outside, of course. He *knew* he'd seen him before. 'Bastard,' he grated.

'Correct,' said Alicia. 'Hold on, Simon.' She turned to the injured man. 'The ambulance will be here soon.'

Mark eyed Donna, worried for her, confused, but most of all so furious he was having trouble restraining himself. He ought to go out there and wipe the floor with the pathetic little creep.

'It was nothing physical,' Donna assured him, hoisting up her shoulders. 'Just nasty threats he's not big enough to back up.'

'Right.' Mark nodded tightly. 'Well you just point him in my direction if he makes any more threats. I'll show the bastard nasty.'

****

Donna watched Jeremy, wondering what she ever saw in him, as poor Simon was being wheeled to the ambulance, Nathan finally allowed to go with him, while Jeremy... He seemed to be gloating. Even with a burly policeman standing over him — she offered Mark's partner a smile of gratitude, Jeremy was still sitting there as if he was a cut above.

God, he was a piece of work.

'Boyfriend off to lick his wounds, is he?' Jeremy taunted as Donna collected her bag,

Mark was at her side in a flash, stepping between her and the spineless man she should have gotten shot of years ago. 'Everything okay?' he asked, glancing from her to Jeremy.

Donna nodded. No matter what had happened between them, Mark did care about her. She knew that to be true. There was no mistaking what she saw in his eyes.

'I'd have thought you could do better than that snivelling idiot you were with, you know, Donna.' Jeremy couldn't resist, as she turned away.

All said for Mark's benefit, Donna had no doubt. He really was pathetic, wasn't he? He didn't want her, but didn't want anyone else to want her either, was that it?

'That's enough.' Mark shot him a warning glance.

'Really are scraping the barrel, aren't you, Donna, running around with anything in —'

'That's *enough!*' Mark moved fast, grabbing Jeremy by the collar and hauling him to his feet. 'Shut up, sunshine' he warned him angrily, '*if* you know what's good for you.'

'Mark, leave it. He's not worth it,' his partner cautioned him.

Her heart wedged in her mouth, Donna's eyes flicked between them. Stop, she willed Mark, knowing there was a line he might step over and be in terrible trouble. Knowing also, as she saw the unmistakable glint of victory in Jeremy's eyes, that that might be exactly what he'd been trying to engineer.

Mark narrowed his eyes, searched Jeremy's for a heart-stopping moment, then, apparently having got his measure, decided his partner was right. 'Do him, Phil,' he said, giving Jeremy's collar a demonstrative twist before dropping him.

'Was that supposed to impress me or *her?*' Jeremy snarled, shooting Donna a contemptuous glare as he fell clumsily back to the chair. 'Well, I hope she's worth being brought up on a charge of harassment, *sunshine*, although I seriously doubt it.'

Mark glanced at Donna, back to Jeremy, then turned away, the look on his face one of utter disgust. 'Come on,' he said, taking Donna gently by the arm and leading her towards the door. 'Phil will make sure he gets what's coming.'

'Jeremy Matthews,' Donna heard Mark's partner behind them, 'I'm obliged to ask you to accompany me to the station.'

'Yerwhat?' Jeremy gasped, his regal tones flying straight out of the window. 'On what charge?'

'Ooh, now, let me see. Causing a public affray. Assault with intent. Damage to public property…'

****

Alicia skidded towards the foyer as Mark and Donna came out. 'Nathan's gone with Simon in the ambulance,' she said breathlessly. 'We're following on... assuming she's all finished here?' She looked at Mark questioningly.

'All finished.' Mark smiled, looking much more his gentle self. Donna was glad. She liked him that way. 'You can go into the station and give a statement later, Donna.' He looked at her, concern clouding his China blue eyes. 'You will do it, though, won't you?'

'Bet your arse, I will.' Donna notched up her chin.

'Good girl.' He nodded, obviously relieved.

Girl? Donna's mouth twitched into a smile. Funny though, she felt like a girl in his company. Not a pathetic, dependent-on-a-man sort of girl. A pretty, floaty, strong, feminine in-the-best-possible-way sort of girl.

He made her feel okay to be her, amazingly. 'Thank you,' she said, so wishing things could have turned out differently between them.

'Any time,' he assured her. 'I'm here to serve. If you need me, call. Okay?'

Donna nodded. He was just doing his job. Not riding his red and white charger to her rescue specifically, but still, she was grateful. He'd handled Jeremy magnificently. The bully got what he deserved, a taste of his own.

'I will. Bye, Mark. And thanks, again.' Donna smiled, and waved, which she felt would be slightly less formal than shaking hands.

'Bye,' he said, hesitated, then brushed her cheek with such a tingling soft kiss, Donna was quite sure she could charge her dodgy car battery on her own. Oh, *sh... ugar*! The AA man! What must he be thinking?

'Mark,' she said as he turned to go back inside, 'about earlier...'

Mark turned back, looking confused.

'The AA man,' Donna elucidated.

'Ah.' Mark's expression darkened.

'He isn't... We aren't, um...'

'He was chatting her up,' Alicia interjected. 'Men do, you know.' She gave Mark an arch look and hooked her arm through Donna's. 'Come on, honey. Poor Simon will have been and gone if we don't get a move on.'

Donna glanced at Alicia miffed as they headed for the VW. 'I wish you hadn't said that.'

'What?' Alicia looked at her, the picture of innocence. 'A little jealousy never hurt.'

'No, just like a little flattery never hurt.' Donna gave her an unimpressed glance. 'In any case, Mark's involved with someone, remember? So there's not a lot of point trying to make him jealous, is there?'

'Yes,' Alicia went around to the driver's side, 'which means you're absolutely not interested in him.'

'Exactly.' Donna plodded around to the passenger side.

'Right.' Alicia smirked over the roof. 'You can take your hand off your cheek now, Donna. His kiss won't get washed off. It's not raining.'

'Ha, ha.' Donna smiled flatly, opened her door, then groaned as Leticia appeared, scurrying across from where she'd been blending in with the trees.

'Donna, can I have a word?' she asked.

Wonderful. Donna sighed. The last person in the whole world she wanted to speak to right then was Leticia.

'Well, it will have to be a quick one, Leticia,' she said. 'We're on our way to the hos… Oh.' She trailed off, noticing Leticia's face, which looked a bit blotchy.

'There's something I wanted to tell you,' Leticia said worriedly.

Oh, Lord. If she was pregnant, Donna absolutely did not want to know.

'And I know it won't make things any better, considering what's happened.'

Bet your Botox it won't.

'It's just… I like you,' Leticia said quickly.

'Pardon?'

'I like you, Donna. I think Jeremy's behaved awfully towards you and I just wanted to let you know that… I suspect he might have lied.'

Suspect? Well, good stock obviously didn't breed brains, Donna thought cattily. Then felt guilty. Again.

'He said you'd been separated for some time, you see,' Leticia continued, wringing her hands together as she did, 'before he and I…'

'Gosh, there's a surprise.' Alicia rolled her eyes.

Leticia glanced at her self-consciously, then visibly steeled herself to go on. 'He said he was staying in the matrimonial home on the advice of his solicitor, because you were trying to cheat him out of his half of the equity.'

Donna's mouth clanged open.

'Go on,' Alicia said interestedly, while Donna gawped, speechless.

'And then when he did leave,' Leticia obliged, 'without a penny...'

Donna almost choked. '*What!?* He damn well did not! My mother helped me buy him out, so his *son* could stay in his home. He had more than his flipping fair share of the equity. It's a wonder he stopped short of sawing the furniture in half.'

God, this was unbelievable. Donna eyed the skies.

'Um, how's his accountancy business doing lately, Leticia?' Alicia ventured.

'Well, not too well, actually,' Leticia admitted. 'He's working terribly hard, but with companies folding, his business property mortgage, and his son to support...'

'Bullshit.' Alicia said, before Donna went apoplectic.

'Sorry?' Leticia managed to furrow a whole brow line.

'He might have a business mortgage, Leticia,' Alicia glanced at Donna for confirmation, 'but he pays Donna a pittance for the support of Matt.'

'But he said —'

'Codswallop,' Alicia reiterated, 'concocted to keep you on board, no doubt. If you ask me, it's his lifestyle he's looking to support. He's after your money, honey, as sure as God made little green apples.

Is he? Donna furrowed so many lines, her brow must have looked like a five-bar gate.

'Where's his car, if you don't mind me asking?' Alicia forged on.

'In the garage, so he —' Donna started.

'He's sold it,' Leticia said over her.

Glances were exchanged three-fold.

Leticia swallowed daintily. 'We were going to get him a new one for his birthday, you see and...'

'*We* as in him, I wonder? Or *we*, as in you?' Alicia fished.

Leticia sniffled. 'Me. I was going to buy it,' she said, miserably. 'A little Lotus run-around, you know, for getting to and from the off...'

'Oh, absolutely. They're just *sooo* handy,' Alicia cut in, with a girly flap of her hand. 'Donna runs around in hers all the time, don't you, hon?'

Donna wasn't listening. She was busy putting two and two together and coming to the conclusion Alicia might be right. Jeremy hadn't been working 24/7. He was never there. As far as Donna could see, he'd spent more time putting horses through paces than going to work, ergo more time in Leticia's company and, more importantly to image-conscious Jeremy, the company she kept.

'Who's, um, paying for the wedding, Leticia?' Donna asked casually, though she almost choked again on the 'w' word.

'Well, Daddy, actually,' Leticia answered, managing a whole baffled expression. 'Jeremy wanted to pay, at least some towards it, but Daddy insisted.'

'How convenient,' Alicia muttered.

'Leticia, just out of interest,' Donna did her best to look only mildly interested, 'where were you going to be living?'

'On the family estate,' Leticia looked at Donna as if it were a foregone conclusion. 'Daddy said he'd have the gatehouse refurbished.'

'In Jeremy's honour,' Alicia growled.

Good God, Alicia *was* right. Donna stared at her astonished. The slimy little weasel. Always fancied himself a man of leisure rubbing shoulders with the landed gentry. And how better to do that than to marry into money and move into the *gatehouse*, where he could no doubt entertain his future dalliances, behind Leticia's back, in more 'salubrious' surroundings.

No wonder he always looked so dapper. He'd probably sold his accountancy business to refurbish his wardrobe. One couldn't move in the right circles wearing *orf* the peg, after all, could one?

Donna dragged her eyes slowly from Alicia, who didn't look at all surprised, to Leticia, who glanced down, her complexion quite pale.

Oh, dear. Donna's sympathy gene kicked in, as Leticia studied the tarmac on the pub car-park for what seemed an awful long time. She was going to cry. Donna braced herself and stepped towards her. She couldn't just do nothing. Even if the woman was the biggest bitch under the sun, which Donna was beginning to doubt, she couldn't let her stand there and cry on her own.

Oh.

Donna glanced at Alicia confounded, as Leticia tugged up *her* shoulders. 'I'm going to ask him to leave,' she said determinedly.

Well, well, kudos to Leticia. Peculiar though it might be, Donna couldn't help but have a growing admiration for the woman.

Chapter Thirteen

By the time Donna had walked around the park with Agnes, the little old lady she'd befriended after the lost ball in the pond incident, things were still as clear as mud, but she did feel more in control.

Mark had been off duty when she'd gone to the station, which was disappointing — Donna would have been bolstered by one of his reassuring smiles, but he'd asked his partner to be there for her, to take her statement and offer her information on taking out a non-molestation order. Donna had to think about that, for Matt's sake. But then, Jeremy had threatened violence. His behaviour, past and present, was certainly intimidating. And the fact was, Matt, Donna believed, was also getting the measure of the man.

She'd left Simon at the hospital looking pale, but determined the show would go on vis-à-vis his fancy-dress party, particularly as it was now a double celebration of his betrothal to Nathan, as well as his birthday.

Donna had a little worry about that. Simon, quite taken, it seemed, by the twinkly-eyed boy-in-blue who'd helped him at the pub, now fancied going dressed as a policeman.

Oh, dear, Donna really was going to have to learn to engage her brain before opening her mouth. Maybe Mark wouldn't mind Simon borrowing his spare jacket though, if she asked him. Donna pondered as she slowed her pace to keep in step with Agnes.

As for Leticia, Donna had felt obliged to offer her a shoulder, though she wasn't entirely sure she wanted Leticia to take up the offer.

'Well, I'm not sure I could love my husband's lover,' Agnes commented, as she fished in her eco-friendly bag for a dog-treat.

'I'm not proposing to go so far as to love her, just lend her an ear,' Donna assured her, then winced as Agnes's totter turned to a near sprint to facilitate her scooping up yet another ball straying in her direction.

'Whoa, that's our Max's ball,' a puzzled dog-owner shouted, running over to her.

'It's for a good cause,' Agnes informed him, plopping the ball into her bag and nodding at Sadie, who was bounding tri-leggedly across the grass in pursuit of the last ball Agnes had purloined.

The owner propped his hands on his hips. 'I don't care what cause it's for,' he said, distinctly peeved. 'Give it back.'

'Shan't,' said Agnes, clutching her bag close to her chest. 'It's not your ball.'

'You what?' The man looked at her askance.

'It's your *Max's*.' Agnes pointed at his dog. 'Have you asked *him* whether he wants me to have it?'

The man frowned, opened his mouth, then closed it again.

'Max said he doesn't mind sharing his balls,' Agnes informed him, with a pious nod. 'You shouldn't presume to make decisions for others, young man.'

'And you shouldn't be out in public, my luv.' The man shook his head as Agnes turned to trot back towards Donna. 'Raving mad,' he muttered, looking bemusedly back to his poor ball-less dog.

At which, Agnes turned back, her peachy cheeks puffed up with indignation. 'It's people like you who are responsible for the downturn in the economic climate!' she said, wagging a finger. 'Greedy! The lot of you! You should learn a lesson from your dog.' She eyeballed him meaningfully, then tottered huffily on.

'What a selfish man,' Agnes said, coming back to Donna. 'The world could certainly do with *less* people like him.'

'Yes, Agnes, but it is his… dog's ball.'

'But the dog didn't mind, dear,' Agnes said, as she tottered on. 'Now, the little autistic boy, that was different. It was the little boy who needed the ball, his dog said. Do you see?'

'Ye-es.' Donna had a little think, then scooted after her, clueless.

****

Mark slowed his run to a walk, and then stopped in his tracks, his heart pumping pure adrenaline. Hardly daring to breathe, he watched Karl run on, the ball in his hand and Starbuck bounding along by his side.

'Stop and sit, Starbuck,' Karl commanded.

Quietly, Mark watched on, mesmerised, as the dog obediently plonked its hindquarters down.

Karl studied the dog for a second, his hair plastered to his head, his chest heaving, that familiar furrow in his brow that had Mark constantly wondering what he was thinking. What went on in a six-year-old mind where abstract ideas made no sense? Where interaction was impossible, Karl lacking the basic tools to interpret thought and feeling?

Mark swallowed, and waited.

Karl threw it.

Mark still couldn't believe it. Just as he'd done three times before, Karl threw the ball.

'Fetch Starbuck,' Karl said, immediately setting off at a run with the dog, giggling quietly to himself as he went.

Laughing?! His boy was laughing. '*Yesss!*' Mark whooped, punching the air. *Jesus!* His son was playing with the dog. He'd thrown that ball *knowing* what Starbuck's reaction would be. What's more, he was doing it spontaneously. It was an absolute bloody miracle.

Okay – Mark tried to ground himself a little, Karl might have copied him initially, and, okay, it was repetitive behaviour to a degree. But the kid was as close to playing normally as Mark could ever hope him to be, and *that* justified an amount of loopy leaping about in Mark's book.

He turned to Jody as she walked towards him, Karl's coat in one hand, bag containing essential dog and boy treats in the other. 'Did you see that? Did you see him?' he asked, breaking into a run to catch a hold of Jody's shoulders and twirl her around.

Jody laughed as Mark hugged her, planting a kiss on her cheek, and acting like a great big kid himself. 'Yes, Mark, I saw him,' she assured him, when he eventually allowed her space to breath. 'I didn't dare look away in case you didn't believe it without witness corroboration. Could I have my arms back now, please?'

'Oh, right, sorry.' Mark unhanded the poor girl and relieved her of some of her baggage. 'It's just so bloody unbelievable. Never, in my wildest dreams, did I ever imagine the dog would have such a beneficial effect.'

And he'd had a few wild dreams, waking up in a cold sweat, worrying even in his sleep about Karl.

Mark laughed again, bemused, then shook his head in wonder at the implausibility of himself laughing — *with* Karl, rather than *at* some of the comical situations he inadvertently created.

Mark recalled the bewildered expression of the woman from the Salvation Army, who'd knocked last week, collecting for charity, to be greeted by a six-year-old kid cursing, 'Bloody door. Shit, now I burnt the toast.'

The lady was *not* amused. Mark couldn't help but be, though he had reminded himself to watch his language in front of Karl, who repeated things verbatim, and who had hearing like radar.

'You should laugh more often,' Jody said, as they walked after Karl. 'Takes years off you.'

'As in I look like a complete miserable git when I don't?'

'No.' Jody thought about it. 'Moody and broody, but still handsome.'

'Flattery will get you everywhere.' Mark smiled his appreciation.

'And miserable,' Jody added.

'You do know Starbuck's a finely honed hunter-killer, don't you?' Mark said after a second, nodding at the great, black, lolloping Labrador, who was obviously as soft as a brush. 'Trained to go for the jugular, should he sense his master has been upset or abused in any way?'

Jody laughed, watching Karl fight Starbuck for the ball. 'Better not upset Karl then, hey?'

****

'Ring him, dear. I've buried two, you know? I know what these men can be like.' Agnes gave Donna the wisdom of her advice based on experience.

Donna looked at her askew, not sure whether she meant she'd buried them *because* she knew what they were like.

'You have one of those walkie-talkie things, don't you?' Agnes asked, mopping a drip of ice cream up her cone with her tongue.

'Mobiles. Yes.' Donna smiled, chasing a drip up her own cone.

'Well, ring him, then. No point waiting for him to make the first move, or you'll end up like me, old and wrinkly.'

'And lovely,' Donna added. 'Sadie certainly thinks you are.' She nodded over her ice cream at Sadie hopping ahead of them, the proud owner of a smart new prickly red ball.

'Thank you, Sadie,' Agnes said earnestly. 'She thinks you're quite the loveliest human in the world, too; unlike some people.'

Agnes stopped and turned with a scowl to a woman who was being overly firm with her dog. 'He's not deaf, you know,' Agnes boomed. 'He is, however, too concerned with the tone of your voice to concentrate on your command.'

The woman stared at Agnes, astounded, taking in her slippers and melting ice-cream. 'I beg your pardon?' she said haughtily.

'As the dog begs yours, my dear. Speak more softly,' Agnes instructed, 'the emphasis on the first letter of the word: *Sssssssit*,' she demonstrated thus, talking to the dog, who obliged in an instant.

'You see? Not rocket science, is it?' Agnes smiled, satisfied. 'Oh, and slacken his collar off, my dear. He said he may be forced to sink his teeth into your rather plentiful rump otherwise.'

So saying, Agnes turned to trot on, leaving the woman staring open-mouthed after her.

Donna scooted to catch up. 'Agnes that was awful,' she said, laughing nevertheless.

'Wasn't it just? Honestly, some people just shouldn't be allowed.'

Allowed to what? Donna wondered as Agnes broke off the bottom of her ice-cream cone, offered it to Sadie, then proceeded to suck her ice cream through the hole.

'Do you really talk to them, Agnes?' Donna asked, as they walked on.

'Well, they do communicate, don't you think?' Agnes answered evasively. 'Can't fail to see the love in her eyes, can you?' She glanced down at Sadie, who was now hopping between them looking up adoringly.

'No,' Donna conceded, though she fancied Sadie might be more in love with her ice cream.

'Come on then, ring your young man.' Agnes said, as they neared the car park. 'No time like the present.'

'Well, I'm not sure.' Donna hesitated. What was the point? Yes, Mark had left the door open for her to ring, but that was only if she needed him to serve her as a policeman... in his uniform. A blob of ice-cream slid mournfully down her throat.

'*Pffffft*, poppycock! You're obviously quite taken by him — or you'd like to be.' Agnes guffawed, giving Donna a nudge. 'You wouldn't be agonising over him otherwise. Ring him. Go on.' Agnes stopped walking, and waited expectantly.

Donna debated, then, 'All right. I will.' She nodded determinedly and ferreted in her pocket for her mobile. They'd parted with a kiss, after all. A friend's kiss, rather than a lover's kiss, but affectionate nevertheless. No reason she couldn't give him a call.

Donna selected his number.

Have a quick chat.

She waited while the call connected.

Update him on things.

Donna smiled as it rang out, then cocked her head to one side. Then blinked at Agnes, baffled.

Uh-oh. Donna's eyes slid sideways, to peer through the sparse foliage dividing car park from park.

'OhmiGod!' The smiled skidded from her face. 'It's him!'

'Where?' Agnes scrunched her head into her neck.

'There,' Donna whispered hoarsely. She nodded towards where Mark — unmistakably Mark — closed the tailgate of his car, then turned his twinkly-eyed smile on...

Wait a minute!

'That's not silken-haired Sally!' Donna tilted her head to get a better look.

Agnes did likewise.

So, who? Ooh. Donna quickly ended the call as Mark said, 'Hi, Mark Evans?' in her ear, his eyes still on the girl he was with.

'They rang off.' He shrugged and pocketed his mobile. 'Thanks, Jody,' he beamed her another smile.

'It's her, Jody-kiss-kiss.' Donna's ice cream plopped miserably from her cone to land with a splat on her Wellington boots.

Agnes glanced at her puzzled. 'Who?'

'His girlfriend. The one with the flexible toothbrush.' Donna ran her hand under her nose and reached for Sadie's collar, before the dog hopped over and announced she was lurking in the bushes, spying on her boyfriend, who never was.

Agnes narrowed her eyes. 'Is he cheating on you, dear?'

'No.' Donna shrugged, embarrassed. 'Not technically. Though he would have been, I suppose, if I, um... If we.'

'With her!?' Agnes looked back to Jody-kiss-kiss. 'But she's *much* younger than he is.'

Yes, thank you, Agnes, Donna's shoulders sagged. 'With two hers, actually,' she confided, not sure why she was. Probably because she knew Agnes wouldn't judge her.

Agnes stared at her, astonished. 'Because you wouldn't part with your virtue?'

Virtue? A smile tickled Donna's mouth, despite her tortured heart. 'No, it wasn't like that, Agnes. He didn't push for...'

'Shush.' Agnes flapped a hand, and turned her eyes back to the car park.

Donna followed her gaze, just in time to hear Mark gasp, 'Pregnant!?' rake his hand through his hair, and stare at Jody-kiss-kiss, quite obviously stunned.

Oh, dear God! Donna's stomach dropped through the floor. She groped in her pockets for tissue, gave up, wiped her nose on her sleeve, and watched on.

Jody shrugging slim shoulders. Confused, Donna wondered, by Mark's reaction?

Donna couldn't see much else of her, her back to them as it was, other than her auburn curls, which were healthy and bouncy — and nothing like Donna's hair could ever be.

'I'm sorry,' Mark said immediately, apparently realising he hadn't been as ecstatic as he should be. 'It's great, Jody. Really great. We'll manage somehow, don't worry,' he assured her, pulling her into his arms — whilst Donna had a mental flash of headlines: *Demented-haired Woman Attacks Policeman in St Peter's Park Car Park.*

Oh, Lord! Agnes?!

Donna gawped as a most definitely demented Agnes broke into her ball-pinching sprint and was up the path in a flash.

'You'll have a spot of trouble managing without a certain part of your anatomy, you... sex-fiend!' she growled, twirling her eco-bag like a pro in the hammer throw and hitting Mark, squarely in the abdomen.

Thank God. Donna closed her eyes, relieved. If the bag had hit home, she'd a sneaking suspicion it would have hurt an awful lot more. As it was, Mark was winded, as white as a sheet, and heading protectively for Jody, to hustle her into the passenger seat of his car.

Well, he would. Quite apart from the fact that Mark seemed to protect people instinctively, the girl was with child.

His child.

Donna's heart sank without trace.

****

'Cheers, Roger,' Mark addressed the manager of The Helliots Nursing Home, on his mobile. 'About ten minutes ago,' he confirmed his run in with the bag-wielding old woman. 'She'll probably head back through the park, but just in case. Okay. Catch you around.'

'Are you going to be all right?' Jody asked.

'Yeah, eventually.' Mark smiled, amused, despite bruises to body and pride.

'Will she, do you think?'

'Who, Agnes? Yes, fine. She wanders around the park most days. Sometimes wanders a bit too far and we give her lift back. She's harmless enough, generally. Can't think why she'd want to attack me.'

'Probably didn't recognise you with your *clothes* on.' Jody smirked.

'Ho, ho.' Mark smiled and climbed out of the driver's side.

'Such a gent,' Jody said as he walked around to hold the passenger door for her. 'You'd never think he was a sex-fiend, would you, Starbuck?' She turned to give Starbuck a pat, then patted Mark's cheek as she climbed out.

Mark smiled good-naturedly. 'Only at weekends, though Jody.'

'What, every weekend?' Jody widened her eyes. 'No wonder you're exhausted.'

Chance would be a fine thing. Mark sighed, as Jody peered back inside. 'Bye, Karl. See you tomorrow.'

'Say goodbye to Jody, Karl,' Mark prompted him, when Karl didn't answer.

'Goodbye to Jody.' Karl obliged.

Mark and Jody exchanged amused glances as they walked back to the pavement, then amazed glances as Karl said behind them, 'You'll have a hard time managing without a certain part of your anatomy.'

Mark squeezed his eyes shut, then prised one open as Jody burst out laughing.

Mark shook his head, then laughed with her. Why the hell not? His pride might be dented, but with the progress Karl had made today, his heart was soaring.

'Let me know whether you need me to pick him up tomorrow,' Jody called, as she headed for her house.

'I will,' Mark assured her, watching her walk off. She looked good, healthy, happy. Pregnancy obviously suited her, though Mark couldn't help wishing she wasn't. He hated the thought of Karl stressed out all over again by the changes in routine a new carer might bring.

That thought in mind, he climbed back in the car, hoping that tomorrow's change in routine would end as positively as today's. Karl was used to the respite home, but Starbuck with him at the home was something new.

Mark had a good feeling about it though. It really did seem that Karl might interact more readily with Starbuck leading the way. He already had, to a degree. Only with the dog, but... Bloody hell! Mark tightened his grip on the wheel as something struck him.

Karl had reacted with him.

Okay, they hadn't had an actual conversation, but Karl had listened to him. Appeared to take in what he'd said.

Hadn't he?

Mark pointed the car towards his dad's to check up on him, and test out his theory while he was there. He was sure he was right. And if he was... Mark felt almost euphoric. Life might have been rubbish on the relationship front... his euphoria dwindled a bit... but today had been a good day.

'We're off to see Granddad now, Karl.' Mark made sure to prepare Karl ahead, as always. 'And then, how about we all have an early night, with Starbuck?'

They might, too, thanks to a certain furry friend.

'All right, Starbuck?' Mark winked through the mirror at the dog panting placidly on the back seat.

'Yes,' said Karl.

Mark's mouth curved into a smile. Bloody good.

****

'Dad?' Mark called over the booming music, once inside the front door. What the hell was going on? He glanced at Karl behind him, hoping the noise wasn't going to destabilise him.

'What do you think, Starbuck? Shall we go through?' he asked warily.

'Yes,' said Karl.

'Right.' Mark glanced at Karl again. Was he answering for the dog? *Jesus.* He shook his head, incredulous, then winced as his dad's affronted tones reached his ears. 'You're on my foot, woman!' Robert bellowed above the din in the lounge. 'Are you trying to cripple me?!'

What in God's name? 'Sit and stay, Starbuck,' Mark commanded. Then, making sure dog and boy stayed put, he inched the lounge door open, stared in amazement, and closed it again.

Christ. He was hallucinating. Had to be. Either that, or... Mark opened the door again and coughed loudly, to no avail. His dad, Evelyn and Dot were lined up in front of the TV, oblivious to his presence and apparently practising the foot moves to Dot's *Strictly Dancing* DVD.

'It's supposed to be the quickstep, Robert, not the jive,' Dot shouted, kicking a legging-clad leg in the air.

'Nonsense.' Robert puffed. 'They didn't call me Elvis for nothing, you know. Rocked around the clock with the best of them, I did, in my…' Robert stopped, obviously having missed a step.

'Pause and rewind,' he called.

Evelyn and Dot danced on.

'Hit the pause button, woman!' Robert bawled. 'I'm off my stride.'

Evelyn stopped and headed to the sofa, looking slightly more stylish than Dot in trackie bottoms and tee, but eye-boggling nevertheless. 'I wish we could hit your pause button,' she muttered, then noticing Mark said moodily, 'Oh, it's you.'

'Nice to see you, too, Evelyn.' Mark looked on, bemused, as the salsa music died.

'Sorry.' Evelyn looked apologetic. 'Your father's being a bit of a handful, I'm afraid. Do come in.'

Mark glanced behind him, wondering whether it might be wiser to make a sharp exit. 'Very kind of you,' he said instead, and turned back to Starbuck and Karl.

'Come, Starbuck,' he commanded. The dog obeyed, bringing Karl along with him. 'Sit and stay. Good boy.'

'My son, Karl,' Mark introduced him. 'I think you've met.'

'Not met, no. I've seen you come and go with him, obviously. I, um… Hello, Karl.' It was Evelyn's turn to stare now. Karl was bordering on hyperkinetic, rocking to and fro, visibly communicating his stress, until Starbuck intervened, thank God.

Mark drew in a relieved breath as Evelyn glanced from Karl to the dog, then to Mark, from which Mark gathered she hadn't realised Karl was autistic.

'But he's…' Evelyn trailed off.

'Easily spooked,' Mark finished. 'Say, hello, Karl.'

'Hello,' Karl said, staring at Evelyn as he did, which Mark knew some people found unnerving.

'I had no idea,' Evelyn looked again from Karl to Mark. 'Dot said he was a special needs child, but…' She trailed off again, then seemed to pull herself together, shoulders up. Like daughter like mother, Mark couldn't help noticing.

'Nice to meet you, Karl,' she said, taking a step towards him, then reaching tentatively out to stroke Starbuck. 'Is this your dog?'

'This is Starbuck. He's Karl's friend,' Karl said, repeating how Sally had introduced Starbuck to Karl, Mark knew, but getting a thrill from it still. It was dialogue, of sorts. It was progress.

'Is he now?' Evelyn smiled. 'He's a very fine friend.'

'He has fur,' Karl said, and reached to stroke Evelyn's hair, to Mark's utter astonishment.

'Bloody hell!' He gasped, disbelieving. Where had that come from? Sally? Jody?

Evelyn glanced curiously at him.

'Sorry.' Mark shook himself out of his stupor. 'He doesn't normally, er... communicate, quite so, er...'

'I'll put kettle on,' his dad said gruffly, placing a steadying hand on Mark's shoulder.

Mark smiled, grateful for the timely interruption. He crouched down, stroked Starbuck, hesitated, then ruffled Karl's hair. Karl didn't react, but that was okay. Mark felt blessed enough for one day.

'Come on, Karl,' he said, straightening up. 'Let's get Starbuck a drink and then take him into the garden... to play.' He glanced meaningfully at Evelyn.

Evelyn nodded, offered him a conciliatory smile, then shook her head as Dot piped up. 'I'll come and lend a hand, Robert.'

'No. No need. I'm sure I can find the teapot on my own,' his dad's slightly panicky reply came back.

'He'll be back in his bunker if she bustles in.' Evelyn rolled her eyes.

Mark laughed, and bent to unhook the tether from Karl. 'Join us, if you like,' he offered.

'No, I won't, thank you. I'd quite like some fresh air, but I need to soak my feet more. Don't we, Dot?'

'Do we?' Dot wandered over.

'Yes, they're killing us,' Evelyn assured her. 'And I think Mark and Karl might need a little less distraction.' She arched a questioning eyebrow at Mark.

'Yes, thanks.' Mark nodded his appreciation. She wasn't so bad, he decided, despite her propensity to hit first and ask questions later.

Chapter Fourteen

Donna cursed her stupidity. She shouldn't have been so impetuous, so full of herself she thought she could do what the professionals couldn't. She wasn't qualified.

She wasn't anything.

Just a volunteer, who'd been here two minutes and taken into her naïve head that she was special enough to make a difference. She forced back hot tears of frustration and looked uselessly on, as the little boy kicked and screamed, a key worker on her knees behind him, desperately trying to hold onto him.

What *had* she been thinking? Trying to get the little boy to wear his shoes, as if it were as easy as helping him on with them?

'Make way for the cavalry,' Peter Lewis said behind her. 'Whoops, sorry, Donna, excuse us,' he said, smiling as he walked past with the boy's dog, who Dr Lewis had taken out for walkies, which was when the little boy had decided to follow, and Donna had foolishly decided he shouldn't with only his socks on.

'Come on, Starbuck,' Dr Lewis said jovially. 'Show us what you're made of, old stick.'

Dr Lewis let the dog off its leash, and Donna watched worriedly, then incredulously, as the dog walked across to the little boy, sat down beside him and placed a paw lightly on the boy's legs.

In a flash, the little boy stopped thrashing, the key worker relaxed her grip, the boy sat up, stood up, and walked across to his dog. 'Good Starbuck,' he said, calmly patting the dog's head.

'That's right,' Dr Lewis said, producing a dog biscuit from his pocket and taking it to the dog.

He crouched down to the boy's level. 'And good Karl, too,' he said, producing a biscuit for human consumption from his other pocket, 'for listening to Starbuck.'

'Starbuck wants to play,' the boy said unblinkingly, taking the biscuit with one hand, the dog's collar with the other, and walking off to play with the alphabet blocks.

'Sit and stay, Starbuck,' he said, plonking himself down next to the dog, so obviously unperturbed by events, a tear escaped Donna's eye.

'Don't be so hard on yourself,' Dr Lewis said, coming over to her. 'We all get things wrong here, as often as we get them right, until we learn what the children's particular concerns or phobias are, and even then... take Thomas over there,' Dr Lewis pointed to another little boy, who was painting away at the desk, and extremely accomplished Donna thought. 'He loves his painting. Give him a paintbrush, he's as happy as Larry. Try to put an apron on him, and we're talking major meltdown. Doesn't like the feel of the cloth on the back of his neck.'

Dr Lewis indicated the back of his own neck, shrugged and gave Donna a good-humoured smile. 'Karl's shoes need more scuffing,' he confided, wrapping an arm around her shoulders and walking with her to the outside play area.

'The world can seem a very unpredictable and confusing place to children with autism, Donna,' Dr Lewis explained, as they watched children with varying degrees of autism playing, some together, some in isolation, a key worker gently trying to encourage social interaction.

'That's why routine is so important to them,' he went on. 'They prefer to have a fixed daily agenda so they know what's going to happen next. Change can be very uncomfortable, and anything unfamiliar represents change. Karl will be less troubled by his new shoes when they're muddied up a bit.'

Donna nodded, understanding. 'Made to look old, as in familiar, you mean.'

'Precisely. But even then, Karl might not be convinced. There's a lot to learn, Donna, but I can see you're keen.' Dr Lewis nodded appreciatively.

'Yes, I am,' Donna assured him, hoping... *knowing* that she could rise to the challenge and maybe, in time, really make a difference, however small.

'Excellent. I'll dig out some study material for you.' Dr Lewis led the way back inside.

'People with autism often find it difficult to engage in social imaginative play,' he chatted on, this time pointing to Karl, who was busy in his own little world with the alphabet blocks. 'Often they prefer to act out the same scene over and over, which brings us back to routine, repetitive behaviours, obsessions, special interests. Here at Blossom Tree, we try to challenge the autism, Donna. Use those obsessions and interests as tools, if you like, with which to help the child develop.

'Do any of the children ever go on to live independently?' Donna asked, somewhat in awe of the man's dedication and obvious enthusiasm.

'Good question,' Dr Lewis nodded thoughtfully. 'And the answer is yes. Depending on the degree of learning disability, some will be able to live fairly independently, although they may need a degree of support to achieve independence. Others require lifelong, specialist support. The overriding factor though, is that people with autism can, and do, learn and develop with the right kind of support. That's where we come in. We could certainly use someone with a bit of artistic skill.'

'I'm your gal,' Donna assured him, and set about proving it by helping the more able children finger-paint for the next hour.

Jean hadn't been that pleased she'd taken the afternoon's annual leave with Simon away, but Donna had already booked it, she'd pointed out, and left Jean to develop her typing skills.

When she wandered over, Karl had moved from the alphabet blocks to the wooden bricks, which he was stacking up in neat columns. 'Hello, Karl,' she said, kneeling down beside him.

Karl didn't answer, but Donna was learning. He wasn't recalling she was the scary woman who'd tried to force his familiar feet into his unfamiliar shoes. He just wasn't relating.

She reached to stroke the black Labrador, thinking about Mark as she did so, her heart flopping loose in her chest. How he'd been walking a similar assistance dog with silken-haired Sally. How ironic would that be? If silken-Sally turned out to be the trainer of this dog, too?

'I like your dog, Karl,' Donna ventured. 'Does he have a name?'

'This is Starbuck,' Karl said, his brow knitted as he concentrated his attention on his bricks. 'He's Karl's friend.'

'Dogs make good friends.' Donna smiled. 'I bet he thinks Karl's a good friend, too.'

'Yes,' Karl said, his gaze still unwavering on his endeavours.

'I have a dog-friend,' Donna confided. 'Her name is Sadie. She's my best friend.'

Karl turned his gaze away from his bricks and reached out to stroke Starbuck. 'Best friend,' he said.

'That's a breakthrough, Donna. Well done.' Dr Lewis smiled, sweeping by.

****

'Donna, are you in?' Evelyn's tones reached her ears before Donna was through her front door.

'Whoops, sorry, babe.' Donna plucked up the phone, almost falling over Sadie in the process.

'Yes, Mum, I'm in,' she said, shrugging out of her coat and making a kissy face at her 'best friend.'

'I've been talking to Mark,' Evelyn said, without further ado.

'Oh.'

'Oh, dear, do I sense a *not-open-for-discussion* note in that *oh?*'

'I don't want to talk about him, Mum. There's nothing to talk about. He's been fine in his professional capacity, but otherwise...'

Donna's heart drooped as her mind conjured up an image of Mark, every inch a girl's fantasy, folding Jody-kiss-kiss into his arms.

'But I think there is, Donna,' Evelyn hazarded. 'I saw him with his little...'

'No, Mum,' Donna cut her short, 'it's *not* open for discussion. Sorry.'

'But there are some things you need to know about him, Donna. I...'

'Mum, I don't want to know anything about him. I know enough already.'

'But that's just it, my lovely. You don't. Or at least, I don't think you do. I think I might have misjudged him. You need to speak to him, Donna. I...'

'I don't need to speak to him, Mum. You speak to him, if you want to, but...'

'Give him a chance, Donna,' Evelyn persisted. 'Just meet up with him and have a chat, why don't you? You've nothing to...'

'Ooh, Mum!' Donna barked. 'He's pregnant!'

'Jody... thingy,' Donna explained in the stunned silence that followed, 'and Mark, they're, um, having a happy event.'

'Oh,' Evelyn said, eventually.

****

Mark snatched up the telephone. 'Hello,' he answered shortly. 'Mark Ev... Karl, slow down!'

Mark sighed, despairing, as Karl backed around the coffee table for the umpteenth time, the tug-of-war with Starbuck in full swing. 'Karl. Starbuck, Stop and... Sit and stay, Starbu... *Jesus*! Hold on.'

Mark dropped the phone and almost leapt the coffee table. Dammit, he knew this would happen. He winced as Karl lurched backwards, his head hitting the TV table with a sickening crack.

'Okay, Karl. Okay.' Mark dropped to his knees, gathering Karl to him, who, stunned for a second, started in on a tantrum that would probably be the mother of all tantrums.

Mark locked his arm around Karl's upper torso, trying to assess the damage to the back of his head, which was nigh on impossible with Karl as rigid as a board, his had slamming backwards into Mark's chest.

'Hold still, Karl,' Mark dropped his own head to his son's. Please hold still, he prayed, seeing blood on his shirt and feeling the kind of panic only a parent can.

Karl bellowed. Of course he would. Mark knew he would, but when he did Mark's heart hammered like a train. It wasn't the raucous roar, the endless screaming that seemed to go on until Karl had got things out of his system.

He called for Starbuck.

Starbuck was there. Sitting right next to them, his tongue hanging out and a paw placed on Karl's leg.

'Starbuck.' Karl cried, but whether from fright or pain, Mark couldn't be sure. Sensory sensitivity meant Karl just didn't feel pain the same way other people did.

'Starbuck,' Karl repeated. 'Best friend.' He held out a hand, Starbuck nuzzled it, and that's when Mark knew — there had been a major breakthrough. He'd wondered whether Karl might be benefiting from the tactile stimulation offered by the dog. Now, he was sure.

His son was gaining comfort from the dog. Expressing emotion.

'Best friend.' Mark swallowed back his own overwhelming emotion and agreed wholeheartedly. 'Come on, Starbuck,' he said, easing Karl into his arms. 'Let's sit on the sofa where it's more comfy, shall we?'

'Yes,' said Karl in a small voice.

Mark hadn't thought it possible to love his son more.

But he did, right then.

****

'Ahem,' Matt gazed upstairs as Donna emerged from the bathroom, 'the steak's a bit… er, cremated. He blinked beguilingly and hugged his defenceless wrath-deflecting bunny closer to his chest.

'Salad's good, though,' he offered hopefully, 'apart from the cheese. It's sort of... eaten. Sadie prefers Wensleydale though, for future reference.'

Donna groaned. 'Oh, Matt, I said not to leave food near the edge of the table...'

She stopped mid-stairs, wincing as something sounding distinctly like the grill-pan hit the kitchen floor with a resounding clang. *Wonderful.* Donna folded her arms and eyed Matt despairingly.

'Medium rare,' Matt informed her Sadie's preference as to how she liked her steak served, 'but she knows better than to diss a cook who's spent hours sweating over a hot stove.'

He smiled wanly, then skidded back to the kitchen as Donna thumped on down, looking not as annoyed as she'd like to in fluffy pink slippers and mismatching pyjamas.

'Uh, oh, Mother alert,' Matt warned Sadie. 'Swallow the evidence, Sade.'

'Oh no,' Donna sighed, studying the pandemonium that used to be a kitchen.

'On the plus side, she is cleaning the floor,' Matt pointed out, by way of compensation, as Sadie made a meal of the mess there.

'Correction, Matt,' Donna gave him a look, 'you're cleaning the floor.'

'Huh, it's not fair, I have to do everything around here.' Matt sloped on in after her, wearing his best put-upon Kenny impression. 'Here you go, Sade,' he plopped Findus safely down under the table and plucked up a lump of steak to feed to the dog, 'but whatever you do, don't tell Mother.'

'Twit.' Donna laughed and readied herself to assist — as in showing Matt which end of the mop was which.

'What say we go out and grab a pizza, now you've made yourself beautiful?' Matt suggested.

'Um...' Donna indicated her un-beautiful state of attire.

Matt glanced at her, taking in the 'Grumpy but Gorgeous' top and cow print pyjama bottoms. 'We'll get one delivered,' he decided, turning to pluck up the all-surface cleaner, then gazing at it as if were some strange new invention.

'Squeeze the nozzle, Matt,' Donna enlightened him. 'I'll go find Jack Bauer.'

Donna hid a smile and went off in search of the latest 24 DVD, and the only man she'd allow herself to fantasise about ever again.

Apart from Mark.

But that was only because he'd snuck up on her while she was in that vulnerable place somewhere between sleeping and waking. Oh, dear, her heart downward-spiralled again. She really did wish she could stop thinking about him.

'Tomorrow then?' Matt called, clanging the grill-pan into the dishwasher. 'My treat. I got myself a Saturday job, sales assistant at *Bench* in Worcester.'

A Saturday job? Donna blinked, surprised, and turned her fluffy pink slippers back to the kitchen. 'But what about your essential beauty sleep?'

'Don't need it, do I?' Matt fluttered girly eyes and sloshed soapsuds onto the floor. 'And we need the dosh, so...'

Donna blinked again, hard. He'd gotten a job. Bless his little Simpsons socks. 'You're all right, you know, Matt?' she said, not wanting to gush too much, lest she make him blush.

'I know,' Matt said, mopping happily. 'Could you wear rollers in your hair when we go out tomorrow though, and a shirt saying *I'm his mother*, just in case there's any hot babes desperate for my body.

'Yes, thank you, Matt.' Donna headed back off, slumping her shoulders.

'Compliment, Mother,' Matt informed her about the bit she'd missed.

****

Mark glanced at Karl on the back seat of the car, Starbuck sitting as close to him as he could get. Mark swore that dog could think. 'Stay awake, Starbuck,' he said. 'Or we'll miss out on that treat when we get back, yes?

'Stay awake, Starbuck,' Karl repeated, sleepy but definitely awake.

Mark's relief was immense and twofold. Karl *was* communicating through the dog. His *son* was talking to him. Mark had no doubt about it now. He wanted to wind the window down and shout it aloud. Wished to God he had someone he could shout it out with. *Forget it, Mark. Don't go there.* He switched his mobile to hands-free as it rang, only to find it was Evelyn, which pretty much meant he couldn't avoid going there.

'Hi, Evelyn. How's things?' Mark took the call in case there was a problem with his dad. Also, he acknowledged, because he wished he could damn well *go there.*

'I was going to ask you the very same thing,' Evelyn said. 'Can you talk at the moment?'

'Briefly.' Mark glanced again at Karl in the back. 'I'm driving. On my way to the hospital.'

'Oh, Lord, is Karl all right?'

Blimey, Mark had gathered Evelyn was perceptive, but that was extra-sensory perception. 'He fell,' he explained. 'Playing with...'

'I know.'

She did? Spooky.

'I heard,' Evelyn went on, 'when I rang earlier.'

'Ah,' *so it had been Evelyn on the phone,* 'got you. So, what can I do for...'

'I spoke to Donna.'

'Right.' Mark tugged in a breath. 'And?'

'And she won't talk to you. Mark, why didn't you tell her?'

Mark sighed. Explanations. There were always explanations or excuses for Karl. He should have told Donna. The fact was, though, he hadn't. He wouldn't make the same mistake again but, dammit, he couldn't wind the clock back. And, right now, he'd had it up to the neck with explanations. 'I'd have thought that was pretty obvious, Evelyn.'

'Very,' Evelyn replied, shortly. 'Right, well, I'll let you tend to your son. Little word of advice though, Mark, if I may?'

Mark rolled his eyes, guessing he was probably going to get the benefit of it anyway.

'Do try and do right by any other ladies concerned. Breaking hearts isn't something to be proud of. Goodbye, Mr Evans.'

Other ladies? Mark almost laughed, as Evelyn signed off. Other ladies in his life since his divorce, apart from Karl's carers, amounted to two, both of whom weren't interested in a relationship with a single father with an autistic son. He could make that three now, he supposed, including Donna.

No problem. At least he knew where he stood. He turned towards the Accident and Emergency department, trying hard to convince himself he didn't care.

****

Five minutes later, Mark stood at reception trying to explain about Starbuck, who in the absence of his identification and a blind person, didn't seem to be passing as an assistance dog.

He was also trying to hold onto his temper, which he was in danger of losing; and Karl, who he was in danger of dropping. He looked at the impassive expression on the face of the receptionist, sighed, and tried again. 'He's a sensory assistance dog,' he explained. 'My son has autism and... Look, for *Pete's* sake, the kid has a gash in his head that needs stitching and is in imminent danger of having a full-blown tantrum. Now, will you please just contact...'

'Mark,' a voice called from the corridor to his side. 'Mark, hi. Come on through.'

'Thank Christ,' Mark muttered, gave the guy on reception a scathing glance and did as bid, Starbuck in tow.

'Hey, Michelle,' He smiled, relieved. 'Boy, are you a sight for sore eyes.'

'Flattery will get you everywhere,' the young doctor assured him. 'What were you doing out there with the masses?' she asked, tugging back a cubicle curtain. 'Why on earth didn't you just come straight in?'

'Minus uniform, plus dog — meet Starbuck, Karl's assistance dog...' Mark nodded towards Starbuck '... I wasn't cutting much ice with your new receptionist.'

He lowered Karl into a chair, rather than onto the trolley, where he'd have access to Starbuck and, more importantly, where Starbuck had access to Karl. 'Hasn't been on his PR course yet, I take it?'

'Yes, but they're more geared to Treating Customers Unfairly nowadays, on the basis that keeping patients out costs less,' Michelle quipped. 'Now then, what have we got here?' She crouched down, postponing attending Karl's wound in favour of petting his dog.

'This is Starbuck,' Karl introduced him. 'He's Karl's best friend.'

'Is he now?' Michelle looked at Karl, smiling her surprise. 'Well I think I'm jealous,' she said, with a pretend frown. 'I thought *I* was Karl's best friend.'

Karl studied her for a second, then reached out and stroked her hair. 'I see I am.' Michelle twizzled her neck to wink at Mark.

She turned back to Karl. 'Can I stroke your hair, Karl?' she asked gently.

Karl flinched as Michelle touched his head, looking to try and assess the damage, Mark knew.

'Er,' he walked across and encouraged Starbuck to give Karl his paw, 'only if his furry best friend holds his hand,' he explained.

****

'Girl done good.' Mark peered through the cubicle curtain two stitches later, to where Karl appeared to be contentedly crayoning, Starbuck and a biscuit by way of reward by his side.

Michelle peeked in alongside him. 'Boy also done good,' she said, looking impressed. 'Both boys.'

'So,' she said, turning to Mark as they stepped away from the curtain, 'does the bigger of the two boys allow himself a reward?'

She scanned his face, her mouth curving into a smile.

Mark reciprocated. 'Sometimes,' he said, with a shrug.

'So do you fancy showing a good girl a good time sometime?'

Mark glanced down, to where Michelle was trailing a finger suggestively down his chest. 'As long as she promises to be bad,' he said, looking back up hopefully.

'You're on,' she said, swapping meaningful glances with him before checking her pager.

'When and where?' Mark asked.

'Got a childminder?'

'Can do,' Mark said, knowing Jody didn't mind the odd occasion he did go out, given she was available to watch Karl.

'Tomorrow. Somewhere cheap and cheerful, then my place for coffee.' Michelle waggled suggestive eyebrows as she turned to attend whichever duty called.

Appreciating the view, Mark watched her walk away. Realising there was more than coffee on offer, he felt fleetingly guilty, then dismissed it. As much as he'd like to have been with a certain someone else, he wasn't. So what was there to feel guilty about?

Chapter Fifteen

Donna decided on a good dollop of frizz-free stuff in favour of rollers. And her new treat to herself in favour of the *I'm his mother* tee shirt.

She shouldn't be splashing out just because Matt now had a Saturday job. That money was his to keep, but Donna would be a little better off now Matt had insisted she cut his allowance.

Feeling guilty nevertheless, she slipped into her new M&S top. Short sleeved, hugging her thighs flatteringly over her jeans, it was just too hard to resist, particularly as the colour, dusty rose, with a rose accessory pinned to the shoulder quite suited her.

There. She pushed her feet into her high-heeled sandals and appraised herself in the mirror. Not too bad, she supposed, then beamed all over her face as Matt wolf-whistled from the landing.

Aw, bless. He was a good kid, turning young man — about to break some poor, hot young thing's heart someday, probably. Donna twirled around. Or not. She noted his *Many Deaths of Kenny* tee shirt, cut-off combats and *Bench* cap and her face dropped.

'I thought we were doing cas...' Matt stopped and nodded. 'I'll just go and get ready.'

****

'More liqueur, Sir, Madam?' The waiter asked with a polite bow.

'No, thanks. Just the bill. Excellent service, by the way.' Mark nodded his thanks.

The waiter smiled graciously and went off looking pleased.

'Tip, I think,' Michelle suggested, sipping back her Cointreau. Her second, Mark noted, on top of two shared bottles of red.

Mark took a swig of his brandy, glad he'd gone out with Michelle, but also sad that it couldn't have been with someone else. It obviously wasn't meant to be though. Donna was probably out with someone else anyway. The AA bloke possibly, or one of the guys from the pub?

Mark swilled his brandy around his glass, then tipped it back. He was dwelling. He shouldn't be, when he'd just spent an evening in very pleasant company. An evening that wasn't over yet, judging by the look Michelle was giving him.

'I thought it was men who were supposed to do the undressing with the eyes bit,' he said, leaning closer, wanting very much to make love to this beautiful, vivacious woman, but beginning to have doubts. Serious doubts. Mark smiled and tried to look more like a suave sophisticate than a clumsy copper as his elbow slipped of the table.

'I think we'd getter bet you home... for coffee.' Michelle giggled, and attempted a flutter of the eyelashes. At least that's what Mark thought it was. She looked a bit cross-eyed.

'I'm going to...' Michelle waved a finger vaguely behind her '... pee,' she announced decisively. 'Here,' she handed Mark her half of the bill. 'No arguments. And no sneaking it back in my bag, while we're making mad passionate... thingy. I'm a jshunior doctor, now, you know. I can make my own way.'

Mark winced as Michelle turned around and promptly made her way into the nearest table.

'Whoops. Sorry.' She smiled at the startled diners, straightened their skew-whiff menus, then felt obliged to straighten the guy's tie. 'See you downstairs,' she said.

'Er, I think she means me,' Mark pointed out as the guy looked uncomfortable and the girl he was with shot Michelle's retreating back a look that could kill.

Mark paid the bill, then loitered outside the ladies'. Michelle, he suspected, might just meet him downstairs a bit quicker than she'd anticipated if he left her to negotiate them on her own. So much for making mad passionate... thingy.

Mark hid a smile as Michelle emerged. '*Ta-dah!*' she said, arms flung wide, took two steps towards him and fell over her shoes.

Mark straightened her up and extended his elbow. 'Allow me,' he offered.

'Anytime.' Michelle waggled her eyebrows and wove him to the stairs, which they took slowly, extremely slowly, with Michelle's tongue wedged in his ear, and Mark half-carrying her.

Michelle went for the full headlock, tongue-and-tonsil job in the foyer, much to Mark's embarrassment and the amusement of the ground-floor diners, bar one or two.

'Nice neck accessory,' one onlooker commented behind Michelle, looking actually far from amused.

'*Jesus Christ.*' Mark hastily tried to extract himself from Michelle's neck-hold.

'Nope,' Matt assured him. 'It's just me.'

If Mark had never known ice-cool contempt, he knew it then.

Donna looked right through him.

And looked utterly, gut-wrenchingly fantastic.

Mark took Michelle home. Then had coffee alone.

****

Donna drove determinedly to the veterinary surgery the next morning. Her heart pulverised though it was, and puffy-eyed though she was, today, she'd decided, was the first day of the rest of her life. She was going to damn well despatch Mark to history, along with dickhead Jeremy and get on with living it.

She was due at the care home this lunchtime. Donna had said she would go and go she would. Little Karl wouldn't notice whether she was there or not, of course, but Donna had had an idea, which just might make that little difference to his life.

Karl had given her the idea himself. Not in so many words, obviously. Four words, actually. 'Starbuck's lead,' he'd said, and, 'Karl's lead,' referring to the tether that bound them and kept him from wandering off, bless his dirty little socks.

But Sadie's would be too small, she'd realised. In any case, she'd need more. Four, rather than three.

Donna slipped into the vets, hoping they had some in stock.

Hastily, she perused the doggy accessories stand, and there, in between Kongo's and chewies, she found them. *Yesss!* And the right size. Perfect. She plucked them off and waved them at the veterinary nurse to pop on her bill, then dashed off to make haste to work, lest mean Jean decide to be even meaner if she were late.

Twenty minutes later, Donna skidded into the office, late, to be greeted by Jean's pointed, 'Morning, Donna,' accompanied by her even more pointed glance at the clock.

'Morning, Jean.' Donna smiled brightly.

Hah! That threw her. Donna popped her coat on the rack and slipped smugly behind her mountain of post, whilst Jean looked on, perplexed, then reached for her bag to check her face in her compact, probably to see if she had visible signs of losing her touch.

Post despatched, and two typed reports later, Donna was starving, but ready to skip lunch. Also on the verge of asking Jean if she could slip off early to allow for travel time, which she was sure Jean wouldn't mind since she was volunteering at one of their very own projects, when…

'Right, I'm off,' said Jean, ending her uber-important personal call. 'Meeting with the Community Services Manager. Back about three... ish. I'll need that report by then, Donna.'

What report? Donna glanced at her in-tray, where, as if by magic, another report had appeared. *Cow.*

'Right.' Enough was enough. Donna braced herself. 'Um, shall I let the Chief Executive know where you can be contacted?' Translated, shall I let the CE know you're two-timing him? Blinkety-blink.

'No need.' Jean said, spraying enough perfume to triple the hole in the ozone layer. 'He's out all afternoon.'

'Oh,' said Donna. 'It's just that he rang, while you were on the phone... to Stephen.'

Donna smiled ever-so-sweetly and let it hang, knowing that Jean knew that Donna knew the Community Services Manager was female and didn't generally go by the name of Stephen. Nor, Donna fancied, would Jean be 'meeting' *her* at Puccini's intimate little Italian.

'I'm sorry, Jean, but I can't type your report for you.' Donna held Jean's flustered gaze. 'I'm volunteering at Blossom Tree, you might recall.'

'Oh, yes,' Jean said, looking very much as if her bluff had been called.

'Dr Lewis is really pleased you're supporting me, by the way.' Donna scraped her chair back, plucked up her coat, and sauntered, shoulders high, out of the door.

****

Dr Lewis laughed, but not unkindly. 'I admire your ingenuity, Donna. Well done,' he said.

Donna fluffed up her chest feathers.

'Let's do it.' Dr Lewis nodded decisively. 'We'll loiter close by in case you need us.' He nodded at a key worker. 'And Donna,' he gave her another smile, 'if Karl does get a bit upset, try not to worry. We're here to help the children develop. Nothing ventured, nothing gained, hey?'

Donna nodded, hoisted up her shoulders, collected up her photographs of Sadie, along with her purchase from the vet's surgery, and went over to where Karl was drawing a picture of Starbuck, his brow knitted in concentration.

'Hi Starbuck.' Donna patted the real live Starbuck by Karl's side, then went to sit on Karl's other side.

'Hello, Karl,' she said, settling down at the table. The table that Karl seemed to be content sharing with other children today. 'Ooh, my, that's a good picture. It looks very much like Starbuck.'

Karl carried on crayoning.

'I bet Starbuck thinks it looks like Starbuck.'

No response initially, then, 'Starbuck thinks it looks like Starbuck,' Karl repeated.

Donna smiled. 'I have some pictures of *my* best friend today, Karl. Would Karl and Starbuck like to see them?'

'Yes,' said Karl.

Donna took a breath, then splayed the photographs of Sadie across the table, some front view, ergo, Sadie being an obviously three-legged dog, but most side shots, Sadie therefore looking like a dog should look to Karl, hopefully.

'What's this, Karl?' Donna pointed to one of the photos.

Karl hesitated. 'Dog,' he said, at length.

Yesss! 'Good boy, Karl. That's right. It is a dog. Her name is Sadie. She's Donna's best friend.'

Karl pointed at the photo. 'Donna's best friend.'

Donna decided not to mention the missing leg. She needed Karl to concentrate on Sadie's paws. More importantly, what was attached to her paws. She reached for another photograph, a close up of Sadie kitted out in her all-terrain paw protectors, which people had thought Donna barking mad when she'd taken Sadie walkies in, but which were essential apparel for a three-legged dog when it was slippery under paw.

'See what Sadie is wearing, Karl?' Donna pointed to the little black shoes, noted Karl's eyes flicker across the photo, pause at the shoes, and was sure he'd registered what he saw there.

Donna moved the photo so Starbuck could get a better view — all-important in Karl's mind. 'See, Starbuck? See what Sadie's wearing?'

'Why? Hmm, good question, Starbuck.' Donna cocked her head to one side, addressing the dog now, employing the 'Agnes' technique, and hoping Karl might go for it. 'Starbuck wants to know why Sadie's wearing shoes, Karl. Do you think we should try to explain?'

Karl crayoned a little harder. 'Starbuck wants to know why Sadie's wearing shoes,' he said, after a moment.

Donna nodded. 'Right, well, I'll tell you, Starbuck.' She moved around to get better access to the dog. 'But I might have to point to your paw to tell you properly. Is that okay?'

'Yes,' Karl answered.

'Thank you, Starbuck. And thank you, Karl.' Donna smiled and lifted Starbuck's paw. 'Do you want to see, too, Karl?' she asked and waited until Karl placed his pencil down and turned his attention towards Starbuck.

'Okay.' Donna started, mentally crossing her fingers. 'Do you see your nails are quite long, Starbuck?'

Karl didn't say anything, but his eye movement meant he was listening, Donna hoped.

She went on, as simplistically as she could. 'Well, that means that sometimes, when it's snowy or icy, you can slip. The rubber bottoms on the boots can stop you slipping, so you don't fall over and hurt yourself.'

Donna heard the door squeak open behind them, but concentrated her efforts on trying to keep Karl concentrating.

'And your best friend wouldn't want you to hurt yourself, would he, Starbuck?'

'No,' Karl said, his brow furrowed determinedly now.

'You have soft pads on your feet, as well, Starbuck, like Karl has soft pads on the bottom of his feet. So, even if it's not icy or snowy, you could still hurt your foot if you trod on something sharp. And then you might not be able to go on walkies. And I don't think your best friend would like that at all.'

Donna glanced at Karl, trying to ignore the murmur of male voices behind them, for fear of losing his attention. 'I think Starbuck might want to try some shoes on, Karl. Does Karl think he does?'

Donna watched and waited.

The furrow in Karl's brow deepened. 'I think Starbuck might want to try some shoes on,' he eventually said.

'Good boy, Starbuck.' Donna breathed a sigh of relief, then moved around the dog, lifting each paw one by one and popping the paw-protectors on, whilst trying very hard to ignore Mark Evans staring at her from where he stood by the door.

Mark kept staring.

Utterly mesmerised.

Quite unable to tear his disbelieving eyes away from her.

Dr Lewis leaned towards him. 'I think we landed on our feet with Donna, if you'll forgive the pun.'

Mark hardly dared to breathe, thinking if he did, he might wake up from whatever hangover-induced hallucination this might be.

'She has a natural empathy,' Dr Lewis went on in the same low voice he'd been addressing Mark with in the last few minutes, rather than distract Donna from her mission, and Karl from Donna.

Mark nodded, at a loss for words that might describe how he felt about Donna just then. How could he have been such an *idiot?* She was smiling at his son. Talking to his son. Engaging with his son. Getting a reaction from him, and he'd been *bloody* fool enough to think she'd walk away at first knowledge of him.

He kept watching, what should be a *Eureka* moment, feeling sick to the bottom of his soul.

'All set,' Donna said, straightening from her task, then cocking an ear in Starbuck's direction. 'What was that, Starbuck?'

'Oh,' she said.

Mark's mouth twitched into a smile.

'Starbuck won't go unless Karl wears his shoes.' Donna sighed melodramatically. 'He says Karl might hurt *his* feet. And then Karl might not be able to go walkies. And then Starbuck will be sad, because he doesn't want to go walkies without his best friend.'

Best friend? Jesus. That's where it had come from. Mark reeled inwardly. Could almost feel a collective holding of breath, a palpable tension as Karl climbed from his chair, walked over to his shoes, picked them up, plonked himself on the floor and pulled them on.

'Good God!' Dr Lewis stared in awe. 'I don't...' He looked from a shoed and ready to go Karl, to Donna, back to Mark, but Mark was gone, half out door.

He couldn't stay to watch anymore.

****

'Mark?' Donna stepped tentatively towards him.

He stayed where he was, his back to her.

'Why didn't you tell me?'

'I, er...' He ran his hand though his hair.

Turned around after a while.

Swallowed hard.

Oh, Lord. He'd been crying.

Donna searched his face. She had no clue what to say to him. Why he was so upset. Why he hadn't mentioned he had a special son. Except...

'Why didn't you tell me, Mark?' she asked again, because she had to. 'Was it because you didn't think I'd be in your life long enough for you to warrant mentioning him?'

'What!?' Mark looked at her, visibly shocked. 'No. I...' He swallowed again. 'I have to go,' he said, dropping his gaze. 'Can I call you, Donna? Will you please let me talk to you?'

He glanced back at her, hopefully.

Donna hesitated, then nodded. He might well have a harem on his landing. She wouldn't be surprised if some voluptuous female popped out of the boot of his patrol car, complete with toothbrush and tassels, but... Her shoulders were broad. She had ears. She could listen if he needed to talk.

Chapter Sixteen

Donna wended her way back home, tired but content.

Jean had been quite nice to her when she got back to the office, wonder of wonders, though Donna didn't have to wonder for too long. The Chief Executive wanted to see her personally, apparently, in his office, Jean informed her, then suggested they had tea.

Then made the tea.

Donna's eyes nearly clunked into her cup when she spotted the biscuit Jean had placed on her saucer. She'd gone into the CE's office warily and come out whooping.

She'd done it! *Yes! Yesss! Yessity, yessss!*

Dr Lewis had telephoned, so said the CE, saying he realised it would be a terrible loss to head office, but that he'd like Donna as a member of his team, training on the job, a.s.a.p.

Would she like to consider it, the CE asked.

Donna considered, for about a nanosecond, then dashed out to dance around her desk and hug a somewhat startled Jean.

Yes, it had been quite the best day in Donna's life for a long time, apart from one teeny negative. Mark hadn't rung.

Donna had no idea what he might say, if he did. Whether it would be worth listening to, but he'd looked so sad, so lonely, despite his female fan club, she couldn't help hoping that, by some miracle, he might be able to redeem himself. At least allow them to be friends.

But he hadn't rung.

She'd checked her mobile at least a thousand times, each time her euphoria dwindling a little bit more. It would have been nice to have someone to share her news with. Someone kind and caring, like the man she'd thought Mark to be. Still did, to a degree.

Donna let go a shuddery sigh, let herself through her front door, and checked the answerphone.

Nothing.

'Not that desperate to call then, was he, hey, babe?' She smiled half-heartedly at Sadie, who hopped enthusiastically to greet her.

'Aw, hello, hon.' Donna fixed a more appreciative smile in place, and bent to give the dog a good fuss. 'You're a star, do you know that? A super-duper star. Come on, let's go and get you some chocy drops, my faithful little best friend.'

Lots of chocy drops, Donna decided. Little Karl happily wearing his shoes and Donna being offered the position at Blossom Tree was down to Sadie and her snazzy paw-wear, after all.

Donna headed for the kitchen to get dog treats and to close the perpetually open back door, before she was instantaneously ice-cubed.

'Oh, dear, he's a bad boy, isn't he, Sade?' Donna despaired of ever getting Matt not to leave the door open, 'just in case Sadie needed to go out.' The garden was secure enough to stop Findus slipping through the fence, but the flimsy bolt on the back fence wouldn't stop people slipping in if they felt so inclined.

'We'll be murdered in our beds one day, won't we, hon? No, course we won't.' She peered out to check on Findus, who was dining happily on dandelions, then smiled down at her dog, who followed her wherever she went. 'You'd fight them off, wouldn't you?'

'Matt!' Donna called up the stairs, once Findus had followed a trail of yoghurt drops back to his cage and Sadie had been duly rewarded her chocy variety 'Will you please stop leaving the back door open. Sadie will let you know when she wants to go out.'

She cocked an ear in hopes of a reply. Nothing, apart from Matt and his friend whooping and groaning, and sound-effects from his computer game, which would explain why he'd left the back door open. With Matt installed in front of his PC, Sadie would have to resort to a flying karate kick to get his attention.

Ah, well, Donna yawned and stretched. A nice warm bath was in order, she thought, it being Friday night — fish and chips night. Also the night before Simon's party, for which she'd need to preen, pluck, and make herself drop-dead gorgeous.

Donna sighed. 'I may be some time, Sade.'

****

After checking on Karl, who was contentedly snuggled under his duvet with Starbuck, Mark walked over to the phone.

It was now or never, he supposed.

Though how the hell he was going to explain that he'd started out thinking Donna would walk away once she knew about Karl, then assumed she had once she did... Christ, how wrong could he have been?

And this was without trying to explain away being locked in a no-holds-barred embrace with Michelle in the restaurant. He doubted very much that Donna would accept any explanations he had to offer about that.

Raking his hand through his hair, Mark picked up the phone, and dialled Donna's number. Whatever her response, he needed to let her know how much he cared about her. Tell her what a special person she was. That he wished he'd been man enough to admit up front — as Donna had — that he was running scared of wrong relationships, too.

He let the phone ring. Was almost at the point of hanging up when Matt picked up.

Mark braced himself, ready to be not-so-politely told where to go. Matt, he'd deduced from the killer look he'd given him in the restaurant, hadn't been too impressed with him either.

'Hi, Matt,' he said, nervously. 'It's Mark. How's things?'

'Who?'

'Er, Mark,' he repeated awkwardly. 'Mark Evans. The, er, policeman.'

'Oh, yeah,' Matt said, after a loaded pause. 'I think I remember the name. Struggling to recall the *two* faces though.'

'Ah.' Mark sensed a little animosity.

'Do you want something?' Matt asked bluntly.

'I, er...' Mark started, faltered, then went for it. 'Another chance?' he asked, hopefully.

'To do what? Mess her about again?'

'No, absolutely not. To explain, that's all.'

No answer.

'To you, initially,' Mark suggested. 'And then, if you want to tell your mum I called, not to tell her to tell me to get stuffed...'

Silence.

'It'd better be good,' Matt said, at length.

'Not good enough, I suspect, but it's all I've got.'

'Try me,' Matt said dryly.

Wasn't going to make it easy, was he? Mark took a breath. So where did he start? How did he explain his own insecurities had had him screwing things up without sounding lame?

'I have a son, too, Matt,' he started, deciding honesty was the best policy. 'His name's Karl. He's autistic. I didn't tell Donna... your mum... up-front, because I was frightened of scaring her away. I didn't give her a chance. My mistake. Big mistake. I'm sorry.'

'Oh,' said Matt.

Mark smiled. Obviously the 'oh' ran in the family.

'So how old is he?'

'Six. Donna has met him now, incidentally. Today, actually. I'm not sure whether she told you, but... Well, let's just say she worked a small miracle. She's a pretty special person, you know?'

'Yes, I *do* know, as it happens,' Matt informed him flatly. 'And the neck accessory?' he enquired, obviously referring to Michelle.

'A friend. Just a friend. I didn't sleep with her, Matt,' Mark assured him quickly, realising that Matt was mature enough for details, and wasn't about to be fobbed off with anything less. 'I might have. Intended to, to be honest. I thought it was over with Donna. I'm hoping to God it isn't. That somehow, I can fix things.'

Mark stopped. That was it. His cards were on the table. Now, as backward as it seemed, it was up to Matt. 'What do you think?' he asked hesitantly.

'I think you should try carrying flowers next time you run into her, rather than a female,' Matt suggested, with due sarcasm.

'Good idea.' Mark conceded.

'I'll be back about eleven-thirty, just in case you should run into her tonight.'

'Er, right,' Mark got the drift, possibly. 'Thanks, Matt.'

Mark signed off feeling as if he should have said, thanks Mr O'Connor. He smiled, knowing he could be feeling a lot worse.

****

'Bye, Mum,' Matt called when Donna turned off her hairdryer. 'We're off to…'

'Have fun,' Donna called back, rummaging in her wardrobe for something to wear between the barely-there sixties dress she'd picked up at the charity shop, and go-go boots, other than goose-pimples.

'… North America.'

'Okey-dokey,' Donna trilled, preoccupied. Aha! She seized on a pair of hold-ups in the absence of tights. But would they look right? Fishnets didn't go with microdot mini-dresses, did they?

'… in search of Bigfoot,' Matt went on, drolly.

'Well, don't be too late. You have your Saturday job tomorrow, remember?' Donna reminded him, deciding she'd just have to try the whole ridiculous fancy-dress ensemble on.

'Yes, Mother. I'll bring us a bear home for supper.'

Oh, whoops. He must be as hungry as one. Donna skidded to the landing. 'Sorry, I was just trying my fishnets on. There's money for food on the cupboard.' She leaned over the banister and beamed him a smile.

Matt shook his head. 'Bye, Mother. Don't get doing anything I wouldn't.'

Chance would be a fine thing. Donna sighed, and skidded back.

God, the dress was miniscule — she held it up to her — to the point of obscene. She had another sigh and wriggled into what might better suit a Sindy doll, then tugged a go-go boot onto one leg, a fishnet onto the other for comparison, and surveyed herself in the mirror.

Hmm? Not quite the luv-in sixties-hippie-chick look she'd been aiming for. She'd be 'pulled in' if she went out in public in this little lot.

Damn! The doorbell. Perfect timing as per… Donna peg-legged to the landing, guessing who it was, but trying to get a peek through the glass nevertheless, lest it be a salesman, who would probably have apoplexy and die on the doorstep.

Donna squinted, then crouched and squinted some more; then almost fell face-first down the stairs when the letterbox flapped and a pair of eyes peered back.

'Cooee, only me,' Simon called. 'Hurry up, Dons. It's raining cats and dogs.'

'Coming.' Donna dashed on down, lest poor Simon end up dead from pneumonia on top of his poor stitched head.

'Ooh!' Simon exclaimed when Donna opened the door to the only man in the universe she was about to let see her dressed... or rather... undressed, as she was. 'I didn't realise we were doing tarts and vicars.'

'Is it really that bad?' Donna asked gloomily, holding the door wide to allow a dripping wet, sou'westered Simon inside.

'Bad?' Simon turned to look her up and down as she closed the door. 'Sweetie, all I can say is I'm glad Nathan's gay.'

Donna knitted her brow. 'Oh,' she said, her mouth curving into a small smile as she realised Simon had just paid her a compliment.

'It's knockout,' Simon assured her, swishing up the hall and dripping all over the floor. 'You'll have single men drooling into their drinks. That's assuming you're not back together with your yummy policeman?'

Simon looked at her, a touch hopefully.

'No.' Donna tried not to look too miserable. 'I'm not sure we were ever together, to be honest. Come on, upstairs. You can tell me whether it's better with stockings off or on.'

'Now there's an offer a man can't refuse.' Simon made eyes at Sadie, then scooted after Donna. 'I promise I'll be quick.'

'How very disappointing,' Donna laughed.

'Like a fireman down a greased pole.'

'You're going as a policeman, Simon, remember?' Donna showed him into the bedroom, then went to the bathroom to try to work out how she was going to wear flowers in her hair when she couldn't get them to stay there.

'So, you didn't actually get it together in the bedroom department, then?' Simon enquired casually, from Donna's bedroom.

'No,' Donna confessed. 'I mean we kissed... a bit.' She trailed a finger over her lips, wishing Mark had been a terrible kisser, wishing he hadn't done terrible things to her when he had kissed her.

'Honestly, Donna, why not?' Simon asked the inevitable question. 'Admittedly I didn't see much of him with half my body's blood supply dripping into my eyes but...' He paused. 'Stop it, Donna.'

'Stop what?' Donna asked, knowing full well what Simon meant.

'Feeling guilty. I know what you're like, Donna O'Connor, and it was *not* your fault. That twit you were married to is such a Neanderthal he ought to exhibited in the Natural History Museum, preferably stuffed. I just hope he gets his comeuppance.'

Which he will, with luck, Donna thought; if Leticia dumps him from a great height, which, hopefully, she will.

'Anyway, as I was saying,' Simon went on, 'from what I could see of your policeman friend, he looked a bit of a dish. I tell you what, I wouldn't turn him down.'

'Simon!'

'I meant if I was *you*, obviously. I'm spoken for, if you recall. Come on then, I'm ready. Come and tell me whether I could ever hope to measure up.'

Simon did a little twirl when Donna went into the bedroom. 'Whadya think? It's me, isn't it?' He flicked his hair theatrically and turned his good side to the light.

'Very.' Donna laughed. He did cut quite a figure actually. Mark's jacket fitted him well. 'Nathan will think it's *his* birthday and Christmas all rolled into one.'

'Do you really think so?' Simon beamed, and turned to admire himself in the mirror.

'Absolutely,' nodded Donna enthusiastically, and lost her flower.

'You, too,' Simon offered, with a reassuring smile. 'But I don't think you're supposed to wear your flower there, sweetie.'

'I know.' Donna tucked it a bit further down her cleavage, for safekeeping. 'I'm obviously not the bells-on-toes and flowers-in-the-hair sort. I'll have to get a headband, or stitch it to my scalp.'

'Ouch,' they both said together.

'Sorry, Simon. Does it hurt much?'

'Only when I laugh,' Simon assured her. 'Oh, do stop worrying, Donna. I'm fine, honestly, thanks to your policeman friend. So are you going to tell me what happened between you two then, or are you going to keep me in suspenders? Talking of which, you'll need another stocking to hitch to yours. You're looking a bit lopsided.'

Simon nodded at her one hold-up, which wasn't holding up very well, then perched himself on the dressing table chair, his face expectant.

'I don't know.' Donna hitched up her fishnet and plopped herself down on the bed. 'We were getting along fine, I think. Then I told him I didn't want complications, and it all got... complicated.'

'You're vulnerable, sweetie. You've been hurt and you don't want to be hurt again, I can understand that. So?'

'So?'

'So is that why you didn't do the deed?

158

Donna looked at him, puzzled.

'On the basis of "you don't give all of yourself, you don't get hurt"; am I close?'

Donna sighed. 'Very,' she admitted. 'Except I do.'

'Except you do.' Simon shook his head sadly.

Donna shifted uncomfortably. 'I did try,' she admitted. 'You know, to give him my all.'

Simon arched an eyebrow.

'I made a mess of it.' Donna shrugged and blushed down to her squashed petals. 'I think I'm a bit...'

'Lacking in confidence after that little turd, Jeremy?'

'Yes.' Donna's blush turned to a hot flush. 'I practically raped him.'

'Pardon?' Simon sat to attention.

'No not... I just, sort of threw myself at him,' Donna tried to explain. 'Gave him the green light, you know, and then when he, um...'

'Revved his engine?'

'Simon, don't,' said Donna, feeling embarrassed more for Mark than for herself. 'Mark was really gentlemanly about it, but... do you think he... You know?'

'What? Lost interest?'

'Uh-huh.' Donna nodded, not sure she really thought he had, not then. He'd rung so many times. But then, he wasn't ringing now, was he? 'You don't think he's one of those *thrill of the chase* sorts? And he suddenly realised it wasn't worth the effort and went off in search of more willing fish?' Donna fished.

'Donna, now you're being paranoid. You're measuring yourself by that dreadful ex's opinion of you. So don't. I'm willing to bet your boy-in-blue's opinion would count for a whole lot more.'

'Yes, I suppose.' She *was* being paranoid. Of course she was. Looking for reasons to blame herself, again. Reasons for him to be able to justify Jody-kiss-kiss and silken-haired Sally, who were obviously on the scene well before her. And what about the woman practically digesting Mark whole in the restaurant?

'Ring him,' Simon suggested. 'Ask him.'

'I would. I might, but...' Donna chewed on her lip. 'He was supposed to be ringing me. Tonight. Just to talk, you know?'

'Ah, so you don't want to ring him, in case he doesn't want to be rung and you'd end up looking the fool.'

'Exactly,' Donna sighed, and peeled off her one hold-up in favour of the other go-go boot. Fishnets, she decided, suited her about as much as they did fish. She'd have time enough to shop for something that looked less trollopy tomorrow.

'I see,' said Simon. 'Um, Donna, just out of interest, you don't think your boy-in-blue might come around in person, rather than ring?'

Donna shook her head. 'No, I shouldn't think so. He wouldn't know whether Matt was in, and he'd realise it might be a bit awkward. He was good like that.'

'Right. So, just supposing he did,' Simon shot off the chair, 'he wouldn't have a nervous habit of any sort, would he?'

Donna stopped ferreting for her flower and looked at Simon.

Simon was looking out of the window. 'Such as running a hand through his hair, perchance?'

Donna's eyes grew wide.

'*Sh... ugar*!' They gulped in unison as the doorbell rang.

'Oh, my God! Simon! You have his uniform on, and I have...' Donna glanced down at her state of no-dress. '*Eeeuuw*, what do I do?!'

'Don't panic!' Simon promptly panicked, heading fast for the stairs.

'*Noooo*, not that way!' Donna threw herself across the room, ready to rugby-tackle him to the floor. 'He'll see you going down.'

Simon turned heel. 'Where then? I know, the bathroom'

'No! The bathroom door's opposite the stairs. Your legs look nothing like mine.'

They both had a quick appraisal of legs and unanimously agreed.

'Well, where else?' Simon looked definitely panicky now. 'Ooh, do hurry up, Donna. I don't have much more blood left to give.'

'Matt's room.' Donna headed for Matt's door.

'Good idea.' Simon rolled his eyes. 'I'll give Matt a wave from under the duvet, shall I, if he comes home while lover-boy's here?'

Hell! He was right. Donna propelled Simon back towards her bedroom. Matt would *not* be impressed if he came back to find Simon in his bed wearing Mark's spare uniform.

Simon dug his heels in. 'Donna, I don't want to appear awkward,' he said, practically clinging to the doorframe, 'but I'm thinking if you kiss and make up, your bedroom is the one place he's *bound* to want to use. *Oui*?'

'Simon, we won't. He won't... For goodness sake,' Donna gave him a shove, 'Simon, *get* in.'

'But can't you just explain?' Simon suggested. 'I mean, it's all perfectly innocent, isn't —'

'*Explain?* Innocent?' Donna gawked. Whatever Mark and she were, or weren't, she didn't want him to see her like this. She'd be a fine one demanding explanations, wouldn't she? 'Simon, we're both in a state of inappropriate undress. Upstairs. Together! What do you suggest I tell him?'

'That we were trying fancy dress on.' Simon tried hopefully.

Donna folded her arms, and looked the length and breadth of him. It didn't really help, she felt not inclined to point out, that his fly was undone and his shirttails were hanging out.

Simon looked Donna up and down, taking in her knicker-skimming no-dress. 'Not very convincing, really, is it? I'll hide in the wardrobe.'

Chapter Seventeen

Donna raced back to the stairs, tugged down her dress, then sauntered — as nonchalantly as one could in white boots and a dress that screamed red light — downstairs. This was awful. *He* was the one who'd been up to no good. So why did she feel like a nun caught out in public in French knickers?

Right, shoulders up, head high and keep calm. He probably won't even notice. She searched for her inner poise, pulled open the door, then almost closed it in his face when Mark's eyes shot to her thighs.

'Donna,' he said, his expression mildly perplexed. 'I, er... How are you?'

'Up here,' Donna suggested.

'Oh, right.' Mark averted his gaze. 'Sorry,' he said, trying to keep his eyes at an appropriate level, only for them to slide slowly back down.

Coming to rest on the flat petals peering not very provocatively from her cleavage, Donna realised, her poise wilting somewhat.

'Interesting... broach?' Mark speculated.

'It's for my hair,' Donna said quickly, lest he think she always used her breasts as a flower press. 'But it wouldn't stay there.'

'Would you like to come in?' she asked, as Mark looked as if he was about to *stay there*, taking in the view.

'Yes, if that's okay. Thanks.' Mark stepped in, with a puzzled little shake of his head.

'You said you were going to ring,' Donna pointed out, as she closed the door.

'I was but, I, er... Is this an inconvenient time, Donna? Because if it is, I...'

'No, no,' Donna assured him. 'Not at all. I was just getting ready for bed, that's all, and I, um... Ahem.'

Donna smiled weakly as Mark looked her up and down bemusedly.

'I just thought I'd try on my fancy dress,' Donna went on, improvising madly, as she lead the way up the hall. 'You know before I put my jim-jams on after my bath.' She pointed the way to the lounge.

'Like you do.' Mark cocked his head to one side, had another little perusal of her aspiring tart's apparel, and his mouth curved into an amused smile.

Thank God. Donna's poise had all but gone-gone. She relaxed a little, much preferring to see Mark smile than look as heartbreakingly sad as he did last time she saw him. 'Can I get you some tea?' Donna offered him a small smile back. 'Coffee?' *Ear plugs?*

Donna smiled slipped as something clunked, then scraped up above, causing Mark's eyes to dart towards the stairs.

Hell! 'Sadie, sweetheart?' Donna called, sounding slightly demented. 'Where are y... Ooh! There you are.' Her eyes went into blink overdrive as a wet nose nuzzled the back of her thighs.

'Damn. It must be the vase falling off the shelf in the bedroom, again. The blind hits it,' Donna explained, squeezing past an ever more-bemused Mark. 'You know, when the, um, wind blows through the, er... Won't be a tic.'

She took the first four steps of the stairs at a run, then stopped, her cheeks flushing furiously as she realised her cheeks below might possibly be on show.

'Do you want to go on in?' She turned her posterior strategically to the wall and nodded towards the lounge. 'I'll just go and, um...' *strangle Simon.*

Mark looked on bewildered as Donna thumped on up, her hands plastered to her bum.

She really was crackers. He shook his head again as he went into the lounge. Crackers in the nicest possible way though, and he couldn't help but love her for...

Love her. It didn't hit him like a thunderbolt. That had happened the first time they'd touched. He'd felt it shake him to the core. As did the high-voltage jolt when their eyes locked. When he saw the vulnerability in hers. The obvious caring, though it was plain from outset she'd had been scared of caring too much.

When their lips met, he'd been lost. Truly lost. Because, though he hadn't acknowledged it then, he knew *he* was in grave danger of caring too much. Of falling too hard, too soon, when he quite simply couldn't afford to.

He had fallen though, big time.

He was in love with Donna O'Connor.

Mark laughed quietly, bent to stroke the three-legged dog Donna so obviously adored, and wondered, could she ever feel the same about him?

Especially now, after he'd been so busy thinking the world revolved around him and his problems. And what had Donna been doing while he had? Determinedly getting on with her life, trying to improve that of others. Of Karl and other kids like him.

Mark had loved her more then, as he'd watched her, empathising with his son as if it were second nature. He'd been in awe of her. *Was in awe of her still.*

He'd treated her badly. Underrated her. Been less than truthful with her. As good as flaunted another woman in her face.

Now, he needed to try to put it right, though where the hell to start? 'What would you do, Sadie?' He smiled, looking into the dog's beguiling brown eyes. Okay, I'm not proud. His smile broadened as Donna came back into the lounge, Sadie immediately bounding over to jump up and greet her. If that's what it took, he'd take the dog's cue and beg.

'Nothing too worrying up there, then?' he asked, straightening up.

'What?' Donna looked at him, looking preoccupied. Probably wondering how she was going to tell him she didn't want anything to do with him.

'Donna…' he said, stepping towards her.

'Mark, I…' Donna did likewise.

And… *Jesus.* There it was again, that jolt. It was physical. Did she feel it? Mark searched Donna's eyes.

'Sorry,' they both said together.

'I…' They both tried again.

Donna dropped her gaze. 'Sorry,' she mumbled.

Mark tilted her chin up and pressed a finger softly to her lips. 'Never apologise, Donna,' he reminded her, grazing her cheek with his thumb, 'especially when the other person *does* have something to apologise for. And, trust me, I have plenty.'

Donna looked at him, confusion in her eyes — and hurt. Hurt he'd put there. Mark hated himself for that. Could he detect a glimmer of hope in there somewhere though? God, he hoped so.

'So, if you have all night, I'll start.'

'As long as I don't have to spend all night in my go-go gear.' Donna smiled, and Mark fought an overwhelming urge to pull her into his arms there and then.

'Do you want to go back upstairs?' he offered.

Donna's eyes shot wide.

Perfect. Mark sighed inside. Why didn't he go for seriously crass and add 'to slip into something more comfortable' while he was at it?

'I meant to, er, get...' He trailed off, running his hand nervously through his hair. 'I'm not doing this very well, am I?'

'Um,' Donna ran the tip of her tongue over her lips, 'I'm not sure,' she said, obviously nervous for reasons of her own, but if she did that again, Mark thought it might be kinder if she just shot him. He couldn't do this, stand so close to her and not hold her.

'Donna, I wanted to explain,' he started again, 'about Karl, about... other stuff. But, before I do, I wanted to say thank you — for being you. For being caring enough to do what you did today with Karl.'

Donna blushed, beautifully in Mark's eyes. 'I couldn't have done it without Sadie and Starbuck. They were the real stars.' She smiled, that same light in her eyes he'd noticed when she first talked about what mattered to her.

'I know,' he conceded, 'but you were the inspiration. It was inspiring, Donna. Truly. You didn't just get a kid to wear his shoes. You helped him take a step towards learning to cope with life. Do you know how amazing that is? How many traumas you've averted? How many tears? And I'm not just talking about Karl's.'

Mark held her gaze.

Donna held his, gauging him, wondering about him, no doubt. 'It's what I want to do,' she said. 'Use my art. Work with children, though I wasn't sure I was capable of rising to the task, to be honest.'

'I gathered.' Mark nodded, more appreciative than she could possibly realise. 'And believe me, you are. You're a special person, Donna O'Connor. No man in his right mind would ever want to lose you, and if I have, because I didn't realise how special you are, because I didn't tell you about Karl, because I thought I would lose you,' Mark tugged in a breath, 'then I probably don't deserve you.'

'Sorry?' Donna blinked up at him, obviously confused.

'I wish you'd stop doing that.'

'Sorry.' Donna glanced down.

Saints preserve us. 'No, Donna,' Mark tilted her chin up, again, 'not that. Well, yes, that.' He shrugged, confusing himself. 'I meant would you please stop looking so damned distractingly beautiful. You see, I keep losing my train of thought.'

And my willpower to resist kissing you is all but depleted too, he didn't add.

Donna laughed.

'Beautiful,' Mark repeated. 'Your hair, your face, your body,' he glanced down, despite his warning to himself that he really should not be doing that. 'Outside and inside, you're a beautiful person, Donna. Don't let anyone ever tell you you're not.'

Donna swallowed, tugged on a strand of her hair, which was sexily messy, and which Mark badly wanted to run his hands through; then glanced down again. 'I bet you say that to all the girls.'

'Not all of them, no,' Mark assured her, with a half-hearted smile.

'Oh?' She said, looking back up.

Mark lost the smile. That *oh?* was loaded. She was looking for answers to questions. And he knew he'd better have the right answers.

He took a deep breath. She probably wouldn't believe him. Michelle, after all, was so hands all over him, Donna might as well have walked in on them half-naked in his bedroom.

'The girl you saw with me with, Michelle… She's just a friend, Donna. An intimate one once, but not anymore,' Mark tried to explain, the only way he could without adding insult to injury and lying. 'And, yes, we might have been intimate the other night, but we weren't, Donna, I promise. I would never even have gone out with Michelle if I'd thought there was the remotest chance, you and I…'

Mark stopped, noting the look on Donna's face, which was a mixture of mistrust and more hurt.

Not surprisingly. Whichever way he said it, the fact that he could go out with an ex-intimate friend at the drop of a hat with a view to picking up the intimacy pretty much said it all, he supposed.

'So,' Donna said, at length, 'not your sister then?'

Mark sighed inside. What did he expect? She wasn't going to say, no problem, let's pick up where we left off. She was more likely to tell him to piss off, which she had every right to.

'No, not my sister.' He glanced down.

'But Jody-kiss-kiss and silken-haired Sally are, presumably,' Donna went on, 'on the assumption you don't have an actual harem?'

Mark snapped his head up. 'Who and who and... *What?*'

'Jody-kiss-kiss, the one who comes with her toothbrush, no doubt wears dental floss in bed, and has an extremely dexterous thumb!'

Mark squinted at her, concerned. 'Donna, have you gone nuts?'

'No,' Donna assured him sweetly, 'but I may claim insanity if you lie to me, Mark Evans! Who is she?'

Donna eyed him narrowly.

Mark shook his head. 'Jody kiss... Jody!' The texts, of course. Mark looked back to Donna, hugely relieved.

'Yes, Jody-kiss-Jody, so flipping low down on your list, you can't even remember her. God, the poor, poor girl.' Donna looked mortified.

Mark looked at Donna, really worried now. 'Donna, Jody's...'

'I don't know how you can live with yourself.' She dragged derisory eyes over him. 'I certainly wouldn't want to live with you.'

'Donna, will you please...'

'And she's so young. She's no more than a mere baby her...'

'Donna, will you please listen!' Mark raised his voice.

Donna blinked, then stepped swiftly back.

'*Christ.* I'm sorry.' Mark realised his mistake. 'Jody is my carer, Donna,' he said, more quietly. 'Karl's carer, that is. I really have *no* idea why you're so upset.'

Donna stared at him, looking more confused than enlightened.

Mark ploughed on. 'And Sally, if that's who you're referring to, is Starbuck's trainer. You must realise that.'

'Well, yes,' Donna conceded, with a shrug, 'I do now, no thanks to you.' She gave him an unimpressed look. 'But, whilst I'm prepared to accept that silken-Sally might not be an 'intimate friend', I'm struggling with Jody-kiss-kiss, who comes to *stay over* bringing a toothbrush and is apparently having your baby.'

'What!?' Mark almost fell over. He stared at Donna, shocked, raked his hand through his hair, smiled, then laughed out loud.

Donna folded her arms. 'I'm glad *you* think the poor girl's predicament is so amusing.' She shot him an ultra-scathing glance this time. 'Couldn't even try to look pleased, could you? Honestly, men like you ought to be locked up for women's safety.'

Mark laughed harder.

'You ought to lock yourself up.'

'Donna,' he managed in between hoots, 'it's not mine.'

Donna's mouth dropped open. 'I don't believe I'm hearing this.'

'The baby's not mine, Donna, I swear.' Mark tried to keep his face straight. 'I doubt Jody's *husband* would be very pleased if it was.'

'She's married?' Donna studied him, the bluster blowing out of her sails.

'Yes.' Mark took his life in his hands and walked over to her. 'To a very nice bloke, who's no doubt ecstatic he's about to become a dad. I, on other hand, am already a dad, Donna; to an autistic child, who's grown used to having Jody around.

'She's Karl's carer, Donna. Of course, I'm pleased for her, but the fact remains, I'm going to have to find a new carer. Someone who cares, you know? And that is going to be hard.'

'Oh,' said Donna, her fury visibly dissipating.

Mark wrapped an arm around her. 'So I take it you were the reason Agnes came flying out of the park like a bat out of hell to wallop me with her ball bag?'

'Um…' Donna looked a bit sheepish.

'I take it you two had a little chat,' Mark enquired interestedly, 'me being the subject of?'

'Yes, but I wasn't running you down,' Donna assured him, looking thoroughly ashamed, which made Mark smile all over again. He doubted she could run anyone down.

'Just girl-talk, you know. The sort one doesn't chat to one's mum about for fear she'll garrotte the subject. It was when we overheard Jody telling you about the baby that Agnes… Wait a minute?' Donna arched a curious eyebrow. 'I didn't know you knew Agnes.'

'Ah, I meant to tell you about that.' Mark nodded, looking uncomfortable. 'I do. We're, er, quite intimate friends, actually. I thought Agnes might have, you know, been jealous when you…'

'Ooh!' Donna narrowed her eyes.

'Uh, uh.' Mark raised his hands defensively. 'Assaulting an officer of the law is a criminal offence, Mrs O'Connor. I may have no choice but to arrest you.'

'Humph.' Donna's mouth twitched into a smile.

'And lock you up… with me, in a very small cell.' Mark took a breath, took a chance and pulled her into his arms. 'In which case, *we* may be forced to become intimate friends. Extremely intimate.' He tentatively sought her mouth, irresistibly drawn to brush her sweet lips with his.

'I think that might be quite, um, cosy,' Donna said breathily, her gaze holding his, soft and inviting.

Mark searched her face, his eyes drinking in the dreamy warmth in hers. This kind, vulnerable, strong woman had bonded with his son, bonded with his very soul. He hadn't thought it was possible.

He lowered his mouth to kiss her, to taste her. He wanted to hold her, to touch and taste every inch of her.

Donna didn't pull away, even when their kiss grew deeper, his hand tracing her back, seeking the soft curve of her hip.

Mark took that as a good sign.

Pausing, out of necessity of breathing, he brushed her hair gently from her neck. Breathed deep the fragrance she wore: feminine and sweet, the scent of the woman he now knew, without question, he adored.

Still Donna hadn't pulled away.

Mark's heart hammered so loud in his chest, he swore she could hear it. He grazed her cheek with his, rode both hands nervously up her thighs.

God, he wanted her.

Wanted to make sweet love to her.

Here.

Right now.

Mark's pulse quickened as Donna's hands found their way under his shirt, nails grazing his back, her lips seeking his, her delicate tongue darting into his mouth.

God, that felt good. And then…

Donna eased back.

Mark's heart stopped.

She glanced down.

Mark eased her chin back up. 'Donna?' He needed her to know, if she said not yet, he'd be fine with it. Desperate, but fine.

Donna chewed on her lip. 'I think this is the bit where the waves lap metaphorically against the shore,' she said, her eyes wide, uncertain, but still inviting.

Mark smiled. 'Whilst keeping one foot on the floor?'

'But of course.' Donna fluttered her eyelashes. 'Even whilst being pursued by a herd of majestic wildebeest, one keeps one's foot...'

Mark kissed her, urgently.

Donna reciprocated, then almost bit off his tongue — as something outside landed not so majestically on the milk bottles.

Chapter Eighteen

'Bloody hell!' Mark pulled back. 'What in God's name was that?'

'I'm not sure.' Donna held tight to him.

'Miaow,' came a very convincing cry from outside.

Thank you, Lord. Donna offered up a prayer of gratitude. It was obviously Simon, who must have dropped from the bedroom window to the porch roof, to the milk bottles and was, thankfully, still in one piece.

'Cats.' She nodded earnestly, and yanked Mark's face back to hers. 'Next door's Tom on the prowl,' she muttered, through lips busy with his, her fingers doing a little bit of walking under his shirt. *Mmm*, but he was toned.

Ooh, how she'd love to get an eyeful as well as a handful. To make love with him. Here and now. Donna felt herself flush scarlet, even as he kissed her, his lovely tongue doing despicable things to her. She couldn't believe it. Where were her inhibitions, her button-up brushed cotton jim-jams?

She was ready to get naked with him, go-go boots a go-go, because he'd made her feel quite beautiful, even if she wasn't, quite.

Alas, inhibitions aside, she couldn't. Not in the lounge. She was a responsible mother, not a good-time girl, even if her dress did indicate otherwise.

Should she take him upstairs? Could she risk it, with Matt due home?

Oh, Lord, what if *he* suggested it. Her eyes sprang open. Mark's were closed. Lovely dark eyelashes. *Mmm*, but she could. God, no she couldn't.

'Damn,' Mark cursed suddenly, reaching for his beeping mobile. 'That'll be Jody. I promised to be back, but some bad person insisted on keeping me out late.'

He glanced at Donna, the lovely twinkle dancing in his eyes. That was better. Donna's heart fluttered in her chest, like magical little butterfly's wings. Twinkly smiles suited him better than tears, though who wouldn't love a man who cried them — for all the right reasons?

'Sorry,' Mark mumbled, grazing her lips again with his, her cheek, her ear.

'For what?' Donna panted, dangerously close now to ravaging him. 'Everything.'

Donna looked deep into his pretty blue eyes. 'So am I,' she said, knowing she'd been hasty and judgemental, factoring out that Mark was human, because she'd lived with someone who'd factored out normal human emotion. 'I shouldn't have jumped to...'

Mark silenced her with his lips. 'I think you probably should have. Can't we just have another go?' he asked softly. 'Try and get it right this time?'

Donna fiddled idly with one of his shirt buttons, knowing things had moved on, and wondering still whether she could live up to what was expected of a person in a relationship.

'No complications,' Mark suggested. 'No demands on each other we're not ready to handle. Just take it one day at a time. What do you think?'

Donna relaxed, marvelling at how she did relax in his company, even dressed like a call girl. 'I think it sounds like a plan.'

'Good.' Mark closed his eyes, obviously relieved. 'Now, what does a man have to do to get a girl to smile around here?'

Fool. She'd been smiling all over, outside and inside. 'You'd be surprised.' Donna laughed, then smothered his gorgeous mouth with hers.

'*Hell.*' Mark groaned as mobile beeped again. 'I really have to go,' he muffled, Donna's lips reluctant to leave his. 'I'll call you, tomorrow, if that's okay?'

'You'd better had,' Donna said with a mock scowl, following him as he walked to the hall, tucking in his assaulted shirt as he went.

'Bye.' He brushed her lips with a last kiss outside the front door, then ran to his car.

Donna waited until he'd started the engine, waving as he pulled off. Then waited again when he stopped.

Mark wound the window down. 'I forgot to say,' he shouted, 'I adore you, Donna O'Connor. Just thought you should know.'

****

Donna had barely reached the top of the stairs when the doorbell rang.

She about-faced on the landing and dashed back down, a gloopy smile all over her face.

'Only me.' Simon beamed as she opened the door.

Oh, no! Donna almost choked, this time on nothing but fresh air. 'Simon, what are you doing?' She glanced worriedly past him. 'Mark has only just left.'

'I know, but I can't go home in this, can I?' Simon indicated his uniformed state of dress. 'My cap and coat are upstairs, with my keys in the pocket.'

Donna closed her eyes, thanking God she hadn't got carried away and dragged Mark up there. 'Quick,' she beckoned him in, leaving the door on the latch.

Simon darted upstairs whilst Donna hovered nervously in the hall.

'Donna, I can't find my cap,' Simon called. 'Any ideas?'

'Dressing table, right-hand side.'

'Nope, not there.'

Hell. Donna flew up the stairs.

'Got it,' Simon announced, dragging the cap from under the dressing table and promptly plopping it on the bed.

'*Noooo!* Not on the bed.' Donna dashed over to snatch it up. Hats on beds were terribly bad luck, didn't he real…?

'Donna?'

Oh, God. Donna's heart stopped dead.

She turned around, trepidation snaking its way icily down her spine.

Mark dragged confused eyes slowly from Donna, to a still-uniformed Simon. 'Jody was texting me to say there was no rush, so I, er…' Mark stopped, his gaze now fixed on the one silly fishnet dangling from the edge of the bed.

He looked back to Donna, trailing his eyes from the top of her boots, to the too-short hem of her dress, to her breasts; then to her face, his own face a kaleidoscope of emotion, from disbelief through fury to contempt.

Donna stepped towards him. 'Mark, I…'

Mark stepped back, the look in his eye freezing the words on her lips. 'Not bad, is she?' he addressed Simon calmly, who stood immobile and apprehensive.

'It's not how it…' Simon faltered. 'We weren't…'

'Right little goer, in fact,' Mark cut him short.

Donna's heart flipped in her chest. 'Mark, it's not what you...'

'But, you know, I'm thinking she might be right,' Mark went on angrily, 'not on the bed, sunshine, because if you do, I might just have to break your neck.'

'He forgot... his... coat,' Donna stuttered.

'Now there's a coincidence.' Mark sneered sarcastically.

'Simon, tell him!' Donna beseeched.

Simon though, under Mark's unwavering glare, was apparently dumbstruck.

'Mark, for God's sake, he's *gay*! You met him in the pub.'

'Right,' Mark laughed contemptuously. 'So, not your brother, rather your sister?'

'No.' Donna shook her head hopelessly. 'Please listen, Mark. I can't explain if you...'

'No explanations necessary, Donna,' Mark assured her, an angry tic going at his cheek. 'Gay, bi-sexual, whatever. It really doesn't bother me what sort of perverse erotica does it for either of you.'

Donna's stomach turned over. 'Mark, don't, please. I...'

'Oh, and I obviously *forgot* something else, didn't I?' Mark dragged disgusted eyes away from her, pulled out his wallet and tossed two twenty pound notes at her feet. 'I'm assuming you're not charging full price as we didn't have full sex?'

Donna stared at him, stunned.

'Maybe I'll ring and make another appointment.' Mark broke the palpable silence. 'Maybe not. Oh, the dress suits you, by the way. Very appropriate.'

He ran a hand across his neck and turned away.

'Look,' Simon found the use of his voice and went after him, 'I know how it looks, but...'

Mark swung around, his fist clenching and unclenching at his side, pure murder in his eyes. 'Get out of my face,' he seethed, 'before I'm tempted to do something I might well regret.'

'Mark, don't!' Donna placed herself bodily between them, her heart racing. 'You're acting like a child. Let Simon...'

She stopped, flinching as Mark raised his hand; to rake it through his hair in that demonstrative way he had, she realised that immediately, but Simon's reaction, born of some protective instinct, was to lurch forward and grab Mark's arm.

He might as well have stung him with a cattle prod. The next few seconds flashed by in fast-forward. Something snapped in Mark's eyes. In one swift movement, he reached over Donna and clutched at Simon's collar. Simon backed off, stumbled and fell.

'Stop it!' Donna screamed, and pushed Mark away, hard. 'Stop it! He's been in the hospital, for God's sake!'

Bewildered, she turned away to help poor Simon to his feet and seat him shakily on the edge of the bed. Then, furious, she turned back to Mark.

'You're no better than Jeremy.' She looked him up and down, appalled. 'Get out.'

Mark didn't budge.

'I said, get out, Mark. Go!'

Ashen-faced, Mark moved hesitantly towards her. 'Donna, I... Is he all right? Christ, I'm sorry. I didn't mean — '

'Don't bother, Mark.' Donna glared at him. 'Just *go,* will you.'

****

Donna tried to see things through Mark's eyes as she held the silly dress against her in front of the mirror. Oh, God, it *was* short. Far too short to be flaunting herself in front of another man in — in her bedroom. How else could it have looked to Mark than how it did? She cringed inside, picturing the scene.

As for the rest of her... Donna looked herself over and groaned. She'd slept so fitfully, her hair had died of fright in the night. It was vertical. All she needed now was a blue rinse and she could go to the party as Marge-flipping-Simpson. Her complexion wasn't up to much either, not so much pale, as grey, apart from a teeny triangle of blusher.

Did she care, she asked herself. Yes, was the short answer. After Mark's onslaught of insults last night, Donna would quite like to find one or two redeeming features, tonight being party night, to which she'd absolutely had to go, for Simon's sake. Right now, she looked like an extra from *Dawn of the Dead* and her only redeeming features were her retro-sixties earrings, which she'd gone to bed in.

What she needed was an outfit that would disguise her haggard bits and enhance her good bits. A sheet, she mused, with peepholes?

He'd had no problem with the length of her dress when he'd slid his hands up her thighs though, had he? Her tummy flipped and dived.

No, it wasn't about the dress, she realised despondently. Mark's problem had been jealousy, which was surely an indication of his true temperament. Whatever he saw, whatever he *thought* he saw. Whatever *erotica* he thought she was into — a word she'd have to look up in the dictionary to know where to start, there were no excuses for violence. And Simon, a kind, considerate man, had been on the receiving end of that violence.

'Cooee,' came a familiar voice outside the bedroom door, 'only me. Are you decent?'

'No,' Donna replied glumly.

Simon came in anyway. 'Oh, dear, no you're not, are you?' He came across the room to peer at her at close quarters. 'Ye Gods, woman, you look dreadful. You'll be scaring the guests away.'

'Thank you, Simon. Most considerate.'

'Come on.' He sighed, plucked the dress from her grasp and tossed it aside. 'Evelyn and Alicia are downstairs, ready to give you moral support and a makeover.'

'Oh, goody.' Donna eyed her bed longingly, as Simon hustled her past it.

The bush drums had obviously been beating then, Simon no doubt having rung Alicia, Alicia then straight on the phone to Mother with hot-gossip.

'Make way.' Simon flapped a hand as they met Matt on the landing. 'Relationship casualty in need of urgent girl-talk.

'Ooh, I like that.' He stopped to peruse Matt's tee shirt, emblazoned *Weapon of Mass Destraction*, his casualty carelessly abandoned behind him. 'Recent purchase?' he asked, hopefully.

'Internet,' Matt informed him, bending to heave little Jack into his arms, who hero-worshipped Matt wherever he went. 'I'll email you the addy.'

'You're an angel.' Simon beamed, and turned back to pluck up Donna's hand. 'Come on then, sweetie, let's get you psychoanalysed and sorted,' he said, heading purposefully onwards.

'*Ping*,' said Donna, indicating Matt's shining halo as she was dragged past him.

Matt glanced at the ceiling. 'Taking Jack into Protective Custody,' he said, heading for his bedroom and PC-play heaven in delighted Jack's eyes.

'An absolute angel.' Donna blinked gratefully over her shoulder, then almost slid down the stairs after Simon.

'Here she is,' Simon announced, leading her into the lounge. 'Make yourself comfy, Dons,' he said, oblivious to the fact that Donna lived there. 'I'll go and make some espresso with a little dash of *hair o' the dog*. That'll put the colour back in your cheeks.'

Donna wasn't sure she wanted any more colour in her cheeks. She flushed furiously as Evelyn flew out of her recliner and immediately demanded, 'What did that despicable man do to you, my darling?' as if Mark had broken the lock on her chastity belt.

'More to the point,' Alicia unfurled her feet from the sofa and patted the seat next to her, '*how* did he do?'

'Alicia, behave,' Evelyn gave her a no-nonsense look. 'Donna's been through a trauma.'

'Trauma?' Alicia sat back with a smirk. 'Snogging a gorgeous policeman? I don't think so.'

Donna blinked. 'How do you know I?'

Simon poked his head back around the door. 'Sorry, Dons,' he said sheepishly, 'but you know what Alicia's like, she wanted chapter and verse – and obviously I couldn't help but see,' he waved a finger at the window '… a bit, when I climbed down from the bedroom.'

Evelyn looked to the window, then to Donna, one plucked eyebrow raised archly. 'So, you were kissing Mark in the lounge, while Simon was up in the bedroom?'

'Snogging,' Alicia offered, sitting up to attention now. 'Heavily. Tongues *and* hands.'

'Yes, but Simon's no threat to anyone, is he?' Donna pointed out, blushing now to the tips of her ears. 'Especially dead,' she added, with a scowl.

'And then Mark caught you both together up there, semi-clothed?' Evelyn asked, incredulous.

'Donna was semi,' Simon supplied informatively, swinging back in with the espresso-laden tray. 'I was suited and booted in Mark's spare uniform.'

Evelyn, normally unflappable, came over all faint and willowy. 'Well,' she said, sinking down next to Alicia, 'no wonder the poor man lost his temper.'

She looked at Donna, astonished. As did Alicia.

Donna laughed, flabbergasted. What was this? A trial? *Her* trial? 'Excuse me,' she huffed, indignantly, 'but would you like to explain why you're all looking at me as if I've been caught posing in the Centrefold of Playgirl?'

'Er, that would be Playboy, Donna,' Simon ventured.

Donna glared at him.

'It's just that Playgirl is… Well, it's where you'll find men on the centre…'

'Shut up, Simon!'

Simon dutifully zipped his lips.

Donna turned her glare back to her mother and sister. 'Now then, first of all, the only reason I was *semi-dressed* was because I was trying on my fancy-dress. Secondly, if anyone here is a *poor man*, it's Simon.' Donna got into the role and pointed at him, deciding if she were on trial, she better blooming well defend herself.

Simon, bless his socks, took his cue and nodded sadly.

'*He* was the one on the receiving end of violent behaviour. *Mark* was the one dishing it out, so why on earth does everyone seem to be leaping to his defence?'

'In his defence though, Donna, he did find us in a rather compromising position,' Simon pointed out.

'But we weren't doing anything!' Donna countered, despairingly.

'That's not quite how it would have looked from Mark's point of view, Sweetie, me in his jacket, both of us in the bedroom, your fishnets discarded willy-nilly.'

'Fishnets!? Ooh, well done, Donna.' Alicia looked mightily pleased for her.

Evelyn looked mortified. 'With go-go boots and a mini dress.' She pressed a hand to her brow. 'Oh, Donna, Donna, where is your fashion sense?'

'I'm not sure.' On the basis that she couldn't afford to follow fashion, Donna felt a bit miffed. 'I think I left it in the charity shop.'

Wondering whose side her mum actually was on, Donna turned back to Simon. 'Simon, I don't like to point out the hole in your defence of your *attacker*, but you're gay, remember?'

'Mark didn't know that though, did he?' Simon paused to pluck up Findus, who'd hopped into the lounge in search of tasty laces. 'We didn't actually converse in the pub, did we, and I don't wear a sign around my neck, Donna.'

'Well, there you are, then.' Evelyn said, helping herself to coffee and biscuits. 'Mark had very good cause, I'd say.'

Mark's side then. Donna stared at her mum disbelieving, who had a ladylike nibble of her biscuit, and completely missed the point. 'Good cause?! He lost his temper, Mum! Hit first and asked questions later. And even if he had asked and didn't like the answers, he did *not* have good cause for violence.'

Donna's cheeks were blazing now. She was close to losing *her* temper. Could they not see? There was no excuse for hitting out like that. For saying the dreadful things he had.

'Donna, I know you've reason to be upset, sweetie,' Simon ventured, 'but I think most people would be inclined to lose it a bit if they found their loved one practically in bed with someone else, don't you think?'

Donna shook her head. Yes, they would, probably, but... Mark didn't know her. If he did, he'd know that that just wasn't her.

'I'd certainly lose it,' Alicia put in. 'I'd boil his bunny *and* serve it up in a pie.'

'There's also one small detail you might be overlooking, Dons,' Simon said, from where he was seated in the armchair, his hands placed sensitively over Findus' bunny ears 'I grabbed Mark's arm first, didn't I? So, if Mark's a condemned man, I suppose I should be hung along with him.' He smiled sympathetically and offered her a chocolate biscuit.

****

'He checks on his father most days, you know?' Evelyn remarked ever-so-casually to Simon on the way out. 'A lot of men wouldn't. And then, there's his little boy, of course, whom he obviously adores. Such a caring man.'

Evelyn sighed expansively and glanced over her shoulder at Donna.

Simon sighed too and placed a hand on his heart, which was obviously all aflutter.

'What are they, a double act?' Donna whispered to Alicia, as they followed them up the hall.

'They're just looking out for you, hon,' Alicia smiled reassuringly.

'I know.' Donna smiled wanly back, but wished they wouldn't.

'I think Donna could do a lot worse.' Evelyn reached for her coat.

'Well, just between you and me, so do I.' Simon nodded sagely as he reached for his sou'wester.

'Simon…' Donna gave him a despairing glance.

'What?' Simon saucered innocent eyes. 'Can I help it if I'd rather have been caught *in flagrante* with your boyfriend, than you?'

Donna blushed, furiously.

'Ring him, Dons.' Simon gave her shoulders a quick squeeze. 'He's scrummy, *and* he's nice with it. You know he is. Give him a chance.'

'Do you want me to speak to him?' Evelyn asked, tugging on her coat. 'I'm round at Dot's tomorrow. He usually calls on Robert on Sunday evenings.'

Robert now, was it? Donna arched an eyebrow. It wasn't so long ago that the man had nil intellect and Neanderthal manners: Mark's father. She hadn't even met him.

'Mum, if I want Mark spoken to, I'll speak to him.' Which she probably wouldn't, Donna suspected, because she doubted Mark would climb down off his moral high horse and speak to her.

'Well, just give me a ring in the morning, if you…'

'Mum! I'm a big girl now. I have a big son to prove it. I can fight my own battles.'

Evelyn looked crestfallen. 'I know,' she conceded, 'but once a mum… Ring me anyway.'

Evelyn headed for the door, then stopped, and turned back. 'I don't mean to fight your battles for you, Donna.'

Simon loitered, not sure whether to get on his bike or not.

'See you later,' Alicia mouthed and steered him on.

Evelyn glanced at the door, once it was closed. 'It's just… Well, I know, you don't want to be like me, Donna, seeing everything as a crusade, even relationships.'

Oh, Lord. Donna glanced guiltily down. Now she'd gone and upset her mum, too.

'The thing is though, darling, I've had to fight — most my life, really. Not to be defined by society. Not to be defined by the men in my life. I didn't want my daughters to be stifled in the same way.'

'Mum, I…' Donna started, feeling awful now. Her mum had always done her absolute best, even with no support from her husband.

Evelyn held up a silencing hand. 'I'm just trying to say I'm beginning to realise a bit of give and take might sometimes be in order. Your Mark has had a small part to play in that. I'm sorry,' she said, as Donna glanced down again, 'but I thought it should be said.'

'As for you,' Evelyn did what Mark did then, eased Donna's chin back up, 'I can see you know what you want in a man. You'll make your own decisions. Just don't make hasty ones based on bad experience, hmm?'

Donna nodded, then gave Evelyn a huge hug. 'I won't,' she promised. 'And I'm quite proud to have a mum who cares enough to want to fight people's battles, actually.'

'So long as I don't do so stridently sometimes,' Evelyn guessed. 'Right, I'm off. I've promised to look in on Robert. Lord knows why. I have to remind him who I am half the time. And then he'll probably insult me. Do you know what he offered me the other day? Iced buns.'

Donna crinkled her much-furrowed brow as Evelyn turned for the door.

'Said I could be his *Calendar Girl* anytime. I mean, do I look like Helen Mirren?'

Donna hesitated. 'Um, now you come to mention...'

'Honestly, men.'

'They're all the same,' Donna finished, smirking as Evelyn's walk developed a definite wiggle.

Chapter Nineteen

'But I've already done my hair,' Donna protested, not happy with Alicia forking out, no matter how generous her maintenance payments.

'Yes, but I didn't know that when I booked it, did I?' Alicia marched purposefully into the beauty salon, Donna trailing behind. 'Anyway, we're having the works, manicure, pedicure and facial, so you might as well settle down and have your hair styled as well. Oh, and we're having a cellulite treatment.'

'Oh, no we are not,' Donna assured her. 'I've learned to love my thighs, thank you. They're the only bit I *don't* need to pluck and preen before I dare be seen in public.' Because they were usually covered up, but still... 'And it doesn't work anyway,' she announced, much to the chagrin of the beautician.

Half an hour later, Donna was as slippery as an eel and her thighs, she suspected, still looked the same as they did when she got out of bed.

Still, by the time that she had her manicure and pedicure, and her face *golden toned and shimmered to add an illusion of radiance and youthful luminosity*, she did feel a lot better. 'Not too bad, I suppose.' She smiled through the mirror at her similarly shimmered sister.

Her hair looked lovely, too. Lord knew how they'd managed to *loosely finger dry it* into bouncy, glossy curls, but Donna wasn't complaining. It looked better than Jody's, she thought in a guilty moment of vanity, then immediately thought of Mark and paused to retrieve her heart, which had dropped to about toned thigh level.

'Come on, chop chop.' Alicia bundled her out of the salon. 'Next stop, *The Shop*,' she announced strutting forth.

'No, Alicia.' Donna eyed *The Shop*-front where all manner of tease-and-please outfits were displayed. 'Absolutely not. Alicia?

Drat. Donna skidded in after her.

'The velour bodice and thong I think.' Alicia mused out loud, having emptied the shop faster than a fire alarm would.

Donna gawked. 'You're not seriously going to wear that?'

'No.' Alicia was now busy eyeing up another outrageous outfit. '*You* are.'

'Oh, no I'm...'

'Yes, Donna, you are. You're Madonna.'

'I'm not,' Donna refuted. 'I'm a hippie-chick.'

'A very sad little chick, judging by the look I saw on your face when you showed me the dress. Ditch it, Donna. It looked great, but it wasn't making you feel very great, was it, after... certain events.'

Donna chewed on her lip. She was right. The last thing Donna wanted to do after last night was put that outfit on again tonight, with or without funny-coloured tights.

'If you're going to get called a good-time girl, then give the guy good reason, I say, and go for it. Let it all hang out and have a blooming good time.'

Donna wasn't sure she'd got that much to hang out, but she was warming to the idea. Strutting her stuff in leather and lace and having a laugh sounded infinitely more inviting than being miserable. And Alicia had been so selfless, bless her stockings.

'In any case, I'm going as Cher and I'm not walking in dressed in nothing but a string vest on my own.'

****

'Oh, *grrreat.*' Mark sighed as he turned the corner into his father's road, to see Evelyn's Mini parked outside Dot's, which meant, if Evelyn wasn't already there, she'd make sure to pop around to his father's. To give *him* a piece of her mind no doubt, demanding explanations that he didn't feel inclined to offer.

'Problem?' Phil asked.

'Donna's mother,' Mark supplied. 'And I really do *not* need this, right now.'

He didn't either. After what happened with Donna, him subsequently driving home like a maniac, torn between anger and guilt, to find Starbuck ill... No, he didn't need this.

'Do you want to give it a miss? We can always swing by later,' Phil suggested.

'No. Thanks, Phil, but I'd better check up on him now with things being so up in the air at home.' Mark smiled appreciatively.

It wasn't often he offloaded his problems onto his partner, but he had tonight, supposing he at least owed Phil an explanation for coming on duty half-unconscious after staying up most of the night with Karl.

'Right.' Phil nodded, as Mark pulled up. 'Good luck,' he said sombrely.

'I'll need it.' Mark rolled his eyes, raked his hand through his hair, and reached for the door.

'If you're not out in fifteen minutes, I'll call for backup.'

'Cheers.' Mark laughed, climbed wearily out of the car and headed for his father's house. He could probably have given it a miss for once, with Dot and their very own warrior woman next door, but he would rest easier knowing his dad was okay.

Dammit, he should've given it a miss. Mark shook his head as he walked in, almost too exhausted to be bemused when Evelyn greeted him, 'You've got a nerve, showing your face —'

'Here?' Mark finished, turning to close the door and counting to five as he did so.

'Anywhere,' Evelyn assured him, standing arms folded and barring his way up the hall.

Mark shoved his hands in his pockets. 'Yes, well, I'm sorry about that, Evelyn. I'd top myself to make the world a happier place for you but, unfortunately, I have people who depend on me. Excuse me.' He nodded past her to the lounge.

Evelyn stood aside, reluctantly.

'How is he?' Mark asked, careful to avoid the well-aimed daggers she was shooting at him as he passed.

'Well, I'm not sure whether he's in the First World War or the nineteen-fifties. He's definitely in the African Queen though.'

Mark's mouth twitched into a smile. And Evelyn was Katharine Hepburn, presumably. He glanced at her. Yep, he could see her sinking the boat for a good cause.

'Hi, Dad,' Mark said, going in. 'What's up?'

'Leeches, son. Leeches.' Robert tsked. 'There's some nasty things in rivers, you know?'

Mark glanced at the TV. 'Humph will save the day though, hey?'

'And the woman.' Robert chuckled. 'Your mother loves this film, you know? Only saw it at the cinema a while back, and now it's on TV. Amazing.'

'It's a DVD,' Evelyn confided, when Mark went back to the hall. 'He was babbling on about it the other night, so...' She shrugged...

... *As if she didn't give a damn about anyone?* Mark hid a smile.

'I can hear you, woman,' Robert shouted from his armchair. 'Anyone would think I was deaf.' He huffed and turned the volume up.

'Early sixties at a guess,' Mark informed Evelyn. 'And I've a sneaking suspicion you're currently his wife.'

Evelyn paled.

Mark did smile then. 'I have to go. I'm on duty. You know where to reach me if you or Dot need to.'

'Yes, pity Donna doesn't know how to reach *you*,' Evelyn said as he headed for the door. 'Or you her. What were you thinking, Mark?'

Mark stopped. 'I wasn't.' He shrugged, his back to her.

'But you said some terrible things to her. And to hit out at someone without establishing the...'

'Evelyn, I have to go. My partner's outside. I can't do this now.'

'But why, Mark? You were getting along so well, apparently, and then...'

'And then, I found her in the bedroom with another man, Evelyn.' Mark turned around. 'How would you have felt?'

'Confused, upset, angry,' Evelyn conceded, 'jealous.'

'All of those,' Mark admitted. 'As for why I lost it,' he shrugged awkwardly, 'because I was toying with the idea of asking you to become my mother-in-law, God help me. I have to go.'

'Wear them,' Alicia instructed, whilst smudging her eye-liner into a sultry Egyptian Cher look. 'They're supposed to look tarty. It's fancy dress. It's allowed. And they make your legs look longer.'

'They make my legs look like two beanpoles.' Donna sighed, glancing down at blood-red stilettos, which were definitely not made for walking.

'Donna, they don't. Your legs are fine. Now come on, let's pop your boobs in and go, or the party will be over.' With which Alicia twanged Donna's bodice forward and stuffed two sock-stuffed polystyrene cups down her frontage.

'There.' She stood back to admire her handiwork. 'What do you think? One in the eye for Mark, or what?'

'Two, I should think.' Donna curled a lip. 'Very fetching, Alicia. Thank you.'

'Right.' Alicia grabbed her purple Cher wig. 'Let's go get 'em,' she said, steering Donna along the landing towards the stairs. 'I just hope there's some worth getting.'

'Actually, I don't want one, thank you.' Donna tentatively tested the stairs with her heels.

'No, well, you wouldn't just now,' Alicia conceded. 'In which case, we'll stick with the original plan of dancing around handbags.'

'Thanks. Alicia,' Donna said, grateful that Alicia was caring enough to give up a night with her new boyfriend to make sure Donna didn't have to go to the party alone.

'We don't need men to have a good boogie,' Alicia assured her. 'Sisters are doing it for themselves. Whoa!'

'Eventually.' Donna tried another step.

'Go on,' Alicia urged her from behind. 'The taxi will be here.'

'I'm trying.'

'Talking of which, I'm going to have to get the taxi to drop me straight back afterwards. Babysitter needs to get back, apparently. Will you be all right?'

'Of course I will. I'm not about to fall apart,' Donna assured her, finally having managed the treacherous descent of the stairs. 'Over, yes.'

'Wow, fit.' Matt wolf-whistled, appearing from the lounge. 'The blonde one's yours, Ed.'

'Cool.' His friend raised an interested pierced eyebrow behind him. 'Er, they're both blonde, Matt.'

Alicia winked and plopped the wig on her head. 'Your lucky night, Ed.'

'Yeah, right.' Ed sloped to the front door ahead of Matt. 'Yours is the purple one, Matt.'

'Mum,' Matt turned back, as Donna teetered towards her coat hanging in the hall, then swung from it, 'as we're in party spirit...'

'Ye-es?' Donna righted herself and eyed her son warily.

'I thought I might invite a few friends around.'

Donna paled under her luminescence. 'When?'

'One night next week, for my birthday.'

'Oh.' Donna pondered, whilst trying out her new spin on multitasking, staying upright in her shoes *and* putting her coat on. 'Well...'

'It'll be cheaper than an alternative present.'

'Which might be?' Alicia enquired, obviously on Donna's wavelength as to whether cheaper was worth risking good neighbourhood relations for.

'Nubile young female and a small island in the Bahamas.' Matt looked ever-so hopeful.

Donna laughed. 'Go on then.'

'Great. I quite like blondes, but...'

'The party, Matt,' Donna informed him, skirting around a sleeping Sadie for fear of spearing her to the hall floor.

'Damn, didn't work, Ed.' Matt sloped on out.

'But no weird-looking friends or alcohol over-indulgence,' Donna called after him.

'Yes, Mother.' Matt cocked a bemused eye over his shoulder as Donna staggered to the hall cupboard to pluck up her party supplies: a four-pack of lager and bottle of wine.

****

As much as Donna didn't want a man, she got one — a cross-dressed one.

'Hi, I'm Daniel.' He leapt on her as she teetered between kitchen and lounge in search of more wine, two glasses not being nearly enough to let go of her inhibitions. 'Area Sales Manager, Winterseal Windows, at your service.'

He offered his hand, then cocked his head to one side. 'Don't I know you?' he asked, squinting at her curiously.

'Possibly.' Donna smiled. 'Madonna. Do you go to many of my concerts?'

'Haw, haw.' He chuckled. 'I can see you're a bit of a wit.'

'Yes.' Donna rolled her eyes, and resisted saying, *and I can see you're a bit of a twit.*

He was actually probably perfectly lovely, but Donna really didn't want to do this. All she wanted to do was *let her hair down*, so long as her new bouncy, glossy look didn't sag, and have a good time dancing around her handbag.

'Are you cold?' Daniel asked, moving around in front of her as she attempted to walk on.

As she was still swathed in her coat, Donna supposed it must look that way. 'A bit,' she said, not ready to reveal her polystyrene boobs just yet.

'That'll be the single glazing.' Daniel nodded knowledgeably, and promptly launched into his sales patter.

The gymslip was a bit off-putting but he was quite reasonable looking Donna supposed, another wine later.

Having learned where her soffits were and the merits of hardwood versus UPVC, she stifled a yawn, then sighed relieved as the cavalry arrived in the form of Alicia. 'Can I drag you away for a sec,' she asked, dragging Donna away anyway.

'He looks all right.' Alicia nodded back at Daniel as they headed for the lounge. 'Nice legs.'

'He seems to be,' Donna shouted as Robbie Williams was cranked up a gear. 'It's just…'

He wasn't Mark. The thought popped into Donna's head uninvited. She was beginning to wish she had rung him. The worst he could have done was hang up. But then, she did have her pride. She hoisted up the shoulders. He should be doing the ringing after the things he'd said. The awful way he'd looked at her.

Recalling the open disdain she'd seen in Mark's eyes, Donna suddenly found herself close to tears. But no, she'd promised herself she wouldn't, and so she wouldn't. She dragged a hand under her nose.

Mark Evans could go to hell. Meanwhile, she, adorable Donna — ho, ho — was going to have herself a blooming good time.

'I know, hon.' Alicia patted Donna's arm tucked through hers. 'Come on, come and dance. There's a girly-group on the floor already.'

'Cooee, Dons!' Simon — who'd apparently been upstairs attending to hitch with his late change of costume — dashed over as they went into the lounge. 'No, don't tell me.' He stood back to take in Donna's attire. 'Got it. A coat.'

'Sorry?' Donna looked at him askew.

'You've come as an overcoat, haven't you?' He nodded enthusiastically. 'It's very good.'

Alicia sighed. 'Take it off, Donna.'

'I will. In a minute,' Donna said, feeling quite attached to her coat for some reason.

'And you're Eddie Izzard in drag.' Simon beamed at Alicia.

Alicia didn't look impressed. 'Cher, actually. And what are you supposed to be?'

'A boxer, obviously.' Simon flapped open his dressing gown to flash his silk boxers.

'Oh, right. Make-up looks good.' Alicia nodded, indicating Simon's black eye. 'It looks just like the real thing.'

Simon glanced worriedly at Donna. 'Um, well, actually...'

Donna paled. 'Oh, no, Simon... You mean... But, he didn't...'

'No, he didn't. Stop with the guilt, hmm? I caught it on the bedside table when I fell. You can hardly see it with concealer on, in any case, so...'

'God, Simon...' Donna's heart sank all over again.

'It happened. It's over.' Simon waved a dismissive hand. 'Forget it.'

Oh, that Donna could forget it, with her mum practically moved in with Mark's dad, little Karl who she couldn't avoid seeing. Her chest heaving under her polystyrene cups every time she thought about Mark. And now this. She looked at Simon's poor eye. He must have worn his concealer this morning. Bless him. He really was the kindest soul.

'I am *so* sorry, Simon,' Donna said, feeling absolutely terrible. And guilty, no matter how many times Simon told her not to.

'Sorry for what, exactly?' Simon gave her a despairing glance. 'It was just an unfortunate accident born of normal human reaction. The man was crushed, Donna. I could see it in his gorgeous blue eyes. And, trust me, I can read men's eyes. So stop beating yourself up with it.'

'I'll try.' Donna made a magnificent effort to arrange her face into a smile.

'You two need to start talking.' Simon gave her shoulders a squeeze. 'I'd say put your pride in your pocket and ring him, but I'm betting he rings you first.'

She would, Donna decided. She would ring him, if only to clear the air for when they did cross each other's paths, which well they might. The whole *I'm not talking to him/her* thing was terribly childish, after all. And in the middle of it was a child, who needed his father to be there for him, not emotionally distracted by nonsense.

'So, come on. What do you think?' Simon tactfully changed the subject and gave them a twirl.

'Rocky,' Donna read daubed across his dressing gown. 'Very good, Simon.'

'And this,' Simon wrapped an arm around Nathan's shoulders, as he appeared with drinks, 'is Rocky Two. My very own personal rock.'

Simon relieved Nathan of the drinks, swapping adoring glances with him as he did. 'However, being not the selfish sort, I'm loaning him to you, Donna. Dance with the girl, Nathan, but be gentle with her.' Simon drew a hand around his chest area and mouthed, 'Broken heart.'

Nathan laughed and crooked his arm. 'Dance, ma'am?'

'Well... Oh, all right then. Why not?' Donna dragged herself from the gloom, and accepted his offer.

'Oh, Dons,' Simon called, as they headed for the Moroccan rug come dance-floor.

Donna glanced back.

Simon waved a hand over his whole body area this time, indicating Donna's camouflage.

Which Donna was feeling a bit hot under, actually. Time for the great unveiling. She had a surreptitious glance around, then shrugged self-consciously out of her coat — and no one batted an eyelid. Humph.

Donna was nicely into the bump to Stevie Wonder's, *Signed, Sealed, Delivered* when Daniel tapped Nathan on the shoulder.

'May I?' he asked, nodding towards Donna, obviously a gentleman, despite the gymslip.

'May he?' Nathan enquired.

'He may.' Donna laughed, and gracefully accepted.

Ten seconds later she was doing a sort of soft-shoe-shuffle with Daniel, when he asked, 'Was I boring you?'

'No, not at all.' Donna smiled warmly and felt a bit bad for giving him the slip. The poor soul probably had a history of boring people to death.

'Good.' Daniel smiled back, and Donna decided he was actually quite sweet.

And she, she realised, as she went over on one spindly-heel, then the other, might just be getting ever-so-slightly tipsy.

Daniel provided her a steadying hand as she swayed, but not in time to the music. 'You okay?' he shouted.

'Never better,' Donna assured him, then in true Madonna persona, did a virginal strut across the carpet, to which Daniel reciprocated with a pouting Mick Jagger strut of his own.

Excellent therapy. Donna was having a ball. Inhibitions? Her? Never.

She was Sandy, bouncy curls, pert bum and all. Daniel was Travolta. Simon, Nathan and Alicia were Pink Ladies, and they were all hot to trot. Move over Dame Edna Everage. Or not.

Dame Edna refused to be sidelined, so Donna had a quick strut with him, too. Or her? Donna squinted cross-eyed, then decided on male when Edna trod on her foot. Undaunted, Donna had a quick *Saturday Night Fever* pointy-finger pose with Alicia, followed by a dizzying fling with Braveheart, who promptly declared undying love and threw himself at her feet.

Wonderful. Donna stopped for a quick drink break. She could quite get into this good-time-girl stuff. She was having a whale of a time. Or she was, until Braveheart decided to have a little breather, perched his posterior on the window ledge, and fell through the window.

Which might not have been so bad, Donna suspected, had the window been open at the time.

'Bloody *hell!*' Simon stopped halfway through a *Hey Margarita* and flew to the front door in pursuit of the flying Scotsman — followed smartly by a houseful of revellers.

'Didn't feel a thing,' Braveheart said from his spread-eagled position on the front lawn. 'Anaeshthetished,' he slurred, then, to the immense relief of everyone, caught hold of two helping hands and heaved himself up.

Alicia gave his rather large kilted rump a pat, as he steadied himself on his feet. 'That'll be the padding, honey.'

'Sorry about the window, Simon,' Braveheart apologised, as soberly as he could.

'Me too.' Simon eyed the missing lounge window forlornly. 'Ah, well, never mind. Hopefully, the insurance will cover it. I suppose we'd better get some of the glass off the lawn though.'

'I'll help,' Donna offered.

'Thanks, guys,' Simon said as Donna and Alicia carefully picked up some of the bigger shards.

'Single glazing.' Daniel shook his head, and pitched in.

'I'll get something to tape over the window,' Nathan said, turning back towards the house.

'There's some cardboard in the garage, I think,' Simon called after him. 'And turn the music down, while you're at it, Nathe, or we'll have the neighbours complaining.'

'I think they already have.' Daniel nodded at the approaching patrol car.

'Oh, no.' Donna shrank in her blood-red stilettos, literally, they being spiked in the mud.

Alicia came to stand side-by-side with her sister. 'You all right, hon?'

'Perfect.' Donna straightened her shoulders, pulled in a breath — and puffed up her polystyrene cups.

****

'At least it isn't him.' Alicia said as the WPC addressed Simon.

'Thank God for small mercies.' Donna breathed a sigh of relief. Whether or not she was obviously wearing fancy dress this time, she didn't think her velour bodice and pointy breasts would go a long way to clearing the air between Mark and her. 'Everything, all right, Simon?' she called.

'Yes, thanks, Dons,' Simon assured her. 'The officer's just taking a few details. You go on in and pop the kettle on, why don't you? And then we can all have some nice chocy biccies. Would you like one?' He fluttered his eyelashes at the woman police officer.

'At least it isn't who?' Daniel asked

'Donna's ex,' Alicia informed him. 'The one Simon had a little run in with. He's a policeman.' She circled her own eye, with a sad sigh.

'Your *ex* gave him the black eye?' Daniel asked, looking at Donna shocked.

'It was an accident,' Alicia supplied. 'He was a bit jealous, that's all. As one would be when one finds one's girlfriend *in flagrante* with another man.'

'Ah, right.' Daniel looked at Donna again, bemusedly this time.

Donna looked nervously towards the officers, wondering whether poor Simon was going to get arrested for causing a public affray or something, which really would put the kibosh on his birthday celebrations.

Oh, obviously not. She looked on relieved as the WPC munched on a chocolate biscuit supplied by Nathan, quite obviously won over by Simon's charms.

'Well, there doesn't seem to have been any aggressive behaviour,' she mumbled, stuffing the last of her biscuit in her mouth and accepting another.

'We do have to issue a warning re noise nuisance though,' her partner pointed out. 'Just keep it down, okay?'

Simon cocked his head to one side. 'Well, of course we will,' he said. 'We wouldn't dream of deliberately causing a nuisance, but... Is that it?'

'Yes. Pretty much. Enjoy the rest of your night.' The WPC offered Simon and Nathan a smile in exchange for a third biscuit, then the officers turned to head back to their patrol car.

'You on tomorrow, then, Rachel?' The male officer asked as they approached Donna and company.

'Not sure,' the WPC answered, through mouthfuls. 'Said I'd cover for Mark if he needed me to. His kid's dog's sick, apparently.'

'His kid's dog?' The PC looked incredulous. 'I've heard them all now.'

The WPC gave him a scathing glance. 'The boy's autistic, Gary. Give the man a break.'

Chapter Twenty

'He must be really ill if Mark's taking time off,' Donna was talking to herself, rather than Daniel, who'd kindly offered her a lift home.

'Who?' Daniel asked, squinting through the wipers sloshing against a deluge of rain.

'Starbuck.' Donna chewed on her lip, worrying about the dog, about Karl, about Mark — and feeling irritated with Daniel, even though he'd considerately swapped his gymslip for his trousers and offered both

Alicia and her a lift home. The thing was, all Donna wanted to do was get home. Go inside, on her own. Get sober and think straight.

'Starbuck's Mark's dog,' she supplied, though Daniel hadn't asked. 'My ex. His son's dog, actually. He's... Well, he's quite an important part of Karl's life.' Donna stopped, chewing on a thumbnail now in favour of her lip.

'I see.' Daniel nodded. 'Sounds like you and your ex were together for some time.'

'No, not really.' Donna sighed, long and hard.

Daniel went quiet.

'Which house is yours?' he asked, after a moment.

'Sorry?'

'Which house?' Daniel smiled. 'I'd prefer to make sure you get in safely, now I've driven you this far.'

'Oh.' Donna blinked, realising they'd reached her cul-de-sac. 'Sorry. It's that one. Just there.' She nodded at her house.

'Well, goodnight Donna,' Daniel said, pulling up. 'It was really nice meeting you.'

'Yes.' Donna paused, her hand on the door-handle. 'Likewise.'

'I would ask to see you again, but I suspect you'd rather be seeing someone else,' Daniel observed shrewdly.

Donna hesitated. 'I, um... I'm sorry, Daniel. It's just that things are a bit complicated.'

'Aren't they always?' Daniel shrugged, good-naturedly. 'Go on.' He nodded her on. 'Get yourself in. I'll wait until you're inside.'

'Thank you, Daniel,' Donna smiled gratefully. 'You're a gentleman.'

'My biggest downfall,' Daniel rolled his eyes.

'No, it's not, Daniel, trust me. You're quite lovely. Someone not as ditzy as me will snap you up. They'd be mad not to. See you at the next party.' Donna jumped out, beamed him a smile, then dashed towards her house, key poised.

What an extremely nice man. It occurred to Donna that she hadn't once worried about any dishonourable intentions he might have had. Yes, Simon knew him quite well, but still... A very, very nice...

Donna ground to a halt on her doorstep, her brow knitted in consternation as she realised the door was ajar.

Silly, she scalded herself, attempting to shake off the heebie-jeebies. It was obvious that Matt had come home and not closed it properly. But... she stopped before going in, feeling the tiniest bit wary... there were no lights on; and Matt wasn't careless enough to go to bed and leave the front door open in reality.

It might not have caught properly, of course. They did have to give a good slam to close it, sometimes.

Okay, yes, that sounded reasonable, Donna told herself, stepping forth, then stepping back. So, where was Sadie?

Oh, God. 'Sade?' Donna inched the door open further, to see nothing but dark.

Sadie wasn't there. The hall was bare. The whole place felt... empty. Her heartbeat escalating, Donna turned around to see Daniel driving off.

'No! Don't go!' Donna flew back down the path. Something wasn't right. She could feel it. 'Daniel, wait! The door... *Damn!*' she cursed, as he turned the corner.

Damn. Damn. Damn! Her legs quite shaky beneath her, Donna headed back, creaked the door wide, and peered tentatively inside. All was still. She tugged in a breath, took a cautious step in, and slapped on the light.

'Matt!' she shouted, taking the stairs two at a time, twisting an ankle. Kicking off her shoes. Damn, damn, *silly* shoes!

'Matt.' She hesitated for a split second, then banged his door open. No Matt. No bed slept it. Donna swallowed back sudden sweeping nausea. Where was? Oh, God, yes! Relief flooded through her. He was at Ed's. Of course he was. He'd said. Ed's was walking distance from the nightclub. He was safe.

She squeezed her eyes shut.

Still, something was wrong.

Donna turned, her heart hammering now. Down again, thundering down, missing her footing, slithering down the last two steps, she flew to the kitchen.

Deep breaths, she commanded herself. Deep breaths, Donna. You have to keep calm.

She reached for the light, seeing immediately the missing glass in the back door, glass that crunched under her feet. The key was still in the lock.

Oh, dear Lord. She'd told Matt, how many times? Never, *ever* leave the key in the lock. Donna whirled around, taking in the chaos. The cupboards and drawers haphazardly open, blood-smudged contents smashed indiscriminately to the ground.

They must have cut themselves on the glass, she thought obliquely. Then swallowed hard. Shit! Where *is* she? 'Sade! Sadie! Sweetie, where are you?'

'Findus!?'

She took two careful steps forward to peer under the table. No rabbit. Cucumber crushed, green slime now underfoot, but no rabbit.

'*Shit*! Findus?!' Carelessly, Donna flew to the utility. He wasn't there. The cage door was open. The cage was bare. 'Oh, no. Please, God...' Donna's heart twisted inside her... *not the little animals.*

'Findus!' Terror vying with blind-fury, she turned to yank open the back door. 'Fin... Oh, baby.' Blinking hard against the rain, tears stinging her eyes, Donna padded across the soggy lawn, catching Findus mid-hop to pluck the disorientated bunny up.

Poor thing, he was shivering. Donna planted a soft kiss on his startled face. 'A damp little puff-ball, aren't you, sweetie, hmm? Poor baby. Poor little...' Her voice cracked. She stifled a sob, failed to stifle a tear, which slid down her cheek to plop onto velvet-soft fur — and nestled Findus close.

'Sadie!' she called.

Nothing but silence for answers, Donna headed fast back to the house.

'Sadie?!' She flew back up the hall, peering out into the night, the only movement the flickering shadows of streetlights.

No scuffle of dog's claws on paving stones. No dog.

'Calm down.' Donna said it out loud, trying to keep rising panic at bay.

She turned back. Went back inside. Needed to call the police. Needed to check the lounge.

She didn't need to turn on a light. She could see from the dim light of the hall that there *was* no recognisable lounge.

Her stomach turned over, every desecration scorching her eyes like a flashbulb. She followed the red trail of blood around the room. Registered the armchairs turned upside-down. The cushions strewn around. Photographs wiped from shelves. Ornaments broken. Books and magazines splayed open.

The walls were moving. This time she could see them.

Donna tried to breathe but her chest was too full.

She walked back to the front door, faster down the path, quickened her pace, then ran, rabbit still in arms and shoeless through the streets.

Park, she willed herself on, heedless of the grit cutting spitefully into her feet. If Sadie was anywhere, that's where she'd be.

And on foot... three feet... this was the way she would go. Donna followed the route they'd taken when Sadie had four, good strong legs, through the trees that shielded the estate from the road.

The main road.

Sadie wouldn't sit.

Why would she, without Donna to tell her to. Damn it! Holding Findus tight to her breast, Donna tore savagely back at the branch that tore at her coat; sodden and wet and heavy with rain. Damn silly fancy-dress underneath. No shoes on her feet.

Useless, *useless* woman. She ran faster.

Down the bank and towards the road, blinded by the rain, the headlights. The sharp blue light, which flickered in time with the siren.

Donna kept running.

Alongside her now, the blue light again. The wail of the siren.

The headlights flashed and dazzled her as she searched for a gap in the traffic.

God, what about the pond? Panic clutched at her throat. *Come on, hurry up.* She willed the car on. A three-legged dog can't swim.

The car passed, at last. The headlights, swerved.

The blue light danced in the distance, then stopped.

Was that her? Donna fancied she saw Sadie. There, across the road. A dog or a fox? Donna squinted against the rain. Too big for a cat. Three legs or four?

'Sadie!' She plunged forward — and an arm snaked its way around her waist, another around her ribs, yanking her back hard, as a car sliced past, mere inches from her bare feet.

Donna turned and buried her face hard in his chest, fear clawing at her insides and her heart thundering, in time with Mark's.

'Donna?' He eased her chin up and searched her face, anger in his eyes; confusion.

Fear? Yes, fear. He was terrified.

'What happened, Donna?' Mark's tone was terse. His face was tense. 'Donna? Talk to me. Tell me what happened, Donna. Can you do that?'

Donna tried, but the words wouldn't come. She felt so tired, suddenly. So very, very tired.

'Donna!' Mark shook her attention back to his face.

'Findus.' Donna held tight to the petrified rabbit and tried to focus her thoughts. 'Sadie... She's gone.'

She pulled in a breath. Breathed in hard. Then stiffened in his arms. 'I can't find her!'

Donna tried to pull away. She had to go. She couldn't stand here in the street, in bare feet, doing nothing. 'There's... blood. On the floor. On the...' she faltered. 'Blood. Everywhere.'

Couldn't stand here. Couldn't stand. 'I have to find her. I have to find her, Mark. Please let me...' Donna choked, the ground seemed to be shifting beneath her, a scream building inside her. She wouldn't. She didn't want to cry like a baby. She just wanted to find...

'Come on.' Gently Mark eased Findus from her to his waiting partner, then scooped her easily into his arms

Donna didn't fight. She had no fight. It felt good to have him so close. Safe. To be held so close to his heart.

****

Mark's partner was being really kind. Donna couldn't drink the tea he'd made for her though. Her teeth kept chinking against the rim of the cup.

'But what about Karl?' she asked, again.

'It's all right, Donna,' his partner eased the cup from her hands. 'Like I said, Mark's called his carer. Karl's being looked after.'

'But he has to go.' Donna tried to stop shaking. Willed herself to stop, but her body wouldn't comply. 'Karl needs him.'

'I think he'd rather be here, just now. Don't worry about Mark, hey? He's not about to do anything that might upset his son.'

'No.' Donna nodded. Of course he wouldn't. 'He's a good man,' she said, distractedly.

'Better one than I am.' His partner sat down beside her and tried to encourage Donna to take a sip of tea.

'But what about Starbuck?' Donna spluttered before the cup reached her lips. 'He's poorly. The lady police officer said...'

'He's fine. The vet came in to see him, and he's doing — '

He stopped as Mark came back into the lounge.

'All finished?' he asked him.

'Pretty much. Thanks, Phil. I can't tell you how much I appreciate —'

'Forget it.' Phil stood up. 'It's what mates are for. I'd better get off though. I'll sort the paperwork, and get Donna a crime reference number.'

Mark nodded. 'Cheers, Phil.'

'No problem.' Phil placed a reassuring hand on Mark's shoulder as he walked to the door. 'Try and get some sleep, hey? You look about done in.'

'I will,' Mark promised.

Raking his hand through his hair as Phil left, he walked over to Donna. 'Okay?' he asked, crouching down in front of her.

Donna nodded. 'Fine,' she said, her foot playing out a nervous tap-dance on the floor.

Mark smiled. 'Obviously.' He pulled the blanket draped about her shoulders tighter.

'Well, I'm not, entirely,' Donna conceded, poking her hand from under the blanket to drag across her nose. 'But I will be. I can cope.' She sniffed and hoisted her shoulders up.

'I don't doubt it.' Mark smiled again, no trace of sarcasm there.

He really was a good man. And she'd compared him to Jeremy. Donna shuddered and studied the ceiling, just long enough to get the stubborn tears in check. She was quite sure Mark would offer her a shoulder to blubber all over. He wasn't a man to be afraid of emotion. But how painful would that be – for her?

'You didn't find her, then?' Donna looked at him. His hair was wet. She stilled an urge to reach out and smooth it. His clothes were wet. Even his beautiful eyelashes were wet. He hadn't said he was going out to look when he'd taken Findus back to his cage, but he obviously had.

He hadn't found her though. She could tell by the disappointment in his eyes. Every emotion he had, it occurred to her then, showed in Mark's eyes. Perhaps she should have been more observant, instead of paying heed to the incessant doubt trundling round in her head.

Mark reached for her hand. 'She'll turn up, Donna. Phil's going to keep an eye out on the way back. The officers who were called to your friend's party are going to keep an eye out, too. And tomorrow, Sadie will have her very own missing persons report. Try not to worry. We'll find her, somehow.'

Yes, but it was the *how* bit that was worrying Donna. In what condition would they find her? And what about Matt? Sadie might just be a dog, but it would break his heart, thinking harm might have come to his little three-legged friend.

Donna closed her eyes and bit back the tears, hard.

'Come on.' Mark got to his feet. 'It's okay to go upstairs now. I'll run you a hot bath. It might help.'

Donna nodded. She couldn't imagine anything nicer, apart from perhaps to curl up with Mark beside her, so why did her legs suddenly feel like two lumps of lead?

'Come on, Madonna. You'll catch your death and have to cancel your next tour.' Mark smiled, squeezing her hand, gently coaxing her to her feet. 'I'll come up with you.'

If only, Donna thought. To be held by him, to lie in his arms and stay like that forever.

Mark followed her up, making sure she didn't trip over her blanket, waited for her to go into the bedroom, then set about running her bath.

He wouldn't come in, of course, after the awful episode in there. And she'd need her privacy, he must suppose. Donna wished he had come in, though. She didn't want her privacy, not in a room strangers had been through. She just wanted her jim-jams.

Donna surveyed the mess. The strewn about bedclothes. The askew wardrobe doors. Tee shirts lolling like tongues from open drawers.

Even her lingerie. What use would that be now? She couldn't wear it. Any of it. She trailed towards the drawer, then stopped.

Oh, dear Lord. She sank to her knees. Plucked the little four-by-four photographs from the floor. One of the Perspex frames was cracked. The birth certificate was torn. She smoothed it out. Swallowed, and smoothed it some more.

Swallowed again, and looked heavenwards.

Donna wasn't sure how long she knelt there. Hadn't realised how badly she was shaking, until Mark pulled her back into his arms. 'Matt's brother?' he asked quietly.

Donna stiffened.

'Talk to me, Donna. Please? Don't shut me out.'

Donna couldn't talk to him. Couldn't speak at all. The walls were too close. Much too close.

Mark tightened his arms around her, pressed his face close to hers and held her. Kept holding her, while the sobs wracked her body. Until the walls came crashing in.

****

Mark wasn't relying on instinct. He knew with certainty what kind of lowlife had been crawling around Donna's home. What he didn't have, was proof.

He nodded his thanks to the doctor, showed him out, and headed quietly back upstairs.

Would there even be any proof, he wondered, as he went back to Donna's bedroom. Fingerprints would be useless if his instinct was right. There were shoeprints in the blood, but too smudged to be of any real use. And DNA evidence from the actual blood depended on forensics. That could take days.

Mark wasn't even sure the bastard who'd broken in *was* bleeding. Donna definitely was, cuts to her feet from the glass. And Sadie? She might well have been bleeding too, given the bloody paw prints he'd found. Prints which couldn't possibly have been put there after Donna had come home to find the dog gone.

She was sleeping now, small mercy. He crept over to the bed and made sure the duvet was tucked up tight around her. That the pillow was there, by her side — a poor substitute for her dog, he knew, but something she could hold onto, until he could find Sadie. And find her he would.

Thank Christ, Rachel had mentioned the call-out to the fancy dress party, which Mark had guessed must have been the one Donna was going to, given the gay friends. He might never have been in the vicinity otherwise. And Donna would have been here on her own.

At least now she might get some rest. She'd been shaking so much he hadn't known how to hold her. What to say. How to make the bloody nightmare go away.

Leaving the door slightly ajar, he made his way back along the landing to Matt's room, and checked again. The PC was there, PlayStation wired up and intact. DVD shelf still stacked.

Ergo, nothing of real value missing in Mark's practised eye.

The sound system downstairs had been taken, but it just wasn't enough to ring true. Why leave the DVD player? Why not take the TV?

Were they disturbed?

Possibly, but not likely. The bloodstains, apart from Donna's, had been dry for some time, which meant the bastards had been long gone by the time Donna got home. Might be that they were disturbed by someone else, but Mark didn't think so. What he was thinking, was that it looked very much like someone had been looking for something specific. That the gratuitous damage, in fact, wasn't.

Mark went back down to the kitchen, to check the list again as to which items Donna thought were missing. A pocket watch and some original Beatles stuff, she'd said, amongst a few other things. Items she'd apparently put up for sale on eBay, if Mark's recollection of what he'd heard at a previous call out was right.

Mark ran his hand through his hair. In which case, his maths was probably right and he damn well intended to do something about it. Tomorrow though. Tonight he was staying put. To make sure Donna was safe. To be here when Matt came home. Likewise, if either of them needed to talk.

He sighed, reading again the letter he'd come across. Why the *hell* couldn't she have talked to him about this?

Yes, right. When? While he was busy keeping secrets from her? Hurling accusations? Or somewhere in between? There hadn't been much of an in between. And now, thanks to his pathetic behaviour on finding that Simon character in her bedroom... He'd blown it completely, no doubt in Mark's mind. Donna had had feelings for him before that unforgivable display of aggression, he was sure.

But then, once someone's feelings had moved on, there was no going back. He knew that. When Emma had walked away, she didn't look back. That was okay. Mark didn't need her to. He could cope, he'd told himself, on his own.

Just like Donna claimed she could cope. Well, not tonight. Love him or hate him, tonight she was stuck with him.

Thereafter... he folded the letter from the hospital cytology department and placed it back on the microwave... if she was going to let him in, he was going to have to work a hell of a lot harder at gaining her trust.

Chapter Twenty-One

Donna lay, pleasantly untroubled. She liked this time of day, when there was no sound in the world, other than the birds' dawn chorus. And, um, the heavy breathing of someone else in the room?

Oh, God?! Donna blinked grainy eyelids against the semi-dark. Slowly, she turned her head to one side, then almost died as whoever it was stirred and rolled over, draping one sleepy arm heavily over her body.

Her heart thudded manically against her ribcage. It was Mark. She could smell his reassuring aftershave, mingled with the comforting scent of freshly washed sheets. Relief oozed from her every pore, swiftly followed by panic.

What was he doing here? In her bed? What was *she* doing in her bed, with *him*?

Her mind was a blank. A complete and utter blank.

Donna eased her head from the pillow, then froze as he stirred again, rolling onto his back, raking his hand through his hair. In his sleep? Did the man's worries haunt him even in his dreams?

Carefully, not wanting to wake him, she eased around to study his profile, watching the steady rise and fall of his chest in the growing light through the window.

She was in her bedroom, she knew that much, but she had no clue how she got into bed. Got out of her... Donna scrunched her eyes shut... good-time-girl's outfit complete with polystyrene cups. *Oh, no.* She gulped, then tentatively traced the contours of her own body.

Perfect. She was wearing a shirt. Just a shirt. Which meant that Mark had seen her. All of her. Parts of her she would have possibly died trying to hide. Donna groaned inside, absolutely horrified.

What happened!? Had she... slept with him? Naked?! And not even remembered? How?! Her stomach churned. Her head swam. She must have been very, very...

Drunk. Yes, she'd been drunk.

Something hadn't been right. Something had happened. Something... bad? She flopped back on her pillow and concentrated hard above the nauseating throb in her temples. Eventually, hazily, the pieces started to click into place.

Sadie? She wasn't here. Donna tried to swallow against the constriction in her throat. Was she out there, somewhere in the unfriendly night? Please, God, don't let her be in pain all on her own.

The photographs. Donna remembered those. Remembered Mark holding her. Holding her tight. Beyond that, nothing, bar a fleeting image of Mark brushing her hair from her face, his face dark and angry. Had she done something awful? *This* was awful. She needed to move. Get up. Get dressed. Matt was due home and ...

Sh... ugar!

She couldn't be here. In bed. With a man! Donna eased a toe from under the duvet, followed by a foot, then a leg.

Gingerly, she glanced back at Mark. Had she dragged him here? Begged him to sleep with her? Passed out?! In which case, what *was* Mark doing lying next to her? She must have consumed a whole distillery, because, beyond a certain point, Donna could remember absolutely nothing at all.

She inched her other leg out, twisted around and slithered the rest of her-wanton-self out, thankful for Mark's shirt as she stumbled to the door. *Mark's shirt?* She turned back to look at him and very nearly did pass out. He was extremely fanciable. Temptingly gorgeous. And naked.

Oh, dear God, she had.

Mortified, Donna made her way to the bathroom on very sore feet, where she dispensed with tradition and sat in the shower, allowing the water to cascade over her, hoping it might wash her awake, or wash her away. She'd had sex with him. A once-in-a-lifetime never to be repeated experience, now he'd seen her in all her naked glory, no strategically placed lingerie, risqué or otherwise. Nothing apart from soggy plasters on the soles of her feet. How awful.

She couldn't even remember how they'd got there. What *was* the matter with her? No complications?! Hah! This was probably as complicated as it got. And she'd no functional brain with which to even try to unscramble any of it.

'Donna?' Mark called as she sat shivering, wondering what her next move should be. 'Donna, are you okay in there?'

'Donna?!'

'Yes!' Donna shouted urgently as he knocked on the door. She couldn't even remember whether she'd locked it. She killed off her brain cells, tossed her last shred of dignity out of the window and turned into an actual floozy. And what a sad old floozy she must be. One she certainly didn't want him to see, wet.

'Yes, yes, I'm fine,' she redressed her tone, lest Mark come in on the basis he'd seen everything anyway.

'Sure?' Mark didn't sound convinced.

'Yes. I'm just, you know,' *drowning myself.*

'Right, I'll make some tea, then,' Mark offered. 'I'll be downstairs.'

Donna's mouth twitched into a smile. She never would have guessed.

Well — she sucked in a breath and blew out a soap sud, whether she remembered or not, it had happened. She couldn't undo it. And, whatever had happened, she had things to do. Her dog to find. Her son to explain to. The mess to clear up. Including the mess she'd obviously made with the off-duty policeman currently making tea in her kitchen. Donna dragged her hair from her face and got unsteadily to her feet, still feeling extremely nauseous.

Served her right. She was old enough to know better.

She towelled herself and reached for a tub of moisturiser in the absence of a handy bag she could wedge on her head. She'd have to go back out in his shirt, she supposed. She couldn't hope to compete with Julia Roberts without surgery, but at least she might look slightly more attractive adorned in a shirt than a faded old towel.

Mmm. It did smell nice. She slipped into it, had a good sniff of it. She'd remember that, when he'd gone, how the smell of Mark had been so lovely to wake up to. Next to the smell of freshly washed sheets, she could think of nothing nice...

Hang on a minute. Donna blinked. The sheets!? They *were* freshly changed. And, if she was too inebriated to remember getting into bed — with Mark, she would hardly have been capable of changing the bed linen beforehand. Which could only mean that Mark had changed it.

Why? When?

It made no sense. She was going to have to ask him. Admit — whatever it did to his ego, or hers — that she couldn't remember any of it.

Donna steeled herself, tugged up her shoulders, tugged down the hem of her shirt, and headed nervously back to the bedroom.

Mark was back. Tea made, as promised. She smiled wanly, wishing her hair was still Madonna not Medusa, and that she at least had on a scrap of make-up.

'Better?' Mark smiled warmly from where he sat on the bed, his uniform on now over his bare torso, which helped Donna's bewildered state of mind not one iota.

'A bit.' Donna nodded, glancing away from him and around the now debris-free room. Her personal things... Donna recalled, with another bout of nausea, how they'd been touched, defiled, strewn about like so much garbage. Mark had obviously tidied up.

'Good,' he said, standing up and patting the duvet. 'Come back to bed.'

Come back to? 'What?' Donna croaked.

'Bed,' he repeated. 'You're probably pretty exhausted after last night.'

Exhausted? Donna felt the blood drain from her face to pool in her feet. 'No,' she squeaked and clutched at the doorframe, 'thank you, but I, um.'

'Donna, what's wrong?' Mark was across the room in a flash.

'... feel faint.'

'Hey, hey, steady. I've got you,' he assured her, sweeping her off her feet. 'Come on, doctor's orders.' He hoisted her high in his arms. 'You need to lie down.'

She did. Absolutely did, but please don't let him lie down with her, she thought woozily, as he carried her across the room to lower her gently onto the bed.

'You're going to have to stop this, you know?' He smiled, sat down next to her and smoothed down the hem of her shirt. His shirt.

'Stop what?' Donna asked guardedly.

'Passing out on me.'

'Is that what I did last night?' Donna wasn't sure she wanted to know.

'Eventually,' he said, brushing her damp hair from her face, then bending to plant the softest of kisses on her forehead, her eyelashes, her mouth.

Donna hesitated, sensation returning, everything tingling. What was she *doing?*

'Mark,' she mumbled, pressing her hands to his shoulders, pushing him away, 'please don't. I can't. I...' Donna trailed off, hoping he'd understand she hadn't a clue what to do, or what she'd already done.

'Sorry, that was insensitive. I shouldn't have.' Mark looked immediately guilty.

'I shouldn't have.' Donna levered herself up on the pillows. 'Look, Mark, about last night,' she said quickly, before the embarrassing situation could get any worse, 'I'd had a lot to drink.'

Mark looked at her bemusedly. 'I know. I —'

'Too much, and I, um... Mark, what happened between us last night, I... I shouldn't have.'

Mark stared at her now.

'I'm not sure when I passed out, but... It shouldn't have happened, Mark. Not like that.'

'Right.' Mark ran his hand over his neck. 'So, you think that you and I... That I...' He trailed off, shaking his head. 'Jesus, Donna!'

He looked back to her, his expression one of utter bewilderment.

Oh, Lord, she hadn't meant... She didn't *know* what she meant. She didn't know... Donna glanced down, wished she could slide down. Crawl under the duvet, curl up and die.

Mark stood up, slowly, his hand going through his hair, a sure sign he was upset. He looked at her, disbelief in his eyes, swiftly followed by anger. 'Donna, do you actually remember what happened last night?'

Donna shrugged, wove her fingers together and studied them. 'Some, yes.'

'Do you recall the doctor coming?'

Doctor? 'What doctor?' Donna's head shot up.

'I'll take that as a no.' Mark searched her face. 'Do you remember coming into the bedroom, Donna?'

Donna nodded, feeling on very shaky ground.

'The photographs?'

Donna dropped her gaze.

'You got upset, Donna. Very upset.' Mark sat back down, hesitated, then tentatively took hold of her hand. 'I called the doctor because you weren't making any sense and you were shaking so much, quite frankly, I was scared.'

Donna looked up at him. His eyes were sincere, yet troubled.

'He gave you something to calm you. A sedative. You slept for a while. A good while. Then you woke up with a fresh bout of the shakes and... I slept next to you, Donna, not with you.'

'Oh.'

'The shirt was because you were ill.'

He'd brushed her hair from her face. Brushed her hair from her face in the bathroom.

'All in all, very nice though it was, I really didn't think you'd be too comfortable in your Madonna outfit. And, yes, there was plenty of your own stuff to choose from…'

Mark paused, holding her gaze.

'… but I was pretty sure you wouldn't want to wear anything that those bastards had had their hands all over.'

Donna bowed her head, shamefaced. The trousers to Mark's uniform, she finally noticed, were covered in fluff from the sheets. He'd obviously slept in them.

She had absolutely no idea what to say.

'Donna, I care very much about you. I know now's probably not a good time, but…' Mark stopped as he heard a key in the lock. 'That will be Matt, I imagine.' He squeezed her hand. 'Do you want me to talk to him?'

Donna blinked up at him. Was that all? Wasn't he going to shout? Feel affronted, slam doors, stomp around? 'Thank you,' she said, squeezing his hand back, in the absence of words that could make right what she'd thought.

She may never take it off. Donna pulled his shirt tight around her as Mark went down to talk to her son, sensitively, she knew he would. How could she have been so insensitive of Mark's feelings?

****

It was obvious why she'd jumped to conclusions. Mark mulled things over as he drove away from the station more suitably attired for a policeman. He'd had a few unmemorable occasions himself. That wasn't a problem.

That Donna thought he'd actually taken advantage of her though. Jesus. Mark was struggling with that. But then, she had woken to find a man in her bed and no recollection of what happened. Dammit, he should have clarified things sooner. Certainly shouldn't have fallen asleep.

He should have apologised too, for the unforgivable things he's said the last time he'd been in that room. Told her how much he loved her — that he'd never intentionally do anything to hurt her.

The timing hadn't been right though, with Matt walking into what was basically a crime scene.

Mark eased the crick in his neck, sighed, and checked his watch. He'd got two hours, before Jody had to get home. She'd been fantastic, child-minding and pet-minding with Starbuck off colour. Mark had no idea how he was going to cope without her. Somehow he would. Right now, though, he had some business to attend to. Unofficial business.

Thereafter, an errand to run that he hoped might make Donna realise that rubbish he'd spouted hadn't been about his bruised ego. Jealousy might not be a better excuse, but that's what it was, pure and simple.

Because he did love her, and he would damn well find a way of telling her, whatever the outcome.

Mark reached the end of the drive that lead to the Grade II listed country house. Wow. He let out a low appreciative whistle. Nice. Wouldn't mind some of that himself. He drove on past an ornamental maze and what looked like an orangery.

Very nice. Gate house. Pool house, too, he noticed driving by to pull up outside the main entrance. Servants' quarters. Stables. Mark could see why, if someone got their foot in this door, they'd go to some lengths to keep it there.

He parked his car discreetly. What he wanted to do was have a quiet word, the uniform lending him a little gravitas if he needed it, which he suspected he might.

Keeping him waiting wasn't a good idea. Mark checked his watch, already annoyed — and growing more so by the minute.

At last, the door creaked open and instead of the airs and graces he'd expected from the person who opened it, Mark was faced with a woman who'd obviously been crying.

Great. Now, he was going to have to tread even more carefully. He nodded an acknowledgement, deciding as she was doing her best to look poised, to try and do the same. 'PC Mark Evans,' he introduced himself, showing his ID card. 'I was hoping for a word with your partner. Would he be in?'

The woman nodded and stepped back to allow him access. Mark followed her through the reception hall into a cavernous sitting room, complete with wooden floors, fireplace, ornate cornicing, and a gargantuan brass chandelier.

Definitely worth marrying into if you fancied top rung social ladder. But the guy wasn't married into it yet. And if this woman had an ounce of sense in her head, he wouldn't be.

The woman turned to extend a hand, retrieved her bunched up tissue from it with the other, then tried again. 'He's in the pool house,' she said. 'He likes to keep himself in shape.' She smiled, but the look in her eye wasn't that of a woman impressed by her man working out. It was more one of quiet disdain. 'I'll go and fetch him. Would you like some tea while you wait?'

'No.' Mark said, with a short smile. 'Thank you.' Drinking tea and swapping small talk with the cretin wasn't why he was here. He'd be doing the talking and the guy better damn well be listening.

'Actually, do you mind if I, er...' Mark nodded in the direction of the pool house. 'It's just that I'm a bit short on time.'

The woman studied him for a moment. 'No, not all. I'll show you the, ahem...' She trailed off.

Struggling not to cry, Mark could see. 'I take it you two had a disagreement,' he asked gently.

She nodded.

'Do you want to tell me about it?' he probed, as delicately as he could.

She shook her head, her eyes still downcast and a tear now rolling freely down her cheek.

Her bruised cheek, Mark was quick to notice. The bastard. He gritted his teeth, disliking this man more by the second.

The woman twisted the tissue between her hands. 'I should have known better,' she said suddenly. 'That he wouldn't change, I mean. That he'd do the same to me as he did to... He didn't even bother to hide the evidence that well.' She laughed, sardonically. 'We don't even use them.'

Condoms, Mark assumed. Christ. He placed a hand awkwardly on her arm. This was never easy, watching a woman cry and protocol allowing him to do absolutely nothing to comfort her.

'You, er, didn't find anything else out of the ordinary, did you, by any chance?' he asked, hoping for a miracle, even a shred of evidence pointing towards the events of last night.

The woman looked up to scan his eyes, the look in hers now a mixture of curiosity and — determination, did Mark perceive?

She straightened up, giving him a small but succinct nod. 'I'll fetch it,' she said, turning to walk to the door.

Her head high, Mark noticed, marvelling — not for the first time — at how women found the strength to get through the most agonising of situations.

The woman came back a few minutes later, her tears in check and her poise intact. 'I'm not sure how much use it will be,' she said, dropping indisputable evidence into the palm of Mark's hand.

Mark nodded his thanks and closed his fist over a metaphorical nugget of pure gold. Got you, you bastard. He sucked in a breath, hugely relieved.

****

Mark slipped quietly in. And there he was, the creep with aspirations way above his station, doing a length of the pool backstroke, keeping his body in shape, probably to facilitate bullying any woman who refused to stroke his pathetic ego.

Mark had removed his clothes to a safe place. Doubted the little shit would want to go walking in the rain in his Speedos, which was basically the only way he was going to go anywhere if he decided he didn't want to listen to what Mark had to say.

He waited for the guy to do his return length, then made his presence known by looming over him as he touched base.

'Bloody hell!' The guy blinked up through his goggles, then spluttered, went under, and emerged spitting half the pool.

So far so good. Couldn't have planned it better if he'd tried. Mark's mouth curved into a satisfied smile. He waited again, patiently, while Jeremy Matthews righted himself, blew water down his nose, twanged off his goggles.

'What the hell?!'

'Your good fiancé said I'd find you out here.' Mark looked him over, noting that Jeremy had backed off a fair way. Excellent. That's where he wanted him. And that's where he'd stay, given the guy would no doubt be petrified of getting a taste of his own.

'*Leticia* let you in?' Jeremy gawped incredulously. 'What in God's name was she thinking?'

Mark shrugged casually. 'That you deserve what's coming, I guess.'

Jeremy backed up some more, glancing behind him, as if Jaws might pop up at any minute. Yep, he was worried, and that suited Mark just fine.

'She's on to you, sunshine. Knows you'd go to bed with her horse if it meant getting your hands on her money.'

'I don't believe this.' Jeremy shook his head and started for the steps. 'I'm getting out. I'd be grateful if you'd leave.'

'No, you're not,' Mark said simply, stopping him in his tracks.

Jeremy paled. 'I beg your pardon?'

'You're staying in,' Mark clarified, 'for as long as it takes. That's unless you want to try and get past me.'

'What?' Jeremy stared at him. 'Are you mad? As long as *what* takes?'

'For you to admit where you were last night, freeze to death, or drown.' Mark shrugged. 'Your choice.'

'You're insane.'

'Possibly,' Mark conceded with a smile. 'Probably, in fact. Worrying, isn't it?'

'I'm getting out.' Jeremy turned around.

'No, Matthews, you're not!' Mark skirted around the pool to block his exit that side. 'Not until you've coughed up or coughed your guts up. Like I say, your choice.'

Jeremy glanced at the chair, where his clothes and mobile no longer were. 'Leticia will call the police,' he said, a slight tremble to his voice. His teeth chattering, which Mark found most gratifying.

'I am the police,' Mark reminded him. 'And, trust me, she won't.'

Jeremy was beginning to look very panicky now. His eyes shooting around the pool in search of an escape. His lips blue-tinged. Serve the bastard right.

'Not nice is it, Jeremy, to be bullied, pushed around, frightened?'

Jeremy wrapped his arms about himself. 'I'm cold.'

'I know. Someone's pumping in cold water.'

Jeremy moved to the side.

Mark shadowed him.

'Donna didn't like it, Jeremy, being reduced to tears by a bully. Leticia doesn't. So you have to stop, don't you?'

Jeremy didn't answer.

'Now, I know you won't unless you know it's in your interests to. And I know you think you'll be able to drag your snivelling body out of there at some stage and get help, but the thing is, in cold water hypothermia can set in quite quickly. Your body constricts surface blood vessels, to conserve heat for your vital organs, did you know that?'

Jeremy wrapped his arms tighter around himself. More from shock at being bullied than being in the water, Mark guessed, which actually no one was pumping cold into, but still he figured he'd have to get him out soon.

'Blood pressure and heart rate increases. Muscles tense and shiver,' he went on, needing the guy to know he was serious, and he was. 'Might make it difficult to climb out, don't you think? Of course, if your core temperature drops below eighty-two Fahrenheit, you're unconscious pretty damn fast, and then dead basically. So,' Mark crouched down, 'are we ready to listen?'

Jeremy nodded, his eyes never leaving Mark's.

'Good.' Mark swung the pocket watch, a Robert Pybus of London, c1790, pendulum-like in front of him. 'For future information, Matthews, women don't like to be cheated on either. They tend to look for evidence of your infidelity. Leticia did, last night. Ready to come out?'

Mark helped him out. Sat him down. Fetched him a towel.

'I could report you,' Jeremy said shakily, after a moment of composing himself.

Mark nodded, sitting in a chair opposite, his hands steepled under his chin. 'You could. But then, if I go down, I take you down with me. We have evidence you were there, Jeremy, make no mistake. We also have witnesses. Do you?'

'Witnesses?'

'Witnesses,' Mark repeated.

Jeremy shrank in his seat. 'What do you want?'

'You to leave Donna alone.' Mark waited for a reaction. Jeremy had the good sense to make none. 'You don't go near her, you don't speak to her, unless invited to. You do not go near her property.'

Jeremy nodded, playing idly with a large plaster on his hand. He might have cut himself then, possibly, but not seriously from what Mark could see, unfortunately.

'The injunction she's taking out isn't in place yet. You probably know that.'

'Donna isn't taking out an injunction,' Jeremy scoffed, cocksure, even now, when he could so easily be having this conversation down at the station — or not at all, given Mark was now feeling very close to acquainting him with the bottom of the pool.

'Oh, but she is,' he grated angrily. 'Don't know Donna very well, do you, Matthews? Mistaking her generosity in giving you a chance in the first place for giving a shit about you. Wrong, sunshine. She cares about her son and the effect his snivelling coward of a father is having on his life. Do you honestly imagine that Donna would put whatever Matt might think of her above his psychological welfare? That she imagines your input is any longer beneficial to him in any way?'

He watched and waited, while Jeremy debated, obviously swiftly coming to the conclusion that Donna would consider her son's welfare paramount. Did he really think she wouldn't? Unbelievable.

'When the injunction is in place,' Mark went on, now Jeremy had registered that as a fact, 'and I aim to make sure it is soon, if you so much as take a step over it... Let's just say, next time I won't let you up for air. Got it?

'Now, in regard to Matt, what do you think would be psychologically beneficial to him, Jeremy? To know you're making your maintenance payments, nice and regularly, i.e. that his father gives a damn about him, or that you've been arrested for breaking and entering into his mother's home — in so doing possibly killing the kid's dog? Your choice.'

Jeremy had paled now to the point of grey. 'I didn't mean to let Sadie out. She slipped past me...'

'Your choice, Matthews!?' Mark shouted, jolting Jeremy in his seat.

'The former,' he said quickly, dropping his gaze.

'Good,' Mark said, more restrained. 'However,' he waited until Jeremy looked back at him, 'if you detract from it, do anything — and I mean anything — to upset Donna or Matt ever again, I'll have you picked up so fast, on any number of charges, your feet won't touch the fucking floor. Understand, Jeremy?'

Jeremy hesitated for the briefest of seconds, then nodded.

'Make sure you do,' Mark warned him, 'because I do mean picked up, Jeremy — what's left of you, that is. Being a policeman, I have some acquaintances in very low places.'

Mark waited again, making sure Jeremy had indeed got the message.

He had. Matthews looked about ready to burst into tears, which is exactly what Mark had intended, distasteful though it was.

Satisfied, he got to his feet. 'For your information, Matt knows nothing about your pathetic exploits, by the way. And nor will he, provided he doesn't have to.' Mark decided to leave with him some small shred of dignity, assuming Jeremy cared enough to care what his son thought of him.

'What about Leticia?' Jeremy asked shakily.

'She wants you to leave. And as her father's loading his hunting rifle as we speak, I imagine she's serious. She said you can keep the clothes you stand up in. Same applies, Matthews. You don't go anywhere near the lady, or the house, unless invited to do so. She has my mobile number.'

Mark resisted a smile as Jeremy glanced forlornly down at his damp Speedos. 'Your mobile is over there along with your other stuff.' He nodded towards the bar. 'You have two minutes to get dressed before I escort you off the premises.'

Mark eyeballed him meaningfully, then walked to the door where he turned to wait, arms folded.

Twenty minutes later, after confirmation from Leticia that that's what she wanted, Mark despatched Jeremy to the town centre, where he waited, looking not very dapper in his coat with track suit under, for the bus.

Confident the guy knew just how serious he was and wouldn't double back, Mark drove off, feeling pretty shaky himself. He'd had no idea how that would go, whether he'd be able to go through with it, or whether he'd have to threaten Jeremy or carry out those threats.

He dragged a hand through his hair, hoping to God Matthews didn't call his bluff re the break in, because the only evidence so far was the pocket watch, which Mark doubted would be enough to put him at the scene. As for the fictitious witnesses, that had been risky, but at least it got the prat's attention.

Chapter Twenty-Two

Mark paused as he left The Helliots Nursing Home to ring Matt on his mobile. He wanted to check on Donna, but without crowding her, he thought might be best.

'Hi, it's Mark,' he said when Matt picked up. 'How's things?'

'Hold on.' Matt went off, presumably to switch off the vacuum. 'Yeah, not bad,' he said, coming back on line. 'I got my badge in housework, at least.'

'Good practice,' Mark smiled, 'for when you find the right woman you don't want to get the wrong side of. How's Donna?'

'Ironing the curtains.'

Mark shook his head, bemused. 'Like you do.'

'It's Mum's way. When she's upset or piss… pee'd off, needs to work things through, you know?'

'Yeah.' Scrubbing away the stench of vermin desecrating her home; keeping herself busy to keep her mind occupied. Mark knew. 'Don't let her work too hard, Matt, okay? She'll need some rest.'

'Don't worry, I won't,' Matt assured him. 'I'm taking her out for a pub lunch and then if she doesn't put her feet up, you'll just have to come around and handcuff her to the bed.'

'Right.' Mark stifled a laugh. 'But don't let on, we'll need an element of surprise.'

'Wilco,' Matt said, then went quiet.

Probably wondering how to ask what the hell was going on with him and his mother. 'Matt, just so you know, I'm not sure where I stand with Donna,' Mark offered. 'But wherever it is, I intend to stay close. Be around, you know?'

'Cool.' Matt obviously approved. 'So, assuming you'll need a few reasons to be around, come to my birthday party Wednesday evening, why don't you?'

Blimey, definitely an approval. 'Great. Cheers, Matt. Do I bring anything?'

'A bottle, obviously. It's my eighteenth. I'm a man. And some flowers. You know those things with petals and leaves?' Matt dropped a subtle hint.

'I'll do my best,' he promised. 'What do you like, daffodils, roses?'

'Ha, ha, careful you don't cut yourself on your razor sharp wit,' Matt retorted drolly. 'Seriously,' he went on, 'bring your son, as well, if you want. If he, you know, can deal with crowds and stuff.'

Mark went quiet now, choked, on two counts. Donna had obviously talked to him about Karl, which meant that Karl and he both had figured in her thoughts, and Matt, it seemed, wanted to try to include Karl in their lives.

'Thanks, Matt. That's more appreciated than you know. I'm not sure though, to be honest. His dog's sick, and without Starbuck, Karl might not manage so well. Can I leave it open?'

'No problem. Um, I don't suppose you've heard anything?'

'Christ, sorry.' Mark slapped his hand against his forehead. 'Yes, I have. Good news, I hope. I'm just off to check it out. Didn't want to say anything before I knew for sure.'

Mark noted the time, and realised he was going to have to get a move on. 'Got to go, Matt. I'll see you Wednesday, if not before. I'll give Donna a ring later, but give her my regards, okay?'

'Right, I'll give her your love as well. Lata.'

'Cheers.' Mark rolled his eyes. 'Oh, Matt, I almost forgot, Alicia's number, do you have it?'

'Obviously, but I'm not sure bringing her sister to the party is going to win Mum over.'

****

Close to giving up, Mark finally spotted who he'd been scouring the park for.

'Hey, Agnes, wait up!' he called, as Agnes tottered towards the bandstand, a certain little friend at her side, who seemed to have developed more of a limp. Poor thing obviously had cut herself on the glass then.

'Agnes?' Mark set off across the grass after her. Then stopped — and sighed — and extracted his shoe from six inches of mud.

Great. 'Agnes!' He skidded to a muddy stop as she lowered herself creakily to sit on the bandstand steps.

'Hey, Agnes, how are you doing?' Mark panted, hands on his thighs, trying to catch his breath. Uh-oh. He straightened up, backing off swiftly, as Agnes got back to her feet in a flash and advanced towards him wielding her ball bag. 'Agnes, don't,' he warned. 'If you do, I'm going to have to take you to the station.'

'Over my dead body!' Agnes marched forth, looking worryingly suffragette-ish. 'You two-timing, sex maniac, you!'

Mark took another step back. 'Agnes, I'm not. I like women.'

Agnes narrowed her eyes.

'As in, I respect women, Agnes.' Mark sighed, and didn't bother looking down. At least now he had a matching pair of shoes, he supposed. 'Agnes, if you take a swing with that thing, I'm going to have to handcuff you.'

Agnes stopped, still eyeballing him menacingly.

'It's not mine, Agnes. The baby you and Donna overheard us talking about, it's not mine. The girl I was with, she looks after my little boy. She's married. A very respectable girl, with a very respectable husband, whose baby it is.'

Agnes regarded him with squinty-eyed suspicion.

'I was a bit taken aback when she told me, that's all, because it's going to leave me without someone to look after Karl, my boy, while I'm at work.'

'The autistic little boy.' Agnes lowered her bag. 'The one whose dog needed to keep his ball.'

'That would be him.' Mark waited.

'Well, why didn't you say so?' Agnes huffed and turned back to the bandstand.

'That's Donna's baby, Agnes, you know that don't you?'

Agnes stopped and delved in her bag. 'But, of course.' She presented Sadie with a multi-coloured prickly ball. 'Sadie wouldn't be anyone else's baby, would you, you clever little girl? We've been waiting for her, haven't we, Sadie?'

'Donna's been waiting, too, Agnes,' Mark pointed out gently. 'For news Sadie was safe, you know?'

'But of course she would be. I was going to ring her, but I don't have a walkie-talkie, you see? Sadie did want to show me where her mummy lived, didn't you, beautiful girl, hmm?'

Agnes eased herself down on the steps next to the adoring three-legged dog, ferreted again in her bag and offered Sadie a treat. 'But her little paws were so sore, we thought we ought to go and see that nice Mr Barnby at the vet's first. Mummy can take you now though, can't she, Sadie?'

Sadie thumped her tail as Agnes had another little ferret in her bag.

'She bit him, you know?'

'She did?' Mark's mouth curved into a tolerant smile. 'How do you know that then, Agnes?'

Agnes looked at him as if he were a bit dense. 'I would have thought that was perfectly obvious, dear boy.' She turned her gaze to Sadie.

Bloody hell. Mark pushed his cap back. Matthews *had* had a plaster on his hand. Nah. He glanced curiously at Sadie, who seemed to be rapt on the old lady's every word. Not possible. Dogs communicated, that he had to concede, but...

'So, are you going to make an honourable woman of her now you're having *her* baby?' Agnes asked puzzlingly.

Mark scratched his head. 'Er, I think I've missed something, Agnes.'

'Well, you are taking Sadie back to her mummy, aren't you?'

'Ah…,' Mark got the drift, 'I thought I might, yes, if that's all right with you?'

'So, there you go?' Agnes looked at him, looking mightily pleased. 'You can ask her then, can't you?'

Mark looked at Agnes totally baffled.

'I know you youngsters all have a get-what-you-can mentality nowadays, but you don't *have* to have sex before marriage, young man!' Agnes boomed.

'Right.' Mark cringed and quite wished he could disappear whole under the mud.

****

'Half an hour,' Mark promised Jody, feeling bad about keeping her waiting. 'And thanks, Jody. I don't mean to take advantage.' Mark hung up and turned to Sadie in the passenger seat. 'Agnes would probably beat me to death with her ball bag if I did, wouldn't she, Sadie?'

Christ, now *he* was talking to the animal. He needed to lie down. Mark ran his hand over his neck and started the engine. 'Don't suppose I could persuade you to wear your seatbelt, could I?'

Sadie replied by way of a cheek-dragging lick, then slid comfortably down, head and one front leg hanging over the seat.

'Thought not.'

****

'You all right, mum?' Matt asked, for the umpteenth time.

'Yes.' Donna sighed distractedly.

'Bad idea, wasn't it?'

'No, not at all.' Donna shook herself, and tried to look the tiniest bit grateful. 'I wouldn't be very hungry wherever we were, to be honest, Matt. But at least I'm out of the house.' Which seemed so empty, even with Matt and Findus there.

Donna eyed the food on her plate, knowing it was a terrible waste, but she really had no appetite. She chewed on her lip instead, wondering whether to ring the dog rescue centre again.

'Come on.' Matt swigged back his Coke. 'Let's go and put those posters up. Someone somewhere must have seen her.'

Donna nodded and smiled proper. How many almost-men would swap a paintball birthday event, arranged by fellow participant and *hottie* Sophie, for lunch with Mum *and* pay for it?

She waited while Matt man-fully footed the bill, making sure to sprinkle 'Mother' liberally into the conversation, lest the bartender also being a *hottie* think he was taken, then waited again while he answered his mobile.

'Matt's phone,' he said, followed by three words, consisting of right, right, and right.

'Sounded scintillating,' Donna commented, collecting her bag from the bar.

Matt's mouth twitched into a smile. 'It was, very.'

Hmm? Another hottie, possibly? Donna turned to the exit with a knowing smile, then quickly sidestepped as someone sprinted through it from the opposite side.

'Whoops, sorry,' the young woman said, turning to hold the door. 'I'm being pursued by a good-looking policeman.'

Donna's ears pricked up. Her eyes grew wide. Then almost fell out of the sockets as a good-looking policeman did indeed bustle his way in, arms full of...

'*Sade*!!!' Donna screeched. 'Oooh! My beautiful, beautiful babe!' She cupped the dog's face and blinked worriedly into her eyes. 'Where've you been, sweetie, hmm? Who did it, hon? Mummy will get them.'

Mark arched an eye as Donna proceeded to plant several sloppy wet kisses on Sadie's head. 'Come on, poppet,' she said, as the dog wriggled, trying to bridge the gap between him and Donna, giving him a whack in the face with her tail as she did.

'Here, Sade.' Matt stepped in, and, between them, they managed to get Sadie safely down on all-threes on the pub floor.

'Oh, babe,' Donna crouched and cooed some more, 'I love you, you know? I really do.'

'I think you may have competition,' Matt observed.

'Yeah.' Mark smiled half-heartedly and glanced down at his mud-spattered uniform, now also covered in dog hair.

He plucked idly at one hair amongst many, then smiled, rather more enthusiastically, as Donna flung her arms around his neck and parted with another sloppy wet kiss.

'You got a brownie point though,' Matt imparted knowledgeably.

Chapter Twenty-Three

'How's things?' Mark asked Jody, finally coming though his front door.

'Okay. They're watching *Fireman Sam to the Rescue.*' Jody came downstairs, nodding towards the lounge, where Karl was watching his DVD. From the sofa, unusually, Mark noticed when he poked his head in.

'He'll have moved his whole bedroom down soon,' Jody said, behind him.

Mark smiled, not quite able to believe that Karl had bought down his duvet set plus pillow, which he'd placed on his lap, Starbuck's head nestled thereon.

He realised that Karl might simply be replaying previous events, once told Starbuck needed rest, rest meaning sleep, sleep meaning duvets and pillows. The odd thing was, though, Karl seemed to be comforting the dog, which must mean he'd realised Starbuck needed comforting. Had Karl actually thought that through?

'He's looking after him,' Jody said, as if reading Mark's mind.

Mark glanced at her in a *maybe* sort of way

'Really, he is,' Jody assured him, turning away to collect her coat from the stair rail. 'He told me. He said "Karl is staying next to Starbuck because it makes Starbuck feel less frightened".'

Mark stared at her. '*Jesus.*' He shook his head, astonished.

That wasn't repetition word-for-word. No way. He'd turned it around. *Starbuck was staying next to Karl because it made Karl less frightened,* Mark had told him when they'd first walked Starbuck out in public. He *was* damn well thinking it through. '*Yesss!* Bloody good,' he said aloud.

'You look like a kid at Christmas.' Jody laughed, tugging on her coat as she walked to the door.

'Remind me to leave Santa a mince pie this year.' Mark smiled, feeling as if all his Christmases had come at once.

'There is a bit of a downside.' Jody glanced at him worriedly. 'Because Starbuck's not eating...'

'Karl's not.' Mark got the gist. 'Right. Okay.' He nodded, knowing he'd just have to deal with it. 'I'll think of something. Thanks, Jody.'

'No problem.' Jody smiled, opened the door and waved at her husband waiting in the car. 'I'll see you tomorrow.'

'No, I mean *thanks*, Jody. It's a small word, I know, but I just wanted you to know. You've made a huge difference to Karl's life and to mine. I'm more grateful than you could ever realise.'

'Like I said, no problem. Just remember to rinse the washing machine when you've washed that little lot.' She nodded at his mud-bedecked trousers and shirt and gave him a mock scowl.

'Yes, Miss,' Mark laughed, closing the door behind her.

He really had no idea what he was going to do without her. Manage, he supposed. At least with Starbuck around... Mark stopped and prayed for another miracle that the suspected intestinal obstruction Starbuck was being x-rayed for tomorrow wouldn't need surgery and, if it did, that it wouldn't be major, for Starbuck's sake, for Karl's sake, and selfishly, for his own.

He headed back to the lounge to try to persuade Karl they needed to get Starbuck to eat something, hopefully therefore prompting Karl to do the same.

'Hey, Karl,' he said, crouching down. 'How's Starbuck.'

'Starbuck's not well,' Karl said, repeating what Mark had told him.

'Yes, I know that Karl. That's why Starbuck needs to be comforted, isn't it?'

'Yes.' Karl nodded and switched his attention from *Fireman Sam* to Starbuck, tucking the quilt around him so that only the dog's head was visible.

Christ, Mark hoped the poor dog's temperature wasn't up.

'Has Starbuck had his water today, Karl?'

'Yes.' Karl was adamant.

Mark nodded. 'Good.' So far, he thought. Now, how to approach the subject of food? He thought about saying that Starbuck needed to eat to get well. But then, if the dog didn't eat, wouldn't that be telling Karl that he wasn't going to get well?

'Poor Starbuck has a tummy pain, doesn't he, Karl?' Mark decided on a different tack.

Karl didn't answer this time.

'Does Karl have a tummy pain?' Mark asked, hoping in a backwards way that Karl just might have some rumblings in there from lack of food.

Karl said nothing, but pressed both hands against his diaphragm, which Mark took as an affirmative.

'I think Starbuck's tummy pain might be worse because he's hungry, Karl. I think Karl might be hungry, too. Shall we see if we can eat something, Karl?'

'Shall we see if we can eat something, Starbuck?' Karl said, easing the duvet away from the dog.

Relating to the dog without doubt. Mark almost fell back on his haunches. 'I think Starbuck might be more comfortable staying where he is, Karl,' he said, quickly, not wanting to disturb him. 'Dad will go and get us some food, okay?'

Mark headed for the door, relieved, then pretty damn pleased when he heard Karl say, 'Dad will get us some food, Starbuck.'

Forty minutes later, Mark was ready to go to phase two of operation persuasion. Starbuck would be having a general anaesthetic, so he'd have to starve him tomorrow, but Mark thought that all the more reason to try and get some sustenance down the dog today. He'd taken a little chicken and rice from him yesterday, so Mark was hoping he might now, which just might encourage Karl to eat something.

'Here we go,' he said, going back to the lounge with boiled chicken and rice mixed up in the dog bowl and his speciality, gluten-free fried chunky-chicken and rice on Karl's plate, portions carefully separated, as usual.

'Karl's dinner.' Mark set the plate on a smoothed bit of the duvet for Karl. 'And Starbuck's dinner, which as Starbuck's so well tucked-up,' he knelt in front of the dog, 'Dad is going to feed to him. Which bit do you fancy, Starbuck?'

Mark mentally crossed his fingers and plucked up a tender bit of chicken. 'Good, hey?' He smiled as the dog sniffed, caught it between his teeth, then swallowed.

'What was that, Starbuck? You want more rice with it?' Mark cocked his head. 'No problem. I'll just give a good stir and...' He made a great show of stirring the food, then offered it to Starbuck, one eye on Karl as he did so.

'Good boy, Starbuck.' Mark sighed, relieved, when the dog took the food.

Then almost died as Karl stirred his food.

****

Bouncing through her last Monday in the office while Sadie was safely back home, Donna was going some way to erasing the awfulness of the weekend. She was quite looking forward to getting to the respite home, she decided, giving Jean, who was on the phone vis-à-vis actual work this time, a smile and blowing Simon a kiss as she left.

She was certainly looking forward to seeing how little Karl was getting on, whether putting on his shoes had become a part of his morning ritual. Getting a glimpse of his dad wouldn't be too hard to cope with either. Donna felt that little flip in her chest again, like the soft flutter of butterfly's wings. She probably wouldn't though. Dr Lewis said that Jody usually picked Karl up in the evenings. Still, it would be nice to meet Jody properly. She couldn't believe how wrong she'd been about her.

About Mark. She smiled, recalling how he'd staggered into the pub with Sadie, looking pleased with himself despite being covered in dog hair and mud, then straightened her face when she recalled what he'd said before he'd gone down from the bedroom to speak to Matt: *I care very much about you. I know now's probably not a good time, but...* what was he going to say after the "*but*'? I don't think we should see each other anymore?

Donna had a little chew on her lip as she drove to the respite home. Had she lost him, her white knight in blue? And he had been. How selfless was a man who'd changed the bed linen, knowing she wouldn't want to sleep on sheets a stranger had touched? A man who'd put her lingerie through the washer, remembering to set the cycle to *delicates*? A man who, after a sleepless night, had looked for, located and brought her dog home, the loss of whom in such circumstances would truly have broken her heart.

She'd thought Mark would be the heart-breaker. Too good-looking, too perfect not to be. He wouldn't have been. The gloss might have worn off a little, eventually, but he wasn't bad at the core. Donna realised that now, now that she'd pushed him away, almost accused him. What a terrible thing to do, after all Mark had done. But then, her home had been invaded and her brain so addled she couldn't think straight. Donna tried to forgive herself, though she doubted Mark could.

Simon, bless him, had been aghast at the news of the burglary, fussing over her and bringing her *two* chocolate biccies with her tea. Then so agog he'd nearly fallen off his chair when she'd mentioned, *en passant*, that she'd woken to find a semi-naked policeman sleeping in her bed. Then so puzzled, he'd wondered if she wanted to *confide* when she said she hadn't actually slept with Mark.

Jean, partaking of girl-talk for the first time ever, thought Donna right to take things slowly.

Slowly? Donna had sighed, then had a little confide — in mean-Jean of all people, that she'd managed to actually move things backwards.

He might well have decided to move on. Donna's buoyant mood deflated as she pulled into the respite home car park. She hadn't been able to reach him on his mobile, via text or voice message and she didn't do telepathy. She couldn't blame him if he had. The man had enough problems without her: a demanding job, single parent to an autistic child. Could she ever have been more self-centred?

Donna tried his mobile one last time, once she'd parked. She took a deep breath when he invited her to leave a message and went for it, hoping to move things backwards to a place where they might have been able to move forward, had he not tripped over another policeman in her bedroom.

'Hi, Mark, it's me again,' she said, trying to sound cheery, 'the neurotic dog-lover who tends to make things terribly complicated. Um, not sure what to say now.' Donna paused, wondering how daft she was going to sound. Did it matter? If she'd lost him, she'd lost him, and it really didn't matter how she sounded.

She steeled herself and went on, 'The thing is, I was wondering if I could take up your kind suggestion to, um, have another bash at it? No demands on each other we can't cope with, obviously. You can't, I mean,' she clarified, not wanting him to think she was still totally focussed on her, 'with little Karl and work, and...' *Stop babbling, idiot.* 'Can we, do you think? Take it one day at a time, possibly? Call me, sometime anyway, whatever. Byeee.'

She ended on as upbeat a note as he could, tugged up the shoulders and went on in to the respite home, determined to be a friend to Karl in a world where, even if you didn't recognise you'd got friends, you certainly needed them.

'Hey, Donna.' Dr Lewis waved at her, from where he was talking to a technically-savvy child, destined to be a whiz-kid in the world of communication by satellite.

Donna waved back, had a quick word with one of the key-workers who wanted some help painting the props for a role-play game, then went straight over to Karl.

'Hello, Karl,' she said, having noticed he'd retreated to his own space, in the obvious absence of his furry best friend. 'Can I play with your bricks, please?' She seated herself carefully next to him on the floor, aware that Karl had only recently learnt the concept of sharing, thanks to Starbuck's help in integrating him with other children.

Karl didn't say anything, but didn't object.

Donna set to building a skyscraper next to his. 'Where's your best-friend, Starbuck, today, Karl?' she asked, after a moment.

'Starbuck's not well,' Karl offered, without hesitation.

Oh, Lord. Of course Starbuck wasn't well. She'd known he wasn't. And she, too preoccupied with her own problems, hadn't given it another moment's thought.

God, sometimes she was so...

Donna chose her moment to have a quick word with Dr Lewis and learned that Starbuck was being operated on that very afternoon.

'Fairly routine operation, I gather. Removal of an intestinal obstruction,' Dr Lewis said, helping to get children who were going home coated and ready to leave. 'Should be right as rain in no time. Karl does seem a bit lost without... Whoa, Jamie, give it back.' Dr Lewis stopped and went off after another little boy to avert an impending crisis.

'Thank God,' Donna breathed, relieved, then proceeded to worry. So why hadn't Mark returned any of her calls? Even assuming it was routine, he'd know that she'd find out if she were here at the respite home. That she might be concerned.

Unless he was on hush-hush op possibly? Or somewhere else no mobiles were allowed. A meeting perhaps? A hospital? Police were often called there. But then, it could be that he didn't want to return her calls, of course. Donna decided not to dwell on that.

Half an hour later — and two masterpieces produced by Karl depicting his furry best friend, Karl was still waiting to be collected.

'Most odd,' Dr Lewis commented, furrowing his brow. 'Jody's rarely late, and when she is, Mark always... that will probably be one of them now,' he said, heading for the ringing telephone.

He came back looking further troubled.

'Problem?' Donna asked, looking up from Karl's new artistic endeavour, depicting Donna's three-legged best friend.

'Jody,' Dr Lewis confirmed. 'Her mum's taken a turn for the worse, which means we have a problem. She can't get a hold of Mark, apparently.'

'Oh.' Donna's *oh* was definitely a worried one now.

'I'd better ring the university, cancel the lecture I'm giving and take Karl over to the accommodation block to wait. Can't leave young Karl here on his own, can we, Karl?' Dr Lewis said, heading back to the phone.

'Karl doesn't like being on his own,' Karl piped up, still studiously crayoning.

'Definitely progress.' Dr Lewis smiled at Donna as he dialled.

'I could take him across and stay with him,' Donna offered. 'It's a bit short notice to cancel a whole lecture, isn't it? Or maybe...' she had a think as to a more suitable alternative than a place Karl wasn't that familiar with '... take Karl on home maybe?'

'That's very kind of you, Donna, but I'm not sure Karl would be comfortable going into a strange environment, particularly without Starbuck.'

'No, no, I meant Karl's home, assuming I can get a key, which I think I can. And, um, I have an idea that Karl might come with me if...'

****

'Well, I never...' Dr Lewis looked on in wonder as Karl slipped neatly into the backseat of Donna's car next to Sadie. 'You're a natural, Donna O'Connor. Have a gold star.'

'Thank you.' Donna gave him a mini-curtsey, before climbing in the driver's side.

'No, thank *you*.' Dr Lewis smiled his appreciation. 'You, too, Matt. I wish my teenage son was half so accommodating occasionally.'

'You need to work on the eyelashes.' Matt imparted his mother's powers of persuasion, fluttering Donna-like beguiling lashes as he headed towards the passenger side.

'I'll work on it.' Dr Lewis had a quick blink. 'Okay, guys.' He patted the car roof, seeing them off. 'I'll keep trying to get a hold of Mark. He has my mobile anyway, but I'm thinking he doesn't know there's been a hitch with Jody if she hasn't been able to reach him. He'll probably be relieved to find Karl's at home. Check in with you later, Donna.'

Donna gave him a wave and pulled off, not sure Mark would be pleased to find the whole world and its dog at his house, including her troublesome self, but at least Karl would be safe in familiar surroundings.

****

'Hello, young man.' Robert, Donna assumed, greeted Karl as they piled out of the car outside Mark's house. 'Hello, Gem...' He squinted at Donna. 'You're not Gemma.'

'Gemma?' Donna glanced curiously at Evelyn.

'Oh, dear.' Evelyn shook her head resignedly.

Obviously expecting her to turn into a suspicious, slitty-eyed monster. Well, she wasn't going to. Donna adopted her serene *woman of substance* expression. Gemma could be anyone. His... Donna tried to give her a label that hadn't already been taken by women in Mark's life... gardener?

'Oh, no, Gemma's the old one.' Robert nodded to himself.

'Old?' Donna mouthed at her mum.

'Previous,' Evelyn translated.

'Ah.' Donna nodded enlightened, then narrowed her eyes. 'Previous what?'

'Childminder, Donna.' Evelyn sighed. 'Which is why Dot and I got confused about Jody's role in Mark's life. Robert thought she was called Gemma, who was actually Jody's pre-de... Oh, never mind.' She stopped, as Donna knitted her ever-perplexed brow. 'Suffice it to say she and Mark were never an item.'

'Is this the latest girl, then?' Robert eyed Donna interestedly. 'I must say he does seem to get through them.'

'Childminders, Donna,' Evelyn supplied patiently.

'Think he'd settle down with one or the other, wouldn't you.' Robert pondered. 'I quite liked that young, slim one myself. What was her name? Ah, yes, Rachel.'

'Rachel?' Donna looked at her mum, boggle-eyed.

'I have no idea.' Evelyn eyed the skies.

'Then there was... who was it? Kath —'

'Yes, thank you, Robert.' Evelyn gave him a swift nudge. 'This is Donna, my daughter. Currently *seeing* Mark.'

'Ah.' Robert smiled. 'Oh.' He looked a bit sheepish. 'Well, why didn't you say so?'

'I did, one or two thousand times.' Evelyn turned to the house with a weary sigh. 'Honestly, Robert. Do try and keep up.'

'Right you are.' Robert saluted, and scooted after her. 'I'd never have thought she was your daughter.' He mused. 'Pretty girl, isn't she?'

'Idiot man.' Evelyn marched on.

Bemused, Donna watched them all troop towards Mark's house: Matt sloping along holding Karl's hand, who was holding firm to the lead of her three legged dog; followed by the odd couple, and decided Mark might do well to avoid coming home.

Was he all right? Donna worried as she trailed after them. Granted, he might not know about Jody's situation, but he must surely have got one of the five million messages Donna had left him.

Perhaps he really was pulling away now he'd helped her put her house back in order. She really couldn't blame him. A mortifying image of herself being sick in the bathroom wearing fishnets and polystyrene cups, flashed through her mind, and she wondered what man in his right mind wouldn't run a mile?

****

Mark shook his head, sure he'd rung the wrong number. 'Evelyn?' he asked, confused.

'Well I was when I last looked, though you'd never think so to listen to your father. If he calls me Hyacinth Bucket again, I may do something —'

'Evelyn,' Mark cut her short, 'where are you?'

'Standing talking to you on the phone, dear boy.'

'I must have rung the wrong number.' Mark shook his head again. 'I'd better go, Evelyn. I meant to phone home.'

'You have. Well done, ET.'

Mark held the receiver away from his ear and looked at it askew. 'Sorry?'

'I'm at your house, Mark. This is why I am answering your phone. Where else would I be when my daughter had to bring your abandoned son home and needed your father's key?'

'Donna?' Mark really was confused now.

'Yes, Donna. The one whose bedroom you were in throwing your weight around, remember?'

'Evelyn, I remember, trust me. Now, I appreciate you'd be concerned for Donna and want to fight her corner, but can we fight later? I'm in a phone box and I really need to talk to her.'

'You can't,' Evelyn informed him shortly. 'She's putting Karl to bed.'

Bed? *Jesus*, did Donna realise that Karl would need to go through his rituals before he got into bed? More so, without Starbuck. What in God's name was going on? The one day he forgets his mobile and all hell breaks loose.

'Okay, look, I don't have my mobile, Evelyn. If Donna needs me, tell her I'm on my way.'

'I'm sure she does need you. If she wasn't busy trying to be so independent, she might…'

Mark left Evelyn talking to herself and ran back to his car, knowing he'd be too late to avert a crisis if there was one. Maybe Donna could cope. She'd been working at the respite home, after all, and he didn't need Dr Lewis to tell him how competent she was. But Donna was not built like a Gladiator. And that's the kind of strength sometimes needed to hold Karl until he calmed down.

Evelyn was there, though. And his dad. Mark tried to calm himself, glancing over to the backseat, seeing Starbuck still flat out there and reminding himself to drive sensibly. What had happened with Jody? He hoped to God she was okay. Why hadn't he given her the vet's contact number, for Christ's sake? Because he hadn't envisaged complications. The sort that you sometimes can't avoid.

Starbuck had needed major surgery, but he'd pulled through. That was something to be hugely grateful for. Whatever mayhem broke loose today, at least Karl and he might be able to get back to some sort of normality tomorrow.

****

Evelyn flapped a hand, shushing him before he was through the door. Mark glanced past her as she pointed to the lounge, then did a double-take as he saw Matt in the hall.

'Crisis averted,' Matt said immediately, obviously noting Mark's apprehension. 'Karl's kipping on the lounge floor.'

Mark raked his hand through his hair, disbelieving. He had to be kidding.

He walked quietly to the lounge door to see for himself, then, 'Bloody Hell!' he was flabbergasted at what he did see. Karl was fast asleep, comfortably tucked under his duvet, another underneath him, and Sadie right beside him.

Jesus. 'How?' he asked quietly, stepping away from the door before he disturbed them.

'Um, well he just sort of lay down, shut his eyes and... Actually it wasn't quite that simple,' Matt admitted as Mark stared at him, incredulous. 'I now have my watching *Fireman Sam* badge and mum has a black eye...'

'A... What?' Mark paled.

'Relax. She's tougher than you think. S'why you'd betta not mess wit her, yo?'

'What happened?' Mark asked, as if he didn't know.

Matt got back to serious. 'Well, he did four circuits of the stairs, landing and the bedroom. Then he just threw a wobbly. Not sure what caused it.'

'Was the bathroom occupied?' Mark asked.

'Not sure. Why?'

'Has to flush the loo, then flick the landing light before he can... Long story.'

'Got you.' Matt nodded, seeming to understand. 'Anyhow, Mum got him in a bear-hug eventually and managed to convince him Sadie wasn't feeling well after all the trips upstairs with her one front leg, so...'

Karl went back down to the dog. Mark got it. Because he didn't want Sadie going away like Starbuck had, who also wasn't feeling well.

Mark ran his hand over his neck, disbelieving, astonished, but above all, jubilant. Did Donna have any idea what she'd done? Widened Karl's scope to accept the abstract? Opened his mind further to the fact that things from the same family tree didn't necessarily come in the same packaging. Starbuck was a dog. Sadie was a dog. Simple. Not in Karl's mind: one with four legs, one with three.

As for getting Karl to break with exhausting ritual: to sleep somewhere different. To most people it might not amount to much. Their kid was camping out. No big deal. To Mark, to Karl, it meant, quite literally, that the shackles were off. That for the first time in his life, his son might be able to go on holiday, to feel the sand between his toes, to paddle in the sea.

'I, er...' Mark glanced down, sucked in a breath, blew it out, and still he couldn't speak. 'Your mum's definitely special, you know that, don't you?' he finally managed.

'Definitely, but in a good way,' Matt conceded as Donna appeared from the kitchen, a frozen haddock over one eye.

'Hi.' Donna smiled hesitantly when she saw Mark. 'Um, Robert,' she explained the presence of fish on her face. 'He's trying to bring my swelling down. Hope this wasn't your supper.'

'I don't mind sharing.' Mark laughed. 'Just be careful where you put the tartar sauce though.' His eyes drifted involuntarily to her lips.

Donna blushed the way she did. And every time she did, it melted Mark's heart just a little bit more. 'And be careful you don't defrost all over your blouse,' he said, stepping towards her to ease a loose tendril of hair from under her haddock.

'I brought Karl home,' Donna explained, looking at him with one uncertain pretty green eye, even now, looking nervous up close to him.

Mark wished she wouldn't be. 'I gathered.' He smiled, mesmerised for a moment, and more in love with this woman who managed to look sexy even with a frozen fish on her face, than he thought he could ever be. 'What did you do, drug him?'

'No!' Donna's fish slipped.

'Ouch.' Mark winced. 'I'm joking, Donna.' He trailed a thumb gently over her bruised cheek. 'And I'm truly grateful. You might not realise it, but what you've done, persuading Karl to step out of the norm, sleep anywhere but where he's used to, is nothing short of a miracle.'

'Oh, it was nothing.' Donna blushed again, pleased with herself this time. 'I've got another eye on the other side, see?' She pointed, and smiled.

Which had Mark smiling right down to his shoes.

'Jody obviously wasn't in a position to with her mum being ill, and it really wasn't too much trouble once the troops were organised.' Donna nodded to the kitchen where Evelyn and Robert were arguing in whispers.

'I assumed you might have been detained with Starbuck, so I left another message on your mobile. Did you get any of my, um...'

Donna trailed off as Mark muttered, 'Starbuck! *Shit*, I left him in the car,' and shot out of the door.

Chapter Twenty-Four

It'll be fine, Donna told herself again as she selected her best, clean and pressed — bless Mark's thoughtfulness — lingerie. Nothing risqué, she decided, racy and lacy not being suitable for the hospital.

No word from Mark. She peered at her mobile whilst applying enough make-up for a brave face, hoping it might flash up a message. Nothing, which meant either he didn't get the bare-all message she'd left, or he had, and wasn't returning her calls by way of his answer.

She wished she'd had a chance to speak to him alone, to ask him outright what he'd meant by *I care very much about you, but...* That had been impossible though, with all the excitement when he'd brought Starbuck into the hall.

Poor Starbuck. They'd had to take a little bit of his intestine away, apparently. And now he was going to be on water and antibiotics, followed by bland food for a while. Donna had offered to help. Mark had smiled and said he'd ring her. But he hadn't; so, even without her odd million messages, that added up to him not wanting to pursue things. Didn't it?

Stop it. Donna selected sensible outer attire to match her sensible drawers and told herself not to be silly. Mark's smile had been his usual twinkly-eyed one — Donna's heart fluttered hopefully — so if he had decided her *no complications* stipulation was just too complicated, at least it meant they were still friends, which was... absolutely no good at all when Donna's inclination was to get good and complicated with him, in any and all compromising positions.

'Do you think he'd notice, hon,' she plopped despondently down on the bed next to Sadie, who with her snout and front paw hanging over the edge of the bed, looked to be missing Mark too, 'if I whipped off his shirt and just bit him next time I saw him?'

Donna glanced down as Sadie glanced up, showing the whites of her chocolate brown eyes. 'No, you're right, babe.' She sighed. 'Probably would be a touch on the excessive side.'

Oh, well. It was her own fault. Drive a man away hard enough and he'd go, she supposed. 'I wished I hadn't, Sade. That I was brave enough to pick up the phone and say, make mad passionate love to me.'

To Mark obviously, Donna added a mental addendum.

Ask him to just love her.

As she loved him.

No complications.

****

She would call him. She didn't like the loneliness of being alone... without Mark. Just as soon as she got back from the hospital she would ring him, depending on when she got back, and whether she got back in one piece.

It occurred to Donna on the way there to extract her head from sand and concern herself about bits of her body other than her heart. She hadn't really had time to think much about her appointment, which was probably a good thing, but now she was almost there. She'd be absolutely fine, she assured herself, popping her head back in the sand.

Donna checked her watch twenty minutes later and strained her ears in hopes of hearing Alicia arrive. She wasn't feeling quite so fine, after all, Donna realised. Very un-fine, in fact.

Where on earth was she? Alicia had said she'd be here, though Donna had tried to wave away her sister's concerns, whilst wondering how she'd found out about the appointment, other than by telepathy.

Not by mind-reading. By *letter*-reading, Alicia had told her, sounding rather miffed when she'd rung. The letter on top of the microwave Donna hadn't bothered to mention, she'd pointed out, and then insisted on meeting her here. Donna had been quietly relieved, whilst telling herself there was no need. Now, she was terrified, and there was every need.

She wanted a hand to hold. What was she doing here, alone? The last time she'd been on her own in a hospital, she'd left empty-handed and broken-hearted, so why on earth had she imagined she could cope on her own, again?

Because she'd had to before.

Because she'd thought she should be able to this time.

Would Mark have been here, she wondered, if things had moved on? If she'd let them move on... enough to confide in him. To ask him to be.

Donna's heart answered for her. *You're a fool, Donna O'Connor. The man tried. But you just kept pushing. I care very much about you, but...* I can't do this, was what Mark had been going to say. She just knew it.

Donna sighed down to her soul, willing herself to stay on the trolley as she heard the consultant coming back, though she actually felt like squeezing out of the open window above her.

'Well, we're all fixed up,' Mr Williams said, smiling warmly as he came back into the examination room. 'If you'd like to pop your things back on, the nurse will take you along for your biopsy. Don't want you getting lost, do we?'

Yes we do. *Biopsy!?* He called it a *fine needle aspiration* five minutes ago. Donna much preferred the former, less scary description.

'I think we're dealing with a non-carcinogenic fibroadenoma,' Mr Williams went on, nodding reassuringly.

Donna didn't feel very reassured somehow. Talk English, she wanted to shout. She really had no idea what he was talking about.

She didn't need to. Her face must have spoken volumes. Mr Williams smiled again, seated himself on the end of the trolley and set about explaining in simple layman's language. 'A benign lump,' he said. 'Nothing to worry about, but until we've removed a sample, we can't be sure. That's where the biopsy comes in.'

'It's a very simple procedure and quite painless,' he assured her. 'You'll have a local anaesthetic, then a needle will be inserted in order to extract a few cells.'

Painless? Donna looked at him, unconvinced.

'The good news is, the results should only take about thirty to forty minutes. Is that all right for you?'

'Fine.' Donna finally offered him a smile. Then smiled at the nurse, because the nurse was smiling at her, but she really didn't feel like smiling at all.

'Don't worry, it might look a bit daunting, but it really is a simple procedure,' the nurse assured her, helped Donna sort herself out, then led her off to the cytology department.

'Dr Smith's ever so sweet, so don't feel intimidated,' she said, once they'd arrived, obviously noticing Donna was about to disappear into her shoes.

Donna nodded and tugged up her shoulders.

'Take a seat,' the nurse said, indicating an empty corridor. 'It should only take about fifteen minutes or so, then you can find your way back to reception.' She smiled brightly and was gone.

The nurse was right. It did all look a bit daunting. Donna worried and waited. She was also right about the doctor, to Donna's relief. Dr

Smith was lovely, thank God, explaining the procedure, outlining everything before she actually did it. And the consultant had been right, too. The procedure was painless, even though Donna was sure she must be rigid with fear.

Twenty minutes later, Donna was trying to find her way back to reception down a myriad of corridors, first one way, then the wrong way, then back on track past the ultrasound department. Then stopping, and walking casually back again.

It *was* her. Donna peered around the open double-doors into the waiting area. Leticia! Looking pale, scared and very much on her own.

So where was he with aspirations to gentleman? Not here, obviously, holding her hand, surprise, surprise. So what did she do? Donna hovered in the corridor. Should she go in and speak to her? Go on and ignore her?

'Leticia Buckland?' A radiographer called her name, and Donna knew her decision was made. She could hardly duck out of sight when Leticia had looked up and looked straight at her. Wonderful. Just what she needed, a chance of meeting with the imminent mother of Jeremy's child? She swallowed hard, and actually felt almost sorry for the woman.

'Donna?' Leticia stared at her, then looked around, no doubt wondering who it was Donna was with.

'Hi, Leticia.' Donna plastered a smile in place and walked over to her. If Leticia was having Jeremy's baby, especially now she'd realised that the man was a self-preserving rat after their conversation at the pub, then she might well need that shoulder.

Donna could do that. She might need a little scaffolding this time, to keep her shoulders broad and up there, but she could be a friend to a woman who would most definitely need one.

'So, how are you?' Donna asked in the absence of anything else suitable to say.

'Good, thank you for asking.' Leticia smiled, though not very convincingly. 'You?'

Donna forced a smile back. 'Oh, fine,' she said, airily. 'You know.'

'Good. I'm glad.' Leticia smiled timidly again, wringing her hands together in that nervous way she did. 'Are you here for, er?' Her eyes flitted to Donna's midriff.

Donna knitted her brow, then, 'Good Lord, no.' Her eyes shot wide. 'I haven't even got... Ahem.' A man, she was going to say. '... an appointment,' she said instead. 'Just visiting someone.'

'Ah.' Leticia nodded, then fiddled idly with her necklace.

'I, um, assume...' Donna glanced at the telltale little bulge lower down.

'Yes.' Leticia looked immensely relieved, as if she hadn't quite known how to tell her. 'I have my three-monthly scan. Just routine, I hope.'

'I'm sure it'll be fine.' Donna smiled, a genuine smile this time, because that's what the woman needed. Not bitchiness or snide comment. She needed support, especially with someone being obvious by his absence. 'Is, um...' Donna hesitated, wondering how to ask after the proud father.

'Jeremy here?' Leticia finished. 'No. And nor will he be.'

'Leticia Buckland?' the radiographer called again, as Leticia hesitated, her eyes conveying a thousand emotions.

'I should go,' she said. 'I, er...'

'Do you want me to wait?' Donna asked, empathising with every one of those emotions.

Leticia beamed, actual smile lines and all. 'No,' she said. 'Thanks so much Donna, but Daddy's collecting me.'

'Right, well, you'd better go on in then.' Donna nodded towards the radiographer, who was looking as if she was about to move on to the next mum-to-be. 'But call me, Leticia, anytime, if you fancy a chat, or a girl's night, or maybe someone to go dog-walking with. You have my number.'

Leticia nodded, her eyes filling up. 'I'd like that,' she said, reaching out to give Donna's hand a squeeze before turning to go in.

Donna's little heart fair burst with pride. She'd done it, extended an olive branch to the woman Jeremy had left her for. The soon-to-be mother of his child. She might be superstitious, neurotic, and judgemental, but right then, Donna was mightily pleased with herself.

She notched up her chin, turned around, and walked — straight into Mark.

'Donna O'Connor...' he cocked his head to one side, looking absolutely perplexed, 'you never cease to amaze me.'

****

'You doing okay?' Mark asked as they sat waiting for her results.

Donna nodded. 'Uh, huh,' she said, her huge green eyes like saucers, which told Mark she was anything but.

'Good.' He took a breath, then tentatively took her hand.

Donna didn't say anything. Just looked straight ahead, then, hesitantly, wove her fingers through his.

'How did you know?' she asked, after a moment.

Mark took another breath. 'Alicia,' he lied, suspecting that coughing up to reading her personal mail and that *he* informed Alicia might not go a great way towards earning her trust.

Donna glanced at him curiously.

'She thought I might be able to get here a bit quicker with the assistance of blue-lights and sirens.'

Donna's mouth curved into a smile.

'Lorry shed its load, apparently. She had no hope of getting here herself. They're taking people off the motorway now; lanes closed both ways, but she said she thought you might need, er...'

'A hand to hold?'

'Something like that.' Mark smiled.

'I do,' Donna admitted.

Mark nodded. 'Hold away.'

Two minutes later, Donna was quiet, but holding on tight.

She'd stop his circulation if she held any tighter.

That was okay. He'd give his hand and the arm attached to it to be able to tell her how he felt and hear the same words back. Now wasn't the right time though. Mark sighed quietly inside, wondering whether there would ever be a right time. Whether what he so badly wanted to say would be what Donna wanted to hear.

If it wasn't, he'd just have to deal with it. Whatever, it would be insensitive to bring it up while she needed to focus on dealing with this.

The results would be good though. Mark was sure of it.

They had to be. He tried hard not to think about his mother's rapid deterioration, whose misplaced pride and fear of the unknown prevented her from seeking the help that could have saved her.

Could he risk telling Donna he'd be there whatever the outcome, if she wanted him to be, without seeming pushy?

He would. As soon as the consultant said what he'd got to say and they were alone, he'd tell her, that much at least.

Mark gave Donna's hand a reciprocal squeeze as the consultant walked towards them. *Christ, just one more miracle please,* he prayed hard.

'Donna,' the consultant smiled, 'and?' He looked at Mark.

'Mark. Mark Evans,' Mark supplied, extending his hand. 'Donna's… boyfriend.'

'Well, Donna,' Mr Williams said, shaking Mark's hand, 'good news. The cytology report is back and normal.'

Donna closed her eyes. 'Thank you.'

'Thank God.' Mark dragged his hand through his hair. 'How reliable is it?' he asked, wrapping an arm instinctively around Donna.

'Ninety-nine point eight percent according to a recent study. Removal would guarantee a clear diagnosis, of course.'

'How would, um?' Donna trailed off.

Mark tightened his arm around her.

'Just a small operation. A lumpectomy, to take away your little alien, that's all.' Mr Williams smiled reassuringly. 'It would be carried out under general anaesthetic, as a day-case, so you'd be back cuddling up on the sofa by teatime. I'll leave you to have a think about it.'

'So, what *do* you think?' Mark asked, steering Donna back towards a chair.

Donna nestled closer. 'That I quite like having the strong arm of the law draped about me in a crisis.'

'It might need surgery to remove it.' Mark slowed their walk to a halt and turned to face her. 'Donna, there's something I need to say…' he started, realising now more than ever, that time was too damn precious to waste '… about us and where we go from here. But…'

'Cooee, Donna!'

Great. Perfect-bloody-timing. Mark groaned quietly inside as Simon and Alicia skidded towards them.

Chapter Twenty-Five

'Uh, oh, policeman alert,' Matt called, from where he was attempting to select cross-generational music to please all of the people at his party. 'Hide the Ecstasy, Mother.'

Donna turned — trying not to look too ecstatic — from where she was helping Simon supervise Nathan grilling his sausages.

'Oh, blimey.' Simon removed his arm from Donna's shoulders *tout de suite*. 'We're just good friends,' he assured Mark, who walked towards them, one arm around Karl's shoulders, who was walking side-by-side with Starbuck, but un-tethered.

Which was most definitely progress. 'You bought the sunshine.' Donna smiled, glad Mark had come, even if friends were all they were destined to be. She could do friends, so long as he didn't stand too close to her with his intoxicating persona… um, aroma.

Mark smiled his twinkly-eyed smile back. 'But of course. Madame's wish is my command.' He gave her a short bow, and prompted Karl, who handed her the box of chocolates he'd been carrying.

'Ooh, Belgian chocolates! Thank you, Karl. They're my absolute favourites.' Donna beamed, delighted with the chocolates and the little boy carrying them, who'd been concentrating hard on his task, if the little "v" in his brow was anything to judge by. 'But how did you know?'

'Never met a woman yet who didn't,' Karl replied smartly.

'Oh.' Donna glanced from Karl to Mark, uncertain.

'Er, shop assistant. She offered me a bit of advice,' he said sheepishly, as he handed Donna a bottle of wine. 'If there's anything else Madame requires?'

'Flowers,' Matt whispered, whipping past to relieve Donna of the wine.

'I'm working on it,' Mark replied likewise, then smiled disarmingly at Donna.

'What are you two up to?' she asked suspiciously.

'Nothing,' Mark shrugged, the epitome of innocence. 'Just man-talk.'

Hmm? Donna wasn't convinced. Man-talk and the *flower* word just didn't go together somehow. Matt had obviously suggested he bring some, and Mark had obviously thought better of it, thinking Donna might read too much into the gesture.

But he'd brought chocolates. Donna's mind drifted back to their conversation, when they'd both been wet through to the skin and shivering in the hall. When he'd held her so close and kissed her so sweetly, he'd set her senses on fire and touched the very core of her. He'd brought a little bit of sunshine into her life then, too. Even through the incessant rain.

'Donna,' Mark cut through her thoughts, stepping towards her to pinch a sausage from the cooked pile parked next to the barbie, 'I can see you're tied up right now, but do you think we could slip off and have a quiet word sometime?'

'About?' Donna asked, her little butterfly's wings flapping manically. Was he about to deliver his *I care very much about you, but...* speech?

'Us,' Mark said quietly. 'I realise it's not a great time, but I was hoping we could...' He trailed off, glancing skew-whiff at Donna, who was now trying very hard to keep her face straight.

'What?' he asked, obviously bemused as Nathan laughed too.

'I'm glad someone's enjoying my cooking,' Nathan chortled, spearing a burger.

'You're dangling your sausage, darling,' Simon enlightened him, spearing one of his own.

'Damn.' Mark tried to snatch the sausage back, but Starbuck was quicker.

'Whoops.' Donna all but doubled up as Starbuck took a fancy to his finger. 'Well, he has been on a light diet,' she pointed out. 'He's probably starving.'

'I'll save him the other nine for afters.' Mark sighed good-naturedly. 'Can we talk, Donna? Please? Somewhere quieter?'

'Well, yes, but I am terribly busy, just now,' Donna said, demonstratively shuffling plates. In truth, she hadn't liked the *I realise it's not a great time* bit. 'Can't we just talk while I work?' She picked up a batch of burgers to deliver to the garden table.

'We could,' Mark said, sidestepping Sadie, who'd hopped out to greet the great benefactor of sausages interestedly, 'but...'

'Mark, how lovely.' Evelyn appeared from the patio doors bearing picky bits. 'We're so glad you could come, aren't we, Donna? Could you go now, please, and take your father with you? He's in there,' she rolled her eyes towards the lounge behind her, 'trying to light the living-flame gas-fire with a match, dim-witted man.'

With which Robert appeared at the doors. 'I might have lost a few marbles, but I heard that, woman,' he boomed, closely followed by, 'Ouch! Bloody hell,' and tossed his lighted match out.

'*Shi-it*,' Mark muttered. 'Could you, er?' He glanced from Donna to Karl, then went to check on his dad.

No, Mark. I thought I'd give him a beer and let him wander around on his own. 'Hi, Karl.' Donna bent down to his level. 'How's Starbuck?'

'Starbuck's doing pretty good,' Karl said importantly, obviously repeating something Mark had said, but his diction was becoming more his own, and his vocabulary seemed to be growing daily, which was progress with a capital P.

'Ooh, I do like your shoes.' Donna glanced down to see Karl was wearing a shiny new pair.

'We went shopping.' Karl said, taking a bite out of his burger. 'Starbuck chose Karl's shoes,' he went on, looking pleased with himself. That little speech wasn't verbatim, she was willing to bet.

'How's the burger, Karl?' Simon asked, looking super-pleased with himself as second master-chef in command.

'Shi-it,' Karl repeated what Mark had said matter-of-factly.

Simon arched an eyebrow. 'We'll work on the recipe,' he said, with a resolute nod. 'Nathan, more sauce, less burning please…'

'Come on, Karl,' Donna laughed and took Karl's hand, 'let's go and find Starbuck a nice bed we can bring out and put next to Sadie's, shall we?'

'Karl's going to sleep next to Sadie, but that's all right, Sadie doesn't snore,' Karl said, referring back to the conversation he and Donna had had when he camped out on Mark's lounge floor.

'Good idea, Karl. We'll find you a cushion, while we're at it.' Donna squeezed his hand.

'Karl's going to sleep next to Starbuck, too.' Karl chatted on. 'When someone's sad or not well, they sometimes need someone who loves them to hold them, and then they'll feel better.'

'That's right, Karl.' Donna blinked, to facilitate seeing where she was going.

She felt quite overwhelmed, happier for Mark and Karl both than they could possibly know, yet sad at the same time. How amazing was it that Karl seemed to be linking up conversations? How devastating would it be if she didn't get to see much of this little boy she'd grown so fond of, which well she might not if Mark and she drifted apart.

Donna sighed, supposing she would have to hear Mark's let's just be friends speech if they weren't to keep skirting around each other, which would be a bit difficult on the back lawn of a semi-detached house.

Talking of whom. She smiled as she came across Mark in the kitchen, dousing his dad's ardour with a glass of beer.

'Back in five minutes, Dad,' Mark said. 'I just need to have a word with Donna, okay?'

'Fine.' Robert took a swig of his ale. 'Leg over, is it, son?'

'Pardon?' Donna glanced at Mark goggle-eyed.

'Old Leg Over. It's a traditional Yorkshire ale,' Mark explained with a wince, 'brewed with, er...'

'Quality grain malts from a traditional Yorkshire maltster,' his dad picked up. 'Takes its name from fell-runners, who have to climb over thousands of stone walls in the Yorkshire Dales,' Robert went on nostalgically

'Yes, thanks, Dad.' Mark ran his hand over his neck. 'Donna, do you think we could...'

'One fell-runner won three races in one day in the nineteen-twenties, you know?'

'Yes, Dad.' Mark sighed and went cross-eyed.

'No mean feat that, lad.'

Mark slapped his hand against his head. 'Yes, Dad. Thanks Dad. Donna could we, please...'

'Babysitters, honestly,' Alicia moaned, cutting Mark short as she stropped into the kitchen, arms full of fractious toddler. 'I'm coated and ready to go, and she rings to say she has a headache. Oh, hello Mark.' She gave him a distracted smile along with her child. 'Hang on to Jack, will you?'

'No problem.' Mark smiled resignedly. 'Fancy going outside for some peace and quiet and a sausage, mate?' he asked as Adele burst into song from the garden. 'Coming, Karl?'

'Find Starbuck a nice bed we can bring out.' Karl furrowed his brow sternly. Mark looked at Donna hopefully and hoisted Jack higher in his arms, who was repeating 'sauthage,' his hand outstretched in toddler-bordering-on-tantrum mode.

'Save it for your husband, honey, I told her,' Alicia moaned on, following Donna to the utility.

And back. 'I mean do they want the job, or not? I have a headache every day. Can *I* just shrug off my responsibilities?'

Alicia walked straight past Mark to help herself to a glass of wine.

Donna hardly dared look up from her dog basket. 'I'll follow you out, shall I?' she asked aware of Mark's hands-full predicament.

'Thanks.' Mark smiled over Jack, and walked straight into Evelyn and Dot coming in from the garden.

'But you're like chalk and cheese, Eve,' Dot said, deep in conversation with Evelyn. 'I'm amazed that you can tolerate him for more than five minutes.'

'Me too, if I'm honest,' Evelyn said as the pair split up to walk around Mark. The man's as mad as a hatter, but I suppose he makes me laugh. And we both enjoy the same things, watching old films...'

'Gone With the Wind.' Robert winked.

'Nostalgia's fine, Robert,' Evelyn replied, haughtily. 'Romance is most definitely not.'

'Evelyn,' Mark tried to get word in, 'do you think you could take Jack...'

'Aw, tha's a reet spoilsport, sometimes, wench.' Robert went colloquially back to his roots.

'Wench?' Evelyn huffed indignantly. 'I'm as likely to serve *you* tea as pork pies are to fly, Robert Evans.'

'Er, Evelyn...' Mark tried again as Jack let out a sausage-deprived howl.

'Like I said,' his dad replied, with a smirk, 'a right spoil...'

'Right, that's it!' Mark shouted, startling Jack along with everyone else into silence. Then, without further ado, he plucked a sausage from Dot's well-stacked plate, presented it to Jack, then presented Jack to Evelyn.

'Donna, we need to talk.' Mark turned to Donna, relieved her of the dog basket and presented it to Matt, who'd wandered in for some legal alcohol and was now looking perplexed under his *Bart Simpson, I have issues* cap.

'But where are we going?' Donna asked as she trailed after Mark, no choice but to with her hand firmly in his.

'To walk Sadie and Starbuck. Coming, Karl?'

Karl hesitated, then took Mark's other hand.

'But is Starbuck supposed to be walking after her op?'

'Short walks only. And we're not walking, we're riding, then walking.' Mark glanced at her. 'If that's all right with you?' he asked, his macho-assertiveness faltering.

'But what about my guests?' Donna asked, confounded as they swung by two cooks debating their latest culinary catastrophe.

'Ooh, a man with a mission.' Simon pressed a hand to his chest. 'I do like a good drama. Come on Nathe.' With which the master-chefs downed spatulas and followed.

'Come, Starbuck.' Mark gestured with his head. Starbuck immediately obeyed, trotting alongside as they headed for the gate.

'Sade?' Donna called. 'Oh,' she said, noting Sadie seemed to have switched affections to tongue-lolling and tail swishing in pursuit of Starbuck.

'Do we have leads?' Donna caught breath to ask.

'Leads.' Matt dutifully replied, bringing up the rear, behind Dot and Alicia, closely followed by Robert and Evelyn, who was clutching Jack.

Matt's mate, Ed, watched the entourage file past, not particularly moved. 'We playing *Mortal Kombat* on your new PS3 then, Matt, or what?'

'Lata, mate. Sorry. Adult-sitting.' Matt trudged wearily on. Then stopped and turned back. 'What PS3?'

'The one that bloke said was for your birthday.' Ed nodded at Mark.

Donna blinked sideways at Mark as he strode on. 'But Mark, how did you ...?'

Mark shrugged. 'Isn't that what all big boys want for their birthday?'

****

Once on the pavement, Mark headed for his car. 'You riding shotgun with the dog posse, Karl?' he asked, and waited, while Karl debated.

'Come on, Starbuck, time for our walk.' Karl made up his mind, scrambling into the backseat after Starbuck.

Mark turned to Donna. 'Promise not to move?'

Donna nodded, perplexed. 'I promise,' she said, allowing him time to help Sadie into the car.

'You're a man of few words, suddenly,' she said, climbing into the passenger side, as Dot and Robert argued over the passenger seat of Evelyn's car behind.

'Do hurry up, children.' Evelyn sighed. 'Before the happy couple dash off to their secret venue without us.'

Donna and Mark exchanged amused glances.

'I'm driving,' Simon announced, standing outside the car beyond that.

'No, I'm driving,' Nathan argued. 'It's my car.'

'But you drove here,' Simon protested, taking the keys.

'Yes, and I was due to drive back, too, wasn't I? Again?' Nathan snatched the keys back. 'Next time I'll do the drinking and you can...'

'Boys, save the lovers' tiff for later, yes?' Alicia relieved them both of the car-keys, handed Jack, whom Evelyn had handed back, to Simon, and hopped into the driver's seat.

'Matt,' she called, patting the passenger seat as Simon climbed into the back, cooing, 'who's a pretty boy, then?' to a mesmerised Jack, while Nathan climbed po-faced in beside him.

'So?' Donna said, as the charabanc finally pulled off.

'So?' Mark repeated.

'A man of mystery, too, I see.' Donna eyed him curiously.

'Actions speak louder.' Mark smiled elusively. 'So Matt tells me.'

'Matt?' Donna's frown went into overdrive.

They obviously had been furtively conversing, which was a darn sight more than Matt had done with his father. Donna smiled. Whatever the future for Mark and her, Matt, she thought, might just have found a role figure worth modelling himself on.

Five minutes later, Mark pulled into the park's car-park, followed by Evelyn, followed by Alicia, then proceeded to drive through the gate towards the cricket pavilion, to Donna's astonishment.

'You're not supposed to,' she hissed, as if the park-keeper was about to leap from behind the nearest bush.

Mark laughed. 'I'm a policeman. I'm allowed.' He drove on, Evelyn and Alicia dropping lumpily down potholes behind.

Finally, Mark stopped and climbed out to let Karl, Starbuck and Sadie out. 'One minute,' he said to Donna, pausing to check Karl had a tight hold on Starbuck's lead, which had Donna's heart fair melting. He really was the most caring man she'd ever met.

'Sadie okay off the lead?' he asked, as Donna came around to his side.

Quite the most caring. Donna nodded. 'Yes, she's used to the park, but where…'

'Come on, then.' Mark took her hand. 'Not far.'

And off they set again, followed by their odd crew of gongoozlers, across the short plain of grass that led to the bridge in the middle of the park.

Up the bridge they went, Donna thanking God for her passé trainers, down the bridge, then…

'Agnes?' Donna gawked, as there on the embankment stood Agnes amidst the entire stock of the local flower shop.

'Ah, Donna,' Agnes paused in her labours, to wipe a hand clutching secateurs across her brow, 'I see you accepted. Wonderful.' She bent to straighten a strategically placed flower, then picking out spaces with her wellies, made her way stealthily towards them.

'I knew he wasn't a sex-fiend,' she announced, collecting her bag, then joining Donna to admire her handiwork.

'So, what do you think?' Agnes looked terribly pleased with herself. 'I've been working all day, haven't we, Mark? We been synchronising; on our walkie-talkies.' Agnes demonstrated thus on her brand-new mobile.

'Um?' Donna smiled uncertainly and looked at Mark.

Mark eyed the skies, sighed, and shook his head.

'It's lovely, Agnes,' Donna finally said, though not entirely sure she knew what the flower arrangement meant.

'Very artistic, isn't it, Nathe?' Simon observed, over Jack's head.

'Gorgeous.' Nathan nodded appreciatively.

'Absolutely,' Evelyn arched an eyebrow, 'if a little bit obscure.'

'Obscure?' Robert scoffed. 'It's as plain as the nose on your face.'

Matt came to stand next to Mark, cocked his head and had a think. 'Nice, try, mate,' he concluded. 'I get it.'

'Yeah.' Mark dragged a hand across his neck. 'Not sure your mum will though.'

'Well?' Agnes looked at him expectantly.

'It's great, Agnes. Brilliant.' Mark glanced at Starbuck loves Sadie spelt out on the grass in white lilies and roses. 'But it's supposed to say...'

'Yes?' All ears cocked in Mark's direction.

'I love you. It's supposed to say...' He glanced awkwardly at Matt.

'Bit slow, isn't he?' Matt rolled his eyes and draped an arm around Karl.

'I love you, too, dear boy.' Agnes batted her eyelids, patted Mark's cheek, then bustled off to join the rest of the eager ensemble. 'But I think your sentiments might be better declared to your intended.'

Intended? Donna's eyes grew wide, her cheeks flushed and her butterfly nose-dived.

'Right.' Mark nodded, tugged in a breath and turned to Donna. 'Donna, I...'

'OhmiGosh, he's going to do it,' Simon interrupted excitedly, squeezing Jack so tight he let out a muffled wail.

Mark raked his hand through is hair, breathed slowly out, and tried again. 'Donna, I wanted to —'

'Oh, dear, it's all so terribly romantic.' Dot reached for her hankie.

'Good God, woman! Show a little restraint!' Robert bellowed as she blew. 'The man's trying to make an honest woman of her.'

'She has a name, Robert. And she's not pregnant,' Evelyn informed him dryly. 'Are you?' She twanged astonished eyes towards Donna.

'It would have to be immaculate-bloody-conception,' Mark muttered, utterly despairing.

Donna dropped her gaze fast. 'Sorry,' she mumbled, wondering whether now might be a good time to lose herself in the pond.

'No, apologies, Donna, remember?' Mark reached gently for her hand. 'I, er, think this might be the bit where the girl's supposed to be gazing deeply into the man's eyes.'

Donna blinked up at him. 'And the man's supposed to pull her into his arms?' she asked, a little bit hopefully.

Mark smiled his bone-melting smile and obliged. 'And declare undying love for her,' he whispered, his breath warm on her red-tipped ear.

'Um?'

He laughed and eased back to lock five-thousand-watt twinkly-eyes on hers.

'I love you, Donna, O'Connor,' he said, his expression now deadly serious. 'I love you today. I'll love you tomorrow...'

'Aw.' The crowd sighed collectively.

Donna blinked, manically.

'One day at a time,' Mark continued throatily, wiping a single tear from Donna's cheek with his thumb, 'I will love you for the rest of my life. Marry me, Donna, please? Be my wife. Let's face life's complications together.'

'What complications?' Donna asked breathily, brushing his tempting lips with hers; and trying to resist stuffing her hands up his shirt. 'I love you, too, PC Mark Evans,' she managed, before giving in to sweet temptation, tasting him, feeling him touching every single one of her senses.

'I will.' She smiled, finally allowing him to draw breath. 'And so will Sadie and...'

Donna glanced at Matt, suspecting he was a little bit in love with Mark, too, but wanting to check, nevertheless.

Matt leaned down to Karl's level. 'Your dad loves my mum,' he explained. 'That's why he's holding her. He wants to marry Donna. What do you think, Karl?'

Karl stared, studying Mark and Donna intently. Then, with monumental effort, he pulled in a breath and said, 'Karl wants to marry Donna, so he can hold her and make her feel better.'

Epilogue

'Cooee, only me.' Simon's tones drifted up from the answerphone, fortunately not at the crucial moment.

'Pick up, or not?' Mark asked.

'Not,' Donna assured him, nestling further under his arm, one finger caressing the poor battle-scars on his chest, a broken-glass wound, he'd said. One of several scars sustained in the line of duty, and which he'd much rather have suffered the agony of than giving birth.

Mark pulled her to him, kissed her sweetly, then yanked her on top of him. Smiling mischievously, he trailed his hands the length of her back, his fingers tenderly tracing her 'battle-scars' before retracing their steps skin-tinglingly up her spine, softly to her shoulders, to her hair, his lips finding hers, kissing her tenderly, stopping.

'Shoot.' He laughed as Simon said, 'Just wondered if you were doing anything special, sweetie, only Nathan and I wanted to pop over with our colour swatches for the lounge. We thought Tibetan Gold with Sunrise, what do you think?'

Donna rolled off Mark and snatched up the bedside phone. 'I think red, Simon. That way they won't see the evidence when I murder you if you ring one more time.'

Donna's lips had barely found their way back to Mark's when, Triiinnng, Triiinnng.

'Hi, hon, me again,' said Alicia, 'So how was it? Good? Bad? Worth waiting for?'

Donna's eyes shot wide. She plucked up the phone. 'Ten,' she said shortly, beamed Mark a smile and plopped it back down.

Finally, lips re-poised for a little nibble of Mark's, Donna closed her eyes in sweet anticipation — then flopped her head onto his chest as the phone rang again.

'Hello, my little blushing soon-to-be bride,' said Evelyn.

Donna groaned and stuffed her head under the duvet.

'Just to let you know Karl's fine,' Evelyn went on breezily. 'He and Starbuck are chasing Robert around the garden wearing Indian feathers. Robert, that is, you'll be utterly surprised to hear. Now then, Donna, I know you'll probably have ideas of your own, but indulge me. My Muumuu is to die for...'

Mark peered under the duvet to swap astonished glances with Donna.

'Designer, of course. Vintage, pleated, quite short, but then, if you've got it... Your legs are your assets, darling, and it will hide any other little, um... Shall we say, lumps or bumps you might have? It's perfect for a late autumn wedding.'

'Oh, no,' Donna balked, 'I can't. Please, please, someone save me from my mother's idea of the perfect wedding dress.'

'Oh, I don't know.' Mark mused, lying back on the pillow, hands behind his head. 'Could look pretty cool with the go-go boots.'

'Ye-es,' Donna slithered up, plonking herself heavily on top of him, 'and I'm sure Simon will think you look darling in them.'

'With stockings, I think,' Evelyn elaborated, 'rather than tights. I suspect Mark's more of a suspenders man.'

'I am?'

Donna almost died as Mark's eyes shot wide.

'Oh, no, no, nooooo,' she groaned, sliding so fast back down the duvet she almost skinned him.

Mark joined her, muffling out Evelyn's further elaborations on how men prefer some things left to the imagination in the lingerie department. 'Do you think if we stay cuddled up under the duvet we could make the world go away?' he whispered, obviously aware of Donna's absolute mortification.

Donna's ears pricked up. She blinked up at him, her heart soaring so high her little butterfly took flight. She had found him. Her soulmate. A likeminded most sensitive lover, who she could happily stay safe and content in the arms of forever.

Mark laughed, and brushed his lips across the tip of her nose. 'Actually, I prefer you like this,' he said, 'beautiful, wearing nothing but a smile.'

Evelyn kept talking, but Mark managed to distract Donna from the detail.

Lightning Source UK Ltd.
Milton Keynes UK
UKOW051633220612

194902UK00003B/22/P